Ice & Lemon

by Pete Hartley

First published in the UK by Pete Hartley.

ISBN: 978-0-9572776-0-1

Printed and bound in the UK by the MPG Books Group,
Bodmin and King's Lynn

*

Cover design and book set by by
Rachel Gledhill of Fat Giraffe Graphic Creations

*

To Marion.

ICE

One : Terminal

The monitor screens retracted while we were still over France. That was the first hint something was wrong. I always liked to watch the monitors on the Airbus as they relayed our speed, altitude and location. I had done that journey several times. They never usually retracted that soon. I felt the plane turn. No one else seemed troubled by this, but I saw something in the eyes of the cabin crew. They knew. I saw them switch to reassurance mode long before it was necessary to reassure anyone. They knew.

The announcement from the captain was professional, slick and entirely unconvincing. I can't remember his exact words but he said something about a possible delay due to traffic approaching Heathrow. I sensed we were shedding altitude. I craved for a window seat. I was seated by the aisle and craned my neck to peer over two passengers to my right and three to my left but the sky told me nothing. After about thirty minutes a real sense of unease precipitated in the cabin. There wasn't any panic at that point, just worried expressions and a rash of displacement activities: people reading intermittently, comfort snacking from hand luggage, making stunted conversations, stopping cabin crew, and peering pointlessly at the business end of the aisle where the flight attendants made themselves as busy as they could. It was as if the crew felt that by adopting some cloak of normality they would make everything all right. The captain made another announcement to say that we were in a stack over Heathrow and would be landing soon. The turns we made did not seem as smooth as usual and I distinctly remember one occasion when the power went on suddenly and harshly and we climbed steeply. No explanation was made for this manoeuvre.

I kept peering to right and left. Many other faces were glued to the windows. The seat belt light came on, the captain warned us of turbulence and we descended through the cloud. I have always enjoyed flying. I will never fly again.

We passed through the cloud layer. People muttered. We caught glimpses of civilisation. We also saw the palls of many fires. Someone said, "Nothing's moving." People undid their seat belts and leaned on complete strangers to look at the roads beneath. Sure enough, all vehicles were stationary and there had been a great many accidents. A good deal of the fires that we could see, in fact all the ones that I saw from the air, were the result of road collisions. We looked in vain for blue flashing lights. No announcement came from the captain. The cabin crew abandoned their charade, converted to our perspective by the spectacle beneath us. One stewardess, who I shall always remember, emerged from the cockpit, mascara streaked from the corners of her eyes to her striking auburn hair. She made her way down the aisle locked into some macabre automated routine, making sure our seats were in the upright position and our belts were fastened but completely avoiding our eyes and ignoring any requests or inquiries. There was some panic in the cabin as it became more and more evident that something, or everything, was wrong. There was that 'we're stuck on a broken roller coaster' feeling. People screamed, hyperventilated, fainted. I think one man had a heart attack. They couldn't rouse him, though they didn't try for very long. I think in the end we just left him on the plane. This sporadic panic continued for perhaps twenty minutes or more then, strangely, a kind of common acceptance and not quite calmness spread over us all as tender nudges signified a familiar pattern of descent to regular fliers. The captain made only the routine announcements to the cabin crew, then with bizarre normality, we landed. The tyres smacked the runway with the passion of an unleashed ugly nymphomaniac. There was a communal gasp and a half-hearted and short-lived round of applause from that uniquely captive audience. It was a sound I recognised all too well.

Once we had cleared the runway the captain spoke to us, and his words set a silence over the cabin. It wasn't true silence of course. There was still the rumbling of the undercarriage beneath us and the hum of the aircraft systems. In those days silence meant relative quiet. Today silence is silence. I have grown accustomed to silence. He said something like "Ladies and gentlemen, this is Colin your captain again. Well, as no doubt you have realised, we're safely down. Please keep your seatbelts fastened and remain in your seats until we've brought the aircraft to a halt and shut down the engines. It may take a few moments while I find us a safe parking space. As I'm sure you can see, things seem a little confused down here."

I was never so relieved to feel aviation tyres thump tarmac as I was on that day. Looking back, it's difficult to see how many air passengers got down so safely. Not all did, we later discovered, but at Heathrow we estimated that over twenty thousand landed safely that afternoon and evening. I wonder where they all are now? The captains of each flight had lost contact with air traffic control but they struck up a dialogue with each other and, as far as we know, managed to keep apart before negotiating an order in which to land. One pilot I spoke to was convinced that many more must not have made it, or must have diverted to quieter airfields. There simply were not enough aircraft to account for all the inbound flights that he would expect on a Sunday afternoon in late May. He said that the automated guidance systems on the ground had remained functional and they had helped, but in many other ways that day had signalled a return to seat of the pants flying.

The situation on the taxi way was chaotic. Aircraft jostled like supermarket trolleys in the turkey aisle on Christmas Eve. The pilots cleared the runways as quickly as they could to allow others to fly in but then they struggled to find places to park. Eventually they were placed wherever there was a gap with many, including ours, taxiing onto the grass. We ended up between a pair of Jumbos, nowhere near any of the terminal gates. In addition to all the aircraft that were landing, there were many already occupying parking places on the ground, and bizarrely there were queues lined up waiting to take off. Their engines idled for days. Once we had stopped, the realisation quickly spread that we were twenty feet off the ground and with no hope that a stair would be brought. We exited the plane using the emergency slides. One of the cabin crew, a stocky, youthful fellow called Graham, switched straight back into the training he had clearly only just completed, efficiently rushing people off, but then a senior colleague, the woman with streaked mascara, eased things and we proceeded at a more sedate rate, some of us, myself included, clutching our hand luggage. As I slid I was reminded of clutching Matthew on his first adventure down the slide on Moor Park. That was an awful moment. I was one of the many passengers who had ignored the regulations and tried to phone from the descending plane. Many more were continually trying now we were on the ground. No one got a reply. Thousands of messages were left on voicemail accounts or an answer phones, never to be heard. I tried my wife's mobile, both my sons' mobiles and of course my home phone. I left messages.

The tarmac was riddled with people, mostly in groups being shepherded by cabin crew, others scurrying individually, others transfixed by one of the many instances of grotesque sculptures of frozen time: a baggage train with the driver slumped against the windscreen, a trio of baggage handlers, one in the cargo hold, one reaching into the caged truck of the train, a third flat on the floor as if trying to smother the case he had been relaying; a fuel bowser attendant ensnared in the coil of his hose, still and unseeing through glasses that had been knocked slightly off his nose as he had hit the floor. Everyone on the ground was dead and all had died instantly and apparently at the same instant. It was surreal, that goes without saying, but the surreal quality stemmed not from the deaths but from the things that still signified normality. Engines were whining, hazard lights were flashing, aircraft were landing. I joined a rush towards the terminal building. We had to discover the extent of this simultaneous massacre. Seven months later I am still plagued by that same question.

Inside the terminal building the situation was the same and the bizarre horror multiplied exponentially. Life had simply stopped. All life. Boarding, disembarking, shopping, eating, working, going to the lavatory, waiting in departure lounges, all stopped at the same moment, mid-purpose and with a sharp execution. There had been no realisation. There had been a dead stop.

One of the necessary side effects of my vocation is the development of a detachment that kicks in as soon as any kind of abnormality occurs however large or slight. I am an observer of humanity and the handiest human to observe is always oneself, so peculiarly at this highest moment of stress I found myself hovering on my own shoulder watching myself and those around me with a bemused glee. Here were rich pickings. Where normally I might expect to happen on a picnic I had, instead, stumbled upon an Epicurean feast that could never be eaten. I saw myself not panicking, not even hurrying, but moving with a measured but dreamlike gait avoiding the distressed as one might evade a consumer survey representative in the high street. I saw myself adopt a fake serenity as if I had ridden above this apocalypse and become a bearer of the sacred vessel of self-control. Normality was there somewhere, and I simply had to find it. Now where was it? Somewhere obvious, of course, like next to the Bureau de Change. Most oddly of all I saw myself observing myself and saw the pointlessness of it. A slightly overweight, rapidly balding, bespectacled forty-nine year old aspiring middle class scrutiniser hunting like a bear trying to smell the fruit on the machines in an amusement arcade. There was nothing humorous about this, and if there was, no one would ever want to hear the funny side of it.

The living occupants of the terminal were inferior to the dead by a factor of about ten to one, though this ratio improved as more and more aircraft landed, but we never came close to matching their numbers. And gradually, of course we all realised that what at first impression seemed like a local disaster, turned out to be only the tiniest of threads on a whole carpet of catastrophe.

Within a matter of an hour or two we understood that whatever had happened while we had been above the clouds had affected everywhere. No contact could be made with any living person anywhere on the planet except for others like ourselves who had been airborne at the same time and who had landed at other airports to discover a carbon copy of our apocalypse. Desperation spread among us. Why could we not reach our loved ones? In our hearts we feared the worst, but we invented many scenarios on which to hang our hopes. World communications were at a standstill. Telephones worked but no one answered. The Internet was there, but with the exception of airports there were no live responses. Some radio channels were silent, others broadcast music for a while before resorting to static. Radio Three, someone told me, worked its way through a Mozart requiem, but I suspect that story to be apocryphal. Radio four lost its voice. Television continued with films and programmes for a few hours. Live news channels showed live news presenters slumped on their desks in a very dead sort of way. These impressions took a few hours to accumulate, by which time many services were starting to go down. More static on the radio, more stillness on the screens. Surrounded by everything for free, for a few hours the only commodity of any value was gossip. People grasped at wafer thin membranes of supposed facts. People said it was some telecommunications bug. Others declared it to be a digital virus spread by radio waves. The theory in both these cases was that the electronic demon was so powerful it short circuited brainwaves and killed people. Unfortunately it also killed the very people who could point out the stupidity of such theories. Who knows, they might have been right, but for me that kind of explanation does not account for the scope of the Event. But in those early days, any explanation that put the emphasis on there being something wrong with systems instead of people, gave hope that loved ones might have escaped, and might be trying as hard to contact us as we were to get in touch with them. The value of the factual plummeted in those first hours, while shares in reassurance rocketed. We quickly learned that someone in terminal three had received a text message. Wow. From someone he knew. Even better. Had he replied? He was trying now. And that was the last I heard of that story. Gas was also a popular hypothesis. This explanation was often explained through clenched handkerchiefs. Three Japanese gentlemen were sighted wearing surgical masks. Children were told to put their hands over their mouths. Someone said there was a strange smell in Duty Free. I didn't doubt them for a minute, but silently questioned how strange it would have to be to cause collisions on the M25. Of course the most popular theory of all was that it was an act of God. We had been spared. We were the chosen ones. If this is what it means to be a chosen one, I resolve to pray twelve times a day for the mercy of being one of God's rejected.

A man, late teens or early twenties in the peak of health and with a supremely honed physique pushing muscular creases into his white t-shirt, sat with a neatly bulging back-pack between his feet. He smiled as if caught in a snap-shot whilst daydreaming. Across the departure lounge the epitome of feminine youth lay on the carpet as if sleeping. Fifteen or sixteen, five foot seven or so, with the form of an over-fed waif, a skin genuinely lightly tanned, face as oval as a geometrician's ellipse, framed by fair hair so fine and shiny it could have sold shampoo or Scotland. Between these two icons of youth, every shape, age and physical variation you could wish to consider. A whole catalogue of moderately imperfect humanity piled haphazardly on each other like a stockpile in the warehouse of humankind. We had to walk among them as if someone had decreed that we should select some. In places we had to walk on them. There was no alternative. Toddlers scrambled over them as if they were fallen Disney World creatures who, suddenly denied animation, turned sinister and still in a totally threatening way. There was a striking middle-eastern looking woman flat on her back as if demanding mummification. A portly eastern-European man lay still smiling as if he was determined to remain everyone's favourite cheerful uncle. A pneumatic Indian lady squatted squarely on the floor upright as Buddha, her family fallen all around her, interlocked awkwardly. Before me humanity was spilled like deck upon deck of playing cards, with business class the most valuable suit suddenly trumped and made worthless by some random factor. One or two of the pinstriped deceased bore the expression that suggested they were still intent on making a killing.

Adrenalin, or something, settled in my stomach and I needed the toilet. How strange it was to be amid this off-the-wall state of affairs to find myself scanning for helpful signs pointing to the loo. Even stranger when inside, to see the man fallen at the foot of the hand drier as if blown down by it. Another slumped across two sinks, his torso depressing the cold tap, his clothing siphoning the water onto the floor. Three of the cubicles were occupied but I found myself gently, almost respectfully pushing at the doors to make sure. The third gave way too quickly as the person behind pulled open the door and stared, scared, right at me. We both recoiled, both apologised. He recovered, returned inside and flushed the toilet. I went into the next cubicle and as I bolted the door and unfastened my trousers I heard him washing and drying his hands. Whilst in there, I tried phoning again and left another message on Claire's voicemail. I washed my hands, an action that seemed both necessary and futile. The me in the mirror, balding, greying, too much weight, seemed balder, greyer but thinner. Me and not me. Looking over or through my rimless spectacles made no difference. Me and not me. How true.

That afternoon and evening I walked miles criss-crossing the airport. I went to all of the departure lounges and through to boarding gates. I went into many places the public would not normally go, catering kitchens, service and security offices, staff restrooms, the chapel which was devoid of the dead and packed with the living. I went to the top of a multi-storey car park and from there saw the roads snaking away, jammed with cars, mostly collided, many at quirky angles, others having veered off the road to find the first available solid obstruction. Some burned. Most had stalled but some engines still ran. None of the living slept that night. All the dead did, and at least half sat or lay with eyes fixed open, watching us.

Electrical power did not fail until the end of that first night. Exhausted by my wanderings and dismayed by any real sign that normality existed anywhere, I had to withdraw, find some sort of solitude, rest and think. I was not hungry, but incredibly thirsty. I helped myself to two bottles of spring water from a shop fridge in terminal two. Finding solitude was much harder. The dead were everywhere and the living clustered in groups or did as I had done: rambling frantically like ants on paving stones rushing from nothing to nothing but occasionally stopping to check it was nothing. By nothing I mean no hope. Had anyone found any genuine evidence of a limit to the disaster or a remedy for any part of it, then that would have been something. No one did, and I realised it was very unlikely that anyone would, so I snatched a Lion bar on impulse and set off to squat in solitude. I thought of returning to the toilet cubicle but that would not have been far enough away from the others. I went outside and ended up beyond the tarmac on the grass beneath an abandoned and silent 747. My watch said 9:17 and the late spring daylight was fading. No planes were landing but the vacuum whine of idling jets still sounded across the airfield from where those queuing to take off still waited. I sat on the grass, drained one bottle of water, ate the chocolate bar and started on the other bottle. There was no one, either living or dead, near enough for me to see and that absence gave me just enough balance to steady myself and think. I detected a physical tremor in my arms and legs and wondered if I was going into shock so I breathed deeply, and for a few moments lay on my back staring at the scattered clouds in the sky. I took stock. Something had happened at some time during our flight from Seville, probably when we were cruising at considerable height. That thing seemed to have affected everyone, everywhere, except those like us, who were high in the air. The enormity of that situation was too great and my mind wanted to keep switching back to the detail and personal. My family. My wife, my children, my sisters and my brother. I believed they were safe, thought this to be highly unlikely, but resolved to believe that they were until I knew for sure that they were not. I would find out. There was nothing else for me to do except survive and see if I could help my family to do the same. Only two hundred miles of chaos could prevent me.

When the evening became cool I went back inside. I stole some more food: a packet of biscuits, some crisps and more water. I remembered a departure gate that had been empty of corpses and returned to it. Two hundred others had already had the same idea but I managed to find a slot of wall to squat against and slumped to the floor. Outside and alone I had felt hopeful but here, surrounded by so many others sharing our communal despair, I sank to a severe low. It was an awful night. Whenever I craved solitude, someone would turn to me or come over and sit by me and talk. Whenever I wanted conversation people turned away or wandered off. Discussion led to disturbing thoughts, silence amplified them. Throughout the night I was ensnared by the tendrils of personal tragedy, as indeed, I had been ever since we disembarked, but now it was much harder to evade them. Everyone was weary of wandering, and optimism was fading. I was told of relatives. I was told of homes far away, that people felt sure were all right. I was told of pets that needed feeding. People spoke about their work and how they had to get home to do it and, if only they could, then somehow everything would be all right. Whilst bemused by all this, I could only do the same. I told them of my family. I told them about my cat. I didn't tell them my occupation.

To say that something on that first day changed my life seems like stating the obvious, but one small aspect of it all directed my future in a precise way. It was just one of the scores of conversations, insignificant in itself but fundamental in retrospect. Kirsty, a diminutive, slightly stocky British Airways flight attendant secured a section of carpet close by me.

"I've borrowed this," she said, slipping a plain black top over her uniform.

"Being pestered?"

"You bet."

I'd noticed how anyone in a uniform had become a human magnet. Airline staff looked the most strained of all because everyone else tended to turn to them for information, advice or solutions. "Want a biscuit?"

"I've got some stuff here," she said, unravelling a Boots bag and pulling out a triangular sandwich pack. "But, yes, I wouldn't mind." She took a biscuit. She was mid-twenties.

"Here, have some wall." We swapped places.

"Thanks a lot," she said. "I'm knackered."

"Edinburgh."

"What?"

"Your accent."

"No."

"Sorry."

"That's all right."

"Where were you then?" This had become the most common exchange between strangers.

"Somewhere between Brussels and here. How about you?"

"On the way from Seville. Just transferring here to head up to Manchester."

"Is that where you're from?"

"Preston."

"Family up there?"

"Yes."

We fell silent. She offered me one of her sandwiches but I declined. I let her eat in peace. After a while we chatted a little more. I can't remember what about. She said she'd promised to meet back with her crew, and off she went.

I went walkabout again in the middle of the night. I peered out of various windows and looked at the glow of the many fires. Somewhere there was a big conflagration sending a ruddy dome across the sky making the horizon Blitz-like.

Lights studded the panorama belatedly proving how many interior bulbs burned even on a summer Sunday afternoon. Had this been a week day many more would have been there. I went back to the tarmac. Here hazard bulbs still rotated like miniature demented lighthouses. Jet engines still idled. Danger warning lights topped tall buildings and aerials and still glowed their warning to low fliers. Nothing flew.

Mains power failed shortly after five a.m. There was a gasping squeal and a moan as the lights went out. In retrospect it was amazing that it had lasted so long. I think other places lost their energy supplies earlier, for I heard of how this city and that had stopped communicating. For example Glasgow had fallen silent as early as eight o'clock the previous evening. At Heathrow we were fortunate, for by the time all went dark, daylight was breaking. The day was overcast and a little drizzly. A dry rubbery aroma tainted the air, a scent I put down to the residue of lots of plastic-fed fires, many of which still burned. There were no lights anywhere save for those on vehicles where engines still ran or batteries still lived. Another exception was the emergency lights within the terminals that burned helpfully for another few hours until their batteries faded. The entire area seemed suddenly dead as if electricity was the lifeblood of civilisation. I imagined this power death right across the nation and the civilised world. I'm sure I was right. At Heathrow it brought with it a resignation akin to being in a lifeboat when the mother ship finally sank. Without electricity we were marooned. For a while people still tried to use their mobile phones. One by one they realised that a cell phone is nothing without a cell, and the indispensable became useless.

On this day, the first Monday, I saw people sleeping for the first time. Children first. When they woke there was a wonderful terrible two seconds when they thought it had all been a dream and then saw it was not. As the day wore on some adults slumped into blissful unconsciousness, but most only managed a few minutes. I did not sleep that day. Curiosity was over, anger replaced acceptance, tears flowed, tempers flared, and fights erupted as one helpless party unreasonably expected another helpless party to do something. People looted. People objected to looting, especially from the dead. People screamed, just wanting the corpses to go away, or wanting someone to clear the corpses away or just wanting it to end. Factions emerged. I heard gunshots. Someone had disarmed a deceased armed policeman, and already a mini mafia was emerging with a group of travellers in designer clothes and Mediterranean tans organising the acquisition and distribution of food and drink. An intellectual party formed. It was an impromptu summer school of academics and cultural tourists in flannels, print frocks and sandals. They held a public meeting round a baggage carousel and agreed that people should agree on how things might be agreed. I happened to be close by and lingered to listen. One of them suggested they held a minute silence to remember the dead. This suggestion necessitated six minutes discussion but eventually was passed by a majority vote and the silence was duly held. The dead joined in. It was during this memorial that I first noticed something mildly pleasing but also terrifying because of its consequences. The dead did not smell. We walked, ate, drank and slightly slept in the company of a hundred thousand corpses. They were not decaying.

Monday was the day that we ventured out from the airport. I did not go. I became attached to a sub-group of the intellectuals who formed a radical offshoot as soon as I drew the non-decaying aspect of our dead brothers to their attention. This total lack of life spurred a sixty-something woman called Margaret into action. We needed to do something she said, and a man called Phillip immediately concurred. We had to somehow find out the extent of the disaster, at least in local terms. Another meeting was called, this time in passport control and it attracted a much more diverse composition. Volunteers emerged. People were willing to go towards London and see if there was any sign of other groups of survivors. Transport was both plentiful and problematic. There were thousands of available cars but every road was blocked with multiple collisions. Then someone had the bright idea of motorbikes. Eventually three bikers were recruited and a little while later two bikes commandeered from riders who no longer needed them. Their accidents had been minor and their engines had stalled rather than starved. Off they went. A fourth volunteer meant that both bikes were sent with pillion passengers. They were gone five hours. Their report was disappointingly predictable. Nothing lived. Except us.

The enormity of this news quickly spread through the airport. That second day was a truly horrible day made worse by the bikers' report, but the real horror was on a much more immediate level. Food ran out. Everything to hand that could be looted and consumed was done so and frighteningly quickly. We had to move outwards away from the obvious, into kitchens, and stores, but these were as quickly emptied as they were discovered, as people hunted, gathered and hoarded. Savage law slammed into place and more meetings were sparked to try to stem the barbarity. When there was nothing obvious to be gained people talked and agreed, and at the slightest scent of personal advantage the debate was over and the pocket was lined. Margaret made the most sense. At a major gathering in the departure lounge of Terminal One she pointed out that we had the biggest larder in the country just a few miles down the road: a capital city of shops. We must leave the airport and flock to find nourishment. No need to panic. One more night first. It was late in the afternoon by this time. We must share what we had and try to rest. Early in the morning we would set out on mass and head for London. Most of the population of the airport were not part of this meeting of course, but those who were seemed largely in favour. Not everyone went along with it, and many sub-groups refused to wait and hence a steady trickle of people set off that evening, but most, like me, decided to stay one more night at Heathrow.

There is a state of mind whereby the grotesque becomes the normal. It doesn't happen at one stroke but gradually, and for me the first phase was the second night as we found ourselves surrounded by our dead companions and without any artificial light. It was seriously eerie, but it was also easier to blank out the horrible sights. I never lost the knowledge that they were there though, just feet away, hundreds of them. I was projected back to infancy and the first great fear dilemma: bedroom light on or off at bedtime. This time there was no choice. In the darkness the dead went away but came closer. Despite this, I did sleep and for longer than I expected. I think I managed three stints with an hour or two each time, and the final session was shallow and fitful, but sleep it was. I didn't return to the place where I had spent the previous night, but camped instead on the high level corridor overlooking the departure lounge shops beneath. It somehow felt safer up there being in a relatively visible position. When awake, I could peer around and scan the area beneath where some of the living and lots of the dead resided. A few others slept close to me and we all kept a respectful and wary distance from two clusters of dead travellers. One or two people had torches and a good many mobile phones were pressed back into service as feeble flashlights, but for most of the time we were in near-complete darkness. There was a biblical feel to it all, a refugee camp atmosphere and an overriding sense of being abandoned. Coughing provided the soundscape. Whenever someone coughed everyone heard it. At times a person, often a child, would call out. Far away a baby cried and it made me think how few babies flew and therefore how few must have survived. The population demographic had just leaped. We were all, on average, older. This thought was in my mind the final time that I awoke that night and it was mingled with a dream, the details of which I cannot remember, but tents and relief supplies were in there somewhere. For a while I just lay there, then I half sat and stared at the nearest of the clusters of deceased, for it was about five thirty and there was a reasonable amount of light. I saw them as something that was not going to go away, something distasteful and distressing and threateningly benign. A part of me was hardening to their presence and I didn't like it.

Of course, my mind constantly hummed with pent-up potential grief. It is the worst kind of grief because there is no satisfaction. Satisfaction comes with knowledge, with certainty, and certainty there was not. We were all subject to this same suffering. We all, well perhaps not all but most of us, secretly held the same belief that our loved ones had perished. That seemed to be the logical presumption. A few clung on to hope, or prayed for miracles, but in my opinion I think that most of those also inwardly knew. But none of us had confirmation, except for a few hundred, whose relatives had already arrived at the terminal to meet them. These formed the saddest groups, and the happiest, for they had certainty. Claire and the children were in my mind, and Claire had visited me in my dream. In the period of semi-wakefulness I began to plan how I would get home. I had to have that certainty. I knew the likelihood of finding good news was virtually zero, but I had to know. The experience of our motorcycle pioneers told me that to take a car would be pointless. All roads were blocked and I would never make it. For a moment I had the crazy idea of driving a four by four along the West Coast main line, but quickly realised the possible frustrations of that also. There would probably be the remains of train collisions, though the dead man's handle safety devices might have prevented them, so it might work, if I could find a suitable vehicle close enough to a main line station. The first phase however was going to have to be by motorcycle. I had ridden a motorbike in my teenage years and even passed the test so that I could take Valerie Rogerson pillion. The more awake I became the more realistic I was in my planning. I may as well take the bike the whole way. I could weave in and out of the traffic and keep to the road network. I would do that, but first into London to find supplies of food and drink, and locate a bike that I could handle.

Tuesday was the day of the mass exodus. A rendezvous had been arranged at seven o'clock in terminal one. We were to set off walking towards London in an organised train, leaving in groups of about fifty at ten minute intervals. The idea behind this was to avoid breaking down into riotous mobs of looters each time we encountered another shop or store. Everyone accepted that there had to be looting but it was going to be done in a managed way. The first groups would fleece the first shops they encountered, then subsequent groups could join in or leapfrog them to find the next place. Nice in theory. I doubted very much that it would work in practice, but I never got the chance to find out, for fate intervened in the form of Kirsty the flight attendant I had met the previous night. I was just about to join the muster when she and a small group of her colleagues passed by. We recognised each other and exchanged nods and she stopped and said, "Daniel, do you want to come with us?"

"What?"

"We've got an aircraft. We're going to fly north."

"What?"

"We've got a 737. We know it's okay because we've found the pilot who flew in on it. Some of us from the north want to try and get closer to home."

"Where are you going?"

"We're going to try Manchester first. There's no guarantees but we think that we'll get in there, or somewhere close, and anyway we've got enough fuel to get back if we have to."

"Yes, I'd like to come."

"Well, tag along."

I began to follow and immediately came face to with the indefatigable Margaret who was on her way to the rendezvous. I was flattered that she recognised me from the day before, as I hadn't contributed anything to the debate, other than to point out the apparent lack of the onset of decay.

"Are you not coming along?" she asked in a distinctly Oxbridge tone.

"No. We're flying to Manchester."

"Oh. Very well." She seemed supportive, but I also detected a slight sense of loss in her voice and this too, I found curiously flattering. "Got any special skills?"

"What do you mean?"

"Well," she said, "what's your occupation?"

"Stand-up comedian."

"I'm sorry?"

"I'm a stand-up comic," I said.

"Ah," she said. Was she disappointed? Or was I less of a loss now she knew what I could or could not offer? She was tactful enough to hide her thoughts.

"Well then," she said, "make sure you stand up for yourself." And off she strode. The strength in her stride made me just a tad sad that I was not going with her.

Only about seventy people elected to join the flight, and the smallness of this number surprised me. A dozen or so were flight crew and they seemed more at ease with the expedition for obvious reasons, though others of that profession declined to join us, even if they lived in the north and this bothered me a little. We were taken first to a departure gate to wait and hence experienced another bizarrely surreal hour or two, but I suppose there was logic in it. We waited while the cabin crew went out to the plane to check it over and make sure they could get it started. Eventually one of Kirsty's colleagues returned and we were led out in a primary school crocodile onto the tarmac. We had to walk for a good twenty minutes because the aircraft that had been selected was some distance from the terminal. Its evacuation slides had not been deployed and a set of mobile stairs had been brought alongside. Its engines were already running and as we got closer they gradually drowned out the hum of those that had now idled for two days. As I climbed the steps I looked back over Heathrow and marvelled that it had all just stopped without any significant damage. There were no fires within the airfield perimeter except beyond the terminal buildings on the public highways. There were no examples of significant damage. There was stillness and a dressing of dead humanity. It was as if the whole place had been simultaneously sedated. Or perhaps this was the work of some celestial hypnotist. And for my next trick: an entire planet. Supposing he snapped his cosmic fingers to wake everyone up whilst we were in the air? Now that would give us a shock when we landed.

Our captain told us his name was Mike. He said not to expect a normal flight. There was no air traffic control and though satellite systems were still working, a lot of the ground aids that he normally relied on were simply not there. For this reason he was going to have to fly rather more brutally than he would normally, varying height and speed so that they could observe what was happening on the ground. The cabin crew had a terrible dilemma deciding whether or not to do the safety routine, and a part of me really begged for it despite knowing it backwards, because I craved for just a second or so of humour watching the demonstration in the knowledge that it would somehow appear so incongruous in this context, but they seemed to sense the inappropriateness of it and did not bother. One of the stewards, clearly uncomfortable at not being able to enact his usual demonstration, started checking that everyone had flown before which was, of course, an entirely pointless question.

Almost exactly two days after I had landed, we took off. The lift off itself was completely normal but we didn't climb rapidly once we were safely in the air. Instead the pilot took us over central London, where we saw some devastation. Major fires filled the sky with filthy smoke in places, whilst other districts remained completely untouched. Everything was still. I looked hard. But nothing moved. Nothing except flames and smoke and items caught in the fire-feeding breezes. In the suburbs, things were more normal. There was stillness, and for the first time long stretches of roads that were not blocked, but pock-marked with a few small collisions. There were fewer fires there, but some houses and some streets or parts of streets burned. These must have been the places where the Sunday lunch was left to cook dry and then ignite, or where someone had been doing the ironing, or smoking. Killed and cremated within the hour. Fortunate. I wondered if the gas mains were still functioning, perhaps fuelling these conflagrations.

Cloud cover was mercifully broken and reasonably high though there was also a smoke haze just about everywhere, but even so we saw a lot of suburbia and eventually some rural areas. How I looked for movement. It was at this point that I first realised the possible breadth of the slaughter, for once over agricultural land we saw thousands of livestock not one of which lived. I frantically tried to remember if I had seen any living creature, no matter how small at Heathrow, but I could not recall any. The corpses should have been troubled by flies, but I hadn't seen one. After about fifteen or twenty minutes we climbed higher and started heading north. We still had good views of the ground between the well broken fair weather cumulus cloud, and in many ways it showed an almost idyllic Vaughn-Williams England with dappled sun on patchwork fields and the higher we flew the more peaceful it seemed, but the detail always unsettled me: roads metalled with unmoving vehicles, pasture dotted with what we knew to be horizontal cattle, palls rising not from cosy Home Counties hearths but from the fabric of the homes themselves. Peaceful streets. Just how peaceful?

Whenever cloud temporarily obscured my view I thought of Claire, of Teresa, of Matthew and Paul. I knew of course. How could I not know? But I still had to be sure. Teresa would be the worst. She lived so far away. Will I ever know?

Kirsty came to talk to me. I'd seen her chatting to two or three others.

"Well," she said in her lovely Scots accent. "What do you think? Good idea or not?"

"Good idea," I said. "I've never liked London."

She smiled. "Me neither."

"Where are you from?"

"Leith."

"That's Edinburgh."

"It is. Unless you're from Leith."

"I recognised the accent. I've spent a lot of summers in Edinburgh. At the Festival."

"Then how the hell did you learn to recognise the accent? Edinburgh folk all leave."

"I had a good friend who came from Edinburgh."

"Had," she said.

"This good friend died some time ago."

"Oh."

"But you're right. It's looking – well . . . . You never know though – further north."

"I doubt it."

"Are we going to Manchester?"

"That's the idea."

"What about you then? Will you carry on?"

"I'd love to. But I can't fly the plane. Mike, the captain, he's from Manchester."

"I see."

"But Manchester's nearer to Leith than London is."

"Yes."

"We're going to share out the stuff from the galley. There's not a lot because it wasn't restocked. They're just dividing it up now."

"Good."

"I'd better go and help."

"Okay."

She got up and sat down again, her eyes moist for the first time in my company. She swallowed, and took a couple of deep breaths.

"What's happened?"

I shrugged my shoulders. "Maybe we'll never know."

She went to share out the Kit-Kats. Eventually I got one and half, and a can of Iron Bru. The captain spoke to us on the intercom to say he expected us to be in the air for about another forty minutes. He wasn't able to tell us what the weather would be like at our destination.

*

My final job had been in southern Spain. There are a number of ex-pats in that area, including a few bar owners, some of whom are old friends from the English club circuit. One of them throws an annual party for his friends and business associates and every two or three years he books me. It's a difficult gig. There are a number of Spaniards in the audience and my Spanish is close to zero. The ex-pats have a satellite and tabloid perspective on the mother country. My act is jaded. I've known that for some time, in fact I've known it since my act was fresh. This is particularly dispiriting for a man whose professional income is derived from observational humour. How can observational humour go out of date? The answer lies in a combination of disenchantment and packaging. Any career can take a downturn, and in my business one downturn leads to a turn down, and then another, and before you know it you're in a spiral. There came a day, in 1982, when to be a comedian you had to be under thirty. I was, but I got older and no-one raised the bar. There were exceptions, but to be an exception you had to be exceptional and I wasn't. Thank god for working wives. Stand-up comic was my Mickey Mouse job. I haven't made a living from it for a quarter of a century. To be honest, surviving the end of the world is the best career move I could have made.

*

Two: Grim Up North

We could not land at Manchester. Both runways were entirely blocked by the wreckage of aircraft. We'd seen a similar scenario at East Midlands Airport. I then had a thought that really puzzled me. These crashes were most likely caused by aircraft that had been flying at low level when the Event took place, and then continued on their line of descent, with passengers and crew already dead, to fly directly into the runway. How had Heathrow, the busiest airport in the world escaped this fate? Somehow it had. How lucky we were. I wondered how many aircraft full of survivors had not managed to find an airfield with a clear runway. Manchester was no use to us. Our captain told us he was going to try Blackpool, and this pleased me even more as it was closer to my home town. I could walk from Blackpool to Preston in a day or so. As things turned out I fared even better, for we landed at Warton, the British Aerospace airfield about ten miles from my home. There was no real democratic decision to land there, Mike the captain communicated his intent and presumed our consent. He surmised, correctly in my view, that everyone on board had wanted to leave London so there was no point going back. But once we were down, we were down, for the emergency chutes were deployed and after that our 737 wasn't going anywhere. We all slid to the ground and once again began to take a look around. I suddenly realised I'd left my hand luggage on board. Ah well, goodbye to that. With a bit of luck I would be home soon and be reunited with a great deal more of my belongings, not that they'd be worth anything. My new situation was in marked contrast to that at Heathrow. There was no one in sight. Warton is an assembly plant but with a relatively small workforce in place on Sundays and they are mostly well away from the runway area. Whilst the airfield was almost deserted, we'd seen enough from the air to realise that the general scenario was going to be the same as in London. Nothing moved, nothing lived, except us. After a few minutes we all gathered in a single group close to our now silent aircraft. One man in his late fifties took our attention for a while. He'd landed badly at the bottom of the escape chute and there was some concern that he'd dislocated his shoulder. Although quite a few of our number were qualified in first aid, we discovered that we did not have a doctor, nurse, paramedic of similar among our number and the significance of that hit all of us at the same moment. We stood for a few seconds slightly shaking like Disney-animated pins at the end of a bowling alley. Sooner or later something would strike us, some of us or all of us, and there was nothing we could do about it. The man with the painful shoulder said he was all right, which he clearly was not. He said he'd sprained it. No he hadn't. Two flight attendants put a sling on him and he said it was much better. It obviously was not. I doubt it ever got better, and what's more, I think at that moment he knew it never would. I often think about him.

So we gathered to decide what the plan should be and Mike told us what it was. We would stock up with supplies from local premises, and then we'd commandeer a vehicle or vehicles and set out en masse for Manchester. Not everyone saw sense in this plan. We had seen from the air that so many roads were blocked. They were not all solidly jammed like those around the capital but they were punctuated with significant blockages and littered with minor collisions. Mike said he felt we would be able to find a way through. We'd simply have to deal with each section of the journey as we encountered it. The next problem was that not everyone wanted to go to Manchester. Mike said no one was forced to go there, but it was a major city and would have lots of things we might need and we all had a better chance if we stayed together. There was disagreement over this also. A sub group broke away and a young eco-warrior called Jenny declared that they were going to head up the coast towards Blackpool. This amused me, as Blackpool was the least eco-friendly place that I could think of, but Jenny's thinking was that being by the sea would be a good idea in terms of finding natural food supplies. At the time, I could see the sense in her idea, but I decided to tag along with captain Mike, as the route from Warton would have to pass through Preston and that was where I needed to go.

Once again, finding a vehicle was not a problem. Finding a vehicle that we could use was. There were hundreds of cars parked at the airfield, but they were all locked and there was no way of knowing which pocket or handbag in the factory contained the key for given car. Mike turned his attention to the airfield transport and set about trying to locate the keys for a couple of minibuses. Someone else had the much more sensible idea of taking cars parked outside the houses in the village of Warton. It meant going into houses disturbing or ignoring cadavers and finding the keys. A team volunteered to do this and within three or four hours we had a dozen vehicles including several four by fours, a couple of vans, three people carriers, and a flat backed truck. I went with a young electrician called Steve. Going in to the houses and seeing people as they had been stopped, in their homes, relaxing or doing ordinary mundane domestic tasks, was heartbreaking and chilling. The first house we went in contained a young family. They were all in the living room. The woman, late twenties I would guess, lay on the floor half smothering a toddler who had been stacking Duplo bricks. Another child, aged about six, and wearing a Preston North End shirt was curled up on the sofa as if sleeping with his eyes open and smiling. The man was in his thirties. He was slumped in the armchair across from the television. He was leaning over at a slightly awkward angle and had a freakily delighted expression on his face. They were not decomposing. There was no smell. There were no flies. We could not find the keys to either of the cars on the drive. The master bedroom had an almost fresh aroma from bowls of pot pourri. It was clean, tidy and a testament to house-proud occupants. A tabby cat lay curled on the lilac quilt, dead as the victim of which it had been dreaming. I went to the window and looked down on the street. A man lay prone across his privet hedge, still gripping with one hand the silent power trimmers. The hedge seemed to be eating him, or cutting him in half. Revenge. Further along the road another man, much older than the hedge-eaten one, was spread-eagled over the pavement with two small terriers close by on leads and on their sides. Beyond him two girls aspiring to be teenagers showed their midriffs to the summer sky. I felt nauseous. It was the first time that the universality of the disaster really hit me. Heathrow had been horrible enough but there had been a veneer of artificiality about it. Now, in an ordinary home in an ordinary street the slaughter struck harder. I hurried to find the bathroom and vomited into the toilet. Vomited, is perhaps, an exaggeration. I retched and spat. There wasn't very much in my stomach anyway. After two or three minutes, Steve the electrician, shouted from downstairs. I took a couple of gulps of lemon-scented air and flushed the loo. I went to rinse my face at the sink but no water flowed. The toilet cistern was silent. I wiped my mouth on a bath towel and went downstairs. The lanky, youthful form of Steve was in the hall. "Can't find any keys," he said, "let's try somewhere else."

"No mains water," I said.

"No water?" he asked.

"No."

"I'm sure it will rain," he said, and strode out of the door.

Round the corner we came across a hire van. "Adelphi Van Hire," I remarked. "I've used them. I'll know where to take it back." The keys were in the ignition. There were no corpses close to the van but its doors were wide open and it was half filled with furniture and boxes of personal belongings. Someone was moving house, I think moving in to the property where we were. "A van is good," said Steve, "but we don't want all this crap."

We threw and pushed the contents out onto the drive and Steve started up the van. "Only a quarter of a tank," he said, studying the dash. As he wove his way through the streets I began to contemplate how we would get fuel for our vehicles. Stations would not pump anymore so I deduced it would be a matter of siphoning from the seemingly endless stockyard of second-hand transport.

When we arrived back at the air base there was a picnic going on. Someone had found a corner shop and brought stocks of food back, a real selection of fresh, canned and packaged goods. We ate like hounds. Three people threw up and many of us were wracked with stomach pains. This spread real panic, and people started saying the food was poisoned. I think now it was just some physical reaction to eating too much after a period of starvation and stress. The day wore on and some people, myself included, felt better, whilst others worried more, but despite all that Mike said it was time to start moving and we would have to divide ourselves up between the vehicles. An elderly gentleman asked if we were sure that everyone who had gone car hunting had returned, but none of us were. We all tried to remember if everyone we had seen on our plane was either with us or had gone with the Blackpool expedition. There were a couple of people we could not be certain about, but Mike refused to wait and called the convoy to order. "Stick together," he said.

Steve reclaimed the helm of the van and was joined by two women in the front, whilst I and two young women climbed in the back. I shouted that there was space and just before we pulled away Kirsty ran across to join us. I wondered why she wasn't going in one of the four by fours filled with cabin crew. "Not going with them?" I asked.

"No way," she said.

As we set off I had that familiar feeling of going home. It terrified me.

We could not see out from the rear of the van so we left the back doors open and watched the devastation unfold behind us. Our fellow passengers introduced themselves as Roxy and Rosie, nicknames I think. They were of Asian descent but entirely westernised in their chosen style of dress. Roxy said they were cousins, and I got the impression she was the elder by a couple of years or so.

"Where are you from?" Kirsty asked.

"Wilmslow. In Cheshire," said Roxy. "Well, I am. Rosie lives in

Rotherham."

"Wilmslow," I said. If we'd have got into Manchester, you'd have been home.

"Yes," she said.

Whoever was leading our convoy did not drive fast, but we made steady progress. Infrequently we had to cautiously mount pavements to steer round obstacles. The majority of vehicles appeared to have trundled on for a short distance after the driver had expired and then stalled, but in some the accelerators must have remained pressed and they had simply motored until they found something solid, which was usually the car ahead. The situation presented to us through the open van doors was therefore a blend of road traffic accidents and surreal friezes of stopped cars with stopped occupants. The eeriest situation was at a set of traffic lights where one car's engine was still ticking over, two days after it had drawn up to wait for green. Here and there pedestrians punctuated the pavements where they had fallen, and I distinctly remember the feeling I had when my eyes were drawn to small crumples of grey, brown or black which at first glance appeared to be discarded rags, but on closer scrutiny were birds that had died mid flight.

All of us had collected bits of the left over food and brought it with us. Rosie was one of the people who had been sick and Kirsty gave her water and encouraged her to try and eat something else, but she refused. Roxy turned to me. "What has happened?"

"I really don't know."

"Is it going to happen again?"

I just shrugged and smiled.

"All over the world?" she asked.

"So it seems," I said, and thought of my daughter Teresa. "Let's hope not."

Roxy was suddenly imbued with maturity. "We're on our own now."

"No we're not," said Kirsty. "We've got each other. We're going to have to stick together."

Rosie said, "But what will we do?"

"Live," said Roxy. And to me that seemed like the most sensible thing anyone had said since the Event had happened.

There was a bit of a hold up at one of the major roundabouts just outside Freckleton, where two caravans and a multi-car pile-up had completely blocked the road. The convoy came to a complete halt and people spilled out to see what could be done. It wasn't pleasant looking at the mangle of aluminium and broken flesh. I felt like a mannequin paramedic or a crash test dummy funeral director and hated myself for feeling that way and smiling at the thought, but already the horrific was becoming commonplace and the numbness that gets disaster rescue teams through the worst wrapped its protective membrane round me. I wondered if guilt-ridden flashbacks and nightmares would subsequently follow. They would.

After some time, the more powerful of our cosmopolitan tractors actually got their tyres dirty and drew on reserves of power from somewhat further inside their design specifications than the school run demanded, and towed, nudged and pushed a pathway through the carnage, and our suburban wagon train rolled again. By now it was evening and a pre-dusk muted brightness settled over the flat agricultural land to the west of my home town. At the junction of the A584 and the main Blackpool route, the A583, we were forced to switch to the opposite carriageway in order to get through. Congestion was much worse in this area and it took several hours to push and wriggle our way through just a couple of miles of main road. Eventually I was able to guide Mike and the pioneering cars off the busier roads and onto parallel routes that had far fewer blockages. We arrived in central Preston close to the University at about nine in the evening, and I declared that was where I was getting off. My announcement brought objections from all the occupants of our van and quickly spread to include the representatives from other vehicles.

"Dan," said Kirsty, "It would be insane. And you will go insane."

"I've been insane all my adult life," I rebuked. "Look, this is why I came north. Now thanks for the lift, but it's where I'm getting off."

"Don't be stupid," said Roxy. "Stay with us. We must all stay together."

"Of course we must," said Kirsty.

"I need to find out what has happened to my family."

Kirsty gripped me by the wrist. "I understand that, but you can't branch off on your own."

"I don't expect anyone to come with me. I'll be fine."

"Oh yeah? For how long? Now wait." She went off to consult with Mike. I could not hear what they said but their rapport had an awkwardness about it, a legacy, perhaps, of their now redundant working relationship. He came back with her.

"Where exactly do you live?" Mike asked me.

"About a mile up that road."

Mike thought for a pilot's millisecond. "It's getting late. We can camp hereabouts and in the morning give you an hour or two to put your mind at rest before we move on."

"It might take longer than that."

Mike took a full second to contemplate his reply this time. "You know the roads. Two or three of you take one of the smaller cars. Someone can report back."

"Very kind," I said. "But I don't know what my wife and kids were doing last Sunday. It might take ages to find them."

"Well it might," he said. "It might not. We'll stop here until mid-day tomorrow. Give us a chance to stock up on supplies. It's a big town . . ."

"Small city," I said.

"Right. If there are any . . . survivors . . . here we ought to try and, well, find out."

"Listen. I appreciate the gesture. But whatever I find at home, I'll be staying round here. It's where I've always lived."

Mike nodded, smiled, frowned. "It's not the same place though is it? Nowhere is. I hope to God, I really do, that we find someone, but . . . well it looks like we're going to have to start afresh, doesn't it. And that means safety in numbers."

I looked straight at him. "Safety from what?"

There was a silence undermined only by the muttering of engines in the convoy.

Kirsty said, "Dan, we're going to have to help each other. And we're going to need all the help we can give."

I smiled. "I don't think I've got anything I can offer."

"Well thanks a bundle," she said.

"Look, I'm a stand-up comic. I'm not much fucking use to you am I?"

Steve said, "I think you could be exactly what we need."

Kirsty cut in. "You've got two hands haven't you? For Christ's sake what use am I? We're not exactly going to be doing daily flights to Barce–bloody–lona are we?"

"Listen. I just don't want to hold you up. I might need several days to get my head round, well everything."

"Fifteen hours," said Mike. "That's all we can give you."

"I'm not even asking for fifteen minutes."

Mike ignored that response and said, "Now who's going with you?"

"I can manage."

"We can't give you a car to yourself, someone must go with you."

"I will," said Steve.

"I don't need a car. It's only a twenty minute walk."

"All right," said Steve. "I'll walk with you."

"Me too," said Kirsty.

And that settled it. I pulled my hand luggage out of the van and said farewell to Roxy and Rosie, and we set off up Brook Street and through the Plungington district. It was a route I'd walked a thousand times before but this was the first time I'd had to avoid the dead on the ground. There were a few extra tense moments, but I didn't see anyone that I recognised.

Within half an hour we were closing on the final stretch of hedge and wall, before the pavement widened at the corner of my street. Within seconds I would see my house. Within a minute I would be in it.

*

I always played on my northern heritage. My audience generally wanted me to be an exotic curiosity who kept whippets and a flat cap, so I took that line to begin with. Wherever I played there was always a degree of prejudice to be faced and I learned, as all stand-ups learn, that you can't demolish the barrier and you certainly can't climb over it. You have to win approval. If you do, then those who build the barriers might deconstruct them. You are always an outsider. You are always a foreigner. If you are abroad, the distinction is obvious, but even in your own country it's there. If you are playing in the south, you're a northerner. If on the other hand you're so far north you are in Scotland then you are a soft Sassenach southerner. If you're in the North East then you're from the North West. If you're in the North West, you're not from this town. If you are from this town you're from the wrong part of this town. Even in your own local club, you're from the wrong street, or the wrong end, or wrong side of it. The best tactic is to attack a local rival tribe. You can use the same gags, you just change the label. Ultimately it's all a kind of cruelty. All humour is cruel. Not in a strict academic sense, I'm sure, but generally it is. It relies on belittling, even if it is only the belittling of oneself. As the focus of the humour falls, so the person who laughs is raised by comparison. Cruelty is constantly with us, but always in a fashionable disguise. Fashions change but the cruel fun remains.

Did you hear the one about the Irish comedian who thinks it's still okay to tell racist jokes?

*

Three: Better and Worse

Claire's car was parked outside our house. I saw it as soon as we turned the corner.

My neighbour from number three had been sweeping her drive. The brush was still in her hand. The evening was almost completely dark now, and she looked American Gothic in the slate grey light, much greyer than usual because, of course, the streetlights were off.

Both doors to my house were locked. My hand found the usual pocket and closed on my clutch of keys.

"We'll wait here," said Steve.

"If that's what you want," added Kirsty.

"Yeah."

I unlocked the front door and went in. I saw everything in one-eighth light, both rigidly familiar and entirely strange, because even at night the streetlight outside our house usually spilled residual glow through the windows of the door. The hall was clear, the living room unoccupied. The Sunday paper was on the dining room table, its supplements separated in the way they always were by the end of Sunday morning. The kitchen was empty. The dishes from breakfast had been washed and stacked on the drainer. I clicked the light switch semi-automatically but knowing nothing would happen. I took a torch from the cupboard and moved like a burglar through my own home, going upstairs slowly as if to delay the discovery that I was desperate to find. I went to the boys' rooms first, because they were the only ones likely to have remained in their rooms all through the Sunday morning. Matthew's room, as usual was a combination of a jumble sale and a jungle, but he was not there. Paul's room was smaller but no more tidy than his brother's. His guitar was on the bed, his school work was on the floor, but there was no Paul. Bathroom: empty. Our bedroom: empty. I sat on the bed at the side where I slept, then stood up, and walked round to sit at her side. This was the worst scenario. I could have been there for seconds, or it could have been half an hour. There was this terrible fusion of knowing and not knowing. Of course I knew. But I could not be sure. There's certainty and uncertainty. Give me certainty every time.

The torch cut a segment of silver across the room illuminating nothing in particular but showing everything. Part of a chair. A cushion. A waste paper basket. Who had sat there? Who'd thrown the cushion at whom? How much trivia had passed through that basket? At that moment I'd have kept every till receipt, every strip of torn envelope, all the hairs from her hair brush, every shop tag from every dress. I reached under the quilt and touched the silkiness of her nightdress but left it there where she had put it. On the wall, pictures of our children when they were younger, just cubist slices in the dimness. Teresa. Why Tibet? For Christ's sake why Tibet?

I could feel a wheel within me start to turn. It was a huge wheel, heavy and thus brim-full with inertia, slow to start but impossible to stop. I didn't want it to turn at this time because I had nothing to steady myself against. I needed normality. Oh god, how I craved normality. This was every parent's worst nightmare. Every husband's worst nightmare. No, nightmares end. Even the worst nightmares end. This would not end.

She might be in the garden. If the boys were out and she was in the garden she would lock the house. I went downstairs leaving the torch to shine on the empty chair in our bedroom.

Of course she was in the garden. There she was, rummaging in the bushes beneath the baking-apple tree, trowel in hand, foam kneeler beneath her knees, hair fastened back in the shortest of pony tails revealing a smudge of soil on her cheek.

"Hello," she said, kneeling up. "How was it?"

"Okay. Why are you digging there?"

"Hazel nuts. I know how much you like them."

"What – harvesting or planting?"

"Recovering. I hid them here last autumn. They don't grow on trees you know." She giggled and her face split into the smile that always slew me. She scooped a handful of soil and hazelnuts from the ground and stood up. She stretched the extra three inches necessary to kiss me, and brought her face so close that I could smell her signature scent, her Claireness. Her eyes closed and the night breeze rattled the apple tree leaves ever so slightly, and she was there no more.

I called her quietly, loudly, frantically, hopefully. "Claire! Claire! Claire! Claire! Claire!"

"Dan?"

I whirled round and there beneath the smaller apple tree, in shades of grey the rounded, youthful, sparkling-eyed face of Kirsty. She touched me and I recoiled in shock, swallowed, breathed, apologised. "Sorry."

Kirsty said, "Is there anyone home?"

"She was . . . ." I turned back towards the larger tree, felt myself breathe in the stuttering way a child does when he's trying not to cry. The earth beneath the bushes was undisturbed. I drew a deep cool breath on which I could taste soil. "No, there's no one home."

I turned back to Kirsty. Another figure stood beyond her leaning against the small apple tree. "Any sign of them?" asked Steve.

"No, well, signs everywhere but just the ordinary things. They could be anywhere. Could have gone out together or separately. Who knows?" I felt dizzy and nauseous. "I need to sit down." I staggered away from the others down the long garden towards the cabin we grandly called the summerhouse. I struggled with the infuriating catches but eventually opened the door and sank into one of reclining garden seats set up inside. Kirsty came and sat next to me. Steve remained outside and perched on one of the steps that allowed the path to fall a couple of feet as it passed the larger tree.

"Okay now?" asked Kirsty.

"Yeah. I'm, I'll, I'm fine. Just a bit . . . weak."

"If we stay here tonight we can look properly in the morning."

"They're not here," I said.

"We might find something that gives us a clue."

"Yeah. Yeah."

Steve said, "Got anything we can eat?"

"Of course," I said, "go and help yourself."

"I'll see what I can find us," said Steve and he got up.

I called after him. "There's a torch, in the, bedroom. Our bedroom."

"Right."

For a while Kirsty and I just sat there and didn't say anything, and to be honest that was exactly what I needed. My hand was on the armrest of the chair and she put her hand on top of it and left it there. It was the kind of thing that Claire would have done. We looked out of the open door of the summerhouse and watched the foliage on the apple tree. It was probably just my imagination but as the leaves flickered in the moving air there was a leathery quality about their dance. The bird-feeder hung almost still, and despite its diminutive size seemed sinister, as if it belonged in some bird dungeon torture chamber. We have ways of breaking your beak.

After a little while I felt better. I wanted it to be daylight because here was the normality I craved. By day the garden would seem as it had a thousand times before as Claire and I had sat in the summerhouse and discussed our joys, our problems, our practicalities. This was where we made lists, made action plans, made amends, drank wine and celebrated anniversaries large and small. She loved this view, loved to watch the birds, the trees, the flowers the occasional squirrel, hedgehog and peculiar white-hooded blackbird. The night denied me the normality I desired because, despite being a long garden, not overlooked from behind, the streetlights still sent their luminous pollution and neighbours' houses sent hums of sound and window glows. That night there was none of that. The garden had never been so dark, so quiet. I resolved to sit there the following morning, regardless of what we would discover by day. I would sit there for just five minutes, alone, and look at the garden. Somehow that would drag back into the present some seconds from the past, some of those precious moments when the world still moved but had stopped for us: times when we were not conscious of time. The best of times.

After a while Kirsty took her hand from mine. I squeezed her wrist in return once, as thanks. I turned to smile at her but she was wiping moisture from her eyes with her other hand.

"Who have you got back home?" I asked her.

"Loads," she said. "Big family." She took a few breaths and sniffed. "Big extended family on both sides. Very complicated."

"Why complicated?"

"Marriages, divorces, remarriages, partners, ex-partners, new partners, old partners taken back again, brothers who swapped partners, billions of cousins, half-cousins, quarter cousins. Mum's calendar has the dates marked on when there aren't any birthdays."

"Big family."

"Not sure that family is the right word."

"Empire?"

She laughed the tiniest of laughs. It was the first time I made her laugh. "My Granny would love the idea of an empire. She calls it the grand clan."

"The clan what?"

"The clan Mcpic'n'mix"

I laughed a little. "And really. What's your surname?"

She was about to tell me, but stopped, looked up at the night sky clouded concrete grey, thought for while then said, "We don't really need them any more do we?"

"Need what?"

"Surnames."

She was right, of course.

There were footsteps and for a fifth of an instant my heart leaped, but it was Steve with two plates of sandwiches. "There's cheese, and there's tinned ham and the bread smells fresh, or at least it doesn't smell not fresh. Tuck in, I'll go back for the drinks. There's loads of cordials, coke, lemonade and beer. Some good beers." We placed our orders and he returned to the house. Kirsty unbolted the other summerhouse door and unfolded one of the director's chairs. We had our late night feast of sandwiches and beer and it tasted delicious. This time our stomachs were ready for it and we had the good sense to not consume too much. Despite everything, we all felt much better.

"Well, you two," I said surprising myself with the most cheerful tone I'd used in three days, "welcome to my garden. Steve, you make a very fine sandwich."

"Not just a pretty electrician."

Kirsty and I smiled. I thought for a moment and said, "Well all three of us are pretty damn redundant now aren't we?"

Both of them grinned, but looked for clarification. "Why," said Steve, "what do you do?"

"I'm a stand-up comedian."

Kirsty smiled wider. Steve chuckled. "Well, he said, "there was an electrician, a comedian and an air hostess . . ." We beamed to fill the silent anticipation, the smiles became sniggers, and then the beer and the wonderful loss we found in the moment let us all laugh.

"Where are you from Steve?" I asked.

"Burnley."

I was about to make some disparaging remark about his football club when a much more important thought barged in to my head. "Fuck, fuck, fuck," I said.

"What is it?" asked Kirsty.

"The play-offs. The fucking play-offs."

"What about them?" said Steve.

"The fucking play-offs. The first leg. North End. Sunday lunchtime. That's where they'll be. Claire and the boys. At the ground. At Deepdale."

*

I visited two stately homes last winter. Each of them proudly claimed to be the most haunted house in the country. It hadn't occurred to either of them that the ghosts might be on tour.

*

Four: Not Singing Any More.

I raced across Moor Park beneath a sky now sliced in two. Half was a crust of grey foam, the other a slab of slate pricked with diamonds. So many stars. With all light pollution gone the celestial crowd had returned to the city sky like fair-weather supporters at a cup final. The moon was still hidden but it was edging towards the boundary of the cloud tinting it silver in a black-and-white TV ghost story style. I had not pelted across this turf in anything like this fashion since I had been a boy imagining the line of trees along the avenue to be the perimeter of the witch wood, and the football and cricket pitches to be the moor suggested by the park's name. I could not sustain the pace and had to frequently slow to a brisk walk to ease my pounding breath and soften the thudding pain in my chest.

I had fought with Kirsty and Steve in the garden. They wanted me to wait for dawn, but what was the point of trying to sleep, and why wait? I had told them to claim my sons' beds, told them the way to the ground and pledged to return. They said they would give me until nine o'clock the next morning.

The problem was getting into the ground. The match had been in full swing. The game had been a televised Sunday lunchtime kick-off, and by the time the Event happened all the turnstiles had been shut. I wondered if one was kept open for late-comers and began to circle the ground, stepping over fallen stewards and prostrate police officers. Sleeping policemen. There was a steel door that was slightly ajar at the junction of the Sir Tom Finney and the Alan Kelly stands. This was the disabled entrance to the Town End and it had remained unsecured during the match. The game had been the first leg of the Championship play-offs against Derby County and it was a sell–out. Somewhere among the twenty thousand were my wife and two sons. They would not be sitting together. Paul had a season ticket alongside his friend and his friend's father in the family section of the Tom Finney stand, but Claire and my eldest son, Matthew, could be anywhere, if indeed they had gone to the game.

As I rounded the edge of the terrace I was faced with a spectacular sight. The crowd lay fallen, tumbled forwards like some bizarre human domino toppling demonstration. This picture of regimented irregularity was wrapped around three quarters of the stadium. The Derby fans sat dead in their seats as if astonished by the display of synchronicity before them. For a few moments I was mystified, but I soon realised there could only be one explanation for this pattern, and on seeing my supposition confirmed, I had to laugh out loud. The ball lay in the back of the Derby net. The crowd must have risen to celebrate then died at the very instant of communal ecstasy. Either this was a first half goal, or North End had lost the toss and been ordered to switch sides, for the ball lay in the net at the Bill Shankly Kop end where the terrace was divided between the visitors and the home team. I felt it was unlikely they'd switched ends for the first half, this rarely happened, in which case I could now pin-point the exact time of the Event to somewhere between noon and one in the afternoon, British Summer Time.

For a moment I shuddered. Had they been aware of their moment of passing, and if so, what must they have thought was happening? A stadium disaster? I felt especially sorry for the club statistician – never knowing he had witnessed the last ever goal scored not only by this auspicious football club, but perhaps by any English club, or for all I knew, by any club in the world. What a moment for the young striker, David Nugent, clearly the scorer, for he now lay, arm outstretched reaching towards the friendly half of the Bill Shankly Kop, a stand of two halves, if ever there was one. Shankly's famous quote that football was not a matter of life and death but was much more important than that, now had a hollow ring to it. Somewhere beneath the slumped fans, half joyous, half dejected, Shankly's face still smiled, blocked out in coloured seats, and cheekily peeping through the green gauze stretched across the unsold columns to separate the opposing fans. You're not singing anymore.

Time to find Paul. I could not remember the seat number but I knew which section of the stand it was in. As if to help the moon broke cover and now the ground was a truly eerie sight: floodlit carnage. I walked in front of the family stand. The problem was that, once everyone had fallen, great slabs of supporters had slid towards the pitch, mostly face down, showing their numbers and the names of their heroes to the sky. Those from the higher seats had tumbled and skidded over those lower down. Paul was not going to be exactly in his usual place, and he may well be buried under those that had eaten all the pies. This turned out to be true and, though in one sense it was not as bad as I feared because the family stand contained a high proportion of not so heavy children, in another sense it was far worse, for I had to pull aside a lot of deceased youngsters.

Moving the dead is a horrible task. Over the months I have become slightly hardened to it, but even now it is close to the top of my list of detestable necessities. That night was the first time I really got hold of and moved a cadaver. And then another, and another and another, until I was wrenching them aside ten to the minute, pausing only to regain my breath and slow the blood pounding at my temples. The initial shock of lifting a body is, of course, the realisation of its true weight. I couldn't lift them, especially not the adults, and especially not one after the other. The best I could do was to drag them aside and let them slide further down the slope. This I did for I don't know how long, but after some time I concluded that I had started in the wrong place and moved to begin again. There was still no sense of any decomposition and the dead did not smell, except slightly in a damp musty way. They made sounds when they moved. This I took to be fluid or gas resettling or rising within them. Some of them moaned as trapped air finally escaped. At first this was frightening, then unsettling then annoying, but as with all other aspects of this grotesque activity something within me found a way of dealing with it. When one teenager sighed and then lay still staring at the stadium roof I turned and said "I told you what would happen if you held your breath too long." After that I spoke to them quite a lot, asking their pardon, their forgiveness, even their permission. I think I got into a sort of gothic trance, talking to the dead and then roughly pulling them aside. Whenever I could I gripped them by their clothes but being a summer daytime match most of them wore short-sleeved football shirts and a lot of skin-to-skin contact was inevitable. Their flesh was dry, cold and clammy like the skin of un-refrigerated chicken. My faked good humour could not last and I became choked and then wretchedly emotional, partly because of the enforced horror of the experience, and partly because of my desire to uncover Paul and my failure to do so. Then I spotted his wristbands.

Paul was at the stage of life where he was designing his way out of the safety of the flock identity and heading towards individuality. He tied a variety of wristbands and bracelets to his arm and I recognised the combination. A particularly heavy man lay on top of him. I swore profusely and removed the man's claim to legitimate parentage over and over until somehow I pulled, pushed and prised him free of my son. This action also liberated a seat and I was able to sit Paul up, place him on the seat and sit next to him, though I had to be content with a tangle of supporters' legs for a bench.

For a long while I just held Paul. His head rocked against my shoulder and I put my hand on his face. His eyes were open and I left them that way.

The moonlight cast a cold slab on the pitch. Fugitive slithers of cloud made a faint shadow blemishes here and there creating ghostly marble. We studied the fallen players' formation as they had been rushing forward to congratulate the scorer: two – one – seven. I told Paul that I was glad that he had died in a moment of happiness. I told him that I was happy that he had lived at all. I told him I was, and would always remain, proud of everything he had done. I was even proud of those things he would have gone on to had he lived longer. I was sorry that he would not be able to play in a band or sing any more. What mattered, however, was what he had done. He had lived. He had been alive and made others more alive by his presence. That was all any of us could reasonably be expected to do. I told him I loved him and always would. He was one of the lucky ones, for so many people now had no one left to love them, and for one shakily profound moment I wondered if in some wondrously mystical way that might have been important. Finally, I told him I had to find his mother and brother, but then we sat there longer, neither of us able to move. I think the cumulative exhaustion of the previous two days overpowered me, and despite having only found one quarter of my family, I had an enormous sense of relief. I fell asleep.

How long I slept I do not know. I don't know what time it was when I arrived at the stadium, or when I found Paul, and I didn't look at my watch when I woke, but I think I must have slept for an hour or longer. It took me a moment to understand where I was and what had happened. Paul's head was still on my shoulder and my head had been against his, and my own body heat insulated by his hair made him feel alive and warm to my cheek. But he was cold, and then so was I.

It was not pleasant to look about me and see a sea of dead football fans. I kissed Paul and in as dignified a manner as we could manage I bore him down sliding over the human mountain side to lay him on the pitch. Then I made my way to the centre circle where a couple of Derby players had fallen, perhaps already lingering in anticipation of the kick-off after conceding a goal. I surveyed the stadium again. Twenty-thousand people. Where would I begin? I think the moon had gone but the very start of the pre-dawn was softening the sky and threatening to add colour to this stadium of the departed devoted. Some irksome instinct in me couldn't resist imagining how it might have felt to stand before this size of audience and make them laugh. I've never played to anything like that number. Sometimes they got singers to entertain the crowds before big matches or at half time, but never comedians. What might I have done? What routine? Which gags? Could I have made them laugh? The players sometimes did. The referee more often.

Claire sometimes bought tickets for the Shankley Kop, less frequently for the Sir Tom Finney Stand, most often for the Alan Kelly Town End, so that is where I would start. I looked at it in dismay. It was full, but here too, the fallen had, well, fallen and many of the highest seats were now empty while the lower parts of the terrace were buried under layers of supporters. My arms were drained. I was over-filled with desire but knew I hadn't the strength to complete the task. Perhaps I would have to do this in shifts, coming back day after day, clearing a section at a time until I found Claire and Matthew. It is really very hard to explain why I felt I had to find them. I knew, I think I knew from the very start, that they could not have survived, but the compulsion to see the evidence with my own eyes was overpowering. It was not a human feeling, odd as that may sound, it was a very animal instinct, and finding Paul confirmed that. I had to touch him, had to kiss him, because at the moment of contact there is scenting, and while Paul did not smell of death, or of anything much, there was something there, very thin, but something of him. Or was that my hope, my imagination? Or did I in some deeply ingrained biological way place my scent back on him and then sense it back again? Who knows, and now no one will ever be able to tell me, but all I know is that finding him and being close to him satisfied something in me, and made my determination to find his mother and brother all the stronger. I would never be able to find his sister, and that thought sickened me.

A figure stood by the corner flag and walked towards me. Female, young, darkly angelic in the last of the night.

"We've brought your wife's car," said Kirsty. "We drove straight across the park."

"I've found Paul," I said and took her to him.

"He reminds me of my brother," she said.

"How many brothers do you have?"

"It depends on how you count them."

Steve was a few yards away taking in the spectacle. He looked towards me and I said, "I think we won."

He said, "I'm not sure about that."

I think he was right.

"Come and get some sleep," said Kirsty.

"I can't. I've got to find Claire and Matthew."

"You need to rest. It's only early. We can go back to your house, you can lie down for a while, then get a few things together before we rejoin the others."

"I'm not going anywhere."

"We thought you might say that. We were worried about you."

"I've got to find them."

"What difference will it make?"

"It just does."

Kirsty indicated the crowd. "It could take weeks."

"Then it will take weeks."

"And what state will they be in by then?"

I sucked the air and said, "I've got a strange feeling they'll be exactly like this."

She frowned deeply. "What?"

Steve came and put his young hand on my shoulder. "Come and get some kip."

"I've slept," I said, and Steve smiled indulgently.

"Come on fella," he said, and started to lead me away.

"We're taking Paul," I said.

Steve looked at him. "Won't he be happier here?"

I picked Paul up in my arms and followed the other two towards the gate. By the corner flag I paused, and with my son in my arms I called out to his brother and mother.

"Claire. Mat. I'll come back."

*

If you're American then you probably don't understand football. The first thing to realise is that it's not about feet or balls. It's a game of pointing. Everyone points. The person who points the best and the most, wins. That's usually the referee. Most referees are very good at pointing. During any given game the referee will point the most and thus win the most points. A player will also point a lot. He'll point to where he wants the ball to be played, or where he wanted the ball to be played. He'll point to a member of the opposition who he is too lazy to chase, meaning that his team mate should chase him. This is also used to direct team mates to deal with, or 'mark' members of the opposition that are likely to be so good that they'll make the player look inadequate. When taking a 'corner' a player may point to the sky with one hand. This point means 'I'm going to try to place the ball at the near goal post, or the far goal post," or if secretly agreed by the team it might mean neither of those things. Two hands pointed at the sky mean exactly the same.

The whole crowd might point, usually at the referee. At such times the crowd are helpfully pointing out why the referee is so good at pointing. Their implication is that the referee is pointing to divert your attention away from what he is doing with his other hand.

*

Five: Shelf Life.

We drove straight across Moor Park to avoid the congested roads of Deepdale. I sat Paul on the back seat of the car with me. When we got home we laid him on the lawn at the end of my long back garden and Steve did most of the digging so that we could bury him. I went to lie on my bed and slept deeply, for three hours or so until Steve woke me bearing jam sandwiches. It was mid morning and the day was bright and begging for suburban normality. Kirsty joined us bringing glasses of coke, including the glass that my elder son, Matthew, always used.

"We've got to think about re-joining the others," said Steve. "Shall we take your wife's car?"

"I'll run you down and drop you off," I said.

"What do you mean by that?" asked Kirsty.

"I'll stay here."

Kirsty drank and slid her tongue over lips that still bore a veneer of the lipstick that she'd applied in Brussels. "It doesn't make any sense to try to survive by yourself."

"It doesn't make any sense to try to survive at all," I said.

"It makes perfect sense," she said with a sharpness that I'd not seen in her before.

Steve drank. I ate. There was silence. Real silence. Then Steve said, "What the hell has happened?"

"We've been spared," said Kirsty.

There was another silence.

"By whom?" I asked.

"By whatever," she said. "We've been spared. We have a responsibility."

"To do what?" I asked.

Steve said, "To start again, I suppose."

"No," said Kirsty. "To carry on."

He looked at her, then at me. "How the hell can we carry on? Carry on

43

with what? Normal life?"

"Just, carry on," she said.

"I've got to carry on finding my family."

Kirsty softened immediately. "Are you sure they are there?"

"That's what I have to find out."

"And supposing that they're not?"

"Then I'll look somewhere else."

Steve said, "Mike and the others won't wait."

"I don't expect him to."

"Dan, we want you to come with us," said Kirsty.

"I'll follow later."

"And how will you find us?"

"Leave markers, along your route."

It's really hard to rationalise the way I felt and I made a very bad job of trying to explain it to Steve and Kirsty, both of whom I really liked. Kirsty had a spirit and a resilience that I first thought to be her way of coping with the extreme shock that we all felt, but that I now believe to be a remarkable aspect of her personality. Steve, I'm sure, was as heartbroken as the rest of us, but he seemed able to deal with it by applying himself avidly to anything physical or practical. Under the circumstances here were two people that I was extraordinarily fortunate to have met. It made perfect sense to stay with them, but a superior force was acting upon me, an instinct, an overwhelming feeling to find my wife and son. This must be something of the way a parent feels when a child has been missing too long to hold any hope of survival. I knew Matthew and Claire must be dead, but I still had to find them and see for myself, and that feeling completely dominated my consciousness.

I drove Steve and Kirsty back to join the others from our flight north but stopped the car as soon as we saw their convoy. I refused to face the waves of persuasion that would surely flow from the group. Steve gave me a hug and Kirsty put her arm round my neck and kissed me on the cheek.

"We'll fly flags, and if we get chance we'll paint messages on the Library door in St. Peter's Square," she said.

Steve said, "Remember – any time you need a fuse changing."

"I'll remember," I said.

"Follow us," said Kirsty.

I turned Claire's car round and drove off in the direction of Deepdale. I made slow progress. The streets were quite heavily clogged by a combination of crashed cars and match day parking. I had to make several detours. On St. Paul's Road I came upon the body of an old friend that I hadn't seen for years, a singer from the club circuit. There he lay, Sunday paper beneath one arm, a line of ash and a filter tip cupped in the one hand. He always smoked like a spiv, with the cigarette pinched between finger and thumb and angled in towards his palm. I used to tease him about his habit and tell him it was bad for his voice. He said that was why he did it, he couldn't handle the big time and so he smoked to damage his voice, harm his career and keep things manageable.

The diversions that I followed brought me to the Kwik Save store on Deepdale road and I decided to go in and grab a few things to eat and drink during my day of searching the stands, but this task was more difficult than I had imagined because, of course, with no electricity available it was pitch black inside. I managed to find a few packets of cereal and randomly grabbed at tins without being able to see exactly what I was collecting. I realised I was going to have to complete this kind of operation on a much bigger scale, and wondered how long I would have in which to do it, and just what I would be able to safely consume. I also realised that there was a certain amount of priority that had to be given to this, and I would have to do raids like this in a much more organised fashion soon. There was a smell of dampness and I soon discovered that this was because all the refrigerated compartments had thawed. Sodden packages floated in them. I stumbled over last-minute shoppers and in doing so spilled half of what I'd gathered. I decided to return to the entrance and get a basket but then had the bright idea of going back to the car because I remembered that Claire kept a small torch in the glove compartment. Once back at the car however, I decided to drive on further just past the football ground and go to Sainsbury's. I was much more familiar with the layout in Sainsbury's because I shopped there often.

The scenario inside Sainsbury's was much the same as that in Kwik Save but I could see much better because of the torch. I commandeered the first trolley I found inside the store opting to keep whatever had already been placed in it, then made my way around the store sticking more or less to my usual route and collecting more or less the usual things, though avoiding frozen items. It occurred to me that was likely to be the way I would have to exist for the foreseeable future. I should not be short of supplies. There were several superstores and a myriad of minor stores within a mile or two of my house and I would be able to help myself from any of them to say nothing of the kitchen cupboards of a hundred thousand houses. The problem was that time was already counting down their sell-by and consume-by dates. I wondered about the fresh food that I was randomly harvesting but I figured that most things would still probably be safe enough to eat. The other problem was going to be how I would be able to cook anything. I stocked up well on barbeque supplies. As with everything else that happened during those first weeks, the shopping trip constituted a grotesque experience. There was a knot of nausea in my stomach. I had to step in and out of those who had shopped till they dropped. It was like being a personal shopper for the Addams Family.

I'd managed to get the car onto the superstore slip road but not as far as the car park because two cars had collided blocking a bend. I manoeuvred the trolley past the wreckage and recognised one of the drivers as an old man who, as a young man, used to collect money at Sunday Mass at the Church I'd attended as a child. I wondered if he'd found his heaven.

There was a surprisingly strong impulse to get the shopping home quickly but then I remembered my new circumstances, and simply wove my way back through the mangled vehicles at the major junction and drew up outside the north end of Preston North End. I walked round to the other side of the ground and entered using the same gate that we'd used the day before. I spent all afternoon moving cadavers in the Alan Kelly Town End, but I didn't find what I was looking for.

That evening I cooked a barbeque in my garden. I had steaks of beef, pork sausages and pre-washed salad and a bottle of brown ale. It was delicious, but soured by the happy memories of family barbeques. I finished the beer by Paul's grave. No tears came.

As the daylight faded I sat on one of the garden chairs in the summerhouse. This was a hallowed place where Claire and I had talked out a thousand and one minor matrimonial difficulties. If a long-lasting marriage has to be worked at then this was our workshop. This was where we'd made plans and reviewed them when they failed, or failed to materialise. This was where we swore at each other out of earshot of the children. This was where we laughed. Where we wept. That night, sitting alone, no tears came.

On the way back to the house I looked for her digging for buried hazelnuts beneath the apple tree. She was not there. The ground was undisturbed.

Twice she walked behind me up the garden path. The first time I caught her scent, the second I heard her laugh. She was laughing at me, of course. Claire rarely laughed at my jokes once the flush of first love had faded into something more solid, but she often laughed at me, at my clumsiness, my innate stupidity, my flawed memory. I remember all this perfectly, though not as perfectly as she would have done. When I scented her I turned round to look but saw only her scent, so when I heard her laugh, I did not look so that she would stay with me longer. She did not follow me into the house. Why should she? The garden was her favourite place. I left the back door open for ten minutes in the hope that she would walk through, but she declined. I understood. She'd know that I would understand. That's why she didn't follow. I locked the front door first and then came back to lock the back. She might have slipped inside while I wasn't looking. I hoped so.

Upstairs, out of habit, I switched the shower on and for a moment was angry when it didn't flow, and then I remembered why. The taps were dry. I lifted the lid of the toilet cistern. It was almost empty but there was an inch or so of water below the level of the siphon and I scooped some of that to wash my face and hands. I stripped naked, and as was customary slapped my over-generous paunch before the bedroom mirror.

"Perhaps now I'll lose this," I said out loud.

The bed was too big. I slept without waking until after nine the next morning.

For a long time I lay in the bed just wishing the world to be normal and not daring to move because I knew an upright perspective would remind me of how wrong everything had become. My bladder hurt, and I thought hard about where I would empty it, as the toilet would no longer flush. I suppressed the irritation to spend more time scanning the bedroom and pretending Claire was downstairs eating her breakfast. If I tried hard I could smell what she had made. Then my eyes fell on the waste paper basket and something buried beneath my thoughts told me it was a pot of gold, but my half-awake head couldn't work out why. I rolled my nakedness to kneel beside it and emptied out the contents, and there it was, a receipt from the Preston North End Ticket Office detailing the time and date when it was issued and the exact seat numbers of the tickets purchased.

I did not dash off to Deepdale immediately. There was a new calmness about me now that I had the key information. I was going to have a proper breakfast. I went into the garden and kindled a small fire in the embers of the barbeque on the patio floor. I was going to heat some water and have my first cup of tea since Sunday morning. I took a small pan from the kitchen and then realised my next problem: where was I going to get the water? I went to the kitchen cupboard and took out a bottle of water. The cupboard was well stocked, for Claire had done her usual weekly shop on the previous Friday. My own shopping still was still waiting to be stored. I had plenty to eat for the next few weeks. Food was not a problem but I would have to adjust to not having power and water on tap. The pan took ages to boil. Where would I get my water from in the future? I could keep taking it from the shop shelves and that was likely to be the best solution for drinking but it would hardly be enough for all my other requirements without an absurdly large and highly frequent number of trips. There is an urban brook that passes close to the end of my garden. This would be my main domestic water supply. I would cut myself a path through my neighbours' gardens in due course. The water in the pan boiled and the tea was excellent. I boiled an egg, and then made toast using a fork taped to the end of a bamboo garden cane. 'Toast' as a classification contravened trades descriptions. 'Carbon bread' would have been more accurate, but warm and with honey on it became supreme cuisine.

I ambled down to Paul's grave and almost without thinking began digging resting places for his brother and his mother alongside him. I marked out the two graves first. I would put Claire in the middle so that she could be close to both sons. I made her a generous space. I decided to dig out both trenches before going back to the football stadium. The soil dug easily but I observed something that intrigued me and caused me to dig more quickly for a while. We had noticed when digging Paul's grave that we were turning over a number of dead worms and I found that to be the case again, but I also noticed woodlice, beetles, earwigs, and every one of them was dead. This was the case no matter how deeply I dug. I failed to unearth a single living creature. The excavation took most of the morning but I made two good trenches, each one at least three feet deep. By the time I had finished it was starting to rain, which ruined my plans for a cooked lunch.

I went into the house and made sandwiches using tinned salmon. I drank lemonade. The rain fell steadily so I further delayed my journey and spent several hours reorganising the house. I managed to avoid melancholy and gloom despite the fact that virtually everything that I touched triggered a personal memory of one of my family. Throughout my new life I have found that the only way to cope is to concentrate on the immediate and actively reject all associations with the past when engaged with essential tasks. Of course there have been hours and hours of remembering, but thoughts of the past contaminate preparations for the future, and I have learned to separate the two. As the rain fell and for the first time I heard rain and only rain, I reorganised my house. I started lists. I found all the essential items that I might need soon: candles, matches, torches, buckets, knives, an axe, tools, two storm lanterns, blankets, sheets, functional clothes. All these things were given new locations in the house and anything with a plug on was evicted to the garage. I removed the decorative base of the gas fire in the living room, for on rainy days like this that would be my indoor stove, and eventually, I supposed my source of heat for my home. I remembered the butane gas cooking stove we used to take camping, and remembered too that we had given it to the charity shop, so I added one to my rapidly growing shopping list. I also thought of trying to get a small petrol electricity generator and used this item to start a second list, what I called my 'fantasy list' of non-essentials that I would move on to once I had a basic survival routine established. I was heartened by home improvements and by the spirit that I detected in myself, but I knew also that there was an element of the charade about this, I was my own morale booster and such an approach is always fragile. I brought remnants of D.I.Y. timber from the garage and made a small indoor fire in my living room hearth to boil a pan and make another cup of tea. It took ages and the chimney was less than effective so the whole house was fogged and I had to remove the batteries from both smoke alarms. A coating of soot settled on my bookshelves, on the window, everywhere. The carpet was stained by trodden out sparks. This was the end of domesticity as I had known it. My class had known luxury for half a century. There was no luxury any more and no class either.

Despite my disheartening first attempt at indoor cooking I still felt encouraged that I could get myself organised to survive reasonably well. I had my yellow pages, and in there I could find suppliers of anything I wanted, so with a little resourcefulness I would be able to establish a solid base for myself. It would be a curious existence with most of what I might need relatively easily to hand and my only occupation being to remain alive, healthy and, most difficult of all, sane.

It rained for the rest of the day so I decided to wait until the next day before collecting my family. I had salad for my dinner that night and cold milk and cereal the next morning. I put the Ticket Office receipt in my pocket but also memorised the seat numbers and with that information I found Claire and Matthew easily. They were partially obscured from the places on the pitch where I had stood to scan the stands. Matthew, who must have stood to celebrate the goal, had fallen to his side landing partly on his mother who was propped against the man to her left and the seat behind her. Both mother and son had peaceful and, slightly cheerful, expressions on their faces.

I was thinking far more rationally during this visit and realised that I had full reign of the ground and that all the exit doors were, of course, unsecured, so I was able to drive the car well into the ground limiting the distance I had to carry the corpses.

There was still absolutely no sign of life whatsoever, and by that I mean no flies, no insects, no rats and, most disturbingly of all, still no scent of decay. There was a smell but it was of damp fabric drying, for although the crowd had mostly been undercover, some moisture had drifted onto the Shankly Cop. The skins of those I touched had a slightly waxy feel to them but they were not biologically decomposing and nothing visible, or as far as I could tell invisible, was eating them. I had refused to confront the implications of this knowledge up to this point but now I had to wrestle with the concept that even life on a microscopic level had been halted. I had no idea what the full repercussion of this might be.

I buried them that evening. The act of burial was very important. I cannot explain why, but it was. It just felt right. Before I covered them I held each in my arms for a time. How long, I do not know. Time had been relegated from premier pressure to non-league non-entity. Day and night mattered, minutes did not. I held my son and wife for as long as I needed to.

Matthew had grown into a thoroughly admirable young man. He had inherited, or learned, his mother's generous spirit and her reserved, but all-embracing warmth. There were parts of me in him too, but even by nineteen, he was more even-tempered, more articulate, more altruistic and less judgemental than his almost-fifty father. As an undergraduate he was in his element, whereas I had been out of my depth. His academic talent was non-specific and generic. He was reading English but could have mastered any discipline written in that language. He was a student of the world whereas his father was a spotter who took notes then took the Mickey. I had been eager for his eventual graduation to see what he would do. He loved the world and was fascinated by it. How would he have contributed to it? Now he would give nothing. Not even himself.

I held Claire for even longer. Even when I eventually set her down I had to touch and rearrange her endlessly. I became jealous of gravity, the only thing for which she reached. We had been in love, then loved, then found that sacred companionship that floats above love. Together or apart it made no difference as long as we knew the other to be alive. This was the Claire who would discuss her stocks and shares with the cat, and furthermore would take his advice. She always treasured our first car because it had a wonderful sense of direction. She once won a tiny compass in a Christmas cracker and subsequently took it with her whenever she travelled because she hated sleeping in a north-south alignment. I used to ridicule her for this, suggesting it was a throw back to her hippy teenage fads, but now I wonder if there was something in it after all. She rarely wore make-up and that pleased me immensely. I hate the fake. She criticised inanimate objects but rarely found fault in people. She loved books and worked for many years as a librarian, firstly in public libraries, then latterly at the University. Like all of us, but perhaps more than most, she could engross herself in something to the exclusion of all other considerations. This would sometimes get her into trouble at work. Order was important, she declared, but it should always be ready to accommodate the exceptional. Classification was a quick route to glorious chaos, not a means of regimenting diversity. She found it difficult to understand why libraries had to close. She considered punctual public transport rude because it didn't have the courtesy to wait for her. She hated being governed by the clock. It was a shame she died when the clocks did.

When I finally let her go, I sat for a long time on the shelf of soil by her head and contemplated joining her. The mechanics of it would be dead simple. A good blade was only yards away in the kitchen. The veins on the inside of my wrists have always been un-endearingly prominent. Unwittingly, or inadvertently, I had carved her grave too wide. There was room, just, for both of us. I considered this for some time. The spade caught my eye. I covered her. I covered Matthew. I spent some time looking for Dawson, our cat. I even called his name. He didn't come. I went inside and slept.

Over the next two weeks I became adept at shelf life. I grew accustomed to the dead who changed very little in their appearance. Their skin tone paled to ash grey but then stayed that way. The sun had an effect on them but it was a shading rather than a discolouration. I soon saw them as distasteful street furniture and blanked them as you might do to obscene graffiti that you passed on the way to work each day. I raided my neighbours' homes at little emotional cost and in this way met most of my immediate needs. I made more visits to Sainsbury's, after first concocting a crude miner's helmet type arrangement by taping a small torch to my spectacles. I shopped like a Dalek footballer's wife.

I evolved a domestic routine in which I ate one main meal per day in the late afternoon or early evening, not that there was any real distinction between those two time phases any more. The main purpose of each day was to prepare for this meal. The weather gradually improved so I cooked and ate more out of doors, on the barbecue patio half way down my back garden. I kept a fire burning there almost constantly. If rain came I ate cold food indoors. I slept in my own bed, except for one balmy night when I slept on the soil close to Claire.

There was, and is, a gothic air to everything. Civilisation becomes a corpse so quickly. Brick becomes bone. Anything with windows is a skull. The urban landscape became a theme park designed by Dali, real and surreal.

This is where we live.

I survived those final days of May through adrenalin-fuelled automation. There were some very bleak moments and I did prepare a self-destruction kit containing lots of pills and a brand new vegetable knife. I put it in the loft to ensure I would have to make a conscious effort to get it. There were a lot of lonely moments but I never really felt alone. I still don't, and this is a source of considerable anxiety and of hopeful comfort. I think it is probably a deeply instinctive sensation. We still do not know how many survived the Event, and I harboured an even less accurate notion of this during those early weeks. It is human nature to presume un-encountered others to be hostile and to attribute any unexplained sound to one of them. The world is full of unusual sounds, it always was, but before the Event unusual sounds were most often made by usual people. Now – who knows? Every sound heralds hope or threat: probably threat. Nature is a Tannoy of terror. It's like Pontin's for the paranoid.

Everyone that I cared deeply about I knew to be dead, except for Teresa my daughter in Tibet. I suppose her survival was the slight hope that kept me going. It was a slim thread to grasp but when there is almost no hope the slimmest of chances becomes the salad-dodger of the century. I also have to acknowledge that the survival instinct is overwhelming. There is a super-hero inside each one of us but they only emerge when there is a real crisis. The thing is, they don't hang around for ever. By day I was Dan Goodwright, by night Adrenalin Man. I transformed a lot during those first few weeks. Since then my powers have faded.

I did not see another soul during the remainder of May except in my imagination. I did not think too much about the future. By the time June dawned it was becoming clear that the impact of the Event was much more comprehensive than we had first realised. I spent a good deal of each day in the garden which was becoming slightly sepia. The lawn looked parched and stayed that way even after rain. Flowers drooped and remained prone. Trees looked weary and had a harsher rustle when blown. May had brought the luscious abundance of natural growth. June came, and brought my favourite season: autumn.

*

My uncle was a funeral director. He was badly hit by a dramatic fall in the death rate. He decided to diversify. He opened a retirement home. He was able to offer an irresistible package: from family cast-off to cremation for a single fee. That went well, so he diversified further and invented the budget no-frills funeral: Easydeath. You can get an internment from as little as three hundred quid, or a cremation from between ninety and one hundred and fifty depending on the price of gas. The only problem is you have to book the exact date six months in advance. You can choose to be buried in one of twelve European cities. You'll be laid to rest sixty miles outside it.

*

Six: Home Improvements.

The sound of a motorcycle made my heart race. It was Thursday 2nd June 2005 and I was cooking a breakfast of bacon outside. I could not tell how close the machine was because I had become so accustomed to the tomb-quiet of dead nature and the empty city. Initially it was travelling at some speed, then it slowed, sped again, then slowed and cruised. I didn't know what to do. Suddenly the most terrible sight was the plume of grey rising from my fire. It could signal my presence and summon friendship or it could betray me. It brought silence, or at least it returned me to the muttering and sinisterly sighing breeze. Whoever it was had stopped his motorbike and I did not know where. Instinct made me remove my frying pan from the fire and throw soil on the contents within it to smother the crackling hiss of the rashers still frying there. I shovelled soil onto the fire itself but there were no tools close by and therefore I could only use my hands, and initially I simply created smoke of a deeper density, but within seconds I had the fire out. Too late. He stood at the top of my garden. He was exactly what you might expect: a leather-clad, helmeted and ginger-bearded male motorcyclist of indeterminate adult age. He looked at me and I at him. We were thirty yards apart. Neither of us spoke. We remained that way for no more than five seconds before he turned and left. A moment later his bike engine growled back to life and yelled out that it was very near indeed. Then away it went, over-revving the way only motorcyclists do.

I felt defiled. There was no logic in that feeling, but then again since the Event I have found little logic in the way I have behaved. I'm starting to think that logic is a more recent and more alien attitude that anyone had previously believed. Perhaps logic came to us in a blast from outer space? Perhaps everything did? Whatever the stars can give us they can also take away. I'm jumping the gun. All I know is that the first months were feral times and I functioned like the animal that I am. I think I am a fawn. That, after all, was why I started telling jokes. Comedy is the camouflage of the playground. When the world went wild I went back to my frightened foraging default self, laying low and scared by sound. I was prey and I'd just been found. It forced me to think afresh about my predicament and make plans. Happy is not a word that I associate with that time, but I had found a kind of undomesticated contentment, absurd as that may seem. I was living day to day and doing so with increasing success and smoothness. Of course, I was emotionally crippled by my personal loss and haunted by my desolate prospects but it was amazing how I was able to cocoon each of those traumas and numb the pain from them, even though I felt sure they would emerge eventually and do their best to consume me. At that time, however, daily necessity was all that mattered and I had competently avoided doing anything so civilised as making long-term plans. Now someone else knew where I was and that forced me to consider whether or not I should stay there.

Most people cannot understand that comedians are essentially solitary beings and most of us actually prefer that state. Some comics I knew were compulsively gregarious, and we all had to feed off mass approval but, along with most of my associates, I loved to retreat into near or total solitude with regularity. The comedy circuit is a lonely track anyway. It's like racing on a slow horse three lengths behind the main pack on a country course, with long spells of near isolation followed by intermittent bursts of blended cheers and abuse as you pass in front of the grandstand. I loved time with my family, but my family was gone. Anyone whose family did not survive the Event did not consider starting one, at least not at first.

Of course, the notion of setting off in search of Kirsty and Steve and the others occurred to me frequently after I'd initially mourned Claire and the boys, but I simply did not have the inclination to abandon my home. I had half decided on making an exploratory expedition at some unspecified time in the late summer. Then summer was cancelled. I still thought I would go. I was frightened by the prospect of making the trip, and the visit of the helmeted beard made me rationalise some of those fears. I was scared of not finding them. What would I do then? How long would I look? I think I was even more scared that I would find them, for how might they have established themselves? Would I be seen as a threat and be rejected? Even worse, might they welcome me into a society I could not stand? Their friendships must surely have developed by then and that notion worried me rather more than it should have done. Either way, what would I find if I returned home? Would it still be home? Would others have claimed it? This was much more likely now that the beard had found it. Would that matter, when I had the whole world to live in, well mainland U.K. anyway? It would matter. But if the beard came back he could probably take it anyway, even if I was in residence, especially if he brought his mates.

He came back. And he brought his mates.

I didn't relight the fire, which was silly. They knew where I lived. You can only be betrayed once. I guess a part of me was punishing the flame. When you are a primitive the fire is your favourite friend. It holds a cruel power over you, and is as possessive as a partner when the au pair starts pouting. You have to feed it, fuss over it attend to it more than hourly. It gives you good feelings and makes you cry in equal measure, but you can't ignore it for long. A tiny part of me hoped that the beard didn't care, or wouldn't remember where I was. How irrational was that? They came in the late afternoon. I heard them as I was slicing through a block of luncheon meat, preparing a salad with lettuce that was still fresh. Their sound said it was either a very big bike or more than one. It was five. Five. One of them rode straight up my drive. They were all garbed in much the same way and were either a clutch of decent blokes dressed sensibly for speed on two wheels, or the leather fetish five. I hoped for the former. They didn't bother to knock and came through both front and back doors at the same time. Their leader was straight out of central casting for standing on the prow of a Viking longboat, as the first extra behind Kirk Douglas. He was a big man in every sense with a beard the colour and texture of wire wool. He was fifty something going on fifteen, and he had clearly found the past in the future the Event had brought. When he took his helmet off it showed a pony-tail that was all length and no root and gathered into a rather puny spring onion stem just above the nape of his neck.

"Good afternoon," he said. His accent was north-eastern and his voice had a moist, whistling quality.

"Come in," I said trying to suppress the sarcasm in my speech.

"Who are you then?"

"Dan. Goodwright."

"This your place?"

"Yes."

"Now, or before?"

"Both."

"Oh," he said and at that point he pushed me slowly but firmly aside and strode into my living room. "Do the survey, boys." The other four set about searching the house. The one who'd found me first went upstairs. He was slim and ginger with a small Jacobean style moustache and a beard. A shorter, stocky, dark man, relatively clean shaven but with long sideburns and tattooed hands took the other two, both portly, early twenties but pushing malt and barley bellies before them, straight to the kitchen. The leader slumped himself in my armchair, his back to the window. "I'm Lucifer," he said. "From Prague."

"Prague?"

He nodded, breathing out at the same time, squeaking like a bronchitic drainpipe. I thought first, but said it anyway: "You don't sound Czech."

"We were in the air. From there. When it happened."

I said, "I was flying back from Seville. Where did you land?"

"Liverpool."

"Is that where you got your bikes?"

"Who else is here?"

"No one."

"Really?"

I told him my story. I'm not sure he believed it, so I suggested he looked in the garden where he would find three shallow graves.

"Three?" piped Lucifer.

"My wife and sons."

There was a minor pause that really bothered me.

"You've got a daughter," he said. There was another pause then he nodded at the family photo on the bookshelves.

"She's in Tibet," I said.

There was another pause, longer this time. I could hear my larder being overturned.

"You're telling me there's no one else living with you?"

"No one."

The ginger scout came down from upstairs. "He's a comedian, Luce," he said and gave him one of the business cards I kept in my bedroom.

"Dan Good," read the self-nominated prince of Prague darkness. "That's not what you said your name was."

"That's my stage name."

"Comedian," he read. I knew the dreaded command was coming. "Tell us a joke then."

I wanted to try one about the number of bikers required to change a light bulb but thought better of it. "I've retired," I said.

"Well, we might just change that. We might want a command performance at our headquarters."

"You know where I am."

"Yeah."

"Where are you living?" I asked.

"We have a place."

"Just you?"

"And anyone who wants to join us."

One of the beer-gutted henchmen appeared in the door chewing my luncheon meat slab as if it were a Mars bar.

I tried not to give him the attention he sought, meanwhile Lucifer considered and delivered his next remark affectedly. "Be wise to join us."

I thought about telling him I was allergic to leather, but said instead, "I'm fine here."

"As you like, Dan my man. We'll drop in from time to time."

"I'll keep the kettle on," I said.

"Don't fuss," he said getting up. "We're always happy to do D.I.Y. hospitality." He sunk a kindly claw into my shoulder. "Remember to tell us, if there's anyone else."

Their bikes started in a flurry of fumes and they began to peel away, into the road.

"See you," shouted Lucifer, "Isn't the afterlife lovely?" When they had gone, I went to my kitchen. They'd slyly stolen the best of the food I'd assembled. They could just as easily have cherry picked it from the shelves where I'd found it but, of course, that wasn't the point.

The visitation by the bikers kick-started my lowest time. The day of the Event itself was not a low period and neither was the immediate aftermath. Mass trauma does not bring depression. It is small human cruelties that switch off the tide of the survival spirit. It is better to feel alone than to feel oppressed, and oppression can be terrible in its subtlety. What had they done? Nothing of any great substance. They had been slightly supercilious in their attitude and sneakily stolen a few things that I could easily replace. So what? Well, they had also firmly established the pecking order. There were only six people that I knew of in my city, and I was sixth in line. That had been made clear. A feudal regime had been established and I wasn't the one in the castle. I wondered how often I would be required to pay tribute. I became angry within and ridiculously rehearsed in my head how I might realign the balance of esteem. Status is a see-saw, however, and if I rose, then at least one of them must sink, and they wouldn't like that. Surviving was not the same thing as starting again, and I really didn't feel like starting again.

Autumn is the most beautiful of seasons. Somehow there is life in the glorious death. The colours are warm, and there is a vibrancy in the peacock display of leaves not shed, as if the tree wants to parade her finery and remind us that she'll be back in all her glory with the spring fashions. Some green plants stay green, others seem to go greener, like the holly that has more sheen than plastic and is stylishly sharper than designer needles. The phoney autumn, the fake autumn, the masquerade season, a shop window for Hades' fashion brought no vibrancy of any kind. No riot of colour, no celebration of recycled fabric. First, everything natural dulled. Beige and muted green was the catwalk. As June aged, in crept brown, pale and dusty like an English drought. Deciduous trees drooped then evergreens stiffened and some shed spikes like novice Christmas trees suffering premature ejaculation. Grass died. This was a gradual process that took all of July and August to complete, but the first signs were evident in early June.

Less than a week passed before I heard motorbikes again. I slipped out of my garden and along the route I'd cleared through my neighbours' gardens to enable me to get to the brook beyond. I sneaked up a garden and hid in a house further along my street. By this time they'd ridden up my drive and out of sight from the bedroom window from where I cautiously peeped. I went into the back bedroom where a small, still, ceramic child lay crumpled over his toys. The view of my garden was limited and I could see nothing, so I returned to the front bedroom where I lay low and waited, peering out with extreme caution. Nothing happened. A considerable time passed, perhaps an hour, then I heard the engines again. Two bikes emerged from my drive and cruised off towards the end of my road away from me. One of them had two riders. The solo rider looked very like Steve, and pillion rider on the other bike was female and almost certainly Kirsty.

They'd left a note on my kitchen worktop.

Dan,
You've had visitors! Hung around a bit for you. We went to Manchester but things turned unpleasant, so a bunch of us cut back and we're camped up in a hotel not far from here. Come and join us. Here's a map.

Kirsty and Steve.
xxx

The sketch map showed a location I knew, just next to the big B & Q

Warehouse south of Preston. I was tempted to go straight away, as I needed to restock on some essentials. I also needed to cook a meal and boost my immediate supply of fuel. This was not a major worry as I was surrounded on all sides by huge quantities of flammable material, but it took time to gather and break down into pieces small enough to use. I carried out another shopping trip and then put my mind to building up my woodpile before cooking. I decided to break up my neighbours' garden sheds first, but took the considered decision to begin with those at the far end of my street. It felt safer to work some distance from my house while I was nervous about the return of the bikers. This was a wise move, because it was while I was setting about a shed that I heard bikes again. I realised they were not the same as the two I had heard earlier, and sure enough I watched a trio of the Prague chapter draw up from the safety of a hedge at the end of my street. They shouted for me and kicked a few things around before leaving. I waited another five minutes then went to survey the damage. They'd taken some more food, including a good deal of my latest hoard. They'd also taken Kirsty's note.

I stuffed myself with biscuits and wondered what to do. I was really worried for Kirsty. I felt sure that they would go in search of her. They were probably already there. Even if they were not, what could I do? She was a part of a community so maybe she'd have the protection of others, but some of those others would be at risk too, and it was my fault. Knowing the likelihood that the bikers would return I should have burned the note. I was curious to know what would happen, or had happened, but I was also nervous about going to find out. I didn't like being on the move following the bikers' first visit, because I was conscious of how audible a single vehicle is when no others are in motion, and the state of the roads meant that speed in a car in town was impossible. It was no surprise that two wheels were becoming the preferred method of transport. This thought provided my answer and I selected the stealth option: my son's bicycle. Riding through the city centre in this fashion was a revelation. I could make very good progress and felt very safe, for I would surely hear any other road user long before they had the chance to see me. I set off and purely by chance I discovered the biker's camp. I was cutting through the centre of the city when I heard them, and after making very cautious approaches on two wheels then on foot I observed one of them using the disabled access ramps to ride his bike right into Preston's parish church: St. John's Minster. I didn't linger, but recovered my quieter steed and headed south.

The city centre was littered, of course, as all city centres are, I imagine, with shoppers and their final purchases. By this stage, the bizarre was already the norm. There was a sickening novelty round every corner but it was the same joke over and over again. There is a moment of twisted satisfaction as you work out just exactly what each victim was doing as the death blow struck, then the gut-wrench of reflection on the life lost, then the heavy numbness because it's everywhere you look. All fall down. A global domino tumble. A world record.

I made good speed but had a few miles to cover, and out of town I felt fairly vulnerable, because I thought I could be spotted from a distance more easily, but I put my head down and pedalled and eventually arrived at the place that Kirsty had indicated on her sketch.

Camp Q was masterminded by exactly the kind of genius you need when the world has all but ended. She is a delightful woman called Clita Shilling. Clita was in charge at Camp Q, closely aided by her two chosen lieutenants, Roxy and Rosie, the young women I'd met in the van from Warton. How they had grown in confidence under her guidance. Clita was also a Prestonian, the only other one I know to have survived. She had been a personnel manager in the National Health Service, so I guess she was pretty used to crises. She was the embodiment of pragmatism, but also burned with optimism and bubbled with humour. Through her I found laughter again. She knew of the hotel and realised that its location, directly opposite a supermarket and adjacent to a huge home improvement warehouse provided the perfect place for a refugee camp. Like the bikers she had flown into Liverpool, though not on the same flight. She, and many others at Camp Q, had been mid-Atlantic on a Jumbo from Boston when the Event happened. Their flight crew had several hours to try and work out what was going on before they struck land. They took lots of calls from aircraft already descending and therefore decided to divert to Liverpool to avoid the runway congestion evident at other airports. Their experience at John Lennon International was not dissimilar to ours at Heathrow but on a smaller scale. In the end the same pattern emerged with people stealing vehicles to set off in search of food and more permanent shelter. Many, like myself were keen to seek out relatives. Sadly over half of her flight companions were United States citizens. Eventually, she and a group of sixteen others journeyed all the way to Preston in a caravan of small vehicles. They began to establish the camp and were later joined by Kirsty and a dozen of the Manchester-bound contingent returning west.

The first sight I noticed as I cycled up was that the superstore's banners had been taken down from the flagpoles and replaced with a long twist of blue and yellow fabric. Heaven knows where this had come from but it was so clearly hastily and roughly hitched that it served well as a flag to signify the fact that a camp had been established in that location, but also as a banner proclaiming confidence. Then I noticed a large ashen heap in one corner of the car park. This, I discovered later, was where Clita had organised the cremation of all the cadavers on the three sites of the hotel, the superstore and the sales warehouse, and all those on the pavements and in vehicles in the immediate vicinity. This meant that those living in the camp did not have to see a corpse for as long as they remained within the designated boundaries. It had been a grim task for her and her companions, but was also one of her many masterstrokes. Everyone had his or her own room in the hotel. Married couples and established partners shared, but everyone else had individual personal space. The sexes were divided, with males on the first floor and females on the second. Males were not permitted above the first floor without the express permission of Clita, Rosie or Roxy. There was no debate about this or any of the other rules. This was Clita's camp and one of her favoured axioms was that democracy is a luxury of civilisation. When we once again could claim civilisation, then we could enjoy democracy, but until that point she was going to operate a dictatorship. And she did. Food was prepared in the hotel kitchen, which had been kitted out with gas barbecues and camping stoves, courtesy of B&Q. Meals were eaten in the hotel restaurant. The larder was the superstore. It wouldn't last forever, but this was intended to be a base camp. There was a very good supply of fuel on hand but water was emerging as a shortage. Toilets were established in the grounds at the rear of the hotel, using gazebos and tents. There was a well-established domestic daily routine and also a schedule of special tasks, and people allocated themselves to each as they wished provided they pulled their weight. Whenever it was necessary Clita imposed duties. The penalty for refusal, and indeed for any misdemeanour, was exile. And she meant it. Somewhere in the locality was an American nineteen-year-old called Nathan, living wild, as Clita put it. Security was high on Clita's list of priorities. She was no fool and knew that she was essentially lord of a remote medieval castle. Any stranger was a threat. I was spotted long before I saw any signs of life and Brad and Duncan came out to meet me with pick-axe handles and an automatic pistol. Fortunately the mention of Kirsty counted as a password, and I was taken for an audience with the mighty Clita in the warehouse, mid way between plumbing and lighting.

I will always remember Clita's smile, for she nearly always wore it. I will also always remember the multi-coloured wrap she wore about her torso. She'd brought it in her hand luggage, an impulse buy in an ethnic-themed shop at Boston airport while she'd been waiting to board her delayed flight. She'd made a simple bandana from a length cut from one end, and this spangled uniform became her trademark, her badge of office.

"So you're Kirsty's friend are you?"

I didn't feel I'd qualified as a friend. "We met on the flight from Heathrow."

"She told me. Want to join us do you?"

"I just came to see her. See if she was all right. She left a note, at my place this morning. Is she here?"

"Oh she won't be back for a day or two."

"What?"

"They've gone on a reconnaissance. It's on our action plan." At this point Clita peeled away and indicated a roll of wallpaper hanging from the shower unit display. On it was a list of things to do, with those done crossed out. One of them said Twenty-five mile radius reconnaissance NSEW. Clita tapped the line with a length of plastic pipe. "There you are. They went north first. We're trying to find out if we have neighbours."

I told her about the Hell's Angels from Prague camped, I presumed, in the Minster.

"Oh we know about them."

I heaved a sigh of relief. "I thought I'd dropped you in it."

"On the contrary, I think, erm, well, we let slip you might be out there. Did they come looking?"

"They did," I said. "Fortunately I wasn't their type."

"They visit. But I'm not having them here."

"Very wise," I said. "How many of them are there do you know?"

"How many did you see?"

"Five."

"Five yes. There were six."

"Six?" I waited for her to elaborate but she changed the subject.

"So, are you going to join us here? Kirsty said you're worthy." She burst into laughter. "I like worthy men." She placed a deep rhythmic emphasis on worthy.

"I'm fine where I am," I said.

"I've got seventeen worthy men and ten worthy women. It's not enough to repopulate Preston."

"Is that what you intend to do?"

"Not me personally, Mr Dan Good, so don't raise your hopes. Or anything else." She cracked into a really dirty cackle, and I laughed spontaneously for the first time since the Event. I felt infected by her humour and loved it.

"It sounds like you need women, rather than men," I said.

"We need to get everybody together. Not necessarily in one place. Though I think that would be best. Well, the right people. The worthy people. Good people. You're a good person, aren't you Mr. Good?" She laughed a great deal longer than her pun warranted.

"Good for nothing," I said, and meant it, but she was even kind enough to laugh at that.

"I don't believe you," she said.

I let the laugh fade, which didn't take long, then said "I'm not sure repopulating will be a good idea."

"It's on our long term decision list," she said, and pulled another roll of wallpaper out from a rack of compression fittings. She didn't unroll it but tapped it lightly against her bandana then slotted it back in place. "I know what you're saying."

"Everything's dying," I said.

"Except dead things," she said with a delighted chuckle.

"I think the bacteria are dead too," I said. "That's why things are not rotting."

"Nuclear Armageddon," she said, closing her mouth but still managing a magnificent Einstein smile topped by eureka eyes.

"But we're still here," I said.

"Final proof that God didn't intend us to fly," she said.

"I often thought that, when I flew Ryanair."

She chuckled and reorganised her wallpaper lists.

I said, "I don't think babies would be a good idea."

"We can only do what we can do."

"Not until there are signs that things are recovering."

She turned to me. "I know what you're saying, but be careful who you say it to. Two of my men and one of my women are children. The youngest is just about to turn seven, and the girl is twelve, which is probably just about the worst age to be right now. Okay, let's allocate you a room, and then give you a few jobs to do."

"I'm not staying."

"Oh yes you are. At least until Kirsty and Steve get back. They really want to see you. And we need all the worthy help we can get."

"I've got things at home I need to attend to."

Clita's face stiffened. "It's not good, being on your own. This is time travel Dan. We've gone back a thousand years. By Christmas it will be two thousand. Got your sword and sandals have you?"

"I've got the sandals."

"We've got the swords. And I'm scared we're going to need them. What we will need is worthy people. Good people. Dan Good people." She chuckled again, but in a controlled way, like well-drilled hiccoughs.

I sniggered and stayed. It was a good decision, because that night my house was burned to the ground.

Kirsty flung her arms around me and hugged me. "Thank god you're safe."

Her scent was charcoal number five. We were in the car park of the hotel. Steve was a few yards behind her, hitching his bike onto its stand. The other rider stood astride the one that had carried Kirsty.

"How are you?" I asked her.

"As good as can be expected," she said with her soft Scottish lowlands lilt lifting the vowels.

She smiled broadly but there was something behind her sparkling eyes. "You smell of smoke," I said.

The smile faded from sincere to forced and then to no smile at all. "Your house," she said.

"What about it?"

"There's nothing left. Sorry Dan."

"What do you mean?"

"We've just been there on the way back. Looking for you. It's just a shell, Dan. Still burning, but just a shell."

"How?"

She shrugged. "Had you lit a fire inside?"

I shook my head. "Not for days."

"Sometimes they can smoulder. Carpets and things."

I shook my head again. "Was anyone else there?"

"Anyone else?"

"See any bikers or anyone?"

"No."

Steve came over, but the other rider did not. Kirsty later introduced him as Tye. Steve said, "Sorry Dan. But you can stay here with us."

I moved into room 113.

With only twenty-seven in the camp it wasn't long before I knew everyone by sight and most by name. We came from a variety of backgrounds and spanned the age spectrum with the eldest touching eighty and the youngest six. The former was a doughty woman called Doris, last remnant of the Dunkirk spirit, and the latter was Dominic the youngest computer wizard I ever met but now his knowledge was all theoretical and like Sean, our ten year old boy, switched his main allegiance to football. They frequently organised evening matches where most people played on one team or the other, even Doris had a spell in goal. We had a dozen Americans in our number and to our dismay they became skilful at soccer and eventually demanded international matches, some of which they won. They taught us baseball, at which we proved mostly useless.

The girl that Clita had referred to was called Lauren, though she later re-baptised herself Thistle as a sign of her determination to grow among so much desolation. She was a slight, sprite of a girl lithe in body and mind and just entering the teenage surge of height. Unsurprisingly, when I first met her she was withdrawn and reflective to the point of being morose for her father was still in the States where he had been working and where she and her mother had been to visit him. Her mother was called Christina. She was a very striking woman, English but clearly of Latin descent. Lauren did not join in with the games and generally kept herself to herself. To begin with I had little to do with her, though I always tried to cheer her with a smile or what I thought was a witty remark. She rarely shared my opinion on what was witty.

I left it about a week before I went to look at the house where Claire and I had made a family. Seven of us took five motorcycles. I used to ride as a teenager so I was quickly competent at driving that form of transport again. Kirsty also came and rode her own bike this time. Steve came too but Tye did not. Duncan, a burly builder who liked to carry an automatic pistol in his tool belt rode shotgun behind a former Boston fire-fighter called Craig. The fifth bike was driven by a real-estate rep called Jolene, and also bore Gordon and his rifle. Gordon was a financial consultant from the Wirral, but on long weekends he'd invested his time in blood sports. By this time the incineration of my property had ceased. The rest of the street was intact. Only my semi and its attached neighbour had burned. The roofs had fallen in and part of the front wall had collapsed. At the rear, the conservatory base stood proud poking through a mesh of metal, molten plastic and shattered glazing. The garage was scorched but otherwise undamaged. I wanted to go in the house and probe the remains but Craig forbade it. The structure was unsafe, he said. His professional opinion was that the seat of the fire had been the living room. More than that he couldn't say.

To be honest I felt very little as a result of losing the house. By that time I'd settled fairly well into Camp Q, but more significantly, personal possessions had become re-aligned in my mind. What's a photograph when, you've lost your whole family? Very important you might think. Actually no. It's the memory that matters. Strangely, the memory reminds you of what you had, while the photo clarifies what you've lost. We found we fared best when we avoided nostalgia for the way things were. They were never going to be that way again, so it was unfair to the present to always expect it to live up to the past. We learned to focus on the now and find new joy in very small bonuses. In the same way a few mundane personal items, mostly acquired after the Event, became more important that the container load of trinkets and gadgets we'd all amassed in the old world. I'm very attached to my Maglite torch and my Swiss army knife. Others find hats to be very important.

The real hurt from the house arose from not knowing how the fire had happened. There was the possibility that it had been started deliberately, but if so, by whom, and why?

My companions allowed me some time alone with Claire, Matthew and Paul. My fear as I walked the length of my back garden was that their burial would have been interfered with, but it had not. I spoke to them, of course, stood by them, then came away.

We avoided the Minster area on both legs of our journey.

On the day of the reunion with Kirsty and Steve they filled me in on their abortive trip. Manchester city centre had proved impenetrable. There was a lot of fire damage and the roads were absolutely grid-locked. The pavements were as bad, so progress was almost impossible, but worse than that was the impact on morale. It had taken them almost three days to cover thirty miles and by now the global picture was quite firmly established in their minds. A dichotomy arose with one group pushing to keep going out into Cheshire and the other to see sense, face the reality of the predicament and withdraw back to one of the better locations they'd passed on the way. People were tired and ill-nourished and a number of personal conflicts arose with several escalating into violence. There had been some kind of altercation between Kirsty and Mike the pilot, and she intimated this was partly a consequence of things that had happened before the Event, but she didn't go into detail. She then placed herself very firmly in the retreat contingent. She said that she wanted to come and join up with me again. In fact she said "they" wanted that, meaning her and

Steve, and he nodded and smiled. They were worried about me being on my own, she said. Someone had then put forward the inspired idea of driving along railway tracks: a notion that had occurred to me during my time at Heathrow. This person had forecast, quite correctly, that the most likely scenario with respect to trains would be that they would have stopped automatically because of the "dead man's handle" safety feature. Furthermore, long stretches of line would be clear, and although the ride over the sleepers would be bumpy, they should be able to make good progress. This is exactly what they discovered. Bizarrely after they had traversed the Manchester track and joined the West Coast main line they caught up with another group doing the same. This group came from Liverpool and had Clita at the helm. She knew exactly where she was going and the whole party then headed for the site that would become Camp Q.

I began to feel at home at Camp Q, but 'home' became redefined. None of us quite knew what it meant anymore because we couldn't see any underlying permanence. The big question of what would become of us in the long run remained the main topic of debate and the main wellspring of superstition or of rejuvenated religion. Clita sensibly allowed and encouraged us to voice our opinions, questions and prayers but even more sensibly confined such conversation to times between tasks. The duties she allocated kept our focus on the immediate, the things we needed to do in order to stay safe and fed for the next few days. Long-term planning was continually put off.

Our biggest concern was water. The mains were useless of course, because pumping stations had ceased to pump. Various theories were put forward as to how we might exploit that source but it seemed riddled with possible complications, so in the short term it came down to loading a truck with numerous containers and taking them to and from natural water supplies to bring in the quantities of fluid that we would require. Several of us also set to work utilising the water conservation devices in the warehouse. Downspouts and drainpipes were diverted and water butts abounded. Ponds were dug, lined and readied to receive rain. These were the tasks to which I was allotted for my first three weeks.

June remained largely dry but July brought some thunder with associated torrential downpours and great joy overflowed as our storage devices filled. Thrift became greed and we became even more inventive to build more. I pulled my weight and my clumsy yet ultimately effective DIY skills gained me some kudos, but the truly talented craftsmen and women constructed and climbed the status ladder at higher speed. A medieval measure of worth returned as practical skills counted for much more than theory. We said farewell to academia and looked once more to value alchemy. Cooks also rose to high esteem. Ingredients remained plentiful but after hours of physical labour flavour was a sensual salary and the only payment we could anticipate. Even by mid July, two months after anything had grown or lived, vegetables, fruit and meat all still remained entirely edible. We stopped using the term "fresh" because it didn't seem fitting and to be honest the taste of raw food was changing, but it was more of a gradual dulling rather than an emerging sourness or bitterness. It was more apparent in terms of texture than flavour. Things did not, and still do not, rot. So the fabric of food does not collapse in the same way, though there is a very gradual change in the nature of the natural. My own opinion is this is to do with the moisture content. Things drain or dry out and hence they become less firmly constituted. A lot of fruit and vegetables became powdery or paper-like sometimes giving you the impression that you were chewing flavoured cardboard. We found that by storing vegetables in baths of water they retained more of their original texture and to our minds at least, more flavour. A dozen baths in the hotel were commandeered just for this purpose, though it meant extra water gathering expeditions to fill them. I was drafted in to help with that.

The nearest natural watercourse was the river Lostock, a small but reliable tributary that winds among and beneath the roads around Camp Q. We engineered several access points to its banks where we could fill our water tubs. The rumourmongers were quick to load its waters with muses of pollution, though we eventually came to the conclusion that both malignant and benevolent bacteria functioned no more. Once or twice we made a trip to the main local river, the Ribble. This was mostly out of curiosity. As it was so much bigger there was a presumption that the flow would be even cleaner, but we saw no evidence of that one way or the other. All water became more littered with natural debris as the premature autumn brought unseasonable leaf-fall and we saw, and sometimes gathered, floating fish, but they soon disappeared as the river maintained its relentless flow.

A kind of normality tentatively emerged in the camp. Routine helped, but Clita's organisation and dominance was, in my view, fundamental not only to our survival but also to our sanity. It was rather like living in an institution for the mentally ill, and in reality I suppose that was exactly what it was. We were all intellectually damaged, our sanity had been infected, incurably. There were frequent outbursts. People became irrationally and explosively violent, usually to inanimate objects, frequently to others and often to themselves, but everyone just accepted it. Blessed were the peacemakers, and many adopted that mantle, but everyone seemed to simply understand that people were going to behave in those ways for the foreseeable future because there was no alternative. As long as the consequences were not too severe we could live with it. But what if someone was seriously hurt or worse? How would we deal with that? Unfortunately I was to find out first hand.

So the abnormal became the normal. We overlooked the anti-social in order to construct a new society, and construct it we did. We became proud of the camp that we built and revelled in our collective ingenuity for turning the twentieth century site into something that functioned in the future because it was based largely on the technology of the past. Food, shelter and safety were our preoccupations. Because of our location the first two were largely taken care of, at least for a while, and the third was centred round an irritating stand-off with the Angels of Prague. Despite the fact they had the whole city to draw on they seemed to become increasingly envious of what we had, yet there was no question on either side that there should be any kind of merger or even truce. We were slow to voice the nub of the problem but even as it remained unspoken everyone knew what it was that they wanted the most. They were all men steeped in bravado, perpetually parading their masculinity to each other. We had the women. Two months into the new era and the tribal animal surged back for the tree-tops. It was a combination of the age-old genetic drive to survive and an overwhelming desire to live for the moment. How clever nature had been to blend those two urges.

The Event had a profound affect on female sexuality. The biological clock of reproduction had been reset. Women suddenly had everything to lose again. A pregnancy had overwhelming consequences. Not only would a woman increase her vulnerability and limit her mobility, but also the notion of running to full term and completing a safe childbirth was terrifyingly daunting, and that was without the deep consideration of what kind of world the child might have to face. In many ways we were, and are, much worse off than our primitive ancestors whose tribes would have had a wealth of hands-on experience of assisting the natural process of reproducing humans. Modern life had removed such knowledge from the many and attached it to the medically qualified few, and we had none of those at Camp Q. From the conversations I witnessed I think it is fair to say that for the first month or so human sexual activity was almost non-existent, but as a certain degree of security began to return the emotional cocktail quickly regained momentum and partnerships restarted the biological bartering that has always plagued and blessed our existence, but women were fearful and reluctant and understandably so. Contraceptives were not in short supply but people were rightly concerned and doubly careful.

Every two or three days one or more of the Prague chapter would parade along the pavements outside, or even within, our compound. We couldn't keep them out because the hotel and warehouse were separated from the superstore by a dual carriageway. We had plans to fence off the entire area but that task was not an immediate priority. We made the hotel as secure as we could especially at night, and similar arrangements were made at the warehouse. This wasn't difficult bearing in mind the tools and materials at our disposal, but it all took time, and priority was given to the main entrances. Because of power failure the electronic key cards of the hotel rooms did not work and we slept in unlocked rooms. That was far from comforting.

Clita was excellent at keeping our minds on task but credit must also be given to many others especially Roxy whose stock rose to almost mythical status despite her youth. She had an excellent perception of personality and her pragmatism was laced with deep empathy. She really understood how people felt and more importantly why they felt as they did. She could talk incessantly, creating as she did a flood of reassurance. I saw signs of exhaustion in her as more and more people drew on her as an emotional resource, but she always found time for them. The more cruel members of the camp complained that talk was all she did, but that was neither true nor fair. She did her share, mostly in the kitchen, but her talk fed us more than her cooking did. It was hard not to feel some emotional attachment to her because when she spoke to you she made you feel as if you were the only person that mattered to her at that time. She was very attractive and I had to work hard to keep the personal bond with her in its proper place. That kind of struggle was replicated all around me as people wrestled with a severely rearranged social code. Pairs of former strangers clung to each other like conjoined twins whilst other individuals continually evaded any kind of close proximity let alone physical contact. To be honest everyone was in hormonal hell. It was as if the whole of society was menopausal.

Most days, in fact every day, Kirsty came to find me, and this was another relationship where I fought to keep our friendship in some kind of perspective. Kisty was another young, attractive woman. She nearly always had a man in tow. Most often this was Steve, or Tye, but occasionally one of the older men such as Craig the fire-fighter would latch on to her. I formed the opinion that she sought me out either to expand the company she was in and avoid it becoming too personal, or to use me to try to shake off the unwanted attention of one of the others. I often asked myself if I was making up that motivation because that is secretly what I wished was happening. At other times I was sensible enough to believe that she saw me as a father figure or, more kindly, a reliable and trusted older brother, much older. Of course I revelled in her companionship. She was very easy to get on with and we had a natural affinity. What was more, as far as the new world was concerned, we went back a long way. I became skilled at deflecting the unwanted attention that Kirsty attracted and she seemed grateful to me for that. In truth though, I had to fight to prevent myself from adding to it.

There were many instances of conflict, too many to catalogue, and most of them too trivial to warrant reflection. Everyone was under a cloud of perpetual anxiety and this made sleep fitful and tempers short. Clita, Roxy and Rosie made a powerful triumvirate, in part because they put a great deal of effort into being positive and good-humoured, but they were not universally liked or respected. Factions arose as they always do, and certain individuals harboured hidden personal agenda and became reluctant workers, sometimes even detaching themselves completely whilst still drawing on the shared resources. That kind of behaviour was not popular but Clita would let such individuals stew for a while before laying down the law quite plainly that in order to benefit from Camp Q you had to contribute towards it. So a set of ground rules emerged. Not everyone agreed with them, but all signed up to them, knowing this was the only sure route to any kind of shared security.

I grew very close to Clita. We had a natural fellow-feeling founded on a similar sense of humour, but we recognised a more fundamental bond in each other. I think each had a respect for the other's calm pragmatism. We were both profoundly disturbed and feared tremendously for the future but realised we could only affect the imminent and the present. The moments when, for one reason or another, we found ourselves alone together increased. I became something of a confidant, a role she both valued and, I think, engineered. My allotted tasks rarely sent me far from the hub of our compound and she frequently sought me out to use me as a sounding board. It was hardly surprising then, that we began ending the day in each other's company. Bottles of Famous Grouse whisky made our laughter come more readily and linger longer. We'd spend time in each other's rooms, in contravention of Clita's own rules, and one of us stopped making excuses to leave and the other stopped loading the silences to solicit them.

Our affection was immature. It had the staccato exploration of fumbling teenagers. This was because we were both still thick in the fog of multiple bereavement and hence we constantly juggled the desire for fondness with the pain of loss. We hugged and wept, soothed and slept and awoke to a cushion of kindness upon a throne of thorns.

It was not long before the intensity of our relationship became the subject of gossip, then of snide sarcasm and then of downright resentment. Despite this, neither of us rose to the bait or openly acknowledged that there was any special bond between us. That may have been a mistake. I ignored the loaded looks and the not so heavily disguised jibes and tried to go about my daily duties as independently and properly as possible. In the end, though, I had to confront my accusers. This was because on the morning of 3rd August Clita did not wake up.

*

Motorcycles are the antidote to traffic jams, a fact that they rejoice in reminding you of whenever you are in one, as they disappear into the distance slipping between lines of cars as smoothly as a lounge lizard's hand between silk stockings. Four wheels bad two wheels good, as George Orwell might have written on the fast road to Wigan Pier. They think of themselves as the kings of the road, but in my opinion they have nothing on the Mods of the sixties with their Italian scooters sporting more mirrors than an egoist's boudoir. Mods famously used to clash with Rockers, the former being fans of flamboyant pop like the Kinks and the Beatles, whilst Rockers invariably worshipped Elvis and the Stones and the relics of the fifties. Rockers were all leather with manes of spidery tassels. Mods were mop-tops with fur-lined Parkas. Only one group evolved.

Rockers turned into Bikers, but Mods turned into Brighton.

*

Seven: Life and Death.

I knew Clita was dead before I touched her. I don't know how I knew, there was just some quality about her that spoke terminally to me. I'd gone to her room to take her a cup of coffee and wake her as she had asked me to the night before. I slid my fingers onto her naked shoulder. It was cold to the touch. Her head was inclined towards me, eyelids closed, mouth open, anticipating a breath that would never come.

Within minutes most of the residents of Camp Q were trying to cram into her room. Duncan, the builder with the automatic pistol and a speed of thought to match, bundled me out of the room and into Roxy's room next door. "Stay there," he said. I protested but he pushed me back in, closed the door and held it shut. I hammered on it, demanding to be let out, but he did not relent and I only have a very sketchy understanding of what happened during the next fifteen minutes before Roxy and Kirsty came to my aid.

When I was let out I demanded to see Clita, but Duncan, Craig the fire-fighter and Tye the biker were keen to keep me out so I never got a proper look at her or her room. By that time everything had been rearranged anyway. She'd been prodded and rolled about and someone had even thought of trying mouth to mouth, though I don't think they got that far.

A cross between a kangaroo court and a mad hatter's inquest was convened in the hotel reception lounge. A thousand years of judiciary history was inverted and I was required to commence my defence with an appeal to the International Court of Human Rights. Unfortunately I was the last person to admit to seeing Clita alive. We had been together for a couple of hours in my bedroom the night before, but she had returned to her own room just before midnight. She had been fine then. Accusations began to fly but Roxy imposed order and Rosie added her voice. The Camp Q lieutenants were suddenly generals in waiting and the urgency to show that they could rise to the challenge was evident on their faces and in their voices, as was their insecurity. I suspected, rightly as things turned out, that with Clita gone their power base would be short-lived, but for the time being they were in control and, to her credit, Roxy did her best to establish the facts.

Clita simply did not wake up. That was all we were able to say. Her demise, as well as being for many of us the first post-Event death we had encountered, also brought home in no uncertain terms the complete absence of expertise that we harboured. No one in our company could successfully establish the cause of her death. There were no marks upon her, no signs of fight or of struggle, and no indications of disease or even of discomfort, she had simply stopped living and none of us could determine how or why. Theories ranged from heart attack to suffocation. There was no way of telling or of proving. Suspects were openly named and of course I was top of the list, though I did not, and do not, see any logic in that. Everyone knew I was the person closest to her, and while we were not keen to openly declare our friendship, neither had we successfully hidden it. Nevertheless in the eyes of many people at Camp Q I became a killer. Annoyingly the things that had fascinated us the most about murder before the Event were relegated to the bottom of the importance pile. Evidence seemed almost as unimportant as motive and people were happy to take their own presumptions as the only basis for conviction. The rumour was that we had argued and I'd put a pillow over her face. Justice was demanded which, from where I was sitting, seemed a tad ironic. I would have welcomed justice with open arms bearing neither scales nor sword, but it was as impossible for me to prove my innocence as it was for anyone else to prove my guilt. Kirsty, who was the closest thing to a defence counsel that I had, vehemently proclaimed that I was innocent. This was an action that, in the eyes of many, placed her dangerously close to me and hence worthy of a similar smouldering acrimony. But one thing she said was especially unsettling for all of us: perhaps Clita had died the same way that all those on the ground had done whilst we had been airborne? Maybe Armageddon was not over yet? This sobering thought settled the proceedings like a judge in need of a tea break and the inquiry was suspended. So I was neither convicted nor acquitted but a new paranoia took root in me and I grew a pernicious weed of fear of a lynch mob. Whilst most people seemed to reluctantly accept that I could be innocent, to my mind at least it was evident that I had been labelled a behavioural leper and sooner or later, one way or another, I would have to leave Camp Q.

I can't honestly say that at the time Clita's death had any great emotional impact on me and that fact played strongly into my accusers' hands. I was shocked and saddened of course, but the instant and clear danger to my own safety got in the way of the kind of catharsis the death of a loved one might be expected to precipitate. I loved her, but it was an immature novelty love, well short of the rich emotional bazaar that I had experienced in my youth. We liked each other a lot and we'd been a real comfort to one another. Our affection had been sincere but not deep, and at times it had seemed like we were saying and doing the things that people would say and do if they pretending to be in love, or perhaps just trying to conjure up some normality. We had provided each other with a distraction in which we could pretend that our close proximity signified a surrounding ordinariness, when in fact all it really did was cloak the extraordinary from view.   We were both too shrouded in mourning for those we had really loved to develop any depth of similar feeling for each other. We had been captivated not by romance but by human survival instincts switching desperately to default settings ready to restart the generation machine, and I think we were both wise enough to realise that.

We cremated Clita three days later. There were arguments that this should not happen, firstly because the cause of death had not been established and secondly that she might resurrect as suddenly and mysteriously as she died. This bizarre suggestion was all too typical of the rampant superstition that erupted in post-Event society. It was the one bacterium that survived and spread like mould on a diet of dung. A special pyre was built in a section of the garden centre, partly because Rosie thought this was a good place for a funeral and partly to shield the incident from the hyena eyes of the Angels of Prague, who still kept a close watch on us from a wary yet intimidating distance. The deception failed miserably. Within twenty-four hours they were shouting jibes, asking to speak to her and when she failed to show, enquiring with mocking sincerity regarding the state of her health. To a certain extent their actions took the heat off me and they became the favoured suspects. I was sceptical. Although the compound was not entirely secure, we did keep an all-night watch and I doubted that they could get to her room without being discovered. Yet, security without electricity is much more difficult. The nights are truly dark now. The hotel was locked, but the weather was warm and windows might have been left open. They might have got to Clita and murdered her just to show that they could, and perhaps as a way of destabilising our camp, but I wasn't entirely convinced by this theory. I don't think they were so disciplined in their scheming and if they had gained entry I think they might have had other priorities. I also rarely saw them sober enough to conduct such a stealthy operation successfully. On the other hand there was a playful quality to their evil, so they may have enjoyed executing such a mischievously malevolent mission. There was one other incident that played on my mind. Two weeks earlier I had been part of the night security patrol. I saw, or thought I saw, an individual moving among the timber and flagstones of the building supplies section of the warehouse, an area that is undercover but out of doors. I had a powerful torch with me, but the person I spotted was some distance away and dodged out of my beam within a second of being caught in it. I shouted for help and my quarry and I played cat and rat for a while, but I never saw him again and my fellow guards unearthed nothing, putting it down to either my imagination or to one of our own number surreptitiously breaking curfew and then successfully returning to his room. At the time I was ready to accept their theories, after what happened to Clita, I wasn't so sure.

Despite the Angels' jibes I remained something of a pariah, at least in my own mind. The three children we had in the camp were kept well away from me and I was taken off the night security rota. Eye contact was rationed and smiles were insincere, brief and few.

"I'll have to move out."

"Don't be stupid," said Kirsty.

We were on a bench in the grounds behind the hotel. The August sun shone and took the chill off the early morning breeze that just occasionally conveyed just a hint of an unpleasant scent from the latrines.

"I can't abide the suspicious stares."

"You're imagining them."

"Does that make a difference?"

"Look, I know you didn't do it . . ."

"No you don't."

"Yes I do. Don't even think of doing anything stupid like moving out. It'll be so much harder than it is with several of us working together. Anyway, the Prague people would hunt you down."

"That depends on how far away I went. Scotland perhaps."

"Don't even say that."

"Wouldn't you like to know?"

She didn't say anything for a moment, and then she rubbed one shoe against the other as she spoke. "It doesn't matter any more. Family. What does that mean now?"

"Same as it ever did I suppose."

"No, I don't think so." Her lowlands lilt softly sounded the pedigree of her heritage. "Family meant something when it was a tiny group among a billion people. Not now. We're all one clan now. The tribe who survived. That's why we have to stick together."

I allowed another silence, then said, "Do you know of anywhere in the Highlands?"

"What do you mean by that?"

"Places where living was always hard. Ironically it might be easier to be self-sufficient somewhere like that."

"Yeah, if things grew, and if you had livestock."

"All you'd need is a truck and a trip to town every two months. I just think I'd find more sanity being well away from streets of shops. Monuments."

"They're pretty good storehouses of supplies."

"Do you know anywhere that's got a generator?"

"Look, I'm from Leith. I did Leisure and Tourism GNVQ and went straight to cabin crew. I never worked for the Scottish Tourist Board and neither am I a farming nerd. I know nothing about generators or who might have one."

This time just a tiny pause, and then I said, "It wasn't a serious question."

She didn't laugh but looked at me askew and gave a little snort.

"Though it is a serious thought. Who knows what lies ahead and how long we can make it work? I can see it makes sense to be here with a good few others and pool our efforts, but I don't know if I can hang on to my sanity living in the city. Everything proclaims the past we've lost. It's too familiar."

"You're just feeling got at."

"Yes, but that's not the reason. I'm sure I'd be happier. Happiness is still important isn't it?"

"Happiness is your job."

"That's not going to happen now is it? Heard the one about the woman who didn't wake up?"

This time Kirsty did laugh. Only lightly and briefly, but for a comedian that kind of response is a foothold on a sheer face.

"I intend to do it Kirsty, but please don't tell anyone."

"You're mad."

"Yes. Always was and always will be. But I used to be mad insane. Now I'm mad angry."

She looked at me for a moment. "You're serious aren't you? About your idea."

"When the time is right. Sooner if things get more threatening. I'll do it. Go. Find somewhere remote."

"Alone?"

I looked out across gently trembling hedgerows nudged by the flirting breeze, then down at her twenty-something hand lightly gripping the bench. "Would you come with me?"

A long pause.

"I might."

It wasn't the answer I expected and to be honest I had no conscious idea why I had asked it, but the reply had been spoken and heard and it was as if the molecules of the air around us had slightly shifted as the breeze paused to take its next breath. There was a tiny click in my mind reminiscent of when a jigsaw piece slots into a gap where you never imagined it would fit. She had more to say.

"You'd have to convince me it's the wisest thing to do. And I'm far from convinced at the moment."

So maybe that's why she'd said it. Just to stop me slipping away one night unannounced as I'd already half planned. Well I wasn't ready to go yet so perhaps there would be time to persuade her. That thought didn't help me sleep any better, but it made dozing off much more delightful.

I was woken at one a.m. by someone rooting through my room with a searchlight.

"What the fuck?" I managed to sit up before being blasted back towards my dream by the sun in someone's hand. I clenched my eyelids and ducked towards the foot of my bed.

"Easy Dan." I recognised Duncan's voice. He was in the doorway to my room with another torch.

"What the fuck's going on?"

Nothing was said. The first figure continued rifling through the chest of drawers.

"What are you looking for?"

"A pen. A big fat marker pen." That was Tye's voice. He blasted me with his torch beam again.

"Okay, okay," I said and stumbled out of bed pushing him aside. "What's the fucking urgency?" I slid open a small drawer in the desk and pulled out a short stubby black permanent marker. "Here."

"Knew it," said Tye, snatching it from me.

"Better put some clothes on," said Duncan.

So I did.

Roxy was in the reception lounge. Rosie was there too, as was Steve,

Craig, Duncan and Tye. I joined them. My pen was on the coffee table its forked shadow diverging in the muted radiance of two battery-powered storm lanterns.

"Sit down please Dan," said Roxie, "thanks for joining us."

"That's all right."

"What does this mean?" She held up a piece of A4 paper. On it was written your next in bold blue marker ink.

"What?" I said still fighting to be fully awake.

"This. What does it mean?"

"I think it means you're next," I said and a second and a half later the universe exploded in my right ear as Tye's booted foot connected with it.

"What the fucking hell?" I spat and leaped for Tye's throat. Duncan separated us.

"Tye! Calm down," shouted Rosie.

"Tye!" shouted Roxy.

"I fucking saw you with that pen last night," shouted Tye.

"Writing fucking notices as I was told to," shouted me. "Grey water, drinking water, grey water, drinking water, fucking grey water, fucking drinking water, fucking, fucking black pen." I snatched my marker pen from the table and ripped the lid off so sharply it flew from my fingers and hit the ceiling. I wafted the nib under Tye's nose then slashed three ink weals on his cheek. "Fucking, fucking, fucking black pen." I threw my pen down on the coffee table where it bounced off close to the paper where the blue ink seemed suddenly all the more blue. Your next it said. Your next.

The violence and the tension evaporated leaving a kind of paralysis. I alone seemed able to move and I walked away in the direction of the bedrooms, turning back briefly.

"And what's more," I said, "I know how to spell you're."

The note had been slipped under Roxy's bedroom door on the second floor of the hotel. Room 213. She'd gone to bed in the late evening, she wasn't sure when, as we were living less and less by the clock. She'd got up during the night to go to the toilet, for which purpose we all had an en-suite bucket, and in doing so noticed the sheaf of paper on the floor behind the door. After my interrogation I went back to sulk in my room but I was aware that the whole camp was being roused and quizzed, as it turned out, to no good effect. No one knew anything. It was all the more perplexing because following Clita's death, the males in the camp were very cautious about breaking the second floor ban and an internal security patrol of two persons was allocated to the hotel. Two people stayed up all night and occasionally patrolled all corridors, though they would not have been hard to avoid. The incident took the worst of the heat off me, not only as a result of my proving my innocence, but also because most people realised that I had been under such close scrutiny that it was unlikely that I would have attempted anything so stupid.

The next morning Roxy announced that she did not wish to be in charge. No corresponding statement was made by Rosie, which I regarded as unfortunate because, much as I liked Rosie, she was the less able of the two in terms of exercising authority. Roxy had a wisdom that belied her youth but the note had really scared her and she wanted to duck right out of the line of fire both metaphorically and literally. She gravitated to the hotel lounge and refused to go anywhere alone, demanding even that she shared a room. A kindly, though somewhat unbalanced, elderly American woman called Mrs. Ventimiglion, obliged and they both moved in to a vacant double room. Mrs. Ventimiglion never told us her first name, and rarely mentioned her surname without also referring to the late Mr. Ventimiglion whose ashes remained in the hold of the Boeing on the tarmac at John Lennon International still en-route to Rome where, in accordance with his wishes, they would be scattered within the walls of the Vatican City. He always wanted to be ranked among the communion of saints and that was his best chance. It would be inappropriate to label Mrs. Ventimiglion as the holy room-mate from hell. Inappropriate but not inaccurate. Roxy slept more soundly. But only for two nights.

Firearms had been accessible from day one. Airports had armed guards and following the Event their firearms were the only live component of the partnership, so the sharp-witted insecure were quick to relieve them of their defensive burden. The determined were able to acquire more relatively easily from police stations, military bases and gun shops, and we had a very small supply stored securely away in a locked cupboard in the hotel. We had plans to extend it in time but somehow that action never rose to the top of our "to do" list. Domestic priorities took precedence, and while the weapons made us feel more secure they also made many of us nervous, and hence people were reluctant to promote the acquisition of more. Duncan was never parted from his automatic and some of the men liked to be armed on night security, but other than that we kept guns well out of sight. It was a cause of some surprise that the Angels of Prague did not furnish and flourish their own weapon collection sooner than they did, but during the second week in August they drew up on the brow of the dual carriageway bristling with ex-army hardware and cheerfully punctuated the fair-weather cumulus with high velocity steel. We all came out to watch them. The magnificent five. A 3D feature for all the family.

For a moment I actually felt happy for them, because they were obviously so blissful showing off their terror toys. In all other respects they looked truly terrible. Unshaven, unkempt, unwashed and permanently exiled from sobriety they sat upon their cycles like mutants. Their cordite flatulence kicked its way into our nostrils. Their demands were straightforward. Anything and everything. They might come and go as they chose, but make no mistake, they were here to stay.

What followed was horrific.

Three of them broke through our improvised car cordon and rode straight for the gates of the warehouse car park. Duncan drew his automatic but for some reason he hesitated and let them ride by. I think that he may have presumed that this was just another display of bravado on the part of the Prague boys but he was wrong. They wanted loot and most of all, living loot. Craig was shot dead on sight, I think by the thin, white-faced biker with the ginger King Charles beard. Kirsty, not far from this incident screamed and the pseudo-Jacobean made straight for her. These two acts jolted Duncan into action and he ran towards them but Lucifer the leader emptied a magazine of automatic shells into him and that was the end of Duncan and of our armed resistance. Our camp degenerated into chaos. People ran in all directions and the micro-universe that we had created disintegrated forever in fifteen minutes of madness. I think and hope that the bikers were high on something, for if they were not then they truly had mutated beyond morality. They fired wildly and almost indiscriminately. From what I could make out they were trying not to shoot the women. To be honest I saw little of what happened for I fled on instinct – blessed instinct – not away from the attackers but towards the carriageway from which they had launched their attack. With hindsight this was the cleverest move I could have made, as that was the one place that they were not heading. I dived into the back seat of a white car, shut the door and squeezed low into the foot-well. I listened to the gunfire, the cries of agony, the screams of the chased, the pleas of the trapped. I did not dare to raise my head. It was a demonic scrap-yard hide-and-seek. I would not peep out until I had counted to one million.

At one thousand and thirteen I stopped counting and listened. Someone, a man, was moaning. All else was quiet. The bikes had gone but I imagined five hells angels silently surrounding my car waiting for my cranium to creep above the base of the passenger door window. I stayed where I was. The man still moaned. I tried to recognise his voice, but couldn't. Something small and metallic fell over or settled, sending another surge of adrenalin in the direction of my bowels. The man cried out not a word but a cry. Then he moaned again, and many more times as I willed the day to pass, to become afternoon, evening, late evening and god-given dusk, that darkness might follow, and then I could raise my head. I wallowed in the cold blood mud of my own cowardice perversely both hating and savouring my security. Waiting. Wishing the moaner would die then I wouldn't have to hear his moan any more. I have no idea how much spineless time elapsed whilst I hid, but hid I did, and would do so again. I will always hide. That's what a comedian does.

The door by my feet yanked open, cold air, a cold stare and a female being leaped in. I yelled instinctively. She shut the door and crouched low on the back seat above me. Lauren.

"I saw you dive in here" she said. "I've been in that red car over there."

"What's happened?"

"I think they took my mum."

Oh no, I thought. A thousand times no. My brain switched to human chess grand master mode and I foresaw the next two hundred possible moves. "Are you sure?"

"Yeah. They made her sit on the back of one of their bikes and tied her to the man in front."

Pawn to queen's bishop three. "You all right?" I asked.

"I'm okay," she said as if she'd had a minor mishap in a sports lesson.

She wasn't okay and never was again. At that moment Lauren became Thistle, though she wouldn't chose that name for a while yet. She had stepped though trauma and now lived in the space beyond it where nothing is everything. There was steel in her now. There was perpetual cold. There was a logic of her own devising instantly created and locked into her consciousness. She would always carry with her an immature maturity that was soldered into her soul the moment that she saw her mother captured. She was destined to see worse.

I looked at Lauren for a while and realised that I heard nothing. Whoever he was had moaned his last. Lauren was sitting up now looking out, so I rose from my trough of terror and surveyed the scene. I could see where Duncan lay, his body draining not far from Craig whose head had spawned a similar crimson lake, but no one else living or dead was in sight and every part of our compound that I could see was still.

"Can't see anybody," I said.
"There isn't anybody," said Lauren

I never found the man who moaned. To be honest I didn't go in search of him. For a while I thought it might have been Duncan but I don't think so. They had pumped too many shells in him for him to survive that long. What do I know? In my first life all the violent deaths I'd seen had been on celluloid. Anyway I believe the moaner must have been slumped somewhere among the tangle of vehicles. We didn't look.

With Lauren in tow I made a superficial scouring of our compound but it was largely deserted. People had fled, been taken or gone so deeply into hiding they were not coming out ready or not. We did find two more dead. One was Terry, an accountant from Boston. He was slumped in the kitchen of the hotel, a room that had been completely wrecked. The other was Roxy. She was in the reception lounge where she had contributed to so many conferences, but she'd clearly had a meeting that she didn't want to convene. We didn't linger. I had Lauren with me. I don't know what killed her. Strangulation I think, but it could have been anything, there'd obviously been a fight and more. Why did they kill her? Why didn't they take her? Why kill her? I thought of the written threat but it didn't look like the product of a promise. It looked like a mess. She didn't even look at peace. We moved on quickly.

"Where's everyone gone?" Lauren asked, almost indignantly.

"To safety, I hope. Lying low."

"Lying dead," she said.

I don't think she was right because we would have seen the corpses. I think they had fled, at least in for the short term and I decided it was time for me to do so too, but for good, however I had a problem called Lauren.

"Lauren, I don't think we should stay here anymore."

"What about my mum?"

"I know, I know."

We observed the Minster from behind the Christian Science building at the foot of the hill on the south side of the church. No one had bothered breaking into the Christian Science building and the Bible in the great public viewing window was still open on the page as set before the Event. The

Sermon on the Mount. Blessed are the peacemakers. Blessed the meek. We meekly peeped. The Minster glowed with surreal normality. Dusk was just thickening into night and two of the Minster's windows were flecked with the amber of candle glow, as they must have been so many times during its history. Someone was inside. That was all we could tell.

"We must go and look," whispered Lauren.

"We must certainly not," I replied. "Death for me and worse for you."

"They won't see us."

"Even if they don't, what do you expect we can do?"

"Mum's in there," she said, wishing and not wishing her hope to be true.

Right on cue there was a female scream, brief and muted but resonant in the ecclesiastical acoustic of the nave. We both just heard it, but we heard it well enough to know the other had heard it too.

"Could be anyone," I said.

"It was someone," she said.

There was another muted sound: a rumble of male laughter.

"We'll have to get on the other side," I said. "There we can watch the door. Count them out. It's the only way to be sure it would be safe to go in. But it might be days before they all ride out."

"Be an orphan by then."

I looked at Lauren in a way that said you may well already be orphaned, and she stared back in a way that said she hoped so but also hoped not. Or was that just my reading of her? I think now that Lauren was the first of us not to hope for anything. Hope is dead. The Event stopped hope. In my head I knew we would be unlikely to get a good opportunity to stage some kind of rescue of Christina, but couldn't bring myself to say that to her daughter. Instead I said, "Come on, let's work our way round to the other side."

We did exactly that but I was taking no risks and we went by a very circuitous route for absolutely safety. We ended up on the north side of Church Street in a passageway that leads to the side of the Guild Hall. We watched for an hour or two but saw and heard nothing. We withdrew into the Guild Hall complex, taking our torches and a small bag of supplies. We didn't switch our beams on until we were inside the building. We were back in the land of cadavers again but there were few inside the entertainment complex where they had been setting up for an evening performance in the main concert hall. Stage crew lay like prosthetic prop corpses so we went to the second performance venue. We torch-lit our way to the dress circle of the theatre like two post-Armageddon ushers. After eating we switched off our torches and settled down on the seating to sleep. I awoke a few hours later to find Lauren gone.

Whilst Camp Q functioned there was no need to reinvent morality, we just clung on to the most pragmatic remnants of old mores. After Camp Q we had to start again. At the time the camp seemed to be a new beginning, but with the benefit of hindsight I know it to have been a leftover of the feast that was civilisation. In my first life I had formulated the theory that success had very little to do with talent and a great deal to do with luck. That hasn't changed, even though success has, greatly. At Camp Q we got unlucky. The Prague Angels survived and moved into the same territory and that was the bad luck that ensured our lack of ultimate success. Fate rules supreme again as it did in ancient times. Just when we thought we might have it beaten, fate came back with a vengeance. Before the Event success was all sorts of things – or perhaps only one: perceived status, a self-assessment of self-esteem. During the Camp Q period success was survival. Now success is sanity. I now know that sanity and morality are interdependent. I wish I'd known that before, for I'd have had such a wicked time, and been so free. No doubt I would not have been the me that I became, and I would not been on that plane. Bliss.

Alone again, in the dress circle of the Charter Theatre I knew I had to redefine my morality. I had a good idea where Lauren might be and I had to decide whether or not to attempt to locate her. I was free. I could simply go and be the free me, and that was a very tempting option for it was more or less what I had decided to do before the sudden demolition of Camp Q. Alternatively I could do my best to discover what Lauren was up to and take her under my wing again. I could revisit Camp Q and see if anyone else had returned yet and then either enlist their support in finding her or pass the responsibility on to them. I graded each of the three options in order of respectability but it didn't help me to decide. As always selfish instincts fought with altruistic logic.

I switched my torch on again. It was powerful and cut through the auditorium air like a follow spot. I played it over the seats and called Lauren's name. Silence replied. I saw the suspension of dust in the beam, it was the finest dust I'd ever seen for any that had to settle had settled long ago, and there were no air currents in the catastrophe-closed theatre. The stage was bare, tidy, black. I shone my spotlight upon it and illuminated Claire.

"Go and find her," she said.

So I did.

She sat with her back against the retaining wall of the raised church grounds, feet splayed towards the kerb. She was alive but there was something sinister about her demeanour triggered by the limpness of her arms and the way her fingers played with dirt while her eyes held a thought by the throat. This I observed from our earlier vantage point in the passageway across the road from her. I dared moved no further for the Jacobean angel stood smoking in the porch entrance. Why smoke there? He could smoke anywhere. He loitered. He paced a little. He loitered again. Even Hell's Angels seek solitude. I felt sure he was unaware that Lauren was there, but I couldn't tell if the reverse was true and I willed her to stay in her stupor safe from his ministration. Time stretched. His cigarette seemed to grow longer instead of shorter its glow seeing off the night as the advance guard of daylight spread a veneer of lesser darkness across the shroud of gothic cloud above the steeple.

He finished his smoke and flicked the butt in an arc of neon towards the flattened memorial stones in the churchyard. He did not go back inside but stood leaning against the doorjamb, meanwhile Lauren was on the move. I dared not shout, but willed her to resettle, to return to her dreadful daydream, but slowly she dusted off her hands and rose to stand, her head prominently above the wall. He saw her straight away and she him, and for a long moment they just swapped stares. His was stiffened and awkward as if he was trying for some pointless dignity that he might find through a kind of cocky stillness. Hers I could not see for her face was turned from me, but I felt its accusation. She won. He smirked, turned unsteadily and went inside. She gently headbutted the wall.

"One after the other," she said. "All five of them."

We were back behind the Christian Science building. Her eyes refused to meet mine. I was a man, why should she deign to look at me?

"One after the other," she said again. "On her. All over her. Eating her. Then they did it with a candle. And they laughed. They never stopped laughing. Holding her down."

"Was there anyone else with them? Any other women?"

"It wasn't the first time. I could tell. They'd done it before."

"Anyone else with them?"

"They were just laughing, the whole time."

"Did they see you?"

"She saw me. She saw me seeing her. She asked me to kill her."

"She asked you?"

"Me, them, God, anyone. She yelled out to be killed. One time she was looking at me."

"Did they see you?"

"They couldn't catch me. They couldn't run straight. They couldn't run at all. That's when the shots happened."

"Shots?"

"They went for me. She got free. Got one of their guns and fired."

"Did she hit any of them?"

"She fired at me."

"You?"

"To make me run out. She shouted at me to run, to go, to grow."

"Grow?"

"Then she put the gun in her mouth."

"What?"

"He was trying to get the gun off her. She put it in her mouth. Her brains went all over him."

After a moment of rigor mortis I hugged her, but she threw me off with animal force. We sat behind the wall in silence, hiding from the Sermon on the Mount. Dawn was close and the clouds above were reddening, threatening to let the sun have a clear view of us as it ascended. I looked the other way. If the sun came it wouldn't be welcome.

I talked to her as we walked but I'm sure her ears were not working. We headed south threading through the streets wending our way back to where we'd left the car that we'd brought from Camp Q. I felt safe. She didn't reveal any more detail but I felt sure that the Prague angels were high on something satanic and were too disoriented to think about hunting her.

"We're living outside time," I told her. "This is the afterlife. Time ended with the Event. I suppose this is a kind of everlasting now. All rules have gone until we make some more, but before we can do that we're going to have to start time again. Start again. That's what your mum meant. Start again. Go. Grow."

Lauren walked in a manner that said I know what my mum meant, but it wasn't in response to what I had just said, she'd walked like this from the moment we set off. She wasn't listening. There was nothing left to hear.

"The terrible thing is we're tied to the past. There's nothing to live on but leftovers and that makes starting again really hard, if not impossible. New rules. We'll need new rules. Perhaps we'll make the new rules you and me. First we have to find some friends."

I had decided I did not want to be alone with Lauren. We must head back to Camp Q in the hope that others would have regrouped there by now. I had to get Lauren some female company. After that I would make off by myself. I was going to make my own rules just for me. Then no one else could break them.

"Without rules people are not people. We're just instincts with muscles. Hormones with limbs. Do you know what hormones are Lauren?"

She scoured the pavement as we walked, cursing it for its absence of weeds. I thought about asking her if she'd done hormones at school but school seemed such an absurd concept now. What purpose did school have in our perpetual detention? What purpose had it had before? How stupid to take people out of the world to teach them how to live. That's what we were doing now and it was impossibly hard. Then I realised that we hadn't been taken out of the world, the world had been taken out of us.

"They're not human anymore Lauren. They're not even animals. And their heads are stuffed with all kinds of things that shouldn't be there. They've dropped right through the animal kingdom to become something below it. The problem is they're still alive. That's the problem. Still alive. Your mum, however, she's above everything now."

Our car had been vandalised. We'd left it at the foot of London Road hill, a steep incline that was too cluttered with wrecks to force a way through. Now ours was the most newly wrecked. It looked almost proud. It was a white Peugeot and it wore a trousseau of glass diamonds. Every window was broken, every panel dinted, every seat slashed. The sight of it jolted Lauren out of her morose semi-coma, but not completely. She will never be completely free of it. She sprang onto the car bonnet like a she-wolf reclaiming a territorial rock, then with twisted crumbled windscreen beneath her feet as she swivelled to scrutinise the landscape to see if anything moved. Nothing did, apart from the clouds and us. If someone had done this to intimidate us then they attained their objective. The smashed car was a statement that they had been there and that they knew we would find it and see what they had done. I knew it wouldn't have been the Prague boys as they were too preoccupied. Who then?

The car could still have been driven except for one thing: they'd taken the keys. There were plenty of other vehicles to choose from but all would have had to have their occupants removed, and I wasn't in the mood for that.

"Come on, we'll walk it."

She didn't object and we set off. I couldn't shake off the feeling that we were being tracked and frequently spun round to try and spot whoever it was, but to no avail. Anyone following us would not find it difficult to stay camouflaged amid a comprehensive range of cover. The natural landscape was now heavily brown. Grass had lost most of its green and the majority of leaves were dull, rusty earth. This premature autumn did not feature the red and gold of old. There was only a light breeze but even so some leaves left the shrubs and trees along the bypass. They would not be replaced.

The walk gave me some proper thinking space for the first time since Lauren had jumped into my car hideout during the attack. I thought about those I'd lived alongside and wondered how many of them still lived and where. I thought of Kirsty. The last I'd seen of her was as the Jacobean was advancing on her. I hope she'd escaped, even if that meant she was dead.

Judging by the position of the sun I would say it was mid-morning by the time we saw the blue and yellow banners of Camp Q.

There was a note from Clita.

*

I had my first sexual experience in a church. I was an altar boy. If you have never been a Catholic you might not know what an altar boy is. It's a like being a choirboy but with access to all areas. You are a God groupie. The priest gets to do all the clever things, like turning wine into blood, but you get to drink the wine both before and after. It tastes just the same.

I got to taste a lot of altar wine, and other things. A Jesuit priest called Father Fitzpatrick used to treat me. At least that's what he called it. He was very fond of dried fruit and we'd have little parties with currants and raisons and sultanas and other delights from his Middle Eastern selection box. We'd wash it all down with the finest sacramental vino and then we'd play games. His favourite was hide and seek in the cassock cupboards with wine and dried prunes. When I grew up it became known as date rape. The older boys, who'd grown out of favour, exhibited a supernatural stoicism, and took the air of those who have ascended above any seedy stain on their cassock or character, and classified it as education under the Jesuits.

Father Fitzpatrick wasn't his real name. It was a nick name. I think he got it because of how close he was to his favourite altar boy.

*

Eight: Location, Location, Location.

The camp still seemed deserted. Lauren wanted to go to her room and shut herself in. I wasn't sure that was a good idea as she had shared the room with her mother. I intended to scour the camp and didn't want to leave her unprotected, but I thought it best to let her have her way. At first I was reluctant to be far from her so I stayed on the same floor checking the other rooms. I spent some time looking round Clita's room. That's when I found the note. She'd left it unwittingly.

On the desk was a pad of notepaper and next to it a pencil. The pad seemed blank but as I sat on the bed and watched the sun creep across the desk I noticed the impression left in the paper by the note that had been written on the leaf above prior to it being removed. In one of those sweetly unsettling moments where a vivid memory is replayed from my first life, I took up the pencil and with bygone Boy Scout excitement softly shaded the pad to heighten the impressed message. It said, harvest the latrines and on a separate line cargo planes. I removed the sheet I'd shaded, folded it and put it in my pocket. For quite some time I sat contemplating what I considered it to be Clita's last command from beyond the pyre, but I couldn't work out what she had meant.

I went and softly knocked on Lauren's door. There was no reply so I gently pushed it open. She was asleep on one of the beds; I think it was the one her mother slept in. I went back to Clita's room and used the note pad to write a message for Lauren telling her that I was going to make a swift reconnaissance of the camp and would return. I left it on her pillow.

I found five more dead. They were all male, though neither of the two boys was among them. Most of them were in the vicinity of the entrance to the warehouse, but far enough inside to not be seen from the road. My imagination began to play all kinds of tricks again as I really expected that others would have returned before I did. Perhaps they were watching me, hoping that I would leave, or waiting for a chance to pounce and avenge the death of Clita?

Maybe they thought me in cahoots with the Prague angels, as here I was unscathed and free? There were so many aisles inside the warehouse, so many places to hide, so many channels to slip along, and even at midday the store was stacked high with gloom. I encountered no one. I considered crossing the road to scour the superstore, but decided first of all to return and check on Lauren. On the way up I called in my own room. And there was Kirsty.

"I looked everywhere for you," she said. There was acid moisture in her eyes and the bone of her skull claimed prominence over the fleshy parts of her face. She was drawn and pale, and her skin was taut with anger. "Everywhere."

"I was with Lauren."

"Don't you dare leave here without me."

"We went into town."

"Don't you dare."

"Looking for her mother."

"Don't you dare."

"Her mother is dead."

"Don't leave me Dan."

"Raped."

"Don't you leave me again."

"Over and over."

"You're the only one I can trust."

"Steve?"

"He ran. They all fucking ran."

"Tye?"

"Got a bullet in his shoulder. They've taken him to hospital"

"What?"

"That's where most of them are. At least that's where they went, where they said they were going."

"The hospital?"

"It's on the north side of town."

"I know where it is."

"Clita used to talk about it. It was her second choice of base."

"I know. She told me."

"Yeah, I'm sure she did." This was said with a seasoning of sarcasm.

I was seeing a side of Kirsty I didn't like. She was obviously traumatised by the attack and by the aftermath of abandonment, but there was an almost marital hatred in her attitude towards me. I had no idea that she felt I had some sort of obligation to her, or indeed that she had formed a kind of attachment to me, we saw each other most days but we had never expressed any special bond, yet here she was berating me with a venom usually brewed by years of cohabitation. And to cap it all she seemed jealous of the friendship I'd shared with Clita. I was confused.

"Why the hospital? Why didn't they stay here?"

"Why didn't you?"

"I told you. I took Lauren to look for her mother. Let me tell you about her mother."

"I don't want to hear it. You've told me. I don't want . . ."

She was struggling now, toying with her sleeve and trembling involuntarily in over-amplified shivers. I offered her a drink from the forlorn file of cans on my shelf. She cracked open a can of Coke and after three swallows she steadied herself somewhat.

"I lost track of you," I said. "During the attack. What happened to you?"

She told me how one of the Prague bikers had grabbed her. She'd struggled, clawed at his eyes and broken free. He was about to grab her again when, somehow, Christina came between them and her attacker switched his attention to her. Kirsty ran into the warehouse and through to the garden section where she shut herself in one of the display sheds and hid until dark. That night she'd looked everywhere for me. For me.

"I thought you'd gone. Gone."

"I came back," I said, being no more precise than that and hoping that the ambiguity might let her imagine I came back specifically to look for her.

"I checked every corpse," she said.

"Who do you know to be okay?"

Between us we drew up three lists, the dead, the definitely alive and the missing. Only twelve of our original contingent of twenty-seven were known to be alive, eight were dead and seven, we hoped, at large somewhere. Apart from Lauren, Kirsty and myself all the other known survivors had decamped to the hospital.

"They're going to take the bullet out of Tye's shoulder."

"There isn't a medic among them."

"There's a couple of confirmed hypochondriacs," said Kirsty. "They should manage it between them."

"What state was he in?"

"Lot of pain. Lot of shock."

"Was he shouting out a lot? Just after the raid."

Kirsty shrugged her shoulders. "Don't know. Not when I saw him."

She drank more of her Coke. She was calmer now. Flesh had reclaimed her face and her colour was returning. The trembles had gone. It was my turn to feel weak, drained and suddenly cold. She must have seen that in me and offered me some of the drink. It was warm, but the sugar hit home quickly and I was bolstered by it. "So what now? Do we join them?"

"God no, god no."

"Stay here?"

"No. They'll be back."

I nodded. "Somewhere else then."

"Somewhere else."

"And Lauren?"

"She'd better come."

I told Kirsty about the vandalism done to the car that Lauren and I had used but she just shrugged her shoulders. She said that the more she thought about it, the more she felt I was right about getting right away from urban conurbations. Who knew who was living where and just how tribal they might have become? Safety lay in space. Big horizons meant lots of warning.

Initially we moved not very far away to a little terrace on the banks of the Ribble at Walton-le-Dale, but we did not feel secure there, and indeed we only intended it as a stopgap measure. We were only a few hundred yards from the vandalised car, a fact that added to my unease, but we'd chanced upon the house, to shelter from a downpour and found it free of human remains but well stocked with preserved food. We only ate cold meals and watched daily for the telltale pencil lines of fires but saw none. Neither did we hear any sound of vehicles. We stayed for four days.

On the drive of a house further along the street was a white van. I found the keys inside the property and siphoned the fuel out of two cars to raise the tank to almost full. That was to be our transport. We would stack it full to the brim and make off. We had no destination but that didn't matter, we would drive until we found somewhere suitable. We loaded it with food, tools and utensils from all the houses round about, blinkering ourselves with Gestapo indifference to the sad human tale each one held. An argument then ensued as to whether or not we should revisit Camp Q. We knew there was useful equipment there that we were familiar with and with which we could quickly strengthen our supplies, but there was something about the place that chilled each one of us. In addition to that trepidation we felt a certain bond between the three of us. Lauren remained distant, uncommunicative but not uncooperative and we worked efficiently together, and I think each of us had become protective of this new security and feared that more people would unsettle it. Nevertheless the lure of a good gas stove with spare bottles was strong and we decided we'd make one last visit, but under cover of darkness. We left late evening and had driven about half a mile when Lauren said, "There's somebody in the back of the van."

"What?"

"I heard them."

"It was the supplies shifting."

"Supplies might shift. They don't cough."

I drove on. Lauren said "There's somebody in the back of the van."

"I believe you. I'm thinking." I looked around the front of the van. Beneath Kirsty's feet was a wheel-brace that I'd spotted in the garage of the house. I'd thrown it in for obvious reasons but also partly because I felt it might be useful as a weapon. I stopped the van but left the engine running and signalled to the other two not to say anything and slip out quietly. Kirsty was clutching a torch. We went round to the rear and yanked the back door wide open, blinding and startling the occupant.

"Whay. . ." he said.

"Nathan," said Kirsty.

"Nathan." I said in confirmation, though I'd never seen him before. I knew who he was as Clita had spoken about him often enough. Nathan was a twenty-one year old backpacker whose worldwide trip to find himself had been rudely interrupted by the Event. Whilst at Camp Q he'd broken just about every agreed rule, and from the outset he'd pestered several of the women and frequently flouted the segregation arrangements in the hotel. After one particularly unpleasant incident with Roxy, Clita had banished him and he'd lived off his own devices ever since. He was a scrawny, lanky longhaired youth born three decades too late, for he would have slotted into dropout culture of the seventies USA seamlessly. Understandably, bearing in mind his recent history, neither Kirsty nor Lauren were enamoured to renew his acquaintance. As soon as his eyes recovered from their mild blinding they fixed securely on the wheel brace I was holding.

"Hi. I'm Nathan and you need me."

"How did you get in there?"

His glance flicked to a pile of coats and other clothing that we'd thrown in. He must have hidden under it whilst we completed the final loading of food and equipment from the street. I told him to get out. He didn't move but said, "You guys need me. I know what's happened and how to put it right."

"What?"

Kirtsy said, "Get him out and get rid of him."

I looked at him with deeper scrutiny and convinced myself that he was the vagrant I'd caught in my night watchman's torch beam weeks earlier.

"You guys need to have me with you."

Kirtsy laughed mockingly and Lauren made a strange hissing sound.

"Lauren," he said.

"Thistle," she said.

"Whatever," he said. "You guys need to have me with you. I have the answer, fella. Really I do."

Kirtsy was starting to lose it. She shouted. "Get him out."

I tried to calm her with a gesture and said to him, "You trashed my car."

"No, not me." His voice was fearful. I think he thought I was about to fracture his limbs. We could break all four and just leave him at the roadside. I was sickened by the realisation that I'd actually formulated that scenario, sickened and strangely empowered by my imagined brutality. The memory of Clita sprang into my mind and my mouth began to form an accusation but some good sense was still operating somewhere in my brain and I held back. If he was guilty I wanted him to damn himself. I returned my tack to the car.

"Why did you wreck the car?"

"I didn't! Why would I? I'd have to trash every car."

He had a point. But I was convinced it was him. In fact there were several things for which he was becoming chief suspect number one. There were lots of questions I could have asked him, but the more I thought about it the less I could see the point. What would I have been proving to whom? Kirsty was anxious to get moving. She just wanted me to throw him out of the van and drive on, but he had succeeded in getting my interest.

"What is the answer then?"

"Not now," he said. "You've not got to hurt me and you've got to take me with you. We have to be together. No more alone. No more solo hobo. I have the knowledge. I know what's happened and I know the secret. The secret to starting again. Knowledge is power. Absolute knowledge is absolute power. I have the knowledge. I'll share it with you guys. But we have to trust each other. Trust. Can't do this by myself. But only I know what to do. Unless someone else has told you. I will tell you. When I trust you. I have to trust you guys. That will take time. Which means you guys have to take me with you."

"All right," I said, and shut the van door with him still inside.

Kirsty went ballistic. I pushed her and Lauren round to the cab of the van and we all got back in. I let Kirsty rant as I wove in and out of the crumpled wrecks that littered the junction by the retail park. Her theme was it was him or her. I stopped the van by the side of the Ribble.

"Okay."

"What?"

"Out you get."

She looked at me with incredulity. "You'd take him over me?"

"Do you have the answer?"

"Do you honestly think he does?"

"I don't honestly know until he tells me."

Thistle said, "There is no answer."

There was a moment of silence. Kirsty put her fingers on the door latch, then spotted the look of horror in my eyes. For a moment I thought she might call my bluff but she was, and is, scared of being alone in this grave new world. We all are. Her eyes held mine, then she looked out at the car carnage ahead of us and spoke with a calmer, slower but even more bitter intonation. "If he's got the answer, he can keep it. He can shove it right up his fucking arse. I can't live anywhere near him."

"Just give it a couple of days," I said. "Until I find out if he's for real. Then we'll off load him. Trust me."

"No," she said.

"There's three of us. No one needs to be alone with him."

"I'll kill him," she said.

"I'll kill him first," said Thistle.

"Neither of you will kill him," I said. "Until I say you can."

We drove on across country east and north and arrived along the southern boundary of the British Aerospace aerodrome at Salmesbury, the sister base to the one where we'd landed. There were three large commercial airliners at the end of the runway. Two of them were 747s. The first had overshot and damaged its nose wheel but it had survived intact even though the cockpit dipped low as if it was bowing for having pulled off a spectacular touchdown. The other two had survived without damage and their emergency chutes fluttered in the wind making the trio seem like ghostly brides still waiting forlornly for husbands that would never come. We drove on towards Blackburn but grew increasingly frustrated by grid-locked roads and so diverted north and west again cutting into rural Lancashire. In general it was far easier to make progress on the minor country roads, because there were fewer obstructions. On the main roads cars had collided with each other but on the narrow lanes they had mostly hit hedges or walls and only infrequently blocked the whole road. We eventually ended up in Ribchester a small town on the Ribble, a place I knew reasonably well, but I didn't feel it was an ideal location as it was liable to flooding and the river looked higher than I remembered seeing it before. I couldn't understand why that should be as we hadn't had very much rain for several days. Nathan said the reason was obvious: all the growing things no longer grew and all the water that fell was left to drain, so rivers would swell. Water was likely to be plentiful, perhaps too plentiful for as root systems deteriorated earth would become unstable and landslides probable. He'd obviously thought about these things.

We occupied two houses on opposite sides of a street. He was to live in one and we three in the other. I warned him that he was under curfew and we would take it in turn to watch his house at night. Whenever one of us was alone for whatever reason he had to be in the company of the other two, or in his house. He readily agreed to this, and my two female compatriots whilst far from enthusiastic were compliant and willing to cooperate on the strict understanding that this was a temporary arrangement. He, on the other hand, was under the impression that we were making some more permanent base, though he wasn't happy about our proximity to the river or indeed to the Prague chapter. We were less than twenty miles from their lair and he was convinced that they would reconnoitre that area sooner or later. I said I though it unlikely, but if they did we'd deal with the matter and I showed him Craig's automatic pistol and the box of ammunition that I'd recovered from Camp Q. That revelation made him feel both more and less secure which was precisely the state that I wanted. He behaved impeccably and complied with all our requests. The women were always frosty with him at best and mostly either ignorant or downright rude, but he never complained. I felt quite sorry for him and even began to like him but Kirsty assassinated any hint of empathy for him that she spotted in me. As far as she was concerned he was a "fucking jackal" and all she wanted to know was when and how we were going to get rid of him. I told her to be patient, but she reminded me of my promise of only being with him for a few days and yet somehow two weeks had passed. That, I explained was because he'd worked hard, been a model associate and most of all hadn't yet shared his grand theory with us. That, she said was because he didn't have one. That, I said, was because he didn't trust us.

The house that we three occupied had a mains gas burning stove that Nathan and I managed to convert to wood burning reasonably well, so between the four of us we succeeded in cooking some very passable meals. One night Nathan made a supreme stew which everyone devoured with relish, though only I offered congratulations to the chef. Afterwards we cracked open an especially fine Australian wine and I decided it was time to probe his mentality. To begin with he was reticent but after a few glasses he loosened up and we struck up a genuine rapport. He had a very quick mind. He told me he'd done well at school but had become something of a rebel because his teachers hadn't known how to extend him and he'd been frustrated by their inadequacy and, in many cases, arrogance. I believed him. I found him sincere. There was something just a touch slimy about him and I could see how he might unsettle female company, though I also think he knew that too and was fighting hard to modify his language and behaviour during his time with us. Kirsty didn't agree. She found him sleazy full stop. I think it may have been another consequence of his intelligence or his obsessive nature. He did come across as a nerd and I think that might have plagued his social development. We drank, chatted and joked and I thanked him for the way he was contributing to our camp. Then I asked him about his big idea.

"It's obvious really. It's from space. From the sun or wherever. A stream of particles of some kind. Perhaps magnetically charged or in some way drawn to the core or surface of the earth. That's why they missed us. Missed planes. Either missed us or only hit us in a dilute way."

I found that last point a little chilling.

"And did what?"

"Killed everything. Switched life off."

"But life isn't the same in everything is it? Human life, plant life."

"We're talking particles here. Who knows what kind? Perhaps a kind we haven't discovered or even thought of – yeah? Sub atomic. And at that level they could affect everything couldn't they? Looks like they have."

I swigged a gob full of Australia's latter harvests. "Possible."

"It's the only way to explain how it missed us."

"Would have hit low flying aircraft."

"Probably."

"Then there should have been wrecks at the big airports."

"There were weren't there?"

"They should have been spread all over the runways like strawberry jam. I got into Heathrow. There's always something on final approach at Heathrow."

He shrugged his shoulders. "I dunno. Perhaps these particles really cling close to the surface? I dunno. But that's what I think happened."

"So what's your answer?"

He seemed to suddenly sober. "That's for another night."

I persisted but so did he. "Knowledge is power. Knowledge is power. You guys have been good to me. You guys. You guys have been good to me. I'm going to bed."

And off he went to bed. And that was the last time I saw him.

After he left, Kirsty joined me, whilst Thistle remained upstairs. Kirtsy opened another bottle of red wine and topped up my glass before pouring a large one for herself. She drank that night with a rapidity that I had not seen her use before. She was very warm towards me, sitting next to me and snuggling into me. She had not behaved in that way before and I wasn't at all sure what to make of it. Kirsty is lovely and very lovable. I always found her attractive but didn't allow myself to respond to her appearance as I didn't think she would want or welcome that kind of attention from me especially in the extraordinary circumstances that we shared. I thought that she appreciated my reticence. She knew, I presumed, that I wasn't immune to her charms and hoped she would appreciate my self-control. She had suffered more than her share of unsolicited attention at Camp Q and I had no intention of adding to the intimidation that she felt. I presumed it was because of my attitude towards her that she wanted to be with me, and so as she wormed her way tighter to my side I was confused and felt both warm and uneasy. Suddenly I was like a twelve year old who'd found an opportunity prior to puberty and didn't know where to put himself or how to respond. I let the arm that embraced her rest tightly but lightly on her midriff and we drank our wine and that was the way we continued for some time, not talking much, but listening instead to each other's breathing. I think that was exactly what she wanted and needed, and for me it provided an episode of unexpected joy and the closest to bliss I've known since the Event, or perhaps ever.

We drank most of the bottle that she had opened. She fell asleep with her head on my chest. I stayed still as a novice babysitter, not counting time, savouring the delicacy, the loveliness, the trust. Too soon she woke, shivered slightly, sipped her drink once more then kissed me, once, lightly and ever so briefly on the lips and then went upstairs to bed. I sat without moving for a very long time, wishing she was still there, imagining that she was, willing her to be there so hard that it almost became real, wishing she had not been so close, rejoicing that she had, revisiting my confusion. Eventually I had to move and so stiff was I that I felt two decades older and had to flex weak limbs to regain any fluidity of movement. I hobbled to the window and looked across to Nathan's house. It, and the rest of the world, was pitch dark. The night was overcast and humid, heavy and dank. On nights such as that the fabric of redundant civilisation stank. I went to bed and dreamed an amalgam of incidents from before and after the Event. There was a recurring episode in which I sat in the middle divan of a three bedded room, the central figure in a frozen troika of affection. To my left slept a drunkenly cosy Kirsty, to my right Clare, eyes open but sleeping and refusing to wake up.

I remained asleep until nearly noon. When I awoke Kirtsy made me a hot instant coffee with sugar. I didn't used to take sugar, but now no one wants to live for ever. Nothing was said about our time together the previous night. Everything was perfectly normal as if no intimacy had been broached. I was relieved and disappointed. My awakening was slow, my sobriety fitful. I had a moment of panic when I realised that we must have spent hours without checking on Thistle, but Thistle was with us, heating soup on the stove we'd adapted. More time passed before I thought to ask about Nathan, but neither of them had seen him and we presumed that he, like me, had been deposited into unusually deep and long lasting sleep by the wine. It must have been early afternoon by the time I went looking for him. His house was empty. We shouted, whistled, waited. No sign. No sound. We found ready meals in an adjacent house and heated them for an evening dinner. We made enough for Nathan, but he did not show.

"We're going to have to look for him," I said.

"Look where?" asked Kirsty.

"Anywhere."

"Everywhere," said Thistle dryly.

"He's got forty-eight hours," said Kirsty.

We gave him forty eight hours, then re-loaded the van and drove on.

So now we were three, and I'd only had half of Nathan's big idea. He hadn't told me his solution – or had he? It was whilst sleeping that I'd remembered the note from Clita's pad. Cargo planes. It was logical that if the Event had occurred as Nathan had suggested then the cargo of aircraft in flight might also be unaffected. So much food was shipped around the world at high altitude that cargo planes standing on airport tarmac may contain valuable vegetable life, plants that would germinate, seeds that would grow. But surely seeds would grow anyway come the new year? Wouldn't they? What about the soil? It seemed sterile to me. And even if we could get plants to grow didn't they need insects to pollinate them? Biology was never my strong subject and when I discussed it with Kirsty and Thistle they were no wiser than I. Nathan's theory was plausible and to a degree attractive, but the solution seemed flawed, if worth considering. I wondered if it was his solution or had he got it from someone else? From Clita perhaps? Had he taken the top leaf from her pad and also taken her life to preserve the idea? Knowledge was power. Maybe he had visited her the night she died to try to negotiate his readmission into camp Q or perhaps he had slipped in simply to get his revenge for her excluding him and seen the note on her desk, taken it and developed his thinking from that, stealing her life and her solution at one go? At that time I thought that I may never know. Now I do, though I am not ready to tell you yet. Of course, we had no idea what happened to him after he left me that night. Did he make off for some reason and deliberately decide to part company with us or did he go foraging as he often did and meet with some accident? I had to consider the possibility that one or both of my compatriots in some way dealt with him. There has been nothing in their behaviour, demeanour or conversation to suggest this might have been the case. I didn't ask them directly at the time. I figured that if they had disposed of him and were not going to tell me of their own accord that they certainly wouldn't admit it if questioned. I felt I would rather bide my time and let them accidentally betray themselves, if guilty. The thought that they might have taken such drastic action put me just a little ill at ease, but neither of them changed their attitude towards me and both seemed somewhat dependent on our triumvirate remaining a solidly three-pronged structure, so on balance I felt fairly safe. Each of them was more content from the moment that we set off without Nathan, but that was entirely the reaction that I expected.

We drove much deeper into the Ribble Valley. Our next home was a static caravan on a modest site. It was Kirsty's idea. In many ways it made sense. There were a lot of empty homes all with bottled gas supplies, which meant not only could we cook but also, come colder weather, we would have heat. There was a small but fairly well stocked store on site and we were not far from a stream. Clitheroe was only a few miles away with plenty more shops for us to plunder. The down side was that there were a number of cadavers littering the place and many were children. We left them alone for a day or two then set to work on the gruesome task of building a bonfire. Human fat burns ferociously smelling of scorched pork. It took three days to get rid of them all and the smell lingered for weeks afterwards. The bodies had remained where they had died for over three months but many were almost perfectly preserved. The ones outside had suffered weather damage from the sun blistering their skin and the rain waxing their complexions. Their clothing was dust ingrained and sometimes the rain had made colours run and mix giving a surreal new-age aspect to their demise: tie-dyed death. Those who had fallen into prone positions, or who had died whilst lying down looked the most normal. Those who sat often had their heads at unnatural angles and the fluid in their bodies had settled downwards bloating their legs and feet. Bodily fluids were our biggest dilemma. A dead person weighs a great deal, and back at Camp Q people had learned that if the bodies are drained they become lighter and a little easier to move. The downside of that is that it leaves lakes of blood in the short term and seemingly interminable stains thereafter. We never did this for people inside caravans, because we wanted to go in and out of their homes freely and with minimum distaste. We sometimes drained the heavier ones out of doors, hoping that in due course the rain would eradicate the stain on the ground. It was an arduous task to clear the site, but ultimately worth it for our peace of mind. As September arrived, warm then windy, we were well settled.

On the third day of that month we saw a miraculous yet entirely dispiriting sight. High above, at thirty thousand feet by Kirtsy's estimation, an airliner cut a single vapour trail across the sky flying east to west going from somewhere to somewhere on a wing and a prayer. Might it possibly mean that not all the world was in as desperate a state as England? Who was up there and what their destination was we had no hope of knowing, and even less hope of letting its occupants know we were below. Its trail, at first a lifeline, was thickened by the wind into a rope, then a banner, then a veil, then a smear of cloud that would have been indistinguishable from any other in the sky, except for the fact that there were none. It was a glorious day.

The breezy beginning to the month stripped the majority of leaves from the trees leaving the landscape January-naked by only the second week in September, but after that a period of high pressure built and we had warm days and frosty, billion star speckled nights. The first of the frosts came, but they were timid compared to what was to follow, vanishing with the initial hint of the late-rising sun. Pleasant as it was, the weather worried me. It all seemed so strange because of the state of the woodland around us and the beige palate of the fields. We survived amid sepia sterility, the sun came every day and there was no rain. Fears grew that more than the obvious had been changed. Life had been halted but what else had been altered? We talked of how the stopping of the animal pulse might have given the climate an unexpected bellyache, changing the atmosphere, and this in turn would have been further compounded by the wholesale holocaust of plants. They would no longer replenish the oxygen in the air, they would not offer up their moisture in transpiration and this must have had an impact on the global ecosystems. Because of the comprehensive strangeness of our new lives minor superstition evolved into major concern at the speed of thought. It might never rain again.

It did, of course, and with a vengeance, but before the cloudburst came a dozen different malevolent spirits or aliens had been talked into existence and, I fear, interceded with in private prayer. The rain came, so the prayers must have worked and thus proved the need to pray again. I fought to hang on to my disbelief in the supernatural but it was hard to draw the lines between talking to one's self, to inanimate objects, to imagined deities, demons and English-speaking extra-terrestrials. Thistle talked to the supernatural all the time, to God, to woodland sprites, to her mother's ghost.

I saw Claire once or twice a week, usually in the distance walking through the woods enjoying flora that only she could see, and just occasionally she was there very close behind my left shoulder when I turned round. She would stay long enough for me to taste her scent, and always smiled before she faded away.

Kirtsy was not keen to talk about God, but a formulated the opinion that she harboured a small belief in him and probably spoke to him in the silence of her mind.

Life at the caravan camp was as good as we might have hoped. We became relatively skilled at sourcing and preparing food. Vegetables, meat and fish, remained edible but continued to become increasingly bland in flavour. Tinned and vacuum-packed food was the tastiest. We used a lot of salt, spice, sauces, and dried herbs to add flavour. We worried whenever we got stomach cramps or headaches, but they were rare, easily treated and always went away. So far as coping was concerned, our confidence grew as the days became cooler but, in spite of our seemingly endless larder, we became more and more concerned about our long-term prospects. Would packaged food last forever? What happened if we did get seriously ill, or had a disabling accident? Were we castaways on a dead planet? How long would we live? How might we die?

Even when all the trees were entirely bare, including of course all the evergreens, our campsite was still very well screened on all sides. That troubled me a little as it gave us no warning of approaching danger, and neither did it offer us a good chance of benefiting from any benevolent travellers if such people existed, but on the whole it gave us a good level of security and we valued that. We saw no one else at all during the months of September and October.

We changed caravans a couple of times as we discovered ones with better cookers and more comfortable beds. We always slept together in the same van. The two women shared a cramped twin bedded room and generously gave me the double master bed to myself.

Winter held back, teasing us that she might not bother to call, but came she did, and brought terrible retribution to torture our souls for daring to stay alive.

*

A caravan is a mobile home. So bad they named it wrongly twice. They're neither mobile nor home. They're too small to live in and too slow to be classified as mobile. A caravan is a machine for imposing your holiday on everyone else. The Americans call them trailers. That's a good name. In the cinema a trailer is the first glimpse of something that you could end up looking at for at least two hours. In England, we're not so apt with words, or maybe we are, after all, a mobile home is something that a snail has.

A caravan is a garage-sized suitcase. No need to pack: just bring the house. And then of course we have static caravans: immobile mobile homes. They're the equivalent of super-gluing a snail's shell to a shed.

*

Nine: Ice.

It is so difficult not to see the pre-Event past through anything other than the rose-coloured memory glass of warm nostalgia, and looking back I feel that the longer I lived the milder the winters became. I may not be correct but my impression is that in the final couple of decades of the last century we rarely had snow on the autumn side of Christmas. It is now December. Snow fell during the final week of October and it has remained on the ground for seven weeks. Don't get the impression that Lancashire became Alaska, though at times it felt that way. To begin with it was sleety and fragile, and after a day or two of frost some of it cleared in warmer rain, but patches in north-facing gullies refused to dissolve and the warm rain went and was replaced during the night by hail and then full-blown thickly flaked snow. For a few hours it looked lovely because it cloaked everything in a thick canopy of normality. We made the most of our Christmas card excursion, though Kirsty and I were concerned by the severity of it so early in the winter, and as things turned out, we were right to worry. The majority of that fall went too, further swelling the watercourses, but before all of it could thaw, frost returned and then a cutting northeast wind followed and refused to abate for days and days keeping the temperature very low. This pattern continued. The airflow seemed to always come from the northern or eastern quadrants, sometimes as tearing gales, sometimes icy winds, sometimes just super-chilled breezes. When there was no wind there was frost. Britain might not be arctic, but it ceased to be temperate. So we lived in a winter wonderland that was part magical part malevolent. I think now, as I did in my childhood, that magic is always malevolent, but during recent decades its biggest trick was to convince us that it was harmless. Well now enchantment has returned to its true colours and black magic is white mischief. The natural is supernatural once more. Nature, always out of control, has reasserted her refusal to be tamed, predicted or held at bay. She does what she wants whenever she wants to do it just as she always has, but now there is no warning and no explanation, and for now, no respite.

The caravan was cosy but we burned a lot of bottled gas and I grew irrationally concerned that we might not be experiencing a season, but rather an epoch, a new ice age. We filled our final choice of caravan with soft furnishings pilfered from others on the site, cushions, rugs, quilts, to make additional insulation wherever we could spare the space. I found a large tarpaulin and roped it to the roof to give yet more lagging. We were warm but after a few really cold days the gas-fired cosiness became claustrophobic and stuffy and I began to think again about finding a farmhouse or similar. Kirsty was against this as it wasn't a good time to go house hunting again, even though she too could see the attraction of a home that we could heat more naturally with a real fire and so still preserve a healthy flow of fresh air. On the other hand it would be difficult to locate a residence that had such a ready and easy supply of cooking fuel and was fully centrally heated. I ventured out on short range surveys to see if there was anything suitable but drew a blank. The long fingers of mains utilities had left many rural homes handicapped in the prevailing climate. Some had open fires and solid fuel stoves but Kirsty refused to view them because their locations were not as secure as the camp site and she feared the tell-tale spire of smoke would draw unwelcome attention. There is no doubt that a chimney plume would be seen for many miles, but I wasn't as fearful of visitors as she. Her anxiety on this matter had swollen to a paranoia and threatened to become contentious as I felt that, in the long run, it would be beneficial for us to communicate with others. By that time those that still survived would surely have put down roots and arrived at a mental stability akin to our own? I began to look forwards to negotiating new interaction and discovering a fresh social fabric founded on emerging conventions of this future past period that we inhabited, but she was ultra-cautious. There was a deeply ingrained fear that I suspected was focussed on an individual or individuals rather than on general strangers, but she wouldn't confess to it, so perhaps I was wrong.

Kirsty and I became much closer. Of course, Thistle was with us, and I suppose we became a kind of family with all the inherent strains of that type of arrangement. What a peculiar bundle we would have seemed to an onlooker, huddling in a cantankerous cluster amid the premature winter of a dead planet, a curiosity in a Dickensian science fiction. We were three generations, with I old enough to be Kirsty's father and she just about old enough to be Thistle's mother, but without a bloodline or even a betrothal between us, and so there was a hierarchy based on forced intimacy but without any legitimacy. We had everything and nothing in common. We argued. We had tiffs and full blown rows but differences could not be resolved on the basis of claiming seniority because we were not related and none of us had lived any longer than the others in this reconstituted world. No one had authority. Consequently we learned to offend and injure, and then to compromise and apologise. Our constricted triangle became at first more widely spaced and stretched and then tighter and stronger. One night when the wind was howling especially strongly, Kirsty climbed into my bed.

I was asleep when she came into the room and I didn't really respond when she lifted the quilts and got in, in fact I think I may have gone back to sleep again for a few moments until she hugged me. Only her hands and face were naked. She wore thick warm pyjamas and socks, as indeed did I. I let her hug me for a while not knowing what to do. After some minutes I shifted position and returned the embrace and she snuggled more tightly to me. I waited some more then kissed her on the forehead. She wormed more deeply into my embrace. I waited a while longer then kissed her again but she shifted her position to signify no further intimacy was to be attempted. Since that night we have always slept together. We have never spoken about our intimacy. We have kissed but always with lips tightly closed. She loves me, I know she loves me, but it is a new kind of love, a strengthening of the present not a pledge for the future. That after all is where we live, in the perpetual present with no foreseeable future and no relevant past. Tomorrow is not tomorrow it is just another today, and as there is no tomorrow, nothing must be done that depends on it being different than today. Do I love Kirsty? How could I not? I should not. I should have a hundred glass doors of normality through which I might notice her, admire her, muse about her personality, envy her lover, but through which I would not normally venture. I would not even try the handle, and I had not done so. Of course she was always a delight to my eyes, and she must have seen my appreciation of her betrayed in my face, but I never wittingly signalled any affection other than one of comradeship and of gratitude for her labours, her kind words, her natural, always slightly professional, warmth. How strange that as she enhanced that warmth, she has delivered to me a new kind of coldness. She desires my affection but keeps a firm boundary. We live on the iced fence of wise intimacy. So far, no further. Do not climb over: the ground is unsafe. We dare not know each other more deeply. We dare not declare a special unity. To acknowledge love is to requisition a slice of the future, and the future is frozen. The future is fear. And overriding all this is the knowledge that it simply should not be happening. Everything is wrong, nature, the weather, our relationship, the world. But it is all we have.

I still see Claire. I see her most when asleep and dreaming, but on occasions when awake, always in sunlight, always in summer clothes, always smiling, always at a distance. Quite often, now, I cannot tell when I am dreaming. Being asleep is more like being awake and vice versa, but sometimes I dream when awake and I cannot distinguish between the dream and the reality, except that when I am asleep, my dreams have fields that are green.

One night in early December, Thistle left us. We looked for her for two hours then stopped, and we felt no guilt about stopping. We were both very fond of her but the loss of her drained away at a rapid rate. We went back to the caravan and made a cup of tea. A weird silence fell upon us, but we broke it with trivial conversation and returned to our routine. Thistle was gone and that was that. She was still gone the next day, and well, that's just the way it was. That was our world now. We lived in post-Event trauma fatigue. Nothing could shock us or deepen the dismay that we felt but kept at the bottom of the freezer of the soul. We had known Thistle and she had gone, just like so much else.

She came back the next day dressed like an Inuit tracker and with a filigree leather of frostbite on her nose. She'd wanted to live rough for three days in the wild and she'd done so. She then went to bed for four days, smug in a leaden euphoria. I was sorry she came back and hated myself for it.

We had to make expeditions for supplies via roads that were increasingly treacherous, but we had all the time in the world, all the time and all of the world, so we trundled and ambled like tourists on a themed treadmill. Each time we went back into civilisation we were reminded how wise we had been to burn the bodies at our base. Yes we were numbed and yes we knew this was now normality, but the sight of the dead, still in position, still just one step from what they were last doing, still, still, still damn them. Still there. Still there to be stepped over. We called it shopping and laughed that we loved it, yet bitterly hated it. Amid all the mundane horrors there was always one fear to spur us on and get us home, the fear that someone would have found our hideaway in our absence. They didn't, and we always sighed when we turned the last corner and saw Doris, our caravan, wrapped in her frosted shawl and with a smile from window to window.

Believe it or not, more than six months on, and "fresh" food was still edible. We still ate it though the flavours were feeble and increasingly similar. Everything tasted shades of cucumber, even garlic and chillies. We called them warm cucumber. Tinned and dried food is far superior. I hate fresh food for not being rotten.

This then is our life. Three go mad in a caravan, except that there is no sign of madness. I wish there was, for then one of us might do something rash. Rashness is not appealing. Nothing is appealing. Nothing is changing. It really does seem like everything is slowing and just waiting for us to catch up. We are not slowing fast enough, but we are slowing, of that I am sure. Soon, but not very soon, we will stop. Avoiding a terminal lethargy is our pact. We keep each other going. Slowly. More slowly. Life has stopped and warmth has gone away. Layer by layer our spirits are turning to ice. Tomorrow is the solstice. Thistle worked it out. Will the days lengthen? Will the warmth come back? Will there be a spring? I used to care.

**

LEMON

Ten: Please Read This.

I hope someone finds this. If you do, please read it. I have written it in the vain hope that one day the hard drive on which it resides will be reactivated and this log will be deciphered. I intend to update it as often as I can. Perhaps you are able to read it from a distance right now? That is our most cherished wish. If you can, please come to our aid. We are in England, not far from Lancaster. It is January, the first after the Event. This used to be the New Year, but we don't really think of it like that anymore because there are no signs of anything new. We haven't actually measured the daylight so we don't even know if the days are lengthening or if the world is still in the same orbit. If it isn't, then perhaps that would explain a lot, though not the suddenness of the Event. If you are puzzled by the context of what I am saying, you will have to be patient. I intend to document my story in full. I will arrange it in nine chapters. That is why this is numbered as chapter ten.

If you haven't read those chapters yet, now would be a good time to do so.

My name is Dan Goodwright. I was also known as Dan Good. That was my stage name. I was a stand-up comedian. I've been low on jokes for the last nine months so don't expect a lot of laughs from this diary. There isn't much to smile about, although my two companions and I did get lucky three weeks ago when we came upon this place. We are now living in comparative luxury, though our mood is still soured by the bleak prospects we all face, unless you can help us. Just a mile or so up the hill from here, ten tall benevolent angels are swirling their wings and we've managed to harness the output of three of them and hence we have electricity. We are the beneficiaries of three of the ten pillars of life that make up a small wind farm called Caton Moor and we are part of a community of forty-eight survivors living on the edge of Caton village. One of them, Brian, helped to commission the wind farm when it first opened in the nineteen nineties, and it is thanks to him that we have the power that drives the lap-top on which I type, and feeds the cooker in the kitchen where Kirsty is boiling potatoes harvested a year ago. Nothing lives in our world, and after death nothing decomposes. None of us know why, but where we are, every living thing except us is dead. Even bacteria. We live off "fresh" food, that is stale in taste and often in texture but not rotten, and off packaged food that is still perfect. Is it the same where you are?

Someone once told me that there are satellites that can read hard drives from space. I hope there are. I hope they can. And I hope that someone somewhere still operates them. If so this may be a distress call, or a prayer. If not, this machine is as sterile as the society in which we know live, and this becomes a testament, an artefact, and electronic archaeology. Perhaps you are reading this far in the future? Read on. I hope I have time to tell you enough to pass on what you would like to know.

Someone set our last home on fire. That's why we had to abandon it. They set fire to it as we slept. We had lived there for nearly three months. The fire ripped through our caravan in a matter of minutes and spread to some of the others on the site almost instantly, driven by the bitter east wind. Fortunately the smell and sound of the burning woke us. Someone had set about causing us a great deal of trouble. We had nothing but the clothes in which we stood. The keys to our vehicle melted inside the inferno as we watched our home burn and had I not had the foresight to anticipate such an attack we should certainly have perished, but ever since the Event I have trained myself to think the unthinkable and wherever possible plan for it. In addition I have long harboured the suspicion that someone was, and probably is, on our trail. I don't know who, or why, but I think they're out there, and I'm sure they must know that we escaped what was a pretty comprehensive attempt to exterminate us. We sometimes used a Land Rover that we found next to a caravan at the top end of the site. I hid the keys beneath a rock at the foot of the quarry face. My comrade, Kirsty, would have mocked me for being over-cautious so I didn't tell her. Now, of course she is angry that I didn't. Three weeks later she is still angry. She says it means I didn't trust her. I didn't. I don't. I love her, but I don't trust her. I don't trust anyone. Not even myself.

The gun we had brought with us was lost in the fire, but that deprivation faded into soft focus because of a much more significant loss: my spectacles. I am not totally blind without them, far from it, but reading is a pain, and whilst

I can still see for miles and miles and miles, all distant detail has gone, except under certain conditions. Sometimes I see with great sharpness, and when that happens I know I am seeing something that isn't really there. Either that or I am seeing a reality that doesn't rely on a retina.

Good job we've lost the gun. I couldn't see straight enough to aim it.

We didn't stay to watch the site burn once we realised what was happening. Our young teenage friend Thistle, bless her, made frantic raids on the northern-most caravans and managed to pick up a couple of very damp and highly inappropriate coats plus a bed quilt, and wrapped in these and with the car heater on full power we fled to Clitheroe where we raided stores for better clothes and emergency supplies. Everything was cold and dank but we had no option, we needed protection and fast. Temperatures in this part of the world have remained below freezing for the last month or more. Despite all we have been through, the first day after the fire was our lowest point. We slid into our new cold clothes, sat in the Land Rover, not daring to switch it off, and waited for its heater to dry us out and give us some fibre of hope. Of course it did not. Its fuel gauge was low and we had no tools to force the petrol caps off other vehicles or tubes to siphon their fuel into our tanks. We sat and waited for the world to solve our problem. It didn't and we three seemed resigned to it. Too sad for self-pity, we just sat and waited until Kirsty seeing the death-wish of our apathy, found a reserve of Celtic anger and suddenly said "Fuck this," before leaping out of the Land Rover and stomping round to my side where she flung my door open and pulled me out, in order to take my place in the driving seat. "You can get in or you can stand there and wait" she said. I tottered round to the nearside and got in. She drove until we came to a hardware store. She went in and I meekly followed, leaving Thistle in charge of the Land Rover with strict instructions to lean on the horn if she saw another living thing, and I meant thing. Even so my absolute distrust made me linger at the store door watching our vehicle as Kirsty fumbled in the darkness to find tools, torches and a hose pipe, from which she sliced several short lengths. We went back to the Land Rover and drove a little further where we forced petrol caps from other cars and siphoned their fuel into our tank until it overflowed. We then drove back to the caravan site to see if we could salvage anything else. We did not. Four vans still burned and we stood in the heat, sort of worshipping it, absorbing it like some act of communion, standing as we did on an island of thawed frost amid an ocean of snow. It was the nicest and the most threatening place in our world. We had avoided fire for so long, afraid of flying the banner of smoke that would tell others where we were, for we feared company much more than we desired it. This surely was the biggest beacon in the county, unless the arsonist was a serial fire-starter who had already moved on. Much more likely he watched us there and then as we warmed.

"Kirsty, you are going to have to tell me who it is you're scared of," I said.

"Everyone," she said.

"Who in particular?"

"Everyone."

"For fuck's sake."

"Everyone."

"When we first met there was someone you wanted to keep clear of."

"Was there?"

"Yes. That first day in Warton, you wouldn't travel with the other cabin crew, and then of course, things didn't work out in Manchester. Things you've never explained."

"And I'm not going to."

"Could this be him?" When a caravan smoulders it smells like grilled tyre.

She shrugged.

"Tell me about the man from Manchester."

"Who said he was from Manchester?"

"Tell me about him."

"No."

I let the sound of snapping coach trim punctuate the conversation as tiny explosions peppered the embers of the nearest wreck.

"Right," I said, "we've tried the isolation thing and it hasn't worked, so I think we should find company."

I expected a bluntly negative response, but there was an extended pause and then she said, "Okay."

"You agree?"

"But not back to Preston."

"We could head for Scotland."

"And how do you know there'll be anybody up there?" she asked with sweet acerbity made melodic by the accent that instantly evoked all the lyrical majesty of her native country.

"I was trying to be considerate."

"Be sensible instead. We should go somewhere where we know there will be people. But not Preston."

"Manchester?" I suggested not opting for the most sensitive tone. She kicked a smouldering prong sending sparks cascading upwards on bonfire thermals then walked away. By chance she was walking westwards. Perhaps this triggered a half-memory. "The coast," I said. "Remember that group at Warton? They were heading for the coast." She paused and thought. "The seaside in January," I jibed. "What could be nicer?"

She shivered a seventh of a smile, Thistle shrugged her shoulders and the decision was made.

We stayed in the Land Rover at the beacon island all that night despite the dangers of discovery. This was the second home I'd lost to arson since the Event and I was beginning to feel victimised. Maybe someone was stalking me? That and other equally irrational thoughts kept me awake as we took it in turns to let the others doze. In due course we made a more organised examination to what was left, and found that there was much more than we had initially realised, but so little of it seemed of use to us now, and we simply didn't have the drive to re-establish a base there, so we steadied ourselves to resume a nomadic existence for a while, gathered what we thought might be invaluable and then set off westwards. Our progress was unremarkable for some time. We were following rural routes, so they were not as heavily clogged with dead traffic and articulated archaeology as the major roads, but blockages were sometimes so complete that we had to retrace our steps and work out diversions. We found several places where we might have stopped but we stuck to our new aim of finding other survivors so kept going, forever scanning the sky for traces of smoke. Eventually we saw a most remarkable sight. Three angelic windmills that later became ten and they were turning. That in itself was not remarkable for we were travelling with a tailwind, but not far from their base we saw something none of us had seen since the night of the Event: light pollution.

And so we hit upon the Caton community.

Our arrival felt mythological: a transition from one testament to another. This was the opening of the second volume of our afterlife story. It was dark but windows glowed with that lovely marmalade hue of cosy occupation. There was a road block and three figures came from the nearest houses, wrapped in military surplus greatcoats and carrying rifles, breathing swirls of mist that turned from grey to gold as the airborne moisture moved between us and their warm, warm window glow, and then to steel cold as their breath was challenged by our headlights. We wound down our windows and told our tale in three sentences. They questioned us, swept torch beams over our faces and our meagre belongings, then unchained the gate across the road and waved us through. We were then led at pilgrim pace, escorted by two of the three while the third secured the gate behind us. This was the new Christmas where every window was a candle of hope, every illuminated home an inn, every smoking chimney a Dickensian hearth. I exaggerate, but at that moment all emotions were exaggerated. There were fewer than twenty properties occupied but to see a row lit, glowing with generated light and heat was like peering through the workhouse window to gaze upon the rich man's table whilst stepping through the wardrobe to another world where we might just possibly be allowed to stay.

We were taken to Brian's house. Brian lives there with Betty, a good earth-mother type who has never dyed her abundant forest of curly grey hair, remembers rebelling to the Rolling Stones and divining the meaning of life to two kinds of Dylan: one Welsh, the other blowin' in the weed. Brian is our leader because Brian brought the angel turbines back to life. Betty brewed us the sweetest cocoa I have ever dreamed of and Brian racked up the coal fire, yes coal fire, with the skill of a footplate-man who could have a stab at a world steam speed record. This was friendly fire, and we were warmer inside and out than we had been for three months. Thistle fell asleep within the hour, while we recounted our new-life stories, though not in full, as Kirsty and I sensed the need to bargain, giving away a certain amount but holding back other things. This was a kind a power poker, for it seems now that experience is wealth and it's best not to share it all until you are sure the recipient can be trusted. Brian and Betty in response served us a potted version of their history along with Cornish pasties defrosted, and heated to piping hot in the microwave, yes the microwave, that pinged in the kitchen like a fairy refectory bell in a fantasy. This was their second defrosting, the first being a direct consequence of the global power failure but as Betty explained, there is no problem refreezing, because she had a freezer and the pasties didn't have harmful bacteria. Our hosts, too, played the power poker game. Not all our questions were answered directly, though all were dealt with politely. I felt biblical again, our new testament life was being told in old, old testament style, for we were true travellers, travelling at a time when most people didn't travel, arriving at an oasis of comfort, the home of another tribe who had overwhelming wealth. We had to be careful and they had to be cautious.

So we learned as much as they wished to tell us. The forty-five who settled at Caton were from a flight to Edinburgh from Stockholm that diverted to Carlisle in order to find a clear runway. They were among the luckiest survivors for their flight was delayed. Another hour and they would never have boarded. The community is mainly the English contingent of the flight. There are a few Scots and a pair of Swedes, but most passengers of those nationalities opted to go north and east towards their homelands. I think that is a simplification but Brian did not elaborate further. The Caton group stayed in Carlisle for a while, scavenging as best they could and in a much less well organised fashion than we had at Camp Q. Then Brian had declared his hand. He felt he could re-ignite the cables at Caton and tap into them to draw power for the local properties. He knew of other wind farms closer to Carlisle, but was fully familiar with Caton and persuaded his followers to decamp to here. It took him less than a week to power the first property. It would have been sooner but they had to wait for the wind. He and Betty live in a modern house about a mile up the access road to the wind farm. It already had its own domestic wind turbine in the field outside, so he had power from the moment they arrived.

The job of linking up the village was a little more complicated. It's not just a question of flicking a switch at the turbines. It involves a couple of substations and three miles of high tension cables snaking overland. This umbilical serpent is the sacred beast of Caton Moor. It is our electric lifeline.

We spent the first night here in Brian and Betty's living room, loving their fire and their oil-filled electric radiators, and sleeping deeply. For a few days following that we were given, the "guest house" a semi at the end of the main electrified row and close to the properties used as gatehouses close to the main arterial road block. We can see now that this was a kind of quarantine period whilst we were assessed. Once it was determined that, despite Thistle's youthful eccentricity, we could be trusted, Brian offered us this lovely cottage at the foot of the turbines. Little was said about its previous occupants except that they had decided to move on due to "differences" with the community, but it is an important house because our job is to guard the turbines themselves, or more particularly, the business end of the supply cables, and for this reason I have been armed with a 1970s self-loading rifle, or SLR, and given a crash course in how to use it by Bash, the ex-RAF policeman. I didn't tell him that, with my eyesight, in order to hit a barn door I have to guess where it is.

So here we are. Happy you would think, and compared to everything we've experienced since May of last year we are certainly happier than at any other time, or at least I am. But who can be truly happy when faced with the monumental uncertainty of a world that shows no sign of defrosting, and seems to hold no prospect of being able to support new growth animal or vegetable even if it warms.

Kirsty shares these worries, but she has others too, and those she keeps entirely to herself. I can't quite work her out. She has really changed, but who wouldn't having lived through the end of the world. I expect we have all changed. Initially Kirsty was a very gregarious person and the kind of woman that thrived off the continuous general rapport-building interaction with others. At our first shared home, Camp Q, she was magnificent in that respect. She got on famously with everyone and they all loved her, which at times she perceived as a threat. She came to me for safety. She has told me that over and over and I have tried to respond to that need. She has never let me forget that I let her down badly in her greatest hour of need when the camp was attacked by the malevolent Prague Angels. Luckily she survived that, but the loss of the Camp camaraderie hit her badly. It was, under the circumstances, a happy place. We found new purpose and new hope together, but it was shattered so simply and so brutally and she has never recovered from that. I couldn't understand her desperate desire to remain so isolated, even though I understood the danger I felt that surely there must be safety in numbers. Once you have established a remote lifestyle, however, it is much more difficult to break it. We are really lucky to have found such a well-resourced group. They seem very welcoming, though I think we are wise to be cautious, and so cautious we remain, Kirsty even more than me.

I found this lap-top at the back of a cupboard in the living room. There were files and photographs on it from the previous owner, but I've deleted them so that if anyone finds it after me, my record will be the first thing that you see. I am going to document what happens to us. If you find this in our time, please come to us with kind hearts and help us. If it's too late and we have gone, it will simply serve to say that we were here, and we did what we could. There are plans to help you. Yes you: the citizens of tomorrow. They are ambitious plans. I think they may be too ambitious, but if you are reading this in the future, then perhaps they have worked.

Thank god for the zoom function. Large text is better than beer.

*

Something really puzzles me when I'm driving. It's the signs people put in their rear windscreens. "Baby on board." Strange, but even if a car doesn't have one of those signs, I'm not usually intending on ramming the rear of it. I had a customised sign made for my car. It says, "No baby on board – O.K. to crash."

*

Eleven: Déjà Vu.

George White is a retired high school Chemistry teacher. He is deputy-chair of a sub-group of a dozen (now fourteen with Kirsty and I) who call themselves The Age of Reason. This is a half tongue-in-cheek title. They regard themselves as the part of the community that likes to put reason before superstition, a task that was hard enough before the Event and near impossible after it. You could deduce from this that the other three quarters are strongly superstitious, and that is not far from the truth, though some people are simply hedging their bets. They like to listen to common sense if it offers ready and effective solutions, but prayer often supplies a quicker, deeper and more promising reassurance. On top of that, lucky charms and superstitious rituals are disturbingly prevalent. George and his like-minded compatriots attempt to eschew the irrational and keep reason to the fore and apply the best post-Event technology they can construct. To their credit, their achievements here at Caton have been remarkable. I thought at first that this may be the only place on earth with a power supply, but it seems they have links with another community operating on a similar basis over near Kendal. Despite these technological restorations, if I am honest, I'm not certain that all fourteen disciples of reason are scrupulously scientific, as between them they harbour a hidden host of hope rituals, and several of them are open worshippers. Everyone in the group tactfully chooses not to voice criticism of this contradiction. I have always had difficulty with religious scientists. I decided long ago that for the sake of peace of mind I would never question the beliefs of a scientist but I would always question the scientific judgement of a believer. So even within the most secular sect at Caton, there are unspoken tensions, but what else could be expected? Acts of God always result in religious earthquakes.

I embraced the Age of Reason group with arms as wide open as my mind. Kirsty, I suspect is along for the ride. She is looking for the most convenient flight, but I'm glad to have her with me. She still clings tightly to me. Socially this is exhilarating and a touch uncomfortable. We have only attended one of their formal meetings. We were a little out of our depth as they were discussing highly specific practical matters regarding the distribution of the power supply and ways of storing it using industrial battery systems of the kind utilised for running emergency lighting after power failures. It all became rather technical and degenerated into a duologue between George and Brian, but most of the rest of us went along with the path that Brian preached despite the fact that Caton is lacking the number of battery systems that we will need. We voted to put our faith in Brian and let him organise a couple of expeditions to locate the hardware and assess the feasibility of relocating it. Towards the end of the meeting George hinted that the next meeting would have to return to debating what he called the Mountain Mission. This set up a rumble among the assembled: a mixture of anticipation and disapproval. Kirsty and I signalled our bewilderment, so George kindly arranged a separate meeting with just the two of us to explain his grand theory. He came to our cottage this evening.

"It has to have been some kind of cosmic bombardment," he said. "And it must have been at a sub-atomic level. And I mean sub-atomic." He brushed grandfather fingers over his badger moustache, which was not unlike that of Albert Einstein, though shorter and smaller than the infamous scientist's, and in complete contrast to him George had very little hair, two shades of grey. "I visualise it as a jet stream, or cosmic wind of sub-atomic particles."

"What kind of particles?" I asked.

George sipped his tea too soon and scorched his lip, but his enthusiasm seared in his next breath and cured the pain almost before he felt it. "I don't know. Maybe of a kind we haven't discovered yet, or behaving in a way we don't know about, but they've surged through everything and damaged the very composition of all living things in a tiny yet catastrophic way."

By this point Kirsty and I were locking eyes. I willed her to say nothing and she seemed to instantly understand and signal compliance. I tried to not look distracted whilst at the same time struggling to remember just how much we'd said to Brian about Nathan, and his precious theory.

"Where did this wind come from?" I asked.

George shrugged his shoulders.

"The sun?" I offered.

He sharpened his focus on me. "Why do you say that?"

"Seems the most obvious suggestion."

"Perhaps. It's clearly a phenomenon about which we are ignorant. Maybe these particle streams don't come from anywhere? Maybe they just exist in the galaxy? Or perhaps they're moving randomly or on some vastly extended solar orbit like comets and only rarely collide with planets?" He was about to try his tea again but a better thought pushed its way in front. "Collide is the wrong word of course. Pass through. It passed right through, through the gaps in the atoms but causing enough collateral damage to destroy life."

Kirsty was pursing her lips now. George wasn't looking in her direction. For the moment I was teacher's pet and rode the privilege proudly.

"But another obvious point," I said. "What about us?"

"That's why I'm convinced it's something sub-atomic. The planet itself was a source of attraction, like a magnet is for iron filings. If this cosmic wind comes close to the earth, the earth itself may bend and focus its path, like an electronic, gravitational or magnetic, lens. We must have been on the fringes of the lens. Perhaps the cosmic torrent only hit us in a very dilute concentration, or if the material of the earth is highly attractive, perhaps the whole stream was concentrated down at this level, missing us altogether."

"Down at sea level."

"And below. The real attraction might be the earth's core. That's where the strongest hit may have been. We all know that everything in the soil is dead, so underground has been bludgeoned at least as heavily as the surface has, but we at thirty thousand feet weren't even scratched. As far as we can tell."

Kirsty shifted a little uneasily in her seat. "As far as we can tell," she echoed almost inaudibly.

"The big question is," said George, "what was the lowest height at which people survived? And is there anywhere in the world where people live on the ground at that altitude." He sat back and smugly swallowed two great gulps of tea.

Kirsty wasn't looking my way anymore, but her eyes were averted to one side where she found deep thoughts. Somehow I didn't think they were about physics. I kept the schoolmaster on task.

"I saw a documentary once about sub-atomic particles from space and how they pass through us and the planet all the time."

"Quite right. They're doing it right now. My thinking is that the Event was a special storm of that kind of particle, concentrated into an interstellar current and focused through the earth like light through a lens.

"I'm not convinced though, especially with respect to our escape. The surface of the planet is a lot closer to thirty thousand feet than it is to the earth's core."

His face lit up. "Excellent," he said, "that's the number one objection to the theory." His glee seemed so genuine I felt confirmed as top of the class. I was first out of two, one of whom wasn't listening. The master leaned forwards. "But all we have is the evidence of our eyes. And we survived, simply by being in the air. So it has to be something to do with the surface or what lies beneath. If it's the surface, my theory is sunk."

"I don't see why. It's the same idea. Perhaps the particles cling to the surface give or take a few hundred feet each way."

"But if it's the surface it's still everyone." His enthusiasm was back in storage. If, on the other hand, it's a question of distance from the core, then maybe whole populations survived? With their infrastructure." His eyes glowed wistfully on 'infrastructure'. "Of course they can't help us unless they know we're here."

"They can't help us if they aren't there," offered Kirsty, who clearly was listening after all. She had become the worst kind of class cheat, the one who fakes indifference but is actually concentrating hardest of all.

George looked at her as an old dog might when he knows he's destined for the ultimate injection. "We have to look for them," he said.

She shrugged. "Where? And how?"

The un-retired man sat back in a new sanguinity, his armchair a throne, the air above his thin hair an invisible crown. "We must find them. That's our vision, our hope, our only hope, our ultimate responsibility. The Mountain Mission starts here. We send out a task force to search the high ground. To find the fertile places."

"Whoah!" I said. "Where's the science gone? You're talking about sending Scott of the Antarctic and Livingstone to scour the surface of Mars on the basis of a supposition that they might stumble on a garden centre."

"Historic: yes," he said and drained his tea. "Difficult: yes. Impossible: no. Reckless: no."

"Remote places don't have corner shops on the way, and it will take you for ever to get there and just as long to get back."

"What's the alternative?"

Kirsty was looking out of the window now, studying clouds, imagining a demise one stop beyond that which the schoolmaster was suggesting.

He said, "Starvation. Eventually. For all of us."

"Not for a long time," I said.

"True," he said. Perhaps you and I will die of unnatural causes, and perhaps Kirsty too, but what of the next generation?"

The clouds put water in Kirsty's eyes. She blinked to keep it in check.

"There's a century on the shelves," I said.

"Do you think so?" He said twisting his empty mug on the arm of the chair. "Can we be sure? It tastes okay now. In the short term it's done us no harm. How about next year? Or in ten years? And even if it is, then one day it will run out. We have only one duty and that is to our descendents."

"Perhaps there shouldn't be any," I offered.

"That's not an idea that has ever caught on in the past."

Kirsty spoke, " Where . . ?" Her throat was tight. She cleared it and started again. "Where will you look? Where will you send this expedition?"

"Expeditions. There'll need to be more than one at once, so this society will have to grow first. As it does so, we will consider your question, which is the fundamental one." He swung towards her and I mourned the loss of his focused enthusiasm. "And you can help."

"Me?" She looked scared. Too scared. Scared by something I couldn't see.

George played with his mug as if it were a treasured artefact in the hands of a historian, meanwhile his senior, ever-so-slightly age-dulled eyeballs oscillated between the void of the cup and the depth of the pupil. "Because of the nature of our survival we have a high proportion of people like you: aviators. We need you. We need your expertise. Firstly, if we can find and question enough of you, we can determine if there is any land mass in the world at an altitude higher than the one at which you were when the tragedy happened. Secondly, we must recruit pilots, and get them flying again. It will be by far the quickest way to conduct the mission. By land, yes, by sea, of course, but most urgently by air."

By saying nothing, we each said our teacher was mad. He ignored the insubordination then undermined it.

"It will take bravery, yes. Immense bravery. But that's more common than you think. But above all we must start now. We can only bank on one generation of sailors and pilots. And we mustn't let their machines rust."

"It was word for word what Nathan said," said Kirsty after George had gone.

"How do you know?"

"You told me."

I rinsed George's cup.

"Well was it?" she asked.

"Was it what?"

"Word for word?"

"Pretty much. From what I can remember. What did we say to Brian about Nathan?"

"You skimmed over him. You mentioned he had a grand theory about atoms and stuff and I remember that he smiled at that point, but you didn't go in to detail, and he didn't ask."

"There are only four possibilities: Nathan got his idea from George, George got his idea from Nathan, they both got them from other people, or they both arrived at the same conclusion independently."

"Do you think Nathan has been here?" Kirsty's eyes were wide and not with glee.

"Brian didn't mention him."

"Do you think he could have been here?"

"Doubtful. I don't think he could drive. Might have worked it out I suppose."

"Could have been, then."

"Well, we'll find out tomorrow."

Kirsty and I are not sleeping together at the moment. We both know it's safer that way. This is a warm house. It has electric heat when the wind blows and an open fire for when it doesn't. The wind is blowing. We are warm. We have separate rooms. Before the death of normality this would have been the most bizarre of relationships, but bizarre is no longer possible because all the world is weird. We have a bond that is deep and strong and along which we signal sincere affection. It is free of romance yet infused with a passion born of a Scandinavian saga, for we are living legendary lifestyles in mysterious times. Our friendship is one part of the living myth that we are making by simply being alive and that realisation adds an unimaginable charm to our partnership. We are a pairing of supernatural beings because we have outlived nature and this is a new kind of love that we know. In one sense it is like the earliest of times with Claire, in the depth of those semi-dark nights when I thought of her and thought that she might be the one to walk with through an uncertain, but well-charted future. Kirsty and I will walk together, but there are no maps, no guides, no victims of circumstance to learn from, no patterns laid down, no dead-ends identified, no safe routes way-marked. Face this future before you tell me about commitment. Kirsty, I know, will stay by me, through poorer and poorer, for worse and worse, until life stops one of us, and I will do the same for her. How can this not be called marriage?

Our friendship, like our new home, has warmth to combat the unnatural chills that beset us and knowing that is a double reassurance because, as well as a morale booster, it is a set of feelings that I recognise. I have been here before. I just wish I could go back and enjoy the first terrors more, knowing as I do now that the imagined fears of the first world were as itches compared to the fear fever symptoms we now face. Yet I see too, that what we now know must have been the norm for the overwhelming majority of our ancestors, living in a perpetually uncertain world filled with fickle nature and living or dying at the whim of astronomical acts. Perhaps they would not have found it so fearful because unlike us they would not know of the world they did not have. Among them may have been people like George, dreamers who, by living in a nightmare, understood that dreaming and living are but one life, and dreams can be brought to life, must be brought to life, or there may be no life.

I see and, to an extent share, George's vision. His theory may be proved to be correct, for there is a logic to it, though I remained troubled by the hope he places on survivors at high altitudes, but let's see how far we can test it. If he is right, then we must pioneer a new living mythology, setting out on epic voyages to find the next Golden Fleece. There is reassurance even in this speculative excitement. We have been here before. Ours will be the second set of ancient myths.

Should there be new generations? There are children among us and in other groups like ours. Will they reach maturation? Will they reproduce? Can we possibly survive or will we deplete until just a few eccentrics remain, slowly starving amid a bewilderment of barren landscapes and rusted shopping centres? Faced with that scenario I would set sail on the new Argos tomorrow. We have to seek those fertile lands. Until they are located, looking is more important than finding, even if we never find them. We are mythmakers. Hope is all that matters.

Yes, I would set sail tomorrow. If Kirsty will come with me.

6th January 2006

Thanks to the painstaking attention to detail by some of our new friends and the battery memory of this computer, Kirsty and I have been reunited with the Gregorian calendar and I am able to attach dates to my blog entries. It's a bit unsettling because we'd become accustomed to a lifestyle that no longer featured days, weeks or even hours. We rose with daylight, made one main meal and retired when darkness came. I grew to like it. When there is no future, you don't need calendars or clocks, but now we are among planners, dates count again. We've been here about a week and have been given this superb cottage just south of the wind farm. We have our own power cable to the turbine substation which makes us feel very important and a little vulnerable. There is a farm on the other side of the fell right at the foot of the turbines. That is occupied by a weighty team of enforcers, part scientists part thugs, and few of their partners. Brian and Betty and another similar team are part way down the same access road in their modern farm with its baby turbine. We are on a road that runs close to the rear of the wind farm, in a delightful house well hidden from the highway, though more visible than it used to be due to the stripping of foliage. One of our appointed tasks is to keep an eye on this approach to the farm. We have been given a stock of marine flares as well as personal radios to keep alongside our self-loading rifle. If only it was self-aiming. I'm not convinced this responsibility is all that was implied. If it was – why risk giving it to three new arrivals, and why leave the property empty? We're not yet in a position to raise that kind of question.

Kirsty has done her best to help George in his quest to establish the height at which aircraft were affected, but it wasn't something that she went round canvassing about in the manic hours at Heathrow. We had been well above twenty thousand feet and most of her interactions with surviving cabin crew led her to deduce that they were in routine procedures mid-flight, so they too would have been at a similar altitude to us. She has a vague recollection of someone saying they were just starting their descent, and while that conversation teased a brighter glow in George's eyes, it was too insubstantial to warrant the raising of hopes that anyone on the ground might have escaped the effects of what ever it was that hit us. I remain very dubious, but continue to be motivated by the drive to do something worthwhile. Kirsty, however, worries me more and more. She is holding something back.

She's done her best to get round the village and meet with all of the community. I won't list them all. There's a good spread of people in terms of outlook, and age. The eldest is in her sixties and we have five under eighteen, all teenagers bar one ten year old. As at Camp Q, some are in pre-Event or post-Event relationships, others are single. Kirsty, as always, has drawn the keen eyes of the males. And I have drawn their suspicious, envious or malicious gazes, at least in my imagination. She seems relieved that Nathan is not among them or known to them, but she is distressed that there aren't any medics.

"What happens when we get ill?" she asked.

"From what?"

"There'll be . . . conditions," she said. "And injuries. Perhaps life-threatening."

"Hurrah!" I said sardonically, but the irony seemed lost on her.

Thistle is much more at home, which is to say she often is not. We are actually about three miles from the village, but already she is in the routine of coming and going between the two as freely as she likes, at whatever time of day and night, and most people seem okay about that. The security people mount night patrols and keep the village shut tight after dark, so she's caused a few scares but they've given her a couple of safety calls to whistle and then left her to it. She's turning truly feral. Under different circumstances people would be outraged, but we've got our backs to nature and that makes the eccentric all the more permissible. There are a few colourful characters evident in the village. They appear to be in the pupating phase, not quite sure yet of who – or what - they are becoming, or indeed aiming to become. There is a polarisation evident, for example Rachel who's just the wrong side of thirty and has assembled an arsenal of cosmetics, and refused to let go of public perfection and hence earned the nick-name The Caton Cleopatra. She is incongruously sharing a house with Rod the builder's mate, who takes me all the way back to the folk clubs of 1971 with his copious long hair, check shirt and work boots. Ah, the memories: Brian Dewhurst, singer and gloriously lewd raconteur with his act and live album Follow That with Your Sea-lions. We're getting frequent visits from wild Winnie the warrior woman who walks and talks like an ambassador from the green wellie brigade, and behaves as if she had a brace of over excited gun dogs writhing round her feet and bounding to and from her in a semi-controlled fashion. To her they are there, and for her, and us, I only wish they were. We have yet to meet Suzuki-Sparks the journeyman electrician who comes and goes between settlements swapping his expertise for sustenance and sometimes for temporary shelter, though he opts to live wherever he chooses. It is thanks to him that we know of other communities. There are a couple of such settlements in the Lake District, one of which, near Kendal, has also managed to tap into a wind farm. Another consists of a flotilla of converted pleasure craft and private boats moored together on Windermere.

I'm keen that Kirsty, Thistle and I find definite roles here and prove ourselves to be worthwhile additions to the community. Despite having some doubts about the overall outlook of Brian and George, I do feel much safer here. They are right of course, about the long term, in that there is no long term. We must either find a way of getting our little corner of the country going again, or we must reach out to others and discover if there is any hope left anywhere on this forsaken planet. There's not much to feel good about, but being here makes me feel better. Thistle is bouncing back in her own way, or at least crafting a protective cocoon. Unbelievably she has found laughter again and I've rejoiced in her all-too-brief moments of mischief. There's a lot of darkness there too but she's fighting it.

I just wish Kirsty could brighten up. She's looking healthier, but her smiles are forced and there's a frightening darkness in her eyes.

*

You've probably heard of the Cern Project. It is a huge underground ring near Geneva known as the Large Hadron Collider. They intend to fire particles round this ring in opposite directions and crash them together in the hunt for clues to the origins of the universe. The television programme Time Team suggested that ancient civilisations got there first, when they excavated a hitherto unknown design of catapult on the Scotland / England border. The Romans built it at the same time that they were working on their wall, hence it has become known as the large Hadrian Collider. Whenever the Scots advanced on the wall the Romans used to fire surplus Britons at them. It had limited effect. The Scots would pick up the catapulted body parts and boot them back. The tradition never really died out and re-emerged centuries later via the English public school system. Today we call it Rugby.

Rugby is almost certainly a form of creation myth explaining the origins of the universe. One team represents time, the other space. They crash together in a big bang of a scrum and out of this cosmic scrotum pops an almond shaped universe. We are able to grapple with this and other myths because of our modern-day diviners of awe: TV sport commentators. Through them we understand time. As Rugby commentator Ray French once said, "It's a shame that half time came as early as it did." It makes you think.

To probe the most profound depths of physics we must turn to the master: motor sport guru Murray Walker, who said "It's not only a race against the clock but against time itself." But even he cannot divine the unfathomable as well as the great Groucho Marx.

"Time flies like an arrow. Fruit flies like a banana."

I had a dream in which Groucho added a line: "And a banana unzips like a fruity fly."

It made my mother laugh.

*

Twelve: Ante Natal.

9th January 2006.

Kirsty is pregnant.

I feel like a shamed father and a betrayed partner and I am neither of these things. She will not tell me when and where it happened or with whose help, but happened it has, and it has happened since the Event. It came to light earlier this evening as we re-ignited our debate about living at Caton. I was listing the benefits. She retorted with the inadequacies.

"No, doctors, nurses, care-workers, paramedics, midwives . . ."

"Midwives? Why the hell should we need midwives? If we've got any sense . . ."

The penny dropped like the cranium of a premature baby engaging with a pelvic portal. I saw her face, flushed with excessive good health, by far the rosiest glow in the community even when she wasn't sitting before a proud paternal coal fire; the bulky sweaters that she'd selected from the Caton community's thoughtfully aired stockpile; her need for cuddles but her reluctance to come too close for too long; the eagerness to sleep apart despite being in a new and scary place; her fidgety relaxation; phases of vomiting; and most of all the fear deep in her eyes.

My first instinct was to reach for the axe of outraged age. In a flash I hated every instant of attraction and affection I'd felt for her. I resented my self-control. Could she even imagine how hard that had been? Was this how she repaid my gratitude? I was a cold war cuckold, annihilated before I'd even considered launching a warning shot. I was riding the falling side of the see-saw, the fool whose sinking status would catapult everyone else to the summit of smugness. I was victim and principal suspect. I was bad man. I was village idiot. I was Joseph before being showered with the sugary snow-shaker respectability of the yet-to-be invented nativity story. Stuff the nativity story. Right now I'd settle for the conception narrative. Short as you like.

Haiku will be fine.

"What does it matter?"

"It matters to me."

"You're not my fucking dad."

"May as well be."

"I don't need this."

"Too damn right, you don't."

"Dan! Please. Please!" She would have burst into tears, but it was too late for that, for they were already racing to be first to her chin. I breathed, she struggled to, and then it was reverse gear anger and a soft-crab embrace. Ah yes, squeeze sensitively and there was the tell-tale tummy contour. I made reassuring noises that were surprisingly warm and calmed me even more than she. I put my hand on her tummy and she put her hand on my hand gently holding the infant where it was, somewhere under the amniotic water of oblivion.

"How long?"

"I don't want to talk about that tonight."

"We'll need . . . we'll need . . . we'll need . . ."

"We'll need so much we haven't got," she said. "And by 'we' I mean it and me."

I began to play a mental slideshow of all the potential fathers but the first ones were too frightening to name, so I simply said, "Who?"

She caught a choke, swallowed that sound, coughed back two more then breathed in deeply. "I've decided, I'm not going to tell anyone that."

Half a dozen objections lined up like a firing squad but I dismissed them. "Okay."

"But I will make it clear it wasn't you."

Suddenly I was a bit sad to lose my Joseph status. "Pity. I always fancied a pet donkey."

She looked at me with genuine bewilderment. "What?"

"Never mind." I sat us both down on the sofa, keeping one arm around her. I looked at the glistening sparks on our coal fire and saw the star of Bethlehem. "But what about him-stroke-her? What will you tell it?"

"That will be the least of its worries. If it lives that long. If I do."

"Hey, hey, people have been giving birth for millions of years."

"Yeah, in the company of people who knew what they were doing."

"We've got more mothers than virgins here."

"I'd swap them all for one midwife." She leaned back into me and found her own apocalypse in the grate. "Who knows what's in there."

"Your imagination that's what. Stop it. It's a baby."

"If it's anything else I'll drown it."

"It's a baby."

"If it's deformed . . ."

"Stop it."

"I'll strangle it."

"Kirsty."

"I might strangle it anyway. Smother it. However perfect it is, it would be kinder."

"Listen . . ."

"You've said it. You've said it so many times. No place for babies."

She was right, and so was I, but I said, "I was wrong."

"I don't think so," she said. "I don't think so."

We fell to a silence, or rather to a deep warm quiet with the coal fire cracking, humming and gently hissing and sending us a glow of domestic bliss that was both comforting and mocking in equal measures, but our embrace had been promoted for there were three of us in there now and I was part of the secret. I nuzzled the top of her head and smelled her 'Kirstyness' while she snuggled tighter to me and gripped my hands. The piece of coal on which I'd seen the star of Bethlehem collapsed sending a choir of sparks skywards via the chimney.

I noticed another pair of feet crossed and declined against the hearth. Claire was sitting in the armchair opposite. It was the first time I had seen her since coming to Caton. She gave me one of her knowing quarter smiles and her eyes out-sparkled the flecks in the fire smoke.

"You shouldn't," I said.

"Shouldn't what?"

"Shouldn't tell people that I'm not the father."

"What?"

"I'll be the father. The baby will need one."

Claire was gone, leaving the armchair looking warmer than ever.

Kirsty squeezed my wrist. "That's not fair on you."

"There's no such thing as fairness anymore. In fact, I don't think there ever was. Anyway, people will presume it's me, so let them think that. It'll save a lot of discussion."

"But I'm betraying you if I say that."

"Then don't say it. Just let them deduce it."

"Folk are bound to talk to me about its father."

"Well that's what I am. I'm adopting it."

10th January 2006

Last night we slept in the same bed. Just slept. Kirsty slept much better than me. I reeled through the possible parents of her child as if I were in cinema hell, chained to a multiplex chair and forced to watch the same roll of credits over and over and over. Lying awake listening to her breathing, to the wind outside and to the gentle moan of turbine number three, I decided not to raise the subject of the father again. If she wants to tell me, she can tell me.

15th January 2006

It's almost a week since Kirsty gave me her news and it is still our secret. I suppose it might be a little while before anyone catches on. The weather is still bitterly cold, so we are usually well wrapped up with plenty of layers to cloak the baby bulge. We are still struggling to find our niche in the community, and living three miles from the centre of operations, which is at the Black Bull pub, doesn't really help. There are a series of formal meetings held there on a weekly basis or more frequently as circumstances demand, but it is also the community hub and some villagers meet there informally every day. One of the problems that we face as a community is that there isn't that much that can be done that has a reassuringly productive outcome. We have no livestock to tend to, (though the snow blanketed fields are still littered with 'deadstock') we can't plant or sow, and the notion of trade or any kind of commerce is absurd, though there are symptoms emerging in the form of personal bartering and exchange of goods or skills. All the essential communal housekeeping here was done before we arrived. Cadavers were cleared and cremated, food stock has been identified and to a large extent sorted, with much of it centralised in former shops. There are schemes to get more premises linked to our primitive grid. It's more complicated than you think. At the time of the Event, Caton Moor Wind Farm was in the early stages of an upgrade, in fact, Brian was working on that project, so we have benefited not only from his knowledge, but also from some of the heavy plant that was on site. He's managed to harness the output of three turbines but we can't simply link ourselves to the national network and send the output from our blessed trinity to fizzle away through all the short circuits caused in the aftermath of the Event. That's why Brian and his team had to lay a new supply cable overland and establish a new substation serving just a cluster of houses close to the pub.

A handful of outlying properties such as ours have their own cable straight from the wind farm. The bulk of the labour is dedicated to extending and improving the supply of power and I volunteered to help with that, but there is an unspoken hierarchy of employment and I was allocated instead to the security team, which sounds very important but in reality is just a daily grind of hammering fence posts into frozen earth and stapling wire mesh to them as part of a project to literally ring-fence the part of the village where we live. Kirsty was offered a place on this team too, and I think that if her personal circumstances had been different she may well have accepted, but instead and somewhat stereotypically she attached herself to the almost exclusively female laundry team. Although we have electricity, we do not have piped water, and whilst we have a strong supply diverted from local rivers, including the mighty Lune, it all has to be finally moved by hand, so most washing is done centrally every third day or so in the sinks of the large kitchen at the Black Bull. Drying and ironing is also done centrally there. Tumble dryers are brought into action if necessary, but all energy is most meticulously conserved, and ironically we can only tumble dry when the wind blows, so mostly the washing cartwheels and back-flips on washing lines like the genuinely athletic linen of my youth. I'm glad Kirsty has joined that team, for they are a warm-hearted and good-humoured bunch and in just a few days I have seen a return to something of the first Kirsty I knew, with a ready laugh and the strength to push problems aside. That Kirsty only appears in flashes though. She can't forget her secret and those laundry girls are so perceptive, that they're bound to rinse it out of her soon.

Thistle has also attached herself to the fencing squad, though she chooses not to work in my team. There are two other gangs, one working on the north of the village and another constructing a narrow snaking passage of protection for the supply cables. It's a kind of exclusion corridor to ensure the safety of our wind energy. That's how precious our power is to us.

Thistle is flowering. She loves it here. Of course, deep within her there is a darkness that will never lift, and she is in touch with that shadow and taps into it whenever she chooses, but I am pleased to say that the pain turns to a protective steel, not an aggressive one. She goes quiet, broods like a thundercloud, but then slips away over the horizon, taking herself out of our sight, going to who knows where? We used to worry, but she always comes back, and when she does the shadow has passed, and there does not appear to be any sign of self-harm, though you can never be sure about that kind of thing. Thistle, in keeping with her chosen name, is a prickly character, though we didn't know her before the Event so we can't say how much that cataclysm and her own personal trauma have shaped her sting. I admire her. Her fieriness fuels her independent spirit and gives her a special strength. The community here seem fond of her too. They see her fortitude and her peculiar freedom and like it. She offers us a kind of hope. We can live through this, we can hunt out a new life and we have the strength within us to forge a future. If only we can make new food.

Kirsty and I had to decide what to say to Thistle about the baby. We decided not to tell her just yet. Kirsty thinks she already knows.

19th January 2006

We've had the Mountain Mission meeting. The proposal has been accepted and, in accordance with a suggestion from me, re-named The Jason Project, because it really does represent the hunt for the Golden Fleece. It was a well-attended meeting with nearly all the village there, and an atmosphere of optimism quickly amplified as gainsayers were gently but firmly put down and people wove a steel hawser from filigree threads of speculative hope. I'm happy to go along with it, as I too now have a greater need for long term happiness, so I voiced support much stronger than good sense justifies. There will be a multi-pronged mission and the aim is to launch the first expedition at the start of the summer, if summer ever comes. (That fear wasn't recorded in the minutes.) The meeting was too large to get down to details so a sub-committee was drawn up to commence the planning. I didn't volunteer. The proviso was passed that the present priorities of securing the village and improving our power supply should remain of utmost importance, so a renewed effort was called for to ensure these projects accelerated. Suddenly a shadow of a previous life returned to hang over us. It is called pressure.

Kirsty was thanked for her attempts to add to the facts surrounding the event, but it was clear much more information was needed, and for the plan to work we would need pilots and planes, sailors and ships. Suzuki-Sparks was mentioned, he being the main link between settlements. He hadn't been seen for a while but on his next visit he would be quizzed regarding the occupations of neighbouring villagers, then deputations could be sent to see if others could be recruited to the cause. Someone said the society on Lake Windermere must include some sailors. I don't think that is necessarily the case, and anyway there's a world of difference between the enclosed waters of Cumbria and the wild seas round the Cape of Good Hope. But at least we have a plan. We don't have a future yet, but we do have a plan.

22nd January 2006.

The secret is out and the congratulations are in. It's bizarre. There are dirty jokes from the men and gushing grins from the women. No one knows quite how to deal with it. Should they be overjoyed or irate? Does it herald a new hope or the ultimate child abuse? Everyone falls back on well-learned responses, but a split second after the good wishes are spoken the eyes signal the condemnation. This is no place for children. It's no place for anyone.

So if you can read this now and you can send help, please do. It looks like we will, eventually be coming to look for you, but it will be dangerous for those who set out, so please, remove the risk. Send help. Or at least a sign.

*

When I was a child I thought Groucho Marx was my father. My mother always told me that she loved him and I took her word literally. Whenever one of his films was on the telly we had to watch it. The thing is I seemed to know the films even before I'd watched them. I think she must have seen them while I was in the womb and I heard them through the amniotic fluid. Or is it possible that a mother can pass on her knowledge of cinematic dialogue through the umbilical cord? All I know is that Groucho always featured heavily in my dreams, and the older I got the more sophisticated the dreams became. The worst was one in which he was present at my birth. My mother had undergone an exhausting twenty-four hours with a day at the races being followed by a night at the opera. It was no surprise that she went into labour. When I popped out Chico, who was the doctor said, "We've delivered a boy."

Groucho looked at me in horror, said, "Wrong address!" and left the room.

*

Thirteen: Friends Reunited.

27th January 2006

I have met Suzuki-Sparks. It's Steve. Steve the electrician who flew north with us from Heathrow and lived at Camp Q. The last we saw of him was during the attack by the Prague thugs. Today he just rode up on his Suzuki 1000cc bike and started talking to some of my mates on the fence gang. At first I was only mildly interested, just curious to see who this legendary figure was, and I didn't recognise him, because his hair is much longer now and much springier with long shock-absorber coils bursting forth when he removed his helmet. He has a beard and the expensive rider gear he has acquired creates the impression that he has put on weight. As soon as he spoke, however, I recognised his voice.

"Steve?"

The fence gang looked at me askance. Evidently no one knows him as Steve. They all call him Sparks.

He looked at me, it took him a moment, for perhaps I too have changed? "Dan! Dan! God!" His locks sprung wider open, prised apart by a hydraulic smile. "Dan Good, God! Good God! Good old Dan!"

"Less of the old. Where've you been?"

"Oh, living wild y'know. Living wild. Roaming. Journeyman magician. Taming the last of the electric magic, where I can, when I can, when I feel like it."

"So I've heard. You're a living legend evidently."

"Evidently. Guess we're all legends now. We will be if anyone outlives us."

A child sprang to mind, but I chose not to tell him. "Kirsty's here."

"Is she?" There was something more than delight in his face.

"Doing the laundry. Down at the pub."

"That's where I usually stay."

"You're staying?"

"Ah, not today, on my way. Jobs promised at Windermere. Overdue, so must go through. Just checking in, to see what needs doing. Where's your specs? Didn't recognise you at first. Got contacts in have you?"

"If only, if only. Permanent squint, more like. Getting used to it. Pain though."

"Lost 'em did you."

"Melted."

"Melted?"

I was about to explain but Leroy, the head of our fencing team, spoke up. "Brian has a few favours to ask."

"I'll bet he has. He always has. Anyone would think I need to work for a living." He turned more intently to Leroy. "Can bring you some stuff on the way back."

"Yeah," said Leroy.

"Thing is, it's a matter of currency."

"Ain't got none, have we?"

"Nothing you want to trade?"

"Anything we've got they've got too."

"Awkward then. I mean he's got a finite supply."

"Don't give me that, he's got a hell of a stash somewhere."

Sparky Steve laughed. "It will run out eventually."

"Yeah," said Leroy. "And tell him he wants to be around to enjoy the last of it."

Steve laughed again and the other labourers chuckled.

Leroy took his gloved hand from the hilt of his sledgehammer and smacked a soil-crusty grip playfully onto Steve's shoulder. "I'd love to pay the man, but I what can I do? Tell him I'll come and lay a fence round his boat. Keep him and his stockpile safe."

Steve laughed again. "He's not going to give me something for nothing, Leroy."

"It's not for nothing. It's for good will. Tell him that." Leroy returned his grip to the sledgehammer, stepped up onto the stepladder and belted the fence post another half inch into the reluctant ground. Steve came over and took me on one side.

"So, you and Kirsty? Anyone else?"

"Thistle."

He was about to say something, but stopped and thought, and after what seemed slightly to long a pause said, "Who?"

"Thistle. Lauren. Liked to be called Thistle. Now won't be called anything else."

"Ah, yeah, Thistle. How's prickly little Thistle? And what about her mum?"

I filled him in with the story and, despite anticipating the worst of it, he visibly crumpled. We drifted to an old dry stone wall where I gave him an edited version of our adventures to date. "And what about you? There was a group that scampered off to the hospital. Were you with them?"

"Decided to go my own way," he said. "Always been a bit of a loner, so cometh the hour cometh the hermit. Got myself a good bike and rode around a bit to find my ideal hovel."

"Which is where?"

He chuckled again. He always was an upbeat guy, but his propensity to chuckle has grown with his hair. "If I told you that, it wouldn't be ideal."

"But you still ply your trade?"

"Well, like to keep the old hand in. And now and then you need a bit of something that you can't always lay your hands on, and if you mix with people you can trade a bit of this and that."

"Doesn't always work," I said looking in Leroy's direction.

"Special relationship," he said with a smile. "I'm just the broker."

"Oh," I said.

The east wind rattled the ribcage of the copse beyond the wall.

"Tell you what though, there's a woman in Kendal, makes the most magnificent pies."

"Pies?"

"Not your post-catastrophe crap. Fresh pies. You know – fresh. She gets all the usual dilapidated ingredients and somehow it tastes magical. Better than pies ever tasted. I mean –ever. I call on her often. In terms of electrical infrastructure she's the best equipped on the planet, I've seen to that."

"They're wind powered there too aren't they?"

"To be honest, they've not got it sussed as well as Brian and his gang here, but that's better for me. I drip feed ideas. Keeps me in pies and things."

"Is that why you come here? To tap into Brian's expertise?"

"I come for a natter. I like the hermit thing, but not all the time. I am human. And to detach yourself from the world you have to keep abreast of it. And it's an outpost isn't it? This is my eastern eye. Me peering towards the Pennines. Works doesn't it? I've found you haven't I?"

"You have."

"And Kirsty."

"Yeah."

"How is she?"

"She was good when I last saw her. At breakfast."

"She's with you, is she?"

"She's with me."

"Lucky man."

"I don't think luck survived did it?"

"Given you a house, have they then?"

"Other side of the fell, just below the turbines."

"On the double bend of the road?"

"That's the one."

"I know it."

The easterly wind sliced at my nose and I began to feel the chill of inactivity. "What happened to the previous occupants? Any idea?"

Steve let the wind fill a gap. "Bit of a puzzle that one."

"Did you know them?"

"Fraid not. Don't know everyone."

"They all seem to know you. Or know of you."

He sniggered. "Eh – legend eh?" He began to unfold the chin strap of his helmet. "Nice community this one." He pushed his renaissance ringlets back off his face. "So long as you stay on the right side of them." He turned into the wind and pulled on his helmet and his hair fanned out of the bottom so that from behind he looked like an inverted flower arrangement. He turned back to me and spoke with syllables modulated by the chin guard. "Kirsty's at the pub, is she?"

"Doing the laundry."

"I'll go and say hello."

And off he went.

Kirsty was back at the house before me, and I got the impression she'd been there some time. The coal scuttle had been full at breakfast and was almost empty now. The wind was strong and we had plenty of power. She had headphones on and was listening to a CD. I kissed her forehead, but there was little response, so after a moment I gently took the headphones from her feathery straw of her hair. She wasn't pleased to have seen Steve.

"He didn't hang around after the Camp Q attack did he?"

"Neither did I."

She was going to say something but replaced it with a bitten breath and then said, "No, you didn't."

"No."

"But you came back. He didn't."

"Did you tell him about the baby?"

"No."

"Why not?"

"Because the questions would come, wouldn't they? And I don't want questions. The others might have told him, after I went."

"Went where?"

"Here. I came home. I wasn't feeling great. Borrowed the blue car."

"It's not here now."

"Sandra took it back."

"Are you all right now?"

"On top of the world," she said. And she put the headphones back on.

5th February 2006

A thaw has arrived. Last night there were terrible storms. I think two almighty weather fronts must have collided and boxed out their differences. It even troubled the turbines and shortly before midnight we lost power. Brian's working on it this morning. The rumour is, that they were struck by lightning, but I think it is just supposition. The rain has mostly cleared and the southerly airflow is obscenely warm. I think it's probably just the acute comparison with what we've suffered through the winter, but it feels almost tropical. People are walking about without coats and this is causing much frivolity. This mildness can't last but, unbelievably, the ice and snow are going. The rivers are swelling and we are expecting floods.

Kirsty looks more pregnant than ever.

I was fanning my face with the warm southerly and scanning the summit of the Bowland hills. I saw the spike of a lone figure on one of the ridges. It was sharply in focus, though the ridge itself was but a blur.

6th February 2006

Steve, or Sparks, came to visit bearing gifts. He brought baby clothes, brand new and smelling ultra-fresh. Believe it or not this kind of item is a rarity. Because of the lack of children and pregnant people, the stockpiling of infant garments was not a priority. There are still endless supplies of clothing for all ages, though it is all last year's fashion. Due to the amount of time it has been stored in cold and increasingly damp premises, a lot of it is less than desirable and some of it has even perished to the degree that it is discoloured or disfigured, but of course there is no sign of mould or of insect damage. The Caton folk have devised a method of moving wanted clothing into a house close to the pub, where it can be processed and dried to make the wearing of it more pleasant. Steve must have done something similar to the baby clothes, unless he had access to a high quality source. Kirsty was delighted by his gift, which has won the premature present race even outpacing the knitting and sewing enterprises that the knowledge of the pregnancy has inspired. Kirsty's attitude to Steve is much improved. It was almost as if she anticipated his visit and had made a mental adjustment. I let them have some time alone together, whilst completing my daily sunset duty of stepping out on the rise behind our cottage and scanning the southern approaches with the binoculars. I made this exercise last much longer than it needed to despite the steady rain. I liked this task, because at least I could see sharply.

I saw the figure on the Bowland Fells again. I am sure it was Claire. She was wearing the outdoor coat she wore on our fell-walking expeditions, the hood pulled up to cup her head and complement the arc of her smile. I could only imagine the smile, for she was far too far away for me to focus on her face. The night Kirtsy told me her news is the only time that she has come to Caton. Why does she stay so far away? She waved in my direction, which gave me a wisp of dilemma, for if it was not her I should report the sighting, and someone should set out to investigate. I won't report it because it was her. Her stance, her hair, her wave. And I could see her clearly.

I went back inside to the apple-sweet sound of laughter. Kirsty appears to have forgiven Steve. Thistle had joined them. She'd slipped into the house during my surveillance. I hadn't seen her. So much for my lookout integrity. We started with coffee then progressed to some rather excellent bottled beer that Steve had brought. We talked of the old times at Camp Q as if we were middle aged contemporaries and those days were our shared youth, and then we divulged more about what we had experienced since August. Nathan came into the conversation and I was about to explain to Steve my puzzlement regarding the similarities between Nathan's grand theory and the one that was driving the Caton community's Jason Project, but he solved the riddle for me before I'd even started.

"Nathan had a big idea regarding the Event," I said.

"I know," said Steve.

"Do you know what it is?"

"Yep."

"He told you?"

"In a way."

"At Camp Q?"

"No."

"When then?"

"After he died."

"What?"

"He's dead then?"

"Of course he is," said Thistle, causing a thunderous silence.

Steve gave a little chuckle to terminate our three-pronged pincer stare at Thistle and said, "He was certainly dead when I pulled him out of the Ribble."

I let the silence set. "When? And where exactly?"

"Oh, two or three weeks after the end of Q. Near the bridge at Ribchester. I was en-route from Salmesbury to, well, hereabouts and riding over the bridge I spotted a body lodged against a gravel bank. Thought it was him, and it was, so I pulled him out."

"Why?"

"Because he'd always said he had the answer. He always said that didn't he Dan? I wanted to search him in case he had the answer on him. And he did. And now I've got it. It took a lot of drying out but I've got it. Except it's not the answer. Can't be can it? We'll it could, but I don't think so." He screwed up his nose. "Nah. Can't be."

I looked at him like an overweight infant who has been offered ice-cream. "Can I see it?"

Steve smiled his deep lumberjack grin from within a forest of unkempt curls. "Sure." He pulled his biker jacket to him then reached into an inside pocket and pulled out a paperback book. "Pulp fiction," he said. "And after being in the water it was more pulp than fiction. Shame. Couldn't read the best bits. If they are the best bits. Can't peel open some of the pages. Tore 'em off and threw 'em away."

I'd only really clung on to one word. "Fiction?"

"Fiction."

It was a novel. Science fiction. The Bosun's Tale by M. Gerard. "Fiction," I said again. "Fiction."

I flicked through the crumbly pages. Steve gave us a condensed account of as much of the story as he has been able to decipher and it is remarkably prophetic. It was set a decade in the future when a bombardment of sub-atomic particles stops all life on one side of the planet. In Gerard's story the cosmic stream comes from the sun and the Earth itself absorbs the worst of the impact with relatively few particles emerging on the dark side, where the eponymous bosun is at sea in the middle of the Pacific Ocean. Those on that side of the planet survive but as time elapses it becomes clear that they have been contaminated and are mutating. Those on or below the surface of the day-lit hemisphere died at the time of impact. Strangely though, those flying high over dusk or dawn regions were completely unaffected because the poisonous particles were attracted towards the Earth's core and away from their aircraft. They are the only pure ones to survive the attack. Animals and plant life in the affected areas suffer too, as comprehensively, though not as instantly, as we have experienced. Salvation is found at the hands of the airborne survivors and the stock that was safely stowed in the cargo holds of aircraft at high altitude.

"So this is where Nathan got his big idea from?"

Steve nodded.

"And George too?"

"In a roundabout way."

"How do you mean?"

"I told him." He smiled parting a beard hedgerow.

"About the book?"

"About the theory."

"Passing it off as your own?"

Steve shook the hedge and his head went with it. "Told him I'd heard it somewhere on my travels. Didn't say where, and I didn't mention the cargo bay theory." He tapped his nose. "Knowledge is power."

"That's what Nathan used to say."

"I know." He lifted his eyebrows as if to imply that Nathan was keeping everything very much to himself now. "Anyway it isn't power is it? Because it isn't knowledge. It's all just a theory. Needs testing. So far it's failed."

"What do you mean?"

"Found a cargo plane. At Salmesbury. Nose wheel collapsed but the plane was okay."

"I saw it."

"Having read Nathan's book, or bits of it, I retraced my tracks to the airfield. I knew the cargo plane had some fruit and veg on board, because I'd snaffled a few and ate them, so I took some more and stuck bits of 'em – seeds and pips and peas and stuff - in some pots in a greenhouse to see what happened."

"And?"

"Nothing."

"Nothing."

"Nothing. But it is only February, and I'm no gardener and don't really know what I'm doing, and the soil might be screwed up, or need insects or something, or more sun or heat or god knows what. Anyway let's see what the spring brings."

"Where is this greenhouse?"

"In your garden."

"What?"

"Of your house. Former house. Well you're not far from Salmesbury are you? And I remembered you'd got a greenhouse."

"Lots of people have got greenhouses."

"And I've got one or two more plantations. Except that's not really the right word, 'cause none of them are showing any sign of growing anything."

"So the theory's crap."

"It's only one cargo plane."

"And you don't know how high it had been flying."

"It got down and the crew got out."

"So the theory's crap."

"Looks that way. And it's the only one we've got."

"No it's not," I said. "But thanks to you it's become the façade to launch a thousand ships."

"Hardly a thousand."

"It was a metaphor."

"Which is what people need isn't it? The harsher the reality the more you need the metaphor to get you through." Steve took the paperback from me and tapped it on the coffee table depositing a barely visible frost of paper ash. "Gives us a purpose doesn't it?"

"It's fiction, Steve. And now Brian and George are asking people to risk their lives based on a myth."

"And good on 'em. That's what myths are for." He put The Bosun's Tale back in his pocket. "And let's face it; risking your life these days isn't risking a lot is it? Now you good trio are the only people in this village to know about the existence of this book, so I'm trusting you to keep it that way." He looked at Thistle. "Got it?" She smiled and nodded. "I want you all to know because I don't want you going off doing daft things on the strength of science fiction. But don't stand in anyone else's way. They might be right, and we four and the little tummy-ensconced traveller need folk to help us find out."

"But what do you think Steve?"

"We just don't know do we? I've seen a plane or two, so either folk like us are looking, or other folk are looking for us, but who knows? Got to look though, haven't we? Stuff the extra. Terrestrial life will do. Life as we know it if you please."

We're putting Steve up for the night. Before he went to bed he joined me on the final security check outside. There are no stars tonight, the sky is quilted with thick cloud. It is still very mild. Part of what he'd told us bothered me and I had to confront him with it.

"You know, when Nathan vanished we had a good look for him. I stood on that bridge twice and looked."

Steve didn't flinch. "I put him back in the water on the other side of the gravel bank. The current took him."

That was possible. "Do you think he'd just drowned?"

"Possibly." Steve toyed with the gravel with his foot. "The cavity on the back of his skull wouldn't have helped."

"What?"

"Something weighty had hit him. And it wasn't theoretical."

Despite the warmth I experienced a rippling chill.

*

My mother loved Groucho because Groucho made her laugh. She loved most comedians and I suppose that's why I eventually became one. My childhood was riddled with comedians in the way that other boys experienced trains, or planes or cars. The Home Service and the Light Programme pushed The Goons, Kenneth Horne, Ken "where's me shirt?" Dodd, Tony Hancock, Kenneth "Rambling Syd Rumpo" Williams and a host of others into our kitchen wireless. In addition to that there was Blackpool down the road with three piers and the Winter Gardens. We saw Jimmy Tarbuck, Bruce Forsythe, Morcambe and Wise, and Al "we supped some stuff tonight" Read. He did an act in which he brought a newspaper on stage and simply read out the headlines in pairs. I copied it and used it for years and I wasn't alone in that. Asking a comic not to steal gags is like putting a pickpocket in charge of a cloakroom. I stole a lot of Al Read's loose change. One of his newspaper lines became my daily echo:

"My father-in-law's getting on a bit. Every night he gets the paper, looks inside, and if his name is not in the deaths he goes to the pub."

*

Fourteen: From Nebula with Love.

8th February 2006.

I didn't sleep that well after what Steve had told me, and to be honest I wondered if he'd have the discipline to confine himself to the living room sofa. Kirsty and I are sleeping separately again as her pregnancy made some nights restless for us both. I rose at about six thirty, having thought I'd heard Steve's bike fire up. I think I had, for he'd gone. The morning was mild. I made tea and drank it outside. It was chilly but I was warm enough with just a jacket and a steaming mug for additional heat. It still feels tropical by comparison to our iced months. There was oppressive cloud cover but as I stood and watched the blanket fragmented to show everlasting patterns of stars upon galaxies upon nebulae. They've seen so much those stars. They know so much. What have they sent us this time? About an hour later I heard Kirsty cough and took her a cup of coffee. She sat up in bed in only a t-shirt and with a sweater round her shoulders. Her bump proclaimed its presence with even greater prominence than hitherto. "Woke me up," she said. "With its kicking." She put my hand on it and I imagined I felt some movement.

"Steve's gone," I said.

"Has he?"

"Said last night that he'd leave early. Said he'd come back."

"Hope so," she said.

"Why?"

"Because he thinks he knows where there is a midwife."

"Seriously?"

"That's what he said."

"Is he going to bring her?"

"He's going to ask."

"Well, that's good news."

"Let's hope so."

She sipped her coffee and seemed to swallow mixed feelings. I decided not to pursue that, but said instead, "Do you think he did find Nathan?"

"He has the book."

"Does that prove it?"

She shrugged.

"He said Nathan had a hole in the back of his head."

"He said that, did he?"   She sipped again. Her swallow somehow seemed more certain. More final.

"Somebody put a hole in the back of Nathan's head."

"Good for somebody."

"What?"

"He came on to me three times at Camp Q."

"When you say 'came on' . . . "

"No, he's not the father."

That was said with conviction, but despite that I couldn't, and can't, be sure it's the truth. I decided to press the more pertinent issue. "Did you kill Nathan?"

"No." She sipped her coffee and saw something in its surface.   I was going to push her further but didn't need to. "The river did."

"What?"

"Seen your wheel brace recently? Or at all, since Ribchester?"

"No."

"It's at the bottom of the Ribble. The wheel brace. Just near the bridge."

"When? That last morning at Ribchester?"

"Yes."

"Why?"

"We said we would. We told you we would. Well we did."

"We?"

"We put him in the river."

"What? Why?"

"Because he kept looking at us."

"Looking?"

"It was only going to be a matter of time."

"Looking?"

"And more."

"More? What do you mean more?"

"There are ways, aren't there. 'Innocent' ways. 'Accidental' pawing. He was good at that. Don't forget that Thistle had seen what had happened to her mother. She took him down to the river."

"Took him?"

"I don't know. She came to find me. You were lost to the world. She was in a bit of a state, but only a bit. There he was, down by the bridge with blood pouring out of the back of his head."

"Had she led him there?"

"I don't know. She said he followed her there, but I don't know. And the wheel brace was there. She wasn't for saying much. And who was I to ask her after what she's been through? Eh? Apart from which I was glad. We put him in the river and that was that."

"Why didn't you tell me?"

"Because she asked me not to, and because, because . . ."

"What?"

"Because I didn't think he was dead when we put him in the water."

"So you did kill him?"

"No. The river did."

I haven't said anything to Thistle and I won't. I can't see the point, and although I still don't know the full story, I can understand why she did what she did. Of course, it's a disturbing story, but I am more disturbed by the fact that Kirsty felt she had to keep it from me. They could have told me straight away and taken me to the river where I could have seen the evidence for myself, before he'd gone in the water. What did they think I would do? I may even have come to the same conclusion and put him in the river myself. If he was badly brain damaged it was probably the kindest thing that could be done.

Kirsty stayed in a strange mood all day. She was monosyllabic and abrupt, though not in a sharp way. It wasn't a laundry day so she stayed at the cottage, but often slipped to the gate to survey the road. She stayed up late, her ears finely tuned to anything that might herald the approach of a Japanese motor cycle.

11th February 2006

I am a broken man.

Steve returned yesterday. He brought his bike but he wasn't riding it, instead he'd slung it in the back of a four-by-four pickup truck disturbingly called a "Warrior". A lot of his other belongings were in there covered with a tarpaulin. It seems he was moving house. He wanted to add Kirsty to his chattels. This was a different Steve, and one that I hadn't seen before, though for all I know this could be the original version. I somehow doubt it. I think we were all reborn in the Event, or re-honed by the aftermath, and my guess is that our braver new world has made warrior braves of us all. We have to fight for life and fight dirty for quality of life. It's no longer dog eat dog, but dog eat dog leftovers. We're scrapping for the scraps and some of us are the tastiest scraps of all.

Warrior Steve crunched the gravel nuggets of our drive just before noon today. Kirsty's face lit up like a child anticipating her first trip to Blackpool illuminations. We stood sharing tea in our kitchen. He had the news that she wanted.

"Yasmin is a very experienced midwife," he said as he handed a handwritten note to Kirsty. I read it after her. In essence it was a chatty curriculum vitae and it seemed genuine. The hand seemed feminine and the mix of qualifications and experience reassuring.

The relief on Kirsty's face was so substantial that a midwife might have weighed it. "Will she come?" she asked.

"Even with the best care in the world, no guarantees can be given . . ."

"I know, but will she . . ?"

"But she should at least be able to look after you, and baby too."

"But will she come?"

Steve smiled and ran a slightly grimy hand through his coiled hair. "We have to go to her."

I asked, "Where is she?"

"That's classified."

I said, "What?"

"Knowledge is power," said Steve. "Her power in this instance. I can't tell you where she is."

"We have to go to her?" asked Kirsty with a slight falter.

"Bearing gifts. We need to trade things of value in return for the most valuable of things: professional experience."

I asked, "What kind of things?"

Steve said, "I can see to that. I have more than enough of the kinds of things she wants."

Kirsty smiled. I said, "So we have to go to her?"

Steve looked me solidly in the eyes and said, "Kirsty does."

A sledge hammer struck me in the belly. "Kirsty?"

"Kirsty. Obviously."

There was a brief trio of forced half-laughs. Then I said, "Just Kirsty?"

Steve said, "And me."

There was a silence.

"Where to?" I asked.

"Can't tell you that."

"For how long?"

Steve drained his mug and thoughtfully rinsed it in the bowl of grey water in the sink. "Depends on the little fella in her tummy. Taking his time, isn't he Kirst?" She looked deep into his cerebral cortex by drilling her stare through his retinas. Something new churned inside me. "Once he's made an appearance we can think again. We might come back, we might not."

Kirsty almost whispered, "We?"

"See how we feel. We might come back here, but we'll probably not come back to this." His eyes surveyed the cottage interior then drove a nail into my mind. "Unless the premises have become vacant."

The time for innuendo was over.

"Let's call a spade a spade Steve. You want Kirsty to go with you, and to stay with you."

"Little fella needs a safe admission to our world, Dan. Think of me as a paramedic. But the national health service is long dead. There's a fee."

"And the fee is me," said Kirsty, her irises still in pile drive mode.

"That's putting it a bit crudely," said Steve.

"What other way is there of putting it?" I asked.

Steve ran his fingers down the flex and along the coachwork of the toaster. "Romance is dead," he said. "It needs a rich diet of affluence, and no one is affluent anymore. We're all commodities. Our skills, our strength, our health, our youth." He leaned back on the granite worktop of our prehistoric kitchen and surveyed the maternal form before him. "You are at a very vulnerable time. I'm your best bet of success. Of safety. Of survival. But there's a dowry."

"A dowry?" She spat the word.

I stepped in. "Listen. It's my child as well."

Steve laughed. His laugh was both genuine and triumphant and was extended under his reply. "No it's not."

Kirsty found a new clarity that seemed to be born of urgency. "Okay, okay, she said, let's not get, let's not . . ."

A sharper thought flashed into my mind. "Is it his?" I asked, then demanded. "Is it his?"

She shouted. "We're not talking about that!"

Steve said, "You haven't told him, have you?"

"What?" I asked. "Told me what?"

Kirsty went louder and firmer. "We're not talking about that!"

Steve said, "You've not told him."

"I've not told anybody."

"Hardly anybody," he said.

"Why don't you tell me now?" I said. There was a silence. Kirsty was silently crying and breathing deeply through a constricted throat. We waited. A tear left her jaw but its bid for freedom had no hope of clearing the birthing mound of her belly. Without looking at Steve she said, "When do you want to leave?"

I drew a breath to speak but she stopped me with two upturned outstretched palms. Looking into my soul with eyes like a Madonna at a crucifixion she said, "When do you want to leave, Steve?"

"Today. This afternoon."

"I'll go and pack," she said.

"Wait a minute . . ." I said, but Steve blocked my way and held me back with a firm grip on both arms. Kirsty left the room.

"It's her decision," he said.

"Oh yeah? What kind of choice has she got?"

"That's life," he said.

I wrenched free of his grip and followed her to her room where she was already making a pile of clothes on her bed. "What the hell do you think you're doing?" I demanded.

"What does it look like?" That was said calmly, then with spitfire venom: "I'm fucking surviving." Steve was in the room and she turned on him. "Get out. Get out. Just give me ten minutes. But get out now."

Steve smiled with contrite smugness. "Okay."

Kirsty shut the bedroom door with her back. There was only the baby between us. I held her face and kissed her lightly on the forehead. "Kirsty," I said, "Kirsty, Kirsty I . . ."

"I know," she said. "And I love you. Really love you."

"Then what are you doing?"

"Do you think I want to do this? Do you really?"

"He's younger, fitter, healthier, better looking and more fucking fun by far."

"Yeah, he is. He's all that. And do you think that's why I'm going with him? Look." She whispered the next bit. "I don't know how, but I promise you I'll come back."

"Oh yeah – sure," I said, peeling from her.

There was a roaring silence, then she said, "I will come back. I burned your house to make you be with me."

"What?"

"I tell you, if I survive this, I will find you."

"You burned my house?"

She jabbed her thumb to indicate the cocksure electrician on the other side of the door. "Ask him, if you don't believe me."

"You . . ."

"I wanted – needed – you to be with me. I had to keep you at Camp Q." Her toned changed. "And when I needed you most, you left me."

"You burned my house! You burned my house! And did you burn the fucking caravan as well?"

Silence.

I exhaled incredulity. She focused through her tears and said quite calmly, "According to my training, the smoke would have killed us before the fire did."

More incredulity held thoughts at bay. After an age I said, "Why?"

"Why not?"

"But . . ."

She erupted venom and jabbed at her belly with two sharpened index fingers. "This! This, this, this, this, this!"

"All right, but listen. I'm sure that somewhere, somewhere, somewhere in this depleted world, there is one person who has already given birth, safely since the bloody fucking Event."

"I want to see that child."

"Kirsty . . ."

"What date is it?"

"What?"

"What date is it?"

I had to think, really think, but I thought, was confident and said, "Tenth of February."

She spoke calmly and in a measured tone but for a moment her voice was more weighty than her swollen body. "That's right," she said, "February the tenth. And tomorrow I will have been pregnant for eleven months."

I shook my head.

"Oh yes," she said. She jabbed towards the door again. "He knows that, because I told him when he tried it on with me whilst we shacked up in a garden shed after the attack on Camp Q. Not sure he believed me at the time, but I think he does now. Perhaps I'm the prize he's after, or perhaps it's the world's oldest unborn baby?"

"Are you . . ."

"Don't ask me if I'm sure. Of course I'm fucking sure. It was a one night stand with the pilot of the plane who flew you out of Heathrow. It happened in Prague on the eleventh of March. I took a pregnancy test the day before the Event. It was positive. I haven't had sex, or a period, or a miscarriage since. So work it out for yourself."

"But you didn't look pregnant until . . ."

"I know, I know, I know. So what bloody happened? Eh? And what is going to happen?"

"You can't . . ."

"I thought I'd lost it, or it had stopped or died within me or something, 'cause for ages nothing happened. Then, when we were in the caravan, it was clear. It was growing again. It's been growing ever since. It's still fucking growing."

"Kirsty . . . "

"You were the only man I could trust. And when I didn't get any bigger I thought maybe the test had been wrong. But I didn't trust any man except you. I wanted to be near you and well away from everyone else. But then I did start getting bigger. I went nuts. I hoped burning the caravan would . . . but it didn't. And we got out. You got me out. And then I needed people. I need medics. I need a midwife."

"You've felt it kicking?"

"Yeah it's kicking all right."

"How many legs has it got?"

"That, is not, funny."

"Then why are you laughing?"

She laughed and cried. I laughed and cried. I took her and her cargo in my arms. We sat on her bed. "Listen, I don't know about gynaecology, but for what it's worth, maybe it was just the stress? Perhaps your body put everything on hold for a couple of months?"

"Never heard of that before."

"No but . . ."

"Or maybe it was that fucking particle. The Bosun's boson? Maybe we did get a dose at twenty thousand feet?"

"Maybe," I said trying not to sound too convincing.

"And maybe," she said, "that was followed some time later by another bloody boson or something, that started it going again?"

"I doubt it."

"What shall we call this one? The First Mate's Mate?"

And so, Kirsty has gone and so has Steve. In the end we left her to do a lengthy pack, though ultimately all she needed was crammed into a couple of suitcases and a rucksack. There was a kind of conversation between me and Steve but it was a strained affair. He knows what I know, but I'm very annoyed he knew it first. He said he thinks it best that I don't tell the rest of the community until the baby is born. The way he said it was laced with threat, but to be honest I can't contemplate sharing it just yet. I warned him about Kirsty's suicidal tendency and he thanked me but shrugged it off. He warned me not to follow him or attempt to find him. He had, he said, spies everywhere. In due course he would get a message to me to let me know if it was a boy, a child, or an alien.

So here I am in the early hours of February 11th. I haven't seen Thistle for two days, but that's not unusual. About an hour ago I summoned up the courage to rummage through Kirsty's room. Her pillow was slightly skewed, which was her way of signalling to me that she'd left a note beneath it. Reading it hurt my eyes even more than usual.

Dan
Can't tell you how much I love you and how I just want to be free
of this fucking bulge and somehow survive with you, or if that doesn't
work, die with you. Sorry. I'm all over the place. Always have been.
But much worse now. If I get through whatever happens next. I will
get back to you. I will. Your the only person I care about.

Trust me.
I promise.

Kirsty.

One phrase burns into my eyes. Your the only person I care about. Your. Your. Oh Kirsty! Oh Kirsty, Kirsty, Kirsty. Your next, said the note to Roxy after Clita had been killed. Your next.

Oh Kirsty.

*

I wouldn't want you to think that my childhood was crammed with stand-up comics and devoid of the fold-up paper kind. I had all the normal boyhood popular culture fantasies. Mum made an old raincoat into a Batman cape and I pelted along Blackpool Road on my bat bike causing petrol tankers to swerve like those demonically depicted in DC comics, while my real-life spinster schoolmistresses tutted and shook their Sunday hat-pinned heads.

I loved James Bond and the Man from Uncle. On autumn nights Andy Shawcross was Illya Kuryakin and I was Napoleon Solo. We crept into our primary school where the parish whist drive was in full swing, found the main fuse box and plunged the players into darkness.

We were apprehended by a caretaker with Politbureau eyebrows, but Andy threw another switch and we slipped between his legs and raced across the playground for the Berlin wall, zig-zagging to avoid AK47 shells.

Even at that age I hoped my exploits would impress Sally Whitworth when I told her, but she just smiled in a very superior way and polished the plastic ring given her by Carl Simpson. What hurt all the more was I know his sister got it free in that week's Jackie teenage magazine.

*

Fifteen: Desperate Dan.

15th February 2006.

I'm eating again. Aching all over. Sweating a lot. Doing nothing.

17th February 2006.

Better now. A touch. Starting to see sense. What sense there is to see. Is there any sense left? I am old now. Today is my fiftieth birthday. Aquarius. Water bearer. Two days shy of a fish. What's better: to carry the water or be carried by it? How many horoscopes told of this future? The papers should have been full of it. It was the astrologers' big chance to demonstrate that all our fortunes lay in the stars. They may yet be proved right.

Fifty years, and feeling more like a teenager than ever. Dumped. Off my food. Writing poetry. Staring into space. Thinking of her. Resenting him. A love triangle contains one hundred and eighty degrees of separation. I am the hypotenuse and hold no hope of touching the right angle at the heart of everything. I should have gone after them. Think I didn't try? Sparks is a very important person in these parts and his departure wasn't unplanned. There were men on the road just by my gate, and they were armed. They also managed to disarm me. My self-loading rifle and the gun I brought from Camp Q have been taken away "for my own safety". My former colleagues drive past frequently to let me know they know I'm still here, but no one has made a courtesy call. I've not been reprimanded for failing to hammer home more fence posts. No one has sent food parcels. Or condolences.

No sign of Thistle.

I'm going to make a birthday cake.

20th February 2006.

Aquarius has set. As a youth I always felt I was defrauded. The age of Aquarius was much heralded. I think it was 1969. The musical Hair was the West End sensation. If you were an Aquarian you went on stage and took your clothes off, and everyone was supposed to be that fluid. I took Frances Leggat to see Hair, but she never took her clothes off. She told me she was a Virgo, and earth was her element and she wasn't ready to feel it move. So much for the freedom of Aquarius. A new age of expression was promised, but as with all astrological promises we're still waiting. Or are we?

22nd February 2006.

An alien woke me in the middle of the night. I was abducted, taken on an adventure and now I'm back in my bed. No one knows I left. I hope.

I was dreaming of a journey. Since turning fifty, each night I have dreamed of journeys. Trains are often involved. Interminable trains with everlasting corridors and a sharp-suited Bond villain in each compartment. In last night's dream I was an MI6 dentist: licensed to drill. I'm not fooling. That was my dream. It's amazing how much Cold War microfilm you can cement into a mesial cavity. It was midnight as we rattled through cinemascope Europe on the Orient Express and I was peering into the gaping mouth of Miss Holroyd, who taught me modern foreign languages but to a sixties teenage mind resembled Ursula Andress, preferably without conch or bikini. Suddenly she was gone from the first class dentist's chair, and I was reclined in it while a smooth headed bug-eyed alien peered over me and sank suckered, triple-knuckled fingers into my chest.

I awoke to my almost pitch black bedroom, and in the seven per cent light from a small torch, saw a diminutive creature with a steel head leaning over my bed, shaking me but stifling my protests with a firm hand across my mouth. I knew the smell of that skin but could not put a name to it, until Thistle raised the visor of the crash helmet she was wearing. She whispered instructions and I obeyed.

"Get dressed," she said. "Wear dark stuff."

There wasn't any need to whisper but it somehow seemed the right thing to do. I got well wrapped up in black attire and following her lead slipped out of the back door of the cottage. We closed it quietly, for now there was a real chance that one of the night guard foot patrol might be in our area. The fields to the east of the cottage had yet to be fully sealed off with fencing so there was a clear route into our complex via an ancient footpath from that direction. Night patrols would survey it. Moving like commandos we kept our heads below the parapet of the dry stone wall and close to the copse of ribcage trees, all the time veering south, and then we scurried over the metalled road and down into the valley. There was broken cloud again but no moon so our cover was good. It was close to two a.m.

We continued in Enid Blyton fashion for some time, being especially careful when close to the roads, though following their line down into the valley at Crossgill. We scurried up the steep road on the southern side of that valley, past the scenic car park to Cragg Wood where Thistle had hidden a motorcycle and a spare helmet.

"Keeps you warmer as well as safe," she said, brushing brittle branches from it.

"I didn't know you can ride one of these," I said.

"Neither did I," she said. "Until I tried."

Ride she could, and once I'd got over the bizarre feeling of riding pillion behind someone yet to turn thirteen, I actually really enjoyed the experience. I felt child-like again, as if I was living out a Biggles fantasy adventure, careering through a naively racist romp and anticipating swarthy spies in trilby hats and gabardine raincoats. Then the slightest of wobbles on the tightest of bends reminded me of the true nature of my driver and the real reason for our mission. "I know where she is," Thistle had whispered when she woke me. "Get dressed. I'll take you there."

To stay clear of Caton we cut a circuitous route right into the heart of Lancaster and then picked up the main A6 route south. It was a road I know well and for a while I thought we were heading home to Preston but we only rode for about twenty minutes before Thistle expertly kicked the bike into neutral, switched the engine off, and let us roll silently downhill for the final mile. We hid the bike in a drive in the small market town of Garstang then crept through the streets until we came to the canal basin at Th'Owd Tithebarn. As always, there was a row of narrow boats hitched to the moorings, but even at this time of night we could tell that at least one was occupied. An odd low voltage light burned, and smoke fluttered from a chimney of a gaily painted vessel. The night withheld the true hue of the decorations but the rural patterns were boldly drawn, and we could even make out her name: Cordelia. Thistle nodded to that boat meaningfully and when I questioned her with my eyes she pointed to the towpath by the basin, where the Mitsubishi Warrior four-by-four stood humbly but smugly silent, like a ninja guard.

"That's where she is," said Thistle. "In that boat."

"How do you know?"

"I've been watching her."

"But how did you find her?"

"Came with them," she said. "Without them knowing. In the back of that." She looked to the Warrior where the tarpaulin still covered the rear of the truck. "I watched the way we came. Stayed here for a bit, then nicked a bike and came for you." She looked at me in a way I'd never seen her look before, with deep pride and a starvation hunger for approval. I hugged her, kissed her cheek. She smiled broadly and her eyes moistened.

We stayed for a while and watched, but there was nothing to see other than what we saw on arrival. After all it was now three in the morning in February, what was there to do at that time on a dead canal in a dead landscape? Give birth perhaps? There was no sign of that. Everything was still, calm and muted. I wanted Kirsty to emerge, to come out, walk about, do anything so that I could see with my own eyes that she was there, but of course she didn't and I had to take Thistle at her word and trust her report, which I did.

"We'd better get back," she said after about half an hour.

I blew Cordelia a kiss for her precious passenger, and then Thistle and I retraced our route in reciprocal fashion, creeping then riding then creeping, all the way to our beds in our cottage at Caton.

Having recorded this escapade, this laptop will have to be more securely stored, which I know would damage its chances of ever being discovered and used for its primary purpose of chronicling these events, but Kirsty's safety and my possible reunion with her is priority number one from now on.

1st March 2006

I'm back on the fencing gang. I've been back for three days now. Nothing much was said, but the working atmosphere has changed. It's not so much that there's an elephant in the room as there is a room full of elephants outside. Large bulky creatures lift fence posts and mallets with kindly smiling faces and arms like serpentine trunks, but behind their almost-lethargic labour there's a knowing glint in the eye that says, if roused I'll trample you in a slow motion stampede. Kirsty is not a taboo subject. Everyone knows she's gone and everyone knows who she left with. If I was younger I may have more of their sympathy but a jilted lover is less pitiable when the mother of his child is young enough to be his daughter. I can't tell them that I'm not the father, not her lover and have not been jilted. They wouldn't believe me. My whine would just be taken as sour grapes.

A part of me is desperate to know if Steve has said anything to anyone in the so called Age of Reason group. Is George White aware of anything to do with Kirsty's peculiar pregnancy? I suspect not, but I simply don't know. Obviously I am deeply perplexed by what Kirsty said. As much as I love her, I've had to entertain all kinds of doubts regarding what happened. I'm sure she did have a one night fling with Mike the flier, and I'm sure the pregnancy test signalled bad news, but they're not infallible, she might not have been pregnant. Even if she was she may have lost it, however, she clearly is with child now and adamant that she hasn't had intercourse since we touched down in May. I don't think she is lying, but she could be deluded, or somehow psychologically blocking out the memory of a terrible assault. I'm no expert, but under normal circumstances I would say she looked to be in her seventh or eighth month. That would place the conception in July or August, or perhaps June at the earliest. So Camp Q fits the bill. I wish, I wish that she'd told me sooner. This dilemma needs a dozen conversations. It makes no sense, but if I am to trust her and accept her account in full, then we surely are in the realms of science fiction. Well the story of the twentieth century was that science fiction became fact. In the twenty-first century, fiction has died, there are no facts, and science has to start again.

The irony of my working day is that I am busy ring-fencing my home and making myself more of a prisoner. I'm thinking I'll have to move out soon, or there'll be no escape. My sense of loss is unbearable but there are minor compensations. Thanks to Thistle I am now ninety per cent sure of where Kirsty is, and there's a change in Thistle herself worthy of rejoicing. She knows she's grown in my appreciation as she did something truly remarkable.

"I heard the row, heard it all," she told me over a late breakfast the day after our trip to Garstang. "I knew anyway."

"How much did you know?"

"I knew everything. From the start. From the day I became me, became Thistle. Kirsty told me. Told me there was someone younger than me, inside her, growing. But she wasn't sure it was still growing." In my eyes Thistle was no longer a child but something slipped across her face at that point that sent her searing back into immaturity. It was a kind of embarrassment and guilt, impossible to hide. "I told Steve."

"What – about the baby?"

"Yes."

"When?"

"At Ribchester."

"You saw Steve at Ribchester?"

"I saw Steve all the time. He's been following us, off and on. Always. It was our secret: mine and his. He told me he loves Kirsty. So I told him about her baby."

My stomach kicked against the cereal I was digesting. I swallowed hard to keep everything in its place. "What did he say?"

"He thought it was yours. Your baby. But I said you didn't know about it. He didn't believe me at first, but I think I convinced him."

"How often did you meet him?"

"Lots. But it was our secret. He said he'd protect me as long as I kept him secret, he'd always check up on me every few weeks, where ever we went. And he did. We had times and places and he always showed up. Brought me stuff. Got you something. Forgotten about it. Was keeping it for your birthday. I'll get it."

She went off to her room and came back with a cardboard box, clearly something electronic. I opened it. It is an adapter to run a laptop from a car cigarette lighter output.

"In case we move on," she said. "You can keep writing your diary up wherever we go. Happy birthday."

"Does he know about my laptop diary?"

Her eyes swelled a little as she nodded confirmation. "But he doesn't know where you hide it, and I shan't tell him."

I was about to tell her that I thought she shouldn't see him again but that sounded too fatherly for the relationship that I was trying to build, so I let it pass. I thought hard before my next statement, but went ahead and bent the truth slightly. "Kirsty said you killed Nathan."

"I suppose I did."

"How?"

"He kept trying to touch me. I told Steve. We made a plan. I took Nathan down to the river one morning and let him try to kiss me. Steve crept up behind him and hit him on the head."

"Steve did? With what?"

"Your wheel thingy."

"How did he get that?"

"I took it down the night before and hid it."

For a few moments I forgot to chew. Thistle looked at me imploringly.

"There's no good and bad anymore, is there?"

"I'm not sure there ever was."

"You'll need to explain that," she said and bit into a nutty chocolate bar.

"Yeah, if there's anyone left worth explaining it to. Did you put him in the river?"

"No, I went to get Kirsty. I'd sworn not to tell her about Steve. I thought she'd be pleased, because I knew she hated Nathan, and that he'd tried to touch her too, but she was a bit, well angry, at first. I said I was scared and wanted rid of him, so I'd hit him. Then we put him in the river and left him."

"Do you think he was dead when you put him in the river?"

She shrugged as if she genuinely didn't care.

Our conversation had clarified a few things but I didn't dwell on it, for I was keen to let Thistle grow through and out of these terrible times, and I wanted to build on our new bond. She's my only ally and until we get Kirsty back, I'm her only safe friend. I'll have to wean her off Steve, he's obviously severely unbalanced, which makes me fear for Kirsty even more. Happily Thistle shows all the signs of embracing a new maturity. She's opted to stay in my company much more, is far less twitchy, and has even started to dress slightly differently by borrowing some of Kirsty's hooded tops, a decision both joyous and painful to my eyes. She brushes her hair more and fastens it back neatly when about the house. She rarely goes down to the village and has opted not to rejoin her fencing team. She spends a good deal of time drawing, something for which she has a genuine propensity. There's a superb delicacy about her work. Sometimes it's a little repetitive, often featuring a curling stem leaf and flower pattern. I'd seen the design before, though it took me a long time to recall just where, then I remembered: it's painted on the narrow boat where Kirsty is.

I wondered about her story regarding Steve. Had he dealt the fatal blow? If so, at what point had he discovered the Bosun's Tale? And if the book had not been in the water, why had he torn pages out? Knowledge is power.

5th March 2006

George White came to see me tonight. He came alone and a little sheepishly, though others must have known he was here. No one gets through the security cordon in a car, either in or out. There was no way I was going to tell him about Kirsty's mysterious extended pregnancy, partly because I didn't see why he should know and partly because I wanted to see if he would tell me. He didn't. We briefly discussed what I described as her 'abduction' and while he sympathised he said the presence of a properly trained midwife would be best for my child. I didn't correct him on the parentage. Instead we discussed nautical nuclear physics.

"I'm just a bit disappointed to discover your facts are based on fiction."

He looked genuinely offended. "I never said they were facts."

"You could have told me their source. Science fiction."

"And that is something that is often prophetic. H.G. Wells put a man on the moon half a century before the Americans did."

"His technology was seriously flawed."

"He had the right idea. Nothing wrong with his basic principles. So what if this Gerard fellow has got the detail wrong? There may not be a Bosun's boson, but the basic idea might be sound. Something like that seems to have happened."

I pushed the boundaries of the discussion a little further, but carefully. "Do you think such a thing could be reversed?"

The question didn't seem to alarm him. "I don't see why not," he said. "But it's not something I think we should rely on."

We debated hypothetical particle physics for a while longer then he came to the point. He said if I wanted to go on the first Jason Project expedition he'd be glad to put my name forwards. This has to be the most elaborate way of exiling someone for a thousand years. I said if it gave me the chance to meet giant stop-motion modelling-clay monsters I couldn't possibly refuse. He smiled politely but didn't look sincerely amused. It didn't matter, he'd brought the message from the elders. In the long run, I simply wasn't welcome. I don't know what I've done to deserve rejection. I think it's simpler than that. Steve is more than a journeyman visitor. As a merchant and a messenger his influence is major, and his links with this community run deep. Perhaps he wants to settle here? If so he won't want me around.

6th March 2006

Thistle's gone missing again. She went four days ago and I've seen nothing of her since. She was getting restless again. Like me I feel she senses that the birth might be imminent and I suspect she went to find out what she could. I'm not worried that she hasn't returned but some of my fellow fencers are. The sideways glances between sledgehammer blows are highly disconcerting.

11th March 2006

A strange glow in the sky this morning. It's probably not strange at all. It's probably happened a billion times before, but I'd never seen it quite like that. I had an uneasy night and was up before dawn. I watched the sky lighten and saw a flamingo pink feathery wash spread across the dome of high pebbled cloud. It didn't last long. Red sky in the morning; first mate's warning.

Not for the first time my thoughts flew far away to my daughter Teresa. Two years ago she went on a mission to Tibet. It was a two pronged affair, partly post-graduate gap and partly to feel she could contribute something to others less fortunate. I'm sure that one way or another she would have made those poor children a little richer. She has, or had, such a generous heart and always made such a quick and deep connection with infants. Tibet is a high country. Perhaps I can persuade the Jason Project to head for there? Too far. Too far. I sent my love on the flamingo clouds. They'll get there.

13th March 2006

Thistle has been gone for nearly two weeks. I'm going to look for her. I'm going to Garstang. I realise that if I leave here I may never be allowed back, so I'm taking the essentials, including this laptop and the adaptor Thistle gave me. I will follow the route we took on the bike. I'll steal a car as soon as I can. I've printed out a hard copy of my diaries and chapters so far. It's wrapped in foil and in brown paper. It's in the loft of the cottage here at Caton.

15th March 2006.

I am in a street near the Tithebarn at Garstang. I visited the basin there this morning in the drizzle just before the dawn. The boat called Cordelia has gone. A rope from her mooring trailed in the canal. It was tied to something weighty semi-submerged in the murky water. I knew what it was before I pulled it to the shore, and with every pull I knew more and more.

*

A comedian is a maker of memes. Memes are viruses of the mind. If you tell a vibrant gag it lives a long life. It goes from brain to brain replicating itself with every telling. The gag doesn't even have to be good, some very bad gags live on like hated tunes that you can't get out of your head. Some even shed their linguistic skin and translate themselves into and onto other tongues. Immigration control never spots them. And gags, good or bad, can reinforce or modify behaviour. Comedy can be the secret service of the soul, and the most unlikely agents can infiltrate the furthest.

If you follow my memeing.

*

Sixteen: Breakfast with God.

15th March 2006.

I cannot tell how long Thistle has been in the water. I do not know how she died. Her head wobbles a lot. I think her neck is broken. The mooring rope was tied round her neck but there is no redness there so I don't think she was strangled or hanged. I have laid her out on the roof of one of the other narrow boats. I have doused her and the boat with diesel and manoeuvred it away from the others. It will be her floating pyre.

15th March 2006 Evening.

It has been a remarkable day. Thistle's pyre has just about burned through. It burned well. It sent a thick plume of grey, white and jet black smoke straight up for three hundred feet or more before the gentlest of breezes took the top and spread it like a bouquet of incense. For an hour, the sixth hour, she was the candle that created her own cathedral. She made her own monument, as monumental as any at Rheims, or York, or Westminster, or Chartres. Notre Dame. Our Lady. God saw the smoke, and came to visit.

The floating fire hissed and the wood of the superstructure cracked and snapped, and for a moment it was provocatively reminiscent of the caravans that Thistle and Kirsty and I watched burn, but then the cracking became a beat and transmuted into a sound too regular for the random appetite of conflagration. I knew that sound, but I hadn't heard it for so long that I struggled to identify it. It was the sound of a helicopter. A blue angel that circled round the smoke then landed in a field on the far side of the canal. I made my way round the basin and pushed through a hawthorn hedge to emerge into the field as the rotors slowed to almost silence, and the sole occupant unlatched his door and stepped out. He was a portly fellow, a Falstaff with wings, a Santa in civvies, white haired, with white trousers and clutching a black-banded white fedora to his head against the psychological downdraft of the nearly motionless rotors. His shirt too had been white once but was dulled to cream now, his jacket was a splendid blue and maroon striped blazer, and round his neck, not a rope, but the simplest of cravats. He sported what at first seemed to me to be an over-elaborate and rather cumbersome waistcoat but on closer viewing was undoubtedly a suicide bomber's body pack. He came striding towards me beaming like Jupiter on his way out of a joke shop. "Hello there," he said, "I'm God." And he wasn't lying. I saw the row of tubes around his waist and backed off. "Don't worry," he said, then stopped and fiddled with his belt for a moment, then threw me a small nine volt battery. "There now," he said, "perfectly safe. I'll want that back before I go." Then he shook my hand. "I'm God," he said. "No one's going to argue with me are they? Even without the battery."

"Not if you've got one of those," I said, pointing to his helicopter.

"Exactly," he chuckled.

"I'm Dan. Dan Good."

"Course you are," he said. "Course you are. I was hoping for an Adam, but you can't have everything. We could have done the old Sistine Chapel thing, you know . . ." He held a pointed finger towards me and made a lightening crackle sound.

"I never strip on a first date," I said.

"Me neither," he said, and laughed, but his laugh hurt somewhere in his belly, though he tried to hide it. "You've made quite a mess of my sky," he said.

"Yes God. I have. But I'm not sorry. She deserved it."

"Did she? Did she? No doubt she did. Are we talking a boat here or a person?"

"Neither," I said. We pushed through the hedge and felt the warmth from the funeral on our faces. I told him who she was and delivered the essence of my epistle, the shorthand letter of my afterlife. He listened, said very little, but made encouraging and sympathetic noises. When I'd finished he said, "I've brought a picnic. Fancy breakfast?"

There then followed the most bizarre half hour. We went to his pristinely polished executive helicopter. He unlocked the luggage compartment and pulled out two folding canvas chairs and a hamper, properly stocked with elastic restrained crockery and cutlery and with copious tins of ham, salmon, olives, biscuits and a flask of lukewarm tea. Over breakfast I took questions and filled in most of the gaps about life with Kirsty.

"We'll look for her," he said. "Can't have got far on a narrow boat. They only do five knots."

"Depends when they left."

He nodded. "We can look. More ham?"

The ham was good. "Where've you been living?"

"Heaven," he said. And smiled to show gravestone teeth, time worn and neither white nor straight. "Heaven," he said. He slouched back in his chair in what appeared to be bliss, his thick faintly downy hands clasping his barrelled belly, then just when I was sure he wasn't going to elaborate he added, "Wales."

"Wales."

"Snowdonia. She's so saintly. So saintly."

"Snowdonia?"

"Snowdon herself. Saintly. Majestic. Queen of angels."

"You've been living on Snowdon?"

"Not on her. But I can see her and she can see me. We're in love. And so are you. Aren't you?"

"Love's dead," I said.

"No, no. Never say that." He drew a short breath and held it. His face reddened slightly and he bit his lower lip. The pain he felt was not emotional. After a moment it passed and he said, "We'll find her."

"You've not seen the Caton community from the air?"

"Not been this far north till now. Shan't look. They'll look up and see me. Don't want to raise their hopes."

"They'd be very interested in this," I said, and patted the helicopter.

"Not having her," he said. "When I go, she goes. They say you can't take it with you. Bloody can. I bloody will." He patted his explosive belt.

"Why do you wear that?"

"In case I go down in the soddin' sea," he said. "Life jacket's no fartin' good. Who's going to come and pick you up? I ain't going to float around waiting to teeth chatter myself to death. If you can't be picked up, best thing to do is blow up."

"Where did you get it from?"

"When you're in the music business you can get anything."

"You a musician?"

"Not according to my fans. According to my fans, I'm God. It's official. The writing's on the wall. Toilet walls. Lots of 'em. I always check. Come on, let's find your trolley dolly."

I looked a little hesitant, but he said it was fine for me to hang on to the nine volt battery as long as we didn't have to cross any major stretches of sea. I went to get my rucksack, including this laptop, from the car while he started his sky chariot. Then I boarded and we took off.

We flew the length of the canal to my home town, but saw no sign of our quarry. He was kind enough to hover low in places. The boat we hunted was green and of course I could vividly picture its hand painted creeping rose decoration. "That's your problem." he said, indicating the newest stretch of canal, the Ribble Link, built as a millennium project and giving access from the canal via the estuary to the rest of the national waterways network, and to the sea. We crossed the estuary and God took his aircraft south for some distance tracing the Rufford branch all the way down to the main stretch of its parent, the Leeds and Liverpool canal but to no avail. He tapped his fuel gauge. "Even God needs gasoline," he said. "What do you want to do? I can take you back or you can come to heaven. But I don't welcome long-term guests. God lives alone and likes it that way."

"If it's no trouble, take me back."

"What will you do then?"

"I don't know. But on the way back, we can have one more look."

He nodded and navigated the return journey. We skirted the outer edges of Preston so I did not see what the state of the centre was, or even snatch a nostalgic glimpse of Camp Q. We drew a blank again then as we descended towards the Garstang basin I realised a fundamental oversight, smacked my forehead and pointed at the canal. "It goes north as well," I said.

God looked at his fuel gauge and grimaced.

"It's all right," I said. "I'll do it on foot."

He shook his white head and said. "What's another ten minutes when you've got eternity?"

I laughed, then he laughed, then he drew breath as the pain in his belly played the devil again. He was kind enough to cover it with a forced smile.

There is a branch of the Lancaster canal that veers off to the old port of Glasson. As we passed it a boat caught my eye, only because it was moving. "She's there!" I said. "She's there." He looked and saw what I saw and nodded. He was about to manoeuvre but my hand was already on his. "Fly on," I said. "Turn away the other way. Take me back to Garstang. I'll come by car. By night." He smiled a wise smile and did as I requested. There was a figure at the helm of the Cordelia, and of course that pilot had seen our flying machine. It looked like Steve, but we were too high for my eyes to tell. God described a very beautiful circle in the sky as we returned to our breakfast field.

There was so much more I wanted to ask him, but his fuel level was falling faster than a de-feathered angel. I almost forgot to give him his battery back, but he made sure to remind me, and I watched him fit it to his belt and carefully position the switch trigger across his lap, before he smiled and took off. His final words to me were, "Blessings Dan. Be good." Then just a millisecond before I shut the chopper door he shouted, "Told you we'd find her."

I was baptised in the deluge of the downdraft and God waved a more than papal hand and went back to the sky.

Thistle's pyre still smouldered.

The car that I stole from near Caton is a Peugeot saloon. After God had gone I sped to Galgate which is where the Glasson spur branches off from the Lancaster canal. I managed to park in a place where I could see the line of the branch for about a mile. If anything moved I'd be able to duck down out of sight. The branch is a water cul-de-sac so I know that if Kirsty is on the Cordelia she is somewhere between me and the sea. They couldn't have had enough time to turn about, cruise back and negotiate the locks before I got here. I pilfered some food and drink from the locals and sat in the car to write up this account so far.

There was a little more to my divine breakfast meeting than I have laid out above. God said he'd heard of The Bosun's Tale, in fact he thought he had a copy somewhere, though he hadn't read it. He felt the theory rang true. He had been aboard a scheduled Air France flight to Nice when the event struck. They'd got down at their destination where he'd had similar experiences to mine at Heathrow. He'd then spent six months crawling his way north, before walking through the Channel Tunnel. France had frozen over too, though not as soon or as persistently as northern England. They had had terrible floods, however. Eventually he'd made his way to Halfpenny Green airfield in Worcestershire where his private helicopter was stored, and after a couple of days getting it serviceable, he took off to his mountain retreat. He hadn't flown during the remainder of the cold period, but now the warmer weather had arrived he'd started to take a look around.

Our conversation was inadequate in many ways, mostly because I was anxious to finish the leisurely English picnic and start searching for the Cordelia, but also because God was, well, deliberately mysterious. I'm not at all convinced that he was the rock star he made himself out to be. He wouldn't tell me his real name, or offer even a stage name. It couldn't be written, he said. Perhaps I'm doing him a disservice? He's certainly very wealthy, or was, or at least has access to the playthings of the previously rich. And he can fly. He's also in fairly persistent pain, and I couldn't help wondering if that annoyance had something to do with the death jacket that he wore. I think God's days are numbered. And I don't think he is who he says he is.

This afternoon I carried out a leapfrog manoeuvre whereby I walked the canal tow path from bridge to bridge, and then went back and quietly brought my car nearer to the point I'd reached. This was only possible twice, because the road is a little distance from the canal and most of the bridges were for farmers and their livestock connecting fields not roads. Fortunately I had the foresight to pack an old ordnance survey map of this area from the collection at the cottage at Caton, so I can clearly see where I am within the landscape. I can also clearly see the Cordelia. She is moored a hundred yards short of the marina at Glasson. There is no obvious activity on deck, but her chimney is smoking. A woman emerged once, but it was not Kirsty. It was a much larger woman, with long wavy hair tied back in a headscarf. She rinsed a teapot over the side of the barge, surveyed the sky and her surroundings, lingered a little then went back below. I'm going to wait until nightfall before venturing closer. I want to listen. I want to hear a Celtic accent.

I have just realised that I was wrong, some weeks ago, when I wrote that I would never fly again. I have flown again. So anxious was I to find Kirsty, that the true novelty of my reconnaissance did not strike me until it was almost over. On our way back northwards I suddenly became conscious of the fact that I was, a thousand feet up, and one of the fewest of the few who have seen this grey new world from a kestrel's vantage. Not even birds fly now. Not even flies fly now. I have flown, and I have to tell you that this new world is indeed grey. There is little other colour in the landscape. We have passed right through sepia and are lodged firmly in the blue planet's grey period. There is eggshell white, bone white, bird shite white, mottled white, slate grey, battleship grey, pencil grey from BB to HH, dry soil, wet soil, charcoal, coal, mud, black and double black. I exaggerate. Of course there is colour, but that colour is mostly confined to the rain-cleansed residue of the markings made by man. Double yellow lines never looked so good. They are more precious than cave paintings. So the landscape is pricked out with playground crayons where the children of the junior school of humanity coloured between the lines of their perspective. Here and there, rust, and brown and beige and very, very rare remnants of natural red or green thrust into view and stand out like a teenage tart's first tattoo, but mostly it is grey. The sky, in contrast, rises above all that like the washing-line of a house-proud mother Earth: radiant blue with whiter than white low altitude lingerie.

A weird thing happened as I walked away from Thistle's pyre this morning. As God's copter chopped to chapel quiet, and the glowing charred rood screen of the funeral boat whispered, a breeze stiffer than its matins predecessor rattled the skeletal choir of the hedgerow, and Claire walked by on the water, the canal was her carpet, and her feet pawed the surface like soft paddles from a fairy boat. This was a Claire I'd never seen before. She was robed like a Roman priestess in purple and blue, with a sparkling veil upon her head. She did not look at me, but rather kept her face fixed firmly on the floating remnants of Thistle's fire. When she reached the boat, she became the smoke, and Thistle's spirit was no longer alone.

This night I will creep close to the Cordelia.

*

My favourite Irish comedian was Dave Allen, who always ended his routine with "Goodnight, thank you and may your god go with you." A lovely touch, but as the years went by more and more people went home alone.

*

Seventeen: Claire Voyant.

24th March 2006.

In the half-light dusk I crept closer to the Cordelia. She was quiet. There was little activity. I began to hear the murmurs of fragmented conversation, but it was far too muted to decipher. It sounded more of a monologue than a discussion. A light came on, the colour of straw through drawn curtains presenting a picture of cosiness amid the shaded pencil sketch of the towpath scene. It was always my intention to storm the boat, the only decision I had to make was when, and in what manner. It had to be this night, but was it the right time? I listened and listened and listened, but heard no infant cries. The struggle with Steve, who I presumed to be on board, could be tenacious and violent. I presumed it was he who had terminated Thistle's short life. God had agreed with me. He said this man wanted custody of this special baby very badly. The child could be the new messiah: the post-Event first born and a prophet for the chosen people. And if this baby bore fragments from far away worlds, he would be superhuman, a carrier of the second Genesis gene. Steve would be the godfather of a new god. Surely that was worth the breaking of a teenage neck or two? So spoke the old god, a rock god, a god of ages gone. And what of Kirsty? What myth mantle would await her? I had to get her back, to reclaim her for planet Earth, to ground her in good sense and save her soul from supernatural promotion.

The inactivity evident on the Cordelia was both worrying and encouraging. It was so quiet that I was convinced there must be very few people on board, hopefully only mother, child, midwife and kidnapper, but I couldn't be sure. I had no firearms, and thought it likely that Steve did. I didn't fancy any kind of combat, especially not in such a confined space, but thought it inevitable that our quarrel would degenerate into one. I considered that the best solution would be to attack the boat herself and force an evacuation, but

I dismissed that thought because it would endanger Kirsty as much as my adversary. A new firearm would be beneficial, and it might be possible find one in one of the vessels in the marina, but the odds were against it and I did not want to leave my vantage position.

My legs were starting to ache. I'd held my crouched attitude for some time, as I was only feet from the stern door and feared, hoped even, that someone would emerge. I had one relic from my days at Camp Q, something that I'd always kept on my person. As a weapon it was pathetic, but it had a blade, in fact it had several blades: my Swiss Army knife. I took it out, selected its least blunt projection and crept closer to the Cordelia.

It was impossible to board her without causing her to sway so as soon as I stepped from shore there was a scuffle within. I braced myself and waited but nothing happened. Nothing was said, nothing moved. What next? Impulse kicked in and I grabbed the door handle, but it was secured inside. I cursed, and could think of nothing but to run for the door at the prow and try that. I leaped onto the towpath and ran straight into two barrels of a shotgun.

"Whoa!" I cried whilst scuttling backwards and just about staying on my feet. The form before me was unclear in the moonless dark, but the voice I heard though coarse and gutsy, was without doubt feminine.

"Go and fuck yourself," she spat. "Or I'll fuck you good and proper and where it hurts the most."

"I want to speak to Kirtsy."

A pause.

"She's not here."

"She's in there," I said.

"She's not."

"Where is she?"

A pause.

"You the father?"

"No."

"You Dan?"

"Yes."

"She's not here, Dan. She's gone."

"Gone where?"

"Too far away."

"Sparks?"

"With her."

"Where?"

"At sea."

"At sea!"

"Soon will be."

"The baby?"

"A girl."

"A girl?"

"Week ago. Almost."

"A girl."

"It's a fifty-fifty chance."

"Is she . . . ?"

"Looks fine to me."

I could still make out two steel barrels levelled at my midriff. "It's just a Swiss Army knife," I said and snapped the blade away. She lowered the gun.

"I'll unlock the door," she said. "Kettle's on."

There was no one else inside. The conversation I had heard had been Yasmin talking to herself, something that she said she did all the time. The birth had been straightforward, she told me. Everything occurred naturally and there had been no need for intervention other than the usual encouragement and guidance. The baby looked well save for a touch of jaundice, had reacted ordinarily and weighed seven pounds eight ounces. Kirsty had recuperated well and was feeding the child naturally. The birth had happened in the early hours of March 11th after a nine hour period of labour. The baby lost its yellow hue within the first three days. It had a bright cap of shiny filigree fair hair. Kirsty had not yet decided on a name.

All this was relayed to me over a steaming cup of, of all things, cocoa. It was the second bizarre beverage in as many days. Having sampled breakfast tea with God I now drank a Boy Scout bedtime brew in the company of an Earth mother. Once the gamekeeper gun had gone I formed an instant liking for Yasmin. She's natural and easy and warm as mulled brandy. Her barge is tidily cluttered with Romany-styled relics, hand painted and higgledy-piggledy arranged, and furnished with rich colourful fabrics. This was her home both before and after the Event. She'd flown back into Blackpool from Dublin which was a short hop and, I suspect, not especially high, so I regard her as doubly fortunate to have been airborne enough to escape the sub-atomic plague. Or doubly unfortunate.

So supper, like breakfast, was extraordinary and filled with anxiety, for I was eager to move on.

"She's not going anywhere," said Yasmin. "Till midnight."

"She's at sea," you said.

"Soon will be. But she can't go until the tide comes. And that's not for four hours yet."

"So where is she now?"

"Other side of the lock. In the sea dock. A yacht called the Erato. But don't get any ideas. She's crewed and they've got more firepower than HMS Victory."

"But why on earth are they going to sea?"

"Because that's the only way to get to their destination."

"Which is?"

"The Isle of Man."

I let this information sink in. "He's not taking her to the flaming Isle of Man."

"You can't stop him."

"Why there?"

"No one survived. No one landed, at least not safely. He's been a couple of times already and set up a base camp with a few chosen followers. He's got wind power, solar power and a whole island of supplies. And now he's got a gift from the gods."

"Is that how he sees it?"

"Oh yes. He's convinced. This child has been sent from the stars and he's going to be the foster father, just in case she turns out to be special."

"And what if she's not special?"

"I don't think there's any chance of that, do you?" Yasmin fiddled with a tiny tassel on the throw over her sofa.

"You mean, he'll make her special?"

"Stuff of legends isn't it? His own fiefdom, on an island, with a child from above."

"What do you think – about the baby?"

"I told you. I've seen more babies than most. I've delivered them in operating theatres, I've delivered them in the backs of camper vans, I even delivered one at Glastonbury while Noel Gallagher sang his heart out. This baby doesn't look particularly different to me."

"Particularly?"

"Lots of babies have something a touch unusual about them for the first couple of days."

"And this one?"

"Skin is a little on the thick side. Some jaundice. That's about it."

"What date did you say it was born?"

"Eleventh."

"It had a gestation of exactly twelve months."

I couldn't decode Yasmin's response. She looked at me with a mixture of intrigue, doubt, accusation and bewilderment. We let it pass. I asked her about Thistle and her face became as painfully plain as a pastor. There was a pause, not while she thought what to say, but while she re-lived something that had happened. "Sparks would kill me if he knew what I've just told you. He has to get that child away, quickly and safely."

"He wants it so bad he had to snap Thistle's neck?"

Yasmin sank her nails into the knot of the tassel with which she still toyed. "Sparks knew someone was watching us, but his guard was down while the birth was in progress. Thistle came close. It must have been the fuss and noise of the labour that intrigued her, but Sparks wasn't on board. I'd banished him to shore. So Thistle found herself between the boat and him. He lunged at her and she leaped onto one of the other narrow boats running across the roof, but she lost her footing and as she fell over the side her head hit the guard rail. By the time he got her out of the water there was no life left in her."

"Did you see this?"

"It's what he said happened."

"And you believe him?"

There was another silence. Then she said, "I wish I could."

"What about Kirsty?"

"We haven't told Kirsty. She was otherwise engaged when it happened. The baby came about ten minutes later."

"Why did you leave Thistle in the water, tied to the bank?"

Yasmin stopped playing with the tassel and shook her head. "You'd have to ask him about that. He was pretty shaken, but also angry. He's completely cracked. He's lost it. It might have been some sort of warning, I don't know. He became worried that if the girl knew where we were, you might follow and foil his plans."

"He's right."

"I'd steer well clear if I were you. I'll be out of here soon, in case he comes back. If he ever needs my services again god knows what kind of nut he'll be by then."

The thought that Steve might need a midwife again sent horrible ripples through my head and redoubled my determination to stop his departure, but good sense told me Yasmin was right. I stood zero chance of rescuing a mother and baby from well-armed pirates about to set sail. As we drained our cocoa, the moon slid into her predetermined position and pulled the tide into the harbour enabling the next stage of Kirsty's journey. The ancients were right, the gods really are up there in the heavens and they really do determine our fate. I've grown to hate the night sky.

Obviously I am pleased that the birth went smoothly, but it hasn't answered any of the more pertinent questions surrounding the conception and gestation. A third of me still thinks Kirsty is wittingly or unwittingly lying and there was a natural conception last June, well after the Event. Another third thinks she underwent some extraordinary pause in her pregnancy during which the foetus simply stopped growing for a couple of months and that this happened because of the exceptional stress that she experienced in the immediate aftermath of our initial survival. And the third third of me, says that the pause was caused directly by outside influence and was perhaps also restarted by cosmic events. A tiny subdivision of that final third attributes that scenario to an intelligent architect. I hate the segment of my soul that voices that version, but it won't shut up. That's the voice that Suzuki Sparks Steve hears, and I think it's the one he wants to hear. If it's correct, then the infant will be a very special child indeed and we will have to watch her development very closely. I can't let her sail away and I won't tolerate Kirsty being taken. These were the thoughts that rattled through my skull as I skirted round the marina at Glasson and hid by the bushes close to the lock to get my first glimpse of the Erato. She's a fine vessel, modern and twin-masted. There was plenty of activity on board, as a crew of four or five, made ready for departure. At my end of the dock the swing bridge was open, it looked permanently so, and the canal lock was closed but dribbling where the seals were not perfect as it strained to hold the pressure of the marina basin at bay. At the far side, away to the west, the huge sea lock gate looked to be open, and I wondered how they'd managed to do that without power, unless of course it had been open when the catastrophe struck. So now the dock was completely tidal, which explained why the Erato was so low beneath the quayside. She was rising though, and soon she would rise so high she could sail safely round the harbour bough and take Kirsty down the Lune to the Irish Sea and to the ancient isle midway between the Celtic heartlands. She may as well be going to the moon.

The choices before me were very similar to the ones I had considered before my feeble and failed assault on the Cordelia, except this time the difficulties were more clearly defined and the odds were stacked even more highly against me. I listed them logically in my mind. I could do nothing. That was the most attractive option, but the one I least desired. I could announce myself and try to negotiate. That was certain to fail. I could storm the boat.

Even if I was able to borrow Yasmin's shotgun, my chances still seemed very poor and I might injure Kirsty or the child. I could try to prevent the boat from leaving by either damaging it or blocking its route. This would be a feasible option if I knew more about boats and had much more time to prepare and if I knew for certain that one of the other vessels in the basin was able to be started and manoeuvred very rapidly, all of which seemed unlikely. I went back to the Cordelia and discussed these options with Yasmin. Time was draining away as the tide in the dock inched higher.

"You've got to let her go."

"I can't do that."

"You can't stop her."

"I've got to try."

"And if they stop you – for good, what hope has she got then eh?"

I ignored that remark. "Can we use the Cordelia to block her in?"

"It takes fifteen minutes to get through the lock, they'll hear us and see us and then there won't be an us."

"What about the other boats in the dock? Any of them serviceable?"

"Ever handled a boat?"

"That's not what I asked."

"They've been sitting there through six months of frost, do you think they're going to start up just like that? And even . . ."

"All of them?"

Her hesitation betrayed her. "There's a little blue and white fishing boat. The Spinaway."

"I saw her."

"You'd need the keys."

"Where are they?"

She reached into a mug decorated with a picture of the Lytham windmill on a shelf by the sink and produced a set of ignition keys. Before handing them to me she walked forward and opened a cupboard near the prow, returning with a lifejacket. "For fuck's sake wear this," she said.

I had to scramble across the decks of three other vessels to reach the Spinaway. I managed to do this in almost silence. She was moored on the opposite side of the dock to the Erato, which was now riding high on the tide with her motor idling. I hoped the proximity of her own engine would drown out the noise of Spinaway's motor when I started her. There was a moment when I was just about to step aboard my vessel from the adjacent one when I completely froze. It was as if the enormity and possible finality of what I was about to attempt hit me in a single wave of realisation. I had virtually no chance of success but some instinct powered me forward. For a moment that power had failed and good sense locked my muscles in a desperate final attempt to make me see reason. I felt myself relax, giving in, letting go, being wise, but something caught my attention. Claire was sitting aboard the Spinaway, just waiting and looking out across the dock in anticipation. She turned to face me, and smiled a third of a smile. What else could I do but join her in the boat? I stepped on board and she went on her way via the very fabric of the salted air. I cast off the bow rope and my tiny vessel began to float free of her neighbour secured only at the stern. This was the moment. I slotted the ignition key into its socket, held my breath and looked for Claire. She wasn't there. I twisted the key. The engine kicked, did not start. I twisted again and the little boat wound her motor's momentum up to a rhythm too strong to stop and I had power. I imagined I heard a distant shout, though in reality I could not have done. I cast off astern and was floating free. I took the wheel and pushed the throttle forwards.

To my utter amazement, I managed to ram the Erato twice before there was any significant reaction from on board, and even then there was a delay before a sharp crack in one of the cabin panes signalled the arrival of a rifle round. By this time I was on my third approach, although I hadn't retreated far enough to build up a good head of speed and my third impact was more of a glancing blow and left little evidence on the hull of my adversary. My first two attempts had been more successful, and the first, in particular, had put a severe dint in the profile of the Erato's hull. The Spinaway had quite a severely pointed prow and both her hull and her guardrail projected sharply so on each ram I was inflicting a double jab, but sadly they were all well above the waterline. Deep in my head somewhere was the hope that the crew of the Erato would be concerned that the damage would be significant once they met the swell of the Irish Sea and that concern would be enough to confine them to port for at least another twelve hours while they checked it out, but Sparks was more determined, or more foolhardy than that, and they cast off and made their way towards the open sea lock and the moonlit river Lune. The next ten minutes are confused in my memory but our floating game of cat and rat continued in a mad swirl of ultimately pointless violent interaction. I ensured the cabin door behind me was closed, and hunched low to gain as much cover as possible from the superstructure. More windscreens cracked and become pock-marked as shells struck home. I made further ram raids and managed to deflect her course a little, but in the end she was too strong for me and she pushed her way out to sea. I was defeated and throttled back but they were not done with me. Someone on the Erato hurled a projectile and I heard it clutter onto my deck just behind the cabin. I jerked the cabin door open and saw it on the floor, and even my limited military knowledge told me it was a grenade. They say that when the mind is near death it goes into hyper-drive and the world is perceived in slow motion. This I now know to be true. My first instinct was to slam the door shut, but another thought fought with the first, to say that action might not save you, the blast might penetrate the door or might even blow up the fuel tank and the whole boat, so look around for an alternative. I looked, and there, fifteen feet beyond my boat, swimming, treading water serenely and smiling a full three-thirds of a smile, was Claire. In one completely instinctive action, I moved towards the grenade and dived over the side of the boat. The cold was sound, the sound of liquid hammers in my head, then the cold was shock, and I was sucking in sea, then the cold was pain, a fast creeping pain clawing its way right round my body. Something bulbous softly strangled me. My lifejacket had inflated and was teasing me with the memory of its name: life jacket. What chance of life did I have now?

The Spinaway had spun away. I had not seen nor heard an explosion and now I was so low in the water amid such darkness I could not see any vessel. My ears were filled with sea or with concussion and I could make no sense of sound. It was March, it was midnight, it was close to freezing. The titanic moon sailed high. There was no Claire, no boat, no hope, and I had sent Kirsty to sea in a vessel that I may have just made unseaworthy.

Welcome to the opposite of pride.

A harbour bell rang. I had never heard a harbour bell, but I heard one then. Or was it a church bell? A bell in the tower of a valley church drowned to form a reservoir. It was a harbour bell. Deep and soulful. Deep. The cold was now on my face in a lace pattern as successive splashes rained a mantilla of spray over the bosom of my life jacket. My reminiscence played with memories of lifejackets in movies. Mae Wests they used to be called. I'd seen pictures of Mae West. She was a big girl. How many fallen airmen and sunken sailors died snuggled in her cleavage? She made a lifejacket so bulbous that you can lose your life in it. Stay awake. I knew how important it was to stay awake, but how seductive sleep was. Sleeping in the bosom of Mae West, warm, soft, maternal. At the point of death big boys always call out for their mother. Every mother is the mother of the whole universe as through her you know all there is to know. Every mother is a god mother. She creates you and your Eden and your hell and all of the world in between. I called for my mother, but it was thirty years since she left me to look for her own. Life is a curious gift: it can be given many times, but only received once. And our little life is ended by a sleep. Soul-welcoming sleep. Seductive sleep. Warm sleep. Painless sleep. Stressless sleep. Eternal sleep. I must stay awake. I had to stay awake, but sleep was warm, sleep was dreams, sleep was rescue. I shut my eyes and smiled at sleep.

Such warmth. Tropical yet fresh and dry. I swam in a lagoon, in a jungle on an island. The water was turquoise and warm and saltless. The sand beneath was as white as sugar, the tangled foliage round the tiny lake was luscious green with tiger splashes of orange, red and deep brown. Creepers dangled. Birds of paradise flitted past flying from song to song. The sky was cloud free and a kindly sun kissed my face as I swam naked as the night I got married. Somewhere deep in the forest a sonorous note rang magically created by falling nature, timber on timber, and at that moment, as if launched by the sound, a raft drifted into view, upon it Claire, garbed now as if she were the subject of a pre-Raphaelite painting, classical yet natural, and amid nature and romance in a composition of fakery so real that a super-reality was created, and there was I within it. She basked in the sun for a while, not bathing but being bathed, washed by Apollo's magic rays because he could not choose to not gaze upon her. All the while she knew I was there and when she'd done with Apollo she trailed a hand in the lake and made her raft turn into the shade of palm fronds. She smiled four quarters of a smile. I swam to her and she pulled me from the water.

We lay on the raft for only a few moments, then it was gone and we walked through temple pillars and beneath geometrically perfect domes to enter an endless marble corridor. I was still naked. The marble was warm beneath my feet. There were rooms off this corridor, with doorways without doors, and the glimpses within often tempted me to veer, but Claire led the way and the way was straight ahead. I looked over her sweet shoulder to see where our draughtsman's course led, but it was too far to focus. I expected there to be a bright light at the end of this marble tunnel but there was only a vanishing point. All else was light. Light radiated and rebounded. There must have been windows somewhere but I could not see them. It was as if the sunlight once in, played among the Arcadian halls and enjoyed itself so much it did not want to leave.

My mother waved from one room that we passed.

"Ah, Mum. There you are."

She smiled her radiant, unconditional, all-forgiving smile, sipped almost milk-less tea from china and tucked into butterfly cakes. She passed the cake stand to her mother who removed a Maid of Honour before passing the stand on to her mother, who passed it to her mother, and there were all my mothers, a hall of mothers and a table of cakes and tea all the way back to where the fruitcake had no cake and was only fruitful.

I lingered at the door and contemplated a million maternal conversations but Claire said, "Mothers only. Come along." And my wife was my mother and I must obey till death us do reunite. We walked on. I said to Claire, "My mother loved children; she'd have given anything if I'd been one." Claire looked over her shoulder with one seventh of a smile. "Groucho Marx," she said and I nodded. We walked on. The next room we passed contained Groucho Marx having tea with his mother. He stubbed out his cigar and spoke to me. "Contraception should be used on every conceivable occasion."

"Spike Milligan," said Claire, and Spike Milligan stepped out from behind a pillar and slapped a custard tart in Groucho's face.

"That's my boy," said Mrs Marx.

"You mean I've got another brother?" said Groucho from beneath his confectionery complexion. "Couldn't you control yourself woman? No wonder they buried you in a Y-shaped coffin."

"Joe Orton," said Claire, and we walked on.

I said, "You know condoms aren't completely safe. A friend of mine was wearing one and he got run over by a bus."

"I wondered why he never arrived," said Claire.

And then there were windows, a whole array of them thirty feet high in a room off to our left. It was a mammoth conservatory filled with palm pot plants and artists all dressed like Manet, and all painting pictures of women all undressed as in Manet's Le déjeuner sur l'herbe. Beyond the windows the bourgeois middle classes top-hatted, tailed and neck-tied leered through the conservatory windows intent on perusing feminine foliage.

"People who live in glass houses might as well answer the door," I said.

"People in ass houses should grow stones," she said, and we walked on past a room where my son Matthew played pool with his undergraduate associates.

"Hi Dad," he called and potted the green.

"Hi Matt," I said.

Claire smiled seven sevenths at our son and we walked on. Matt leaned out of the room and called after us. "Hey Dad! If your parents didn't have children, the chances are you won't either." I laughed. "Thanks Matt." I reached for my working notebook but found neither pocket nor trouser and made a mental note instead. Further along the corridor my younger son, Paul was busking by singing and strumming on a sunburst red guitar. He was playing one of his own compositions. A small crowd of Impressionist artists and their naked female models had gathered to listen and watch. There was a rash of gold and silver coins at his feet. We stopped and listened and when he'd finished I said, "I'd give you something son, but I'm a bit short of change." He looked at my absence of trousers and said, "No Dad, you're just short." Claire laughed, he laughed, I laughed, the Impressionists laughed with blurred lips, their models giggled and wobbled. How we laughed. I patted him on the back and we walked on. Over my shoulder I heard him say, "I shall now play one of my own songs backwards whilst decomposing." No one laughed. And he couldn't play it.

We walked on.

The warmth became dryer and the corridor had gritty tails of recusant sand outlining the Corinthian feet of the pillars and the bizarre became bazaar as we wove between men and women in Arabic attire, the men in cool swathes of white, or deeply dyed, linen, the women all veiled except for hands and feet and averted eyes. And there I walked naked, under-endowed and with a paunch that anticipated all the excesses of a sixth decade. To the men I was risible, to the women invisible. Amidst all these one man stood out so starkly, a Sikh among Arabs, he stopped me, held my shoulders, looked me in the eye, and said, "My son has taken up meditation. Well it's better than doing nothing." His beard split into a beam and he laughed halitosis in my face. One of his teeth was gold. Then he was gone, and the others were gone, and our way was cool, the air thin and there was a door to one side, a door of stone, tightly shut. I wanted to try it, but it was secure and had no handle. Claire was waiting for me. She identified the room behind the door.

"Tibet," she said.

I tried the door again. She shook her head.

"Teresa?" I said. "Our daughter."

But Claire had no answer for me, no words to form, no expression to adopt on her face. She took my hand and we walked on.

Our path was plainer now. Walls, ceiling and floor were glossy white marble patterned by nature with other shades and textures of almost white marble. I tugged on Claire's hand. She stopped. I said, "Could we find my father here?"

She said, "How would you recognise him?"

I said, "From the look on his face. On my seventeenth birthday my Dad tried to surprise me with a car, but he missed."

She said, "Did it hurt? When you got to that part of your routine? How much joy can a comic get from severely biographical jokes?"

I said, "My parents accepted me for what I was: a punishment from God."

"Your mother loved you Dan, and for all we know, so did your father."

"Love's a funny thing."

"It was, the way you made it."

"Mum always said Dad loved me. And when she said that I always knew she meant my real dad. She said he loved me the way God the father loved his son. Me and Jesus, we had something in common: our dads never played football with us."

"And does that bother you?"

"No, but I'd have trust issues if my father allowed me to be crucified."

"We're not here to run through your standup routine."

"Why are we here?"

"To have the last laugh."

"He who laughs last didn't get it in the first place."

"I'm serious, Dan," she said.

"I'm desperate Dan," I said, and I wasn't joking.

"This is serious."

"Comedy is a serious business."

"It paid the bills," she said.

"That's what you think. When you thought I was going to gigs I was actually just delivering pizzas. Didn't get laughs, but I think I made more people happy. And they nearly all said thank you. Behind every door was an overweight person who thought they were starving."

"Behind every door," she said and I saw that the corridor had gone. We stood on nothing, surrounded by nothing except a sphere of sky above, about and beneath us, but between us and the sphere of sky was a golf ball pattern of identical doors. How many? Who knows? Fifty at least.

"What is?" I asked. "What is behind every door?"

"The same thing," she said. "Choose one."

"Which one?"

"It's up to you."

"But if it's the same behind each one, why does it matter which one I choose?"

"It doesn't."

I scanned the doors. "What's behind them?"

"The same thing," she said.

I thought about this. "Do you mean that there is the same thing behind one door that there is behind any other, or do you mean there is just one thing there behind them all? Beyond here there is just one thing? And it's behind every door."

"You're catching on," she said.

I looked at her. "Are you there too?"

She smiled a billion billionths of the smile I married her for. "Everything is behind each door. It is all the same. The same thing. And yes, I will be part of it. I will be it."

"And Matthew? And Paul? Teresa? Mum, both fathers and . . ." I wanted to form the G word but my doubts would not let me."

"It's all the same," she said.

I found myself moving towards one of the doors, and then I was close to it, my hand on the cold gold marble handle. A tiny thought fought the multitude in my mind and commanded a pause. I looked at Claire. Beyond her were shadowy forms I knew to be my two boys, my mother, my stepfather and the man he had replaced. I had a question for Claire. She had the answer ready, I could see it behind her anticipation. "And Kirsty?"

Her billionths shrank to millionths and she shook her head almost imperceptibly. I took my hand from the handle and felt the gush of cold, cold gale as we rammed back through marble halls bouncing off marble walls, and feeling pain, pain and more pain until there was no more pain to be perceived, but through the pain came claws, claws of ivory, claws with supernatural strength, working their way down my back as a bench slammed into my stomach and I spewed sea, and the sound of water and of swearing cut the cold out of my ears. I lay crumpled on something solid that moved and rocked and settled and had a shape.

"Got you," panted Yasmin. She slapped my face as if it were a baby's bum. "Now breathe you bastard. Breathe! Breathe!"

I breathed. It hurt. But I breathed and breathed and breathed.

Yasmin had done a remarkable thing. She'd watched my feeble and failed attempt to stall the departure of the Erato, seen me dive into the harbour, seen the grenade blast and watched both vessels float off into the night. She lost sight of me in the water and had no idea where I was, so she went back to bring the Cordelia single handed through the marina lock, by which time I could have been anywhere, and by which time my body temperature was already bordering on fatal. She scanned the dock with her strongest torch but to no avail and presumed, correctly, that the turning tide had taken me round the bough and into the Lune estuary. In essence, she took her canal barge to sea and began to survey the ever-widening midnight expanse of the Atlantic ocean. She was about to give up when she heard a cry, though I have no recollection whatsoever of calling out, and she brought her angelic beam to bear on my bobbling form. Bringing me and the Cordelia together was no mean feat, but with admirable skill and the help of a boathook she brought me alongside and heaved me aboard. She then threw me under cover, tore off just a few of my wet clothes and buried me under bedding before returning to the helm of her vessel, which by then was in serious danger of drifting out into the open ocean. She fought against the combined tide and Lune flow but time was against her and the levels were falling too fast and we became beached on a sandbank in the estuary. In one sense this was a blessing in disguise for she switched off the engine, came below and concentrated on me. She was my second midwife. She brought me back to life. I remember nothing of the remainder of that night or of the next day and Yasmin tells me I spent nearly all of it unconscious. She stripped me, rubbed warmth into me, and put me in her bed under completely dry bedclothes and with two hot water bottles. She somehow got some lukewarm water into me, and later some lukewarm milk. Meanwhile rain pelted down outside and she waited for half a day for the tide to lift us off the sandbank. She then had to pilot our vessel through the downpour working it skilfully up river to arrive at the dock gates with the tide still rising and high enough to allow us through, despite the eddies and currents that plague the river at that point. Exhausted, she tied up the Cordelia, wisely with a good deal of slack to allow for the falling sea level, and then collapsed into sleep. To her relief we both awoke later that day, and there my memories re-start. She gave me vegetable soup and I blessed the person who had sealed that can so many months before. On the next tide, we moved back through the canal lock and returned to our original mooring beyond the inland edge of the marina. It feels like the heart of England.

Miraculously I appear to have no lasting injuries. For a day or two we feared frostbite to my fingers, but they seem fine now. Yasmin brought my laptop from the Peugeot and I have written up these wondrous events. She is reading my whole story. We have discussed my memories of marble halls, of warm lagoons, of reconciliation in the afterlife, and of failure to find my true father or my daughter. I dismiss it as a dying dream. She shrugs her shoulders and says that dreams are a kind of reality. The other world I suggest is just an invention of my brain, my mind trying to make sense of tangled memories. She accepts that might be the case, but says even if it is, it should still be attended to: "Your spirit is still you. And it doesn't sleep."

I shrugged my sea-stiffened shoulders. "I just wonder why I didn't carry on and open the door."

"You're in love with Kirsty and Claire understood that."

"My imagined Claire."

"Is there another Claire? Hasn't Claire always been the Claire you imagined? Can we ever know another person except through our perception of them? Through our imagination?"

"I can't see what I can do for Kirsty now."

"I don't think it's just about Kirsty. I think it's the baby too. I think that child is as important to you as she is to Sparks. You can't afford to lose two daughters."

"They're equally remote."

"Don't be silly. Tell me about Teresa."

I told her about Teresa. My daughter went to find herself as many teenage daughters do. Most these days go to the Far East but Teresa first tried a throwback to the mind-expanding expeditions of my generation and went to Marrakech. I had many nightmares while she was there, mostly involving endless searches through bazaars. After that she went to India and then on to Tibet. I haven't seen her since she was seventeen: six years ago. I haven't known her for much longer than that. I would say she went off the rails in high school where she fell in with New Age rebels. I didn't disapprove, but it's hard to support campaigns against third runways when you're sick of queuing up to get on the second one. She didn't really appreciate my humour or my frequent absences from home. I always felt we would eventually find common ground and I craved for that to happen. As time went on, Claire and I became more and more convinced that we had lost our daughter, and we both underwent a kind of mourning combined with a sense of failure. It was a prime ambition of mine to resolve those feelings. I believed all could be put right by a single act of reconciliation and quietly plotted to bring one about, but at every opportunity Teresa seemed determined to extend the distance between us by increasing her geographical remoteness. It was as if she was pushing the whole planet between us.

The story of my missing father is even simpler. The plain fact is, I never knew him, for he'd left my mother before I was four, and I have no recollection of his face or of the man behind it, at all. I was twenty-one before my mother saw fit to tell me that my step-father wasn't my father. What she didn't know is that he'd told me ten years earlier, and I'd suspected it even before that as a consequence of something an aunt had said when she didn't know I was under the tablecloth landing Thunderbird Two. So I grew up with a deep sense of suspicion about who I was and a vague feeling of being unworthy and of rejection. Aged nine I'd been brought before my step-father with a group of friends. We'd been caught, quite literally red-handed, after raiding the fruit bushes of a neighbour's garden. My step-father said no son of his would steal, and then later, when we were alone, he left me in no doubt that indeed I was no son of his. It was no easy matter for my mother to undergo a second marriage in 1960, and so my whole childhood was conducted under the thinnest veneer of respectability, the fragility of which I always detected, but never understood until the truth was told. Yasmin is just the latest of many people to suggest that my chosen occupation was a lifelong search for approval. If all stand-up comics were rejected children with low self-esteem I could accept the argument, but they are not. We all seek approval. All of us. All the time. We seek it ultimately from ourselves, but for most of us that self-appreciation is entirely a function of the perceived appraisal of us by our peers.

So I have known rejection, but who hasn't? Get over it. Life is disappointment, and many of us experience fractured relationships with our families, but sometimes those missing people become ghosts more tangible, more persistent and more powerful than any spectre of a stranger.

Yasmin has returned me to the here and now. We have slowly navigated our way back to the main course of the Lancaster canal and moored close to the place where Thistle's altar lays charred and partly submerged near Garstang. Being within sight would be too close so we sailed a few yards further downstream. We won't stay here for long as Yasmin is anxious to get well away and lose herself in the tangle of Britain's canal network. She has no desire to have further dealings with Sparks. I, on the other hand, cannot break off my seemingly impossible pursuit of Kirsty. After all I have turned back from the door of eternity to find her, and my best chance lies with divine help from on high. I have dug out a pattern of soil spelling the words GOD HELP ME in the field where his helicopter landed. Next to it I also managed to use my spade to sketch out a representation of a nine volt battery. It's rather a good sketch, even if I say so myself. It made Yasmin smile. "But I'm not staying long," she said, "I'm going south."

"That's fine," I said, "show me the ropes and I'll set up in one of these other boats."

"I'm not leaving you until you are fully recovered," she said.

"I think I more or less am," I said.

"No you're not," she said. And she's probably right.

I really like Yasmin.

1st April 2006

God has not come back. Yasmin has moved on. She's somewhere on Queen Victoria's midlands M25 waterway. She showed me the ropes and I mastered another narrow boat called Northern Nights. I didn't like the name, so I painted over most of her letters and added an 'a' and she is now Nora. Nora and I get on just fine. She gives me shelter and motion, heat and light and even mains voltage electricity to power this, my pixelated past, my electronic epistle, my legacy on a laptop. I'm on my own again, and heading home again, because I've remembered something that Steve said which was made clearer by something Claire said. And I want to see Claire again, and she hasn't been back since I left her at the brink. She always said I was pushing her over it. Perhaps this time I did?

The parting from Yasmin was not easy for either of us. We made a wish phrased like a promise that we will meet up again sometime in the future. It would have been so simple to stay together. We got on so very well and on top of all that I owed her my life. She is a loving, warm, tactile woman and we were very comfortable in each other's company, but she was adamant that she needed to use her barge to move on. I am learning that there is something about Steve that instils fear in those who encounter him. Outwardly he is light-hearted, high-spirited and amiable, but beneath there is a self-centred ruthlessness that knows no bounds. Thistle is the latest evidence of this. Yasmin needed to put as much distance between Steve and herself as she could, or at least find a place where she felt it was too much trouble for him to seek her out. She would have gone south sooner, but she had felt for Kirsty when Steve had first told her of the pregnancy, and stayed to see her through it, and to claim her fee, part of which had been the shotgun she had levelled at me. I said with me and the shotgun she was well protected, but she shook her head. That was nowhere near enough protection against Sparks, she said. I don't think that was the complete reason for her departure. She had a boat and there were thousands of miles of England she could navigate, and I think that she wanted to see for herself just what state the country was in, and if there were people making more of a success of surviving in it, than those we'd experienced. I said I thought it unlikely that there were many groups better organised than the one at Caton, and she immediately responded with a retort that both shook and convinced me. She said they were not organised, they were conditioned. They were not a society, they were a cult, and their leader, not with them but not far away, was the man who had brought them their new holy book, the Bosun's Tale,   and that man was now holding court with

Kirsty as his queen.   My observations of Sparks' interaction with the people of Caton did not really fit with her appraisal of him. They had treated him very much as some travelling tinker. He was a bit of a celebrity but also often the butt of witty jibes, he was not held in any reverence or especial respect, but I had never seen him in the company of the community leaders, and the attitude of their internal militia certainly changed after he had taken Kirsty from me. This perspective, given to me by Yasmin provided moments of deep thought, but also convinced me that, no matter how hard it was going to be, I had to find some way of setting Kirsty free. Yasmin understood this, and with much affection, she kitted out my new boat, showed me the ropes, then piloted our tiny flotilla south to Ashton, before a final kiss sent her onwards to the Ribble link, the estuary and the rest of the country.

6th April 2006.

I moored Nora only a short mile from the house where Claire, Teresa, Matthew, Paul and I ripped half an acre of wrapping paper from virgin Christmas gifts as we clocked up a month of Decembers. The place where children's pyjamas became indecent women's club ware and unwashed male underwear in less time than it took to notice the time pass. A twentieth century house was full of timers and not one counted the time. Only the unchanging things noticed the time passing: the picture of the gardener on in the dining room, the vase from the Riviera, the rubber stop that prevented the back door handle from demolishing the kitchen wall, a wall that is no longer there. The house is there. I can see it rebuild itself from the charred rubble, restacking its Accrington brick by sheer force of pride in its own workmanship, and rebinding each course with mortar mixed from west coast sand, Ribble grit, Lancashire limestone and horizontal rain. I can stand before my house and watch it rise up. What I cannot understand is why Kirsty had to burn it down. All she had to do was speak to my heart without going through my head. She is forgiven, and one day I will tell her that.

Of course, I did not return to my house to find Kirsty. I went looking for my wife. I walked her garden. I stood by her grave. The mound, her mausoleum, was more rounded, more convex, more sculpted, more solid than I had left it, and made so by vertical rain. I suddenly realised, with delight, that when I had buried her, I had laid her in an east-west alignment, and how much that would have pleased her. Funny she never mentioned it in Arcadia.

Knowing all that I do know, I knew, thought, hoped, that she would be exactly the same beneath the soil as she had been eleven months earlier when I covered her. The mantle of earth over her face looked too smooth, too well-proportioned, to perfect to disturb, but disturb it I would. I must. I did. I used my fingers. Only my fingers. Anything else would have harmed her. It didn't take long. There was her face, perfect as the day she died. A little more porcelain perhaps, and drained even more the bloom of lifeblood, but pretty as a parcel of memory and intimacy could ever be. I don't know how long I stayed with her, but a light drizzle came and I let it dance on her face for a while, before dabbing her dry with the inside of my coat cuffs, and covering her with her beloved loam once more. In all that time, I did not speak to her once. When that was done I went and sat for a while in her favourite chair in our summerhouse. I wasn't looking any more. I wasn't thinking what to do. I went home knowing what I must do for she had told me in my near death dream.

"People in ass houses should grow stones," she'd said.

I sat in the summerhouse for some time then went to Claire's greenhouse. I'd glanced in on my arrival in the garden so I knew that what I was looking for was there, and it was now time to investigate it more closely. There were a number of small packages of oranges, lemons, limes and nuts that Steve had left on the floor, and on one of the shelving units was an array of ten or eleven small plant pots. The soil in them was rock hard, as they hadn't been watered for months and they were so dry that the contents had shrunk a little creating air gaps between the soil cylinders and the pots. Some were just terribly cracked. I empted out the contents and crumbled the soil in my hands. Sure enough in each one I found citrus stones, or nuts and not one showed any sign of any germination or growth having taken place.

My next action is a touch unpalatable to describe but I believe it may prove to be central to our future survival. Claire's remark had puzzled me when I first heard it in my near death dream, but even at that point I realised there was more than one layer to it. During my convalescence on board the Cordelia I thought about it a lot. Yasmin was reading through these memoirs and she asked me about Clita's note, and suddenly the full power of Claire's pun was evident. It linked with Clita's message, and took me back to a conversation that Kirsty and I had had shortly after her death. It wasn't the subject of that conversation that mattered, but our circumstances, our environment. I'd noted in my recollections, that as we chatted the early morning breeze conveyed a hint of an unpleasant scent from the latrines. If all bacteria had died, then what was causing the unpleasant smell? Of course not all bacteria had died:

lots of it still lived in our stomachs, in our guts, in our bowels and eventually in the content of our latrines. Clita had told us to harvest the latrines because she had realised that the fertility of the future lay in the sweet smell of shit. Steve's greenhouse experiment may have worked if he had returned frequently enough to tend to his test crop, but what Clita had realised was that the most potent prospect of fertile soil was in human faeces. Not only was there bacteria in there, it is possible that undigested material may have been present too. So I went to my garden lavatory, the part right at the end, next to the tip, what Claire might have called my ass house. I knew exactly were it was, and it was that soiled soil that I used to refill the plant pots. Then I took them, along with some of the citrus and nut samples that Steve had brought from the cargo plane at Salmesbury airfield and went back to my barge. I also took a couple of small polythene cloche kits that Claire had stored in our shed. I made mini greenhouses on the roof of my narrow boat. I watered them well and waited for the spring sun.

So perhaps my seeds will grow. I'll have to wait and see. Meanwhile I'm going to take a careful look at the city centre. I'd like to visit the Harris library. I want to read up on boating. If I can get to grips with a more seaworthy vessel and learn how to navigate it, then I could attempt a day trip to the Isle of Man.

*

Comedians have always had to evolve to survive. Tell unfashionable jokes and you're history. Tell taboo jokes and you're dead. How we crave for the long-gone days when we could be the true kings of comedy, the all-licensed fools at the court of the monarch who knew that many a true word is spoken in a jester. Humourists are the masters not of light, but of the dark arts, for humour cuts more than it tickles. It can deliver death by a million quips.

We have been the Nazis of the liberal mentality. Ask the Jew in the joke shop. We have been the racists of the global village and the sexist sons of bitches. We have sought celebrity by sniping at it.

A comic is a predator. We prey on the living and the dead. We pick away at their habits, their clothes, their skin and their bones. There is no such thing as a vegetarian comic. We are all carnivores.

We are also cowards. We are the all-licensed fool hiding in Lear's shadow, and in that shade we mutually mutilating vultures ravenously feed from each other's carcases, for there is no such thing as a new gag.

If I have achieved anything in my professional life, it is because I have stood on the shoulders of dwarves.

*

Eighteen: Out of Hell.

13th April 2006.

My first week on the canal in Ashton was uneventful. I moored on the towpath alongside the park. Most mornings I went for a walk round the park. It was strangely reminiscent of the long gone days of normality, though of course nothing looked normal. I have described how our world had turned to all shades of grey and there, for a while, it resided, but April has brought a new hue. Firstly the sky became washed with amber. It was only faint and could only be detected at dawn and dusk when the rising or setting sun caught it, but I saw it on several occasions and relished its appearance without worrying too much about what might be causing it. Then on some days there is the finest veneer of yellow on the roof and sides of Nora. It looks like sand, and reminds me of those rare incidents when, according to meteorologists, southerly winds deposited sand from the Sahara on our cars and pavements. The world is very dusty now, for more and more vegetation is breaking up and being swept, gathered and deposited by the wind. The majority of the dust is grey and soil based but at times a contrasting dusting of pale brown is evident. The prevailing weather in this part of the world has always come from the west and I think the golden beaches of the Fylde coast are taking flight and sometimes sugaring our slate grey palette. There were two days towards the end of the month when a heavy smoke-like cloud covered the sky, and a distasteful odour of combustion pervaded the air. That was very worrying. Everything is so dry.

I was disappointed that God did not return and see the plea that I had carved into the soil of the field at Garstang, and upon leaving, I was worried that he would turn up and land there and be unable to find me. I wanted to carve a forwarding address but realised that it could also provide a clue for anyone else trying to locate me, even though they wouldn't know I had carved it or really understand for whom it was intended. In the end, I added a footnote: "10m S" and an arrow pointing towards Preston. I carved a fresh message in the open expanse of Haslam Park, in Ashton, the suburb where I moored the Nora.

I stole a cycle and went into the city. My memory was redundant, for nothing at all had changed. Everything was exactly as it was the last time I had seen it, barring a few minor adjustments made by wind, sun and frost. There was a new eeriness as the permanence of the macabre devastation was underlined. The same corpses lay still caught in the same interruptions of their lives, still smothering un-stored shopping, still rushing to nowhere. Still late. Still still. If you take the time to study their shape you can find fascination in the distortions caused by long-term stillness and the settling of muscles and the misplacement of the moisture of the body, but it is not a pastime for the easily disturbed. My town, which spent so much of its time planning, planning, and planning to be a metropolis has become a necropolis. John Lennon is said to have said that life is what happens while you are making other plans. There are no plans now. My little life, that always seemed so insignificant when squeezing through the jostling multitudes of market places, now seems so large and yet so pointless. So many of us strive to stand out from the crowd, but you can't stand out when there isn't a crowd. It's the crowd that matters, not the standing out.

It was important for my own peace of mind that I investigated the Minster. I couldn't move freely in the city centre, if the Prague angels were still ruling the roost. Of course I was cautious but there was something that spoke to me of safety from the outset. I don't know what it was, but at no point did I detect even the threat of a threat and as things turned out, I was right. Once inside the church all was supremely tidy. Someone had been very busy. The chairs were all neatly aligned. Litter, debris and detritus had been banished. Walls had been washed. Wood had been dusted. The floor had been swept, though stains remained. Brass had been polished. Memorials remembered having their inscriptions lovingly and recently wiped. Only high above the high reach point was there any hint of dust. A tide mark betrayed the extent of arm, mop and step-ladder, although in one corner the level was raised as if somehow the next phase of cleaning had started and then I noticed a long ladder lying neatly on the floor against the foot of the wall.

There was a small congregation. It was incongruous, decorous and deceased. One living person had assembled seven dead persons and seated them side by side in the front row of the nave. They were, I subsequently discovered, four of the Prague bikers, and three others, one of which was Thistle's mother, Christina. Whoever had positioned them had also dressed them. They had been given hats, for it seemed that most, like Christina had ended their own lives with self-inflicted bullets to the brain, and their hats had been positioned with a poise that melded incongruity with dignity, covering the escape routes of their brain shattering shells. In some cases scarves had been placed to cover the entry point. The two next to Christina I did not recognise, but they were women. They had all been given coats, and these were slotted over the backs of their pew chairs and then fastened so that they sat more or less upright. Someone had gone to a lot of trouble to place these former people in this way, and I got the impression that they, like their surroundings, received regular and reverent attention. Before them was the altar, but between them and that now pristinely prepared sacramental table, was a bird-embossed lectern with a great illuminated bible opened upon it. The page on view was from the Book of Exodus.

"Ah!" Came a proclamation from behind me. "A lay reader."

I turned and saw a man in liturgical vestments, but they provided an insufficient disguise. "Lucifer," I said.

He shook his head.

"Not any more," he said with his Tyneside whistle still tunefully intact. "I'm climbing my way back up. There are a lot of rungs. Do I know you, brother?"

"I'm a good man," I said. His face was immaculately scrubbed and though he still sported a full beard, it was much more neatly trimmed. The rat's tail of hair at the back of his head has been snipped off. "I'm Dan Goode. You came to my house." His eyes narrowed, his lips pursed as I elaborated. "On your bike." I turned to his macabre congregation. "With your. . . angels." His pupils suddenly widened and the curtain of his grey beard parted to allow the white stone tablets of his teeth to smile, then after a moment, his face reshaped to presage a thought, and he raised the first finger of his right hand in an ecclesiastical gesture of recollection. His proclamation brought shock, delight and pain in equal measure.

"You have a daughter!"

It was said in exactly the manner that might be expected of a kindly priest, and suddenly here was a man who could have been a vicar all his life, well practised in cosy conversation decorated by the subtlest residue of plainchant inflection.

"I have," I said.

His face changed again. Now there was real worry there, and fear, but also resolve. "Did we violate her?"

"No."

"Oh good." The worry, fear and resolve evaporated. His face reported one sin less, so there would be no need to carry out that stint of penance.

"She's in Tibet," I said. "I hope."

"Hope," he said. "We have to hope. There is hope."

"I hope there is."

"There can't not be can there? So long as we hope, then there is hope."

I smiled an agreement.

"Have you come for the service?"

"No, I just . . . came to see if you were all right."

"I'm sick of chocolate, but otherwise I think I am all right."

I indicated his propped up parishioners, but didn't quite know how to phrase my question, so I just asked, "Have you put these people here?"

He seemed to understand the true point of my question. "We realised . . . we realised that . . . we just realised." I let his final syllable resound round the gilded angels on the beams above our heads. He took a deep breath and continued. "The alcohol ran out. It eventually ran out. Well it didn't. There's a whole Soddom of it somewhere out there, but the will to drink it dried up. And the bullets went. And in the end there wasn't one left for me. Well, I'm sure there is if I look hard enough, but I'm not looking just yet. I'm reading the Bible, a page a day, and I'm praying. I'm praying a lot. And we have daily service. Do you require a hymn book?"

"No, thank you, Lucifer . . . we no longer call you Lucifer?"

"He was an angel you know, before he was a Hell's angel."

"Yes, I know."

"I was christened Luke. Not a hugely popular Christian name in Newcastle in my generation. It quickly became Lucifer. A nickname. One of the devil's own. Anyway Luke it is." He turned towards the Bible on the lectern. "I'm looking forward to getting to my bit. It's a long way off yet."

"Was this your occupation before . . ?"

"Oh good God no! I was higher than this."

"Higher?"

"Oh yes." His word whistled supremely through the nave. "I was a roofer."

"A roofer?"

"Come and see."

He led me outside and took me round to the south façade, the way Thistle and I had first approached, from the Christian Science building. What he then showed me raised and plummeted my spirits on a single high speed rollercoaster loop. Firstly I saw a fine array of specialist ladders, the lowest section of which was missing and the highest length was looped over the apex ridge of the church. A message had been painted in twelve foot letters on the slate of the Minster roof. It said: GOD HELP ME.

At first I laughed out loud, then my heart sank as I wondered how long it had been there and whether it might have distracted and diverted my possible airborne saviour.

"Do you really think God needs that?"

"I'm doing everything I can to show him I'm on his side."

"Well it would catch the eye of any pilots flying by."

"One chap came in a helicopter," whistled Lucifer. My heart touched down. "Landed on the bus station, came to see me and claimed to be God almighty. Saw right through him."

"You did?"

"Big fan you see."

"Of God?"

"Of Meat Loaf."

"Meat Loaf?" I would not classify myself as a fan of Meat Loaf, but I'm confident the man with the helicopter was not the artist formerly known as Meat Loaf. I challenged Lucifer. "Meat Loaf came to see you in a helicopter?"

"No!" he said. "Come with me."

He took me back inside the Minster to one of the offices tucked up by the choir loft. The rooms up there were not in the tidy state of the church itself, in fact there was clutter everywhere. This was obviously where Luke lived. Evident amongst the accumulated garbage was a number of music and 'lads' magazines. One was readily to hand and open on the relevant page. It was an article about Meat Loaf. He was on the roof of a high-rise block in a sky-scraping city. He was stepping from a helicopter and through the open door the pilot was clearly visible. Both aircraft and pilot were familiar to me.

"Recognised him straight away. It's the hat."

Sure enough, despite his regulation headphones, the pilot of the chopper wore a white fedora with a black band, just as he had when he met me and when I flew with him. Luke went on, "I've seen this picture before, it's been used a lot down the years." He went on to tell me God had been none too pleased to be recognised, but still stuck to his story of being a rock icon in his own right. I was fascinated to see his cover blown but anxious to know the more pertinent facts of Luke's encounter with him. He wasn't very precise but said it had been a few days ago, perhaps a week. It was likely that God flew in just about the time I tied up at Haslam Park. I hadn't heard any helicopters and Yasmin and I had been especially vigilant, but we did have irregular sleep patterns, and if we were below decks with our motor running we might not hear an aircraft unless it was close overhead. Surely God would have scanned the canal. Luke said God hadn't asked after me, or anyone. He came down because of the message on the roof, and he didn't stay long after being shown the magazine picture. Surely he must have checked the canal? Surely he would have flown to Garstang and seen my message there? Maybe he saw that one first and then saw the one on the Minster roof? After that he could have been so annoyed that he went straight back to Wales. Even if he'd flown over Haslam Park, it's possible he did so before I'd carved out my message in the grass there, and he wouldn't have recognised the Nora, and the Cordelia may have been well clear of there by then. That could be it: my best chance gone, for he was the quickest, safest and surest way of determining if the Erato had arrived on the Isle of Man, and the best way I could imagine of getting there.

I took my leave of Luke, wished him all the best and said I'm sure his redemption was a good thing. He didn't make much sense. The longer we talked the more he alternated between the lucid and the ludicrous. He went on about chocolate and the plagues of Egypt, and the best way of getting brains off walls. I told him to be careful on ladders but he said he was bringing them inside so that he could clean higher up.

I went to the central library to look for books on sailing. I found a few but it all took much longer than I had anticipated, and despite it being April, the light was starting to fade by the time I emerged. I found a newsagent where not all the confectionary had been looted and thought of Luke as I tucked into a pair of Twix, some crisps and a can of Seven Up. After that I wandered the streets of central Preston, the streets where I'd shopped for toys, then for teenage fashion, engagement rings, a wedding suit, children's clothes and toys again. Places where mortgages had been secured, overdrafts negotiated, loans agreed. Then off the main street to Winckley Square where sixth form windows in Georgian terraces failed to keep our minds on General Studies and off the specific anatomy of the convent girls who ran the gauntlet of our cavalier eyes. After that I returned to my bike and cycled the two miles north with a heavy pack on my back and a heavy heart in my chest. I'd glanced at the books whilst in the library and realised that, even if I was by some miracle, able to secure a good seagoing vessel, my chances of putting to sea and then finding the Isle of Man were on the wrong side of zero. I would read the books, I would visit Preston Marina, I would go back to Glasson, but without skilled help I really couldn't see how I was going to get to Man, and even if I did, what would I do then? My prospects were poor, my purpose pointless. My existence? Futile. I had seen in God and in Lucifer two polar examples of post-Event futility. Two people completely unbalanced: one at the self-indulgent end of delusion, the other desperately seeking redemption by ritual. There comes a point when survival is the only point to being alive, but traditionally survival held the hope of a return to comfortable normality amid the prospect of a happy future. Survival no longer held that promise. To survive simply meant things would get worse. I felt I wanted to join Luke's congregation. Pass the communion gun.

I didn't sleep well that night and what transpired was the strangest of all my experiences. I would not testify that it had happened at all were it not for the fact that by the end of the night I held in my hand the physical evidence of where I had been and what I had done. It began with a dream and I cannot discern where the dream ended and the waking began, and perhaps there was no division, perhaps I sleep walked, or walked through the hinterland between wakefulness and sleep, sensing both worlds in a super-imposed super-reality. Perhaps I have experienced the dream-state of the shaman? Maybe I have seen the mental moonscape of the mystic? If I have then they were not self-induced. I thought that I was taken there by Claire, but it is possible if I dare to think a cruelty of cruelties, that my imagined, dreamed, sensed, and deeply desired haunting by Claire may have been conjured by another. Another who is just as deeply loved and even more missed.

To begin with, it was definitely a dream and it presented me with a fairly normal re-working of the abnormal day's difficulties. I was back in the Minster and Luke was both writing and reading his gospel. His zombie congregation were responding with the ritualised enthusiasm of those under the duress of losing their afterlife. Then the service was over and I collected their hymnbooks. Their volumes were identical, as you would expect, but rather more battered than a good vicar would tolerate, and they looked to have been water damaged and some pages were melded together, and on the cover, no crucifix, but instead a curious but simple design of a vertical ellipse cut by a straight line close to the top end. They were lemon-mustard in colour, identical to another volume I had held a few weeks previously and, of course, they bore the same embossed title: The Bosun's Tale. I returned the books to their rightful place of storage and that was in the Harris Library, but they refused to reside on the fiction shelves, falling off each time I put them on. I worked harder and faster until my labours became frantic and I became so frustrated that I put them instead under the label for science. At that point I remember sitting up in my barge bed, sheathed in sweat, and only then did I fully realise just how much effort I had exerted trying to place them under fiction, and how the success of cataloguing them under natural philosophy had opened a portal from dream to consciousness. I think. For what happened next, really happened. It must have. All was quiet. If there is no wind, all is quiet, deathly quiet, and why not? Everything is dead. Only the wind lives, and the world itself, that turns, spinning, as if trying to shake off its dead skin.

Someone was on deck. I cannot tell you how I knew, I just knew. I sweated again. There was someone on deck. There was a presence beyond my bolted cabin door. I got out of bed, dried myself with a towel and got dressed, then, like a reluctant but diligent schoolboy, put on my shoes and sat on my bed waiting for the command, or the bell. The person was no longer on deck. She was on the towpath. I just knew. So I went on deck. She was no longer on the towpath, at least not by the boat, but was further along, just out of sight. I followed. We walked the dead midnight streets. I never saw my guide, but always knew her to be there, just ahead, just round the next corner, just out of sight but just within earshot, and I knew that pace, I knew the sound of her feet, and every time I thought I had lost my way I tasted her scent in the molecules of the dry dead air of the dry dead night. We went, of course, to the Harris library and she led me, invisibly, to the fiction shelves and my hand rose involuntarily to the spines of novels and their Dewey decimal classification labels. My mind was in my index finger now leading me along the Sci-fi shelves speeding and then slowing as it found the three letter vertebrae GER. And then there was a gap, an absence, a void, a grey hole where a whole imagined universe could have been, and a little like Holmes but more like Watson, I worked out what was missing. This was the place where The Bosun's Boson should have been, but it wasn't there. I came to my senses and was about to leave, but her scent was too strong and it wouldn't let me go. There was something that I wasn't seeing and it was more than a gap, and then there was a draught, and there was nothing strange about that, for this was an old library and there were draughts, but there had been no draughts that night until then. The draught made a sound. It was crisp and brittle but brief and small. On the floor, a few feet to my left was a fragment of paper caught against the footing of the bookshelves, and my eye caught sight of it as it moved once, like the wing of an almost dead moth. I picked it up. It was a page from The Bosun's Tale, the page on which the library's loan record insert was pasted. There were the dates on which it had been due to be returned when it had been borrowed. There were fourteen stamps of ink in a disorderly stack of one and a half columns. Ironically the final date was three days after the Event. It had been returned in good time. But who had torn this page out? And why would they do that. The fact that it was still there suggested it had been done since the Event. The scent that had led me and kept me there was stronger than ever now, as if it was telling me to think more. The only thought I had was of Nathan. I had always presumed that he had brought his copy from the States, but perhaps he had found it here during his exile from Camp Q? It must have been gold dust to him.

I looked at the first date stamp. It was almost eight years ago. Claire might have read this book. So might Teresa.

I absorbed the momentousness of my night walk and tried to understand why I had been brought there at that time, and also expecting that now I might be released, but the scented and unseen presence still held me in an overwhelming sense of benevolent threat. I tested it by trying to leave, but an unseen intimidation was so strong that a sweat of fear returned. I wandered the library, trying to find and follow a path of no resistance despite a dearth of clues, but ultimately I arrived at the issues desk, where close by there stood a display and at once I knew why I had been brought. The display was headed "Recent Acquisitions" and there not far above the floor a new novel with a dust-cover that sported only the newest of dust, but through the new dust and the cellophane sleeve burned a subtitle more poignant than that of any classic. The book was called The Sea of Troubles. The subtitle described it as a sequel to The Bosun's Tale.

I do not remember my journey back to my boat, but it seems that as soon as I removed the sequel from the display stand I was free to go. I do not remember sitting upon my bed and reading the first three chapters as the dawn eased in, but I awoke hours later with my finger still inserted between pages forty-six and forty-seven. I read the rest of that book through that day and night. It charts the rebuilding of society by the elite who survived the celestial bombardment of the previous story, and the subsequent conflict of the mutants and the relatively pure who had, like us, been airborne or at places of very high altitude. In their scenario, which was much less comprehensive in its destruction than ours, communities had set up secure bases on islands. Most of the trouble they then encountered came from the sea as rival tribes came in search of wealth and health. I immediately wondered if Sparks had read this book and thus been inspired to withdraw to the Isle of Man, but from what I can glean, that idea may have also been instrumental to the plot of the final water-damaged chapters of The Bosun's Tale. He hadn't mentioned that, but neither had he mentioned another key element referred to in the sequel:

the idea of special births. The Sea of Troubles contains special children whose lives were paused and re-started in the wombs of those who had been on the fringes of the sub-atomic contamination. These special children had extraordinary intellectual and spiritual attributes for they had more than two parents. Stitched into the DNA of every one of their cells were coded strings from other worlds. This was explained in both volumes. Sparks must have seen it, unless it was in the damaged sections of his version, but even if that was so, Nathan knew and Nathan might have told him. Perhaps Thistle's protection was not the sole motive for Sparks' murder of Nathan? M. Gerard was the author not just of the book in my barge, but also of the beliefs in Sparks' head and the fates of Kirsty and her child.

In this volume, Gerard explains the cosmic background to his fiction, and for all I know, to our fact. The diagram on the cover, of an ellipse cut by a line, represents the orbit of the Earth intersecting with a stream of sub atomic particles. The stream cuts the orbit in two places with a gap of about three months between them. Three months. The pause in Kirsty's pregnancy lasted three months. Gerard says the line may not be a line at all but might also be an orbit of immense radius, or a super long string stretching between galaxies. The particles carried upon it vary and have different effects at different times. It all happens, he says, according to laws way beyond the most advanced theories of our natural philosophy and at a point where science and spirituality are one and the same.

I thought a great deal about M. Gerard. Michel Gerard. The blurb on the jacket of his second work tells little of him, other than he is French and grew up in the foothills of the Italian Alps, and in Montreal before returning to the south of his native land and then moving to Morocco. Inside, however, are two very telling sections, each of which sliced through me like an iced scimitar. The first is the dedication. I must surely have seen it when I started the novel, but I do not recall doing so, and if I did it made no impression upon me. The second, comes at the end of the volume. As the tale goes on the author's voice becomes more and more prominent and after the conclusion he pens a declaration that may or may not be intended as part of the fiction. He suggests that what he has written has no clear place in the librarian's listings. He feels that some humans may have been affected by a 'herald' attack of interstellar particles that contained foreknowledge of what was to follow, and that individuals may have responded by voicing or writing of what they mysteriously knew. Of course he counts himself among that number. He is part storyteller, he says, and part prophet. If I had read his work over a year ago I could, and would, have dismissed such a claim. That dismissal is not so easy now. It was not that section that seared my soul however, or the date subscribed beneath, September 2004, but the single line of address beneath: Tibet.

Having felt that thunderbolt, good sense surged in to throw aside any remote link he may have with my family, but I was acting involuntarily again, perhaps only on a memory of something I'd read the day before, and I flicked back to the start of the volume to focus with an unbelieving and acid stare on the simple line of dedication: To Teresa.

I am ashamed to admit that what followed was a period of self-neglect that deteriorated to a dangerous level, and my lowest point. I found a strength to ignore hunger, a phase which passed remarkably quickly and I began to survive on water and the fat in my pig-like physique. A headache became a leaden skull that I was destined to eternally carry. The days were warm but I grew cold and wore the coldness as a badge of condemnation with a shameful pride. Within days I would have died, but I live in a time when dying is not allowed. I went to bed one night with every intention of never getting up again, but I awoke the next morning, or the one after that, or the one after that to the salted scent of bacon frying. With some difficulty I sat up in my bunk and pushed aside the drawn curtain on my porthole to see a neat shining bottled gas grill merrily flicking blue angel flames beneath a frying pan, and next to it, expansive and resplendent in his angler's folding chair, a beaming portly man in a white fedora and suicide belt. God had come back. He smiled a Santa smile and bellowed "Morning Dan!" or was it "Morning Man?" I blinked crustily. He said, "I'd offer you a bacon butty but you are one of my chosen people and it would be sacrilege."

"And make you sick," said a softer, warmer, deeper, life giving voice, much closer. Yasmin was on board. "We'll try a touch of soup, shall we?"

More days were lost as I fumbled back to health and strength. God and the midwife stayed with me and nursed my body and soul. God slept in his helicopter which was parked on the park by the sign I had dug for him, Yasmin slept on the Nora. Her own vessel, the Cordelia was tied up in Preston Marina on the docks by the Ribble. God had found her before he found me. At that point she had sailed far beyond the Ribble and was navigating the Cheshire ring but there were ominous clouds on the southern horizon. As God explained, "A country the size of Wales is on fire."

"Which country?" I asked.

"Wales," he said.

From the first moment of the Event, fire has been our constant foe and now its army is fully organised and on the march. Our world is tinder. A spark in southern Wales has razed the whole country from the coast to the highest heather. God's heaven burned like hell and he was forced to take to the clouds. He spotted the Cordelia on the move, landed hoping to find me, and warned Yasmin of the danger ahead, after all Wales is joined to England and the prevailing south westerly would drive the demon flames to Cheshire. Such was the ferocity of the firestorm that canal water would not protect her and her only sensible choice was to retreat northwards again. She sailed, he flew ahead and he found me first and evidently he tended me within the days of my deepest self-deprivation, but I have no recollection of that. He gave me water and let me sleep and ferried Yasmin to and fro from her vessel as she worked her way back to the Ribble. God and I discussed his earlier visit to meet with Lucifer at the Minster but we each skimmed over the detail. We were sure that at the point I had not carved my sign on the park, and I did not broach the Meat Loaf angle with him. As far as I am concerned he has brought me back from the dead and so he is still God. I might have preferred to slip away however and be once again in the arms of Claire, but hey, he's God and so can rise above goodness. Despite his girth, he doesn't look well. He has a new companion, a silver hip flask that he says contains milk and honey, but it's neither of those things, and I don't think it's alcohol either, but what ever it is it helps him to endure his personal eternity.

So here we are. I'm back to strength. I have company. I am a little clearer with respect to what has happened, but perplexed and intrigued by the prophet who might just have something to do with my Tibetan exile daughter and what he knew in advance, and by what might be special about the child who is fifty miles across the sea from me with her young mother. Kirsty, I'm sure, will be deeply unhappy. I have my health. We have a helicopter. I think we'd better attempt a rescue.

26th April 2006.

God knew exactly where Sparks and his entourage were encamped. He'd been and looked long before I came round from my starvation slumber. Yasmin told him where the Erato had been bound and he'd found her and then found the only sign of life on the entire Isle. Furthermore he knew the place. It belonged to a record producer from the seventies. He'd stayed there as a guest. I wondered if Meat Loaf had been the actual guest, or did God work for an executive air taxi company? I didn't pursue my suspicion. I did press him on the absence of life though. The Isle of Man had an airport very well situated for aircraft not able to get in to Liverpool, Blackpool, Manchester, Belfast and even Glasgow. It seemed unlikely that there were no survivors there unless they'd survived the catastrophe but failed to survive the aftermath.

It was not possible for God to determine how many were ensconced in the luxury property as they weren't exactly keen to come out and be counted, and he wisely decided not to linger. It didn't matter. Only God and I would be flying over on our mission and we made a pathetic Special Forces unit. Despite my recent starvation diet I was still portly fifty-something and God was an overweight sixty-something. Yasmin called us the SAS: Sweat and Sag. Subterfuge and sabotage were out of the question our only hope was confrontation and negotiation, for we had two things that Sparks might covet: God's helicopter and the Sea of Troubles. Furthermore we had the way of destroying both: God's suicide jacket. Our mission seemed foolish, but we were determined to try. I must acknowledge that much of the impetus came from God. I wanted to take more time. Now that I knew of Kirsty's circumstances I thought it unlikely that they would change in the short term, and while I was less than happy about the company she was keeping, I considered that Sparks would not want to do anything to endanger the care of her baby. I argued that we should do more reconnaissance. The island was big enough for us to approach and land unseen and for me at least to take a closer look at things from the ground, but God talked me out of my Boy's Own mentality and back to reality. All we could do is go over there and talk. Nothing else was realistic. In addition to that God was looking less and less well. His sharp breaths occurred more frequently and his grimaces lasted longer. His face looked less robust, his beard more fierce. He started to use expressions like "eternity beckons" and "apocalypse imminent" whilst looking me solidly through watery eyes underpinned by wry smiles. I said we should delay whilst I found firearms but he had the sense to make me realise that the only real threat we could pose would be via his belt.

"If we land upwind and stay by the copter one nine volt battery could take out the entire island," he said.

"And you and me," I said.

"Eternity beckons," he said. "Doesn't bother God. How about you?"

I had a memory of Claire and an array of doors. I smiled and shook my head.

As we approached the Isle of Man it rose out of the sea like a cuttlefish bone. It's pallor of death matched that of England, but if anything, it was whiter than the grey and unpleasant land we had left behind. "Tinder dry," said God, just before a scary moment when he suddenly bent forward in his straps, his teeth cramped together, and his eyes screwed close. The helicopter pitched slowly but sickeningly, but he and it recovered and without comment from either of us we flew on. We landed on the lawn upwind of the whitewashed villa overlooking the east coast about mid way between Douglas and Castletown. Sparks came out to meet us flanked by two muscular t-shirts with rifles. One I recognised from the altercation we had in Glasson Dock, the other was Tye from Camp Q. I asked him how his shoulder was. He said they'd prized the bullet out and he'd put it in the gun he was holding. His witticism wasn't logical or funny but I wasn't in a position to not laugh so I threw him a corporate snigger. Sparks advanced on us with a forced smile and extended hand. I signalled him to keep his distance and introduced God and his long life death battery trigger. We roughly outlined the consequences of God completing his circuit. It would be goodnight Vienna for those of us in close proximity, and then the copter's fuel tanks would ignite the crisp garden kindling and commence the cremation of Man. We told them about Wales. Sparks tried to avoid an action movie cliché but failed when he said he had men everywhere with weapons trained on us. I said I didn't doubt it, but I held an additional trigger linked to God's belt and even if we both received the ultimate bullet one of us would ensure we took the copter with us before we expired. This was a lie, we had rigged up another trigger on the end of a long thin cable, but it was entirely benign. I wasn't prepared to kill God. It looked impressive and that was all that mattered.

Kirsty emerged from the house.

"Hello Kirsty," I said.

"Hello Dan."

She wore a bright yellow t-shirt and new jeans and new trainers. She looked well. She looked better than I had ever seen her look before.

Sparks held a thoughtful smile. "What is it you're after Dan? New fuse box?"

I said. "Brought you a present." I held up the Sea of Troubles and explained what it was. Sparks' expression was in place too rapidly for him to bluff indifference.

"How thoughtful."

"Present is probably not the best choice of word. You know how these things work Steve. It's merchandise. Something to barter."

"I think your price will be too high."

"Pity. Knowledge is power. The knowledge in here is . . . mind blowing."

"Well, you keep it. If you've got a copy, it shouldn't take us long to find one."

"Perhaps not. But what about the third part of the trilogy?" This was not complete elaboration on my part. The final part of the trilogy entitled Ocean Queen was promised in the volume I held. "Gerard is at his most prophetic. You'd be surprised at what we can expect to happen next, and how we should prepare for it." I let him see me look at Kirsty before I added, "How we should prepare the golden children."

Sparks doubted me. "We could find that too."

"Doubtful. It's not in print. Not published in time. But I have a proof copy." A lie.

"Show me."

I pointed towards England. "It's over there."

He looked at the sea, then at me. "Why should you have a proof copy?"

"Gerard is, or was, in Tibet. So is my daughter. This book is dedicated to her." I held The Sea of Troubles open on the relevant page, not that he could read it at the distance he was from me. "Teresa sent the third book to her mother, my wife."

He dwelt on that then said, "We burned your house."

"We?"

"Kirsty and me."

I let his words wound me for a moment. "Teresa sent the book to my wife at work. At the university. I doubt there's another one this side of Istanbul."

He shrugged. "I've got the child. I don't need the book."

I shrugged. "Fair enough. Except the book tells you what you need to do with the child."

He thought about this. "Then you can tell me." He glanced at Tye who lowered his aim towards my legs. "Couldn't you."

"I thought you might say that. So I only read the introduction."

He fired a snigger, and then went significantly silent. "So what's the deal?"

"Kirsty for the books."

"What use are the books if I haven't got the baby?"

"Who said anything about the baby?"

"You don't want the baby?"

Kirsty stepped forwards her voice sharp as any shipyard steelworker, her Scottish accent hard as a steam hammer. "So not only am I to be negotiated over but . . ."

Sparks raised his hand to silence her. He said to me, "Mother stays with child."

I shrugged my shoulders. "Then book stays in England. God knows where." I slipped a choirboy grin in God's direction then cancelled it and turned back to Sparks. "You might find another copy in Tibet."

The westerly breeze caught the electrician's ringlets and for a moment he could have been the principal in a rock opera. He said, "How would this work?"

"We fly Kirsty and you, or one of your . . . associates . . . to England and I give you the book. God will fly you back, or your water taxi can come for you. Your choice."

"The child stays here."

"I'm sure Tye's as good with a baby's bottle as he is with a gun barrel."

Sparks considered. I heard God draw a sharp breath, but I disciplined myself not to draw attention to it. Sparks nodded. "All right."

"Wait a tiny fucking minute," said Kirsty. "I'm not going anywhere." She came forward. No one stopped her. She stood six feet from me. Gorgeous as ever and fiery-eyed, she spoke forcefully but calmly. "Go back Dan, and take your god with you."

"Is this what you want?" I asked, scanning the backdrop behind her.

"As a matter of fact it is."

I searched for insincerity in her face but found none. Over her shoulder were three young men and a luxury villa with solar panels and a wind turbine. "Are you sure?"

"Yes Dan, I'm sure. Look, I'm really grateful for . . . well for what you did. But the baby's born now . . ."

"Have you any idea how special that child . . ."

"It's my child," she spat. "No one, no one needs to tell me how special she is. She is my child. She has a future. I have a future. This is the best place for it."

There was a golden light in her skin that I had not seen before. Motherhood and the Isle of Man were agreeing with her. I loved her, but the love was transmuting. "Okay," I said, and turned towards angelic rotor blades.

"Get on board," said Sparks and I swung back to see him clutching her arm.

"I'm not fucking going," she said, trying and failing to get free.

"We both are," said Sparks and he started frog-marching her towards the helicopter.

Tye objected. "Sparks!"

"Bring me the Springfield," he yelled.

"No weapons," said God.

"No weapons," said I.

Sparks paused for a moment then continued the struggle towards us.

"No woman," said Kirsty and broke free.

Sparks turned to me with addiction in his eyes. "Just me?" he asked.

I shook my head. "No woman no fly," I said. God chuckled then caught his breath. "After all, she's cabin crew."

"I want that book," said Sparks.

"I thought you might." There was desperation in his voice, so I toyed with the dummy suicide trigger just to keep things in perspective. "Take it from me; you'll not be able to put it down. And as for part three . . ." I peered into the blue between the clouds. "Beyond belief."

Sparks didn't touch Kirsty but his voice found grand prix grip. "Kirsty, please! For the child. The child is so . . ."

"I know!" she said. "So important, so precious, so powerful . . . so mine!"

"We have to get this book."

"It's fiction!" she spat.

"Yes," said Sparks. "But it's gods' fiction."

"Excuse me," said God.

"The fiction of the gods," clarified Sparks. "Whoever and wherever they be. Their message, their story, sent to you and me. And we have their child."

"She's my child!" screamed Kirsty.

"Look, you can think what you like, but one day she will prove the prophecy to be right or wrong. Only she can do that."

Kirsty gave one of her resigned sighs and I watched the sea change in her stance and face. "I'll get her," she said.

"No!" said Sparks with venom. Tye and the sailor with the rifle twitched trigger fingers like synchronised slaughtermen. "The child must stay here."

Kirsty was stunned and then puzzled and looked to me for clarification. "That's fine," I said. "Start her up, God. Let's ascend."

Sparks gave a few mundane orders to his crew as God went through the preliminaries, meanwhile I tried to put Kirsty at ease and told her that I would abide by her wishes, just as long as her decision was made without duress and on neutral ground. She didn't seem convinced. God was sweating profusely, and he stepped out of his seat to strap Kirsty and Sparks in the rear of the cabin, taking too much trouble for my liking. Then doors were secured and we rose above the bemused expressions of those on the ground. As we climbed a car stopped on the road beneath us and several people emerged including a couple of young women. The men were too small for me to identify but I suspected they were part of Spark's entourage. One produced a rifle but thankfully decided not to use it. They stared in awe and wonder. So did I, but without the awe.

We flew unsteadily from the start and I threw concerned stares in God's direction. He didn't look at all well. He'd given me a set of headphones but hadn't afforded the same luxury to our backseat passengers. I could hear him clearly on the intercom but if we kept our voices low they couldn't determine what we said.

"You all right God?"

"Eternity beckons. Apocalypse very imminent."

We only needed fifteen minutes. I bit my tongue but then noticed that uncharacteristically he hadn't topped off his headphones with his white fedora and a sweaty skull glistened beneath scarce straw threads of hair. "Can we do this?" I asked. He didn't reply. We flew on like a tipsy moth towards the sun. I had a double anxiety, once for my immediate safety, and secondly from desire to get Kirsty to England. I needed to talk to her, to say things that could not be said on the tinder lawn of her island prison. I had to tell her what Michel Gerard said about her child. I wanted to rehearse that conversation but instead I scrutinised the movement of our craft and the grip of my pilot on the controls of the copter. Man was behind us, the water was beneath. God's left leg suddenly stiffened and we yawed violently. I thought he must be avoiding something, but there was nothing to avoid. He'd locked himself rigid in some kind of seizure of pain. Sparks cried out. Kirsty screamed. I gripped my seat. God gained control, and blinked sweat from his eyes. He shook his head and put the aircraft into a steady turn. Sparks was shouting something, but we weren't listening. God located the isle we had just left and set course for it. "Eschaton," he said over the intercom.

"What?"

"The four final things," he said. "Two are getting away. To live another day."

"What?"

"Apocalypse now," he said. "Sorry. Can't make Blighty." He looked pale, his facial veins became a purple delta. "When we touch earth, grab the girl. Run like hell. Run from hell. I'll make us a little patch of hell."

I felt my mind began to accelerate. We were losing altitude. Kirsty yelled something. Sparks shouted, "Get us down! Get us down."

The copter jolted, skidded across sky, putting my stomach just beneath my scalp. More shouts. God's eyes were closed. He looked to be at peace. I prodded and clawed at his arm. The copter's engine raced and we climbed. God's eyes opened and a touch of colour returned to his skin, it was a parchment yellow. We were over land but he did not go straight down. "Downwind," he said, "downwind."

"We are downwind," I said not knowing why or what I was saying, but implying with completely inappropriate subtlety that I just wanted to land.

"More west, more west," he said.

"We are west."

He looked at me and smiled. "Get ready to grab the girl. Get her out. Fast as you can."

"Fast as I can," I confirmed like some robotic co-pilot.

He smiled again. "Fast as you can," he said. He looked beyond pain now, his face filled with life lived and a vision of afterlife offered. For a moment he held my eyes and I felt he was willing me to say something particular. A phrase flashed into my mind and I considered saying it, but didn't. He chuckled and said it for me. "Like a bat out of hell."

My eyes laughed with his. "You took the words right out of my mouth."

Moments later we hit the ground hard. "Out, out, out!" commanded God.

I was out, I wrenched the cabin door open, releasing Kirsty's belt whilst Sparks was struggling with his. I pulled Kirsty clear, and as we rolled on brittle heather the helicopter leaped skywards with Sparks still on board. It swept away from us but flew for only half a minute before exploding in a ball of apocalyptic flame that seared in all directions but especially earthwards as tongues of dragon breath sought the deliciously inflammable foliage of Man.

"We've got to get a boat," I said. "We've got to get to England."

The horizon was a belt of orange flame and grey and black smoke. It was barely ten minutes after the explosion. The combination of a strengthening westerly sea breeze and the atrophied vegetation was every bit as volatile as I had anticipated. The flames radiated across the island busily cooking up a firestorm that would surely not stop until it reached the northern shore, and half of Man would be seared back to bare earth. The villa could not survive, and thanks to God's dying navigation it was merely minutes from being consumed.

"My baby!" breathed Kirsty, and then with throat-tearing anguish, "My baby!"

A shameful concept demanded a place in my mind. The death of the child might be a desirable outcome. I struggled to find the words to voice that prospect, but of course I could not. I grabbed her wrist. "Kirsty. We get your baby, then we sail to England."

"Yes," she said. "Yes." It was not an agreement. It was a desperate plea for help. We scrambled towards the nearest road and ran off in pursuit of the flames.

As things turned out we came upon the car that we had seen as we took off. It was still on the same stretch of road, engine running, and with doors flung open but with no one on board or in sight. I can only imagine that the occupants watched our erratic flight, then saw the explosion and ran towards it, then found themselves cut off from the road by the spreading flames and so headed for the villa. If we were to attempt to rescue the child then the only option was to drive straight into the curtain of fire, even though we had no way of knowing how thick it was. We closed all the windows and I put my foot down convinced I was following God and Sparks into certain oblivion. We were in the heat for no more than ten seconds, the stench was terrible, and there was a ripping sound which I think was the rubber of our tyres trying to adhere to the molten tarmac, then we were bouncing off stone walls in a cloud of swirling smoke. It cleared a little and with Kirsty's aid we swerved and jostled our way to the villa. The wind was up now, perhaps the effect of the fire itself generating a forward draught, but it worked to our advantage, spreading gritty, eye-stinging smog ahead of us. I roared into the drive. There was no one in sight.

"This has to be a snatch and run," I said.

"Turn the car round," she said and leaped out.

I did as she had instructed as she disappeared into the villa. Seconds passed disguised as hours. I waited, revving the engine. I was going to have to go in after her, I knew I was. A figure appeared from the door, indistinct through the deepening smoke, but clearly not Kirsty. I dipped down in my seat anticipating trouble, but none came and when I eased my head up, he'd gone, and then there was Kirsty pelting round the side of the house, a bundle in her arms. She skirted the bonnet of the car and fell into the passenger seat.

"Drive. Drive!" she demanded.

I slammed the stick into first gear as something cracked against the door over my right shoulder. I didn't look but slammed the accelerator pedal towards Australia and heard the gravel pebbledash the wheel arches as we lurched forwards. Another thud. Another. But we were moving, and then there was another figure, Tye I think, spreading himself on the drive ahead of us.

"Oh shit!" I thought, and I think I said it out loud, but by now I was in third gear and my accelerator leg was at double its natural extension and no part of my brain gave permission to shorten it. We hit him with a sickening thump. I expected him to bounce against the windscreen but instead we felt a nauseous triple jolt as we bounced over him, then it was joyous gravel again and I clipped the gate post as we galloped into freedom.

"North!" I yelled. "We can't go back though that fucking furnace."

We drove to Douglas. No one followed.

I got my first glimpse of the baby. She is abnormally normal. I cannot put it any other way. She looks like most other babies, but there is a slight rind-like texture to her skin. There is still a residue of jaundice in her colour. She has very fine, very blonde hair. Her eyes are almond in shape and in iris colour, and they signal secure, unchallengeable arrogance.

We stole a boat. A cabin cruiser. It was not difficult. The corpse of the captain was still on board. Kirsty said he breathed when we moved him, but I remembered shifting the stadium crowd and the gasps and noises they made. We put him in the harbour, and his limbs softly twitched as if he was trying to swim. Dead fish moved out of his way and one of them spiralled off as if he too suddenly remembered swimming. We powered our way out of Douglas harbour as, away to our right, the cloud of cloud-bound ash that had been the shrubbery and architecture of the island made new structures in the sky. Navigation wasn't difficult, for as long as I kept the prow on the eastern side of north or south we were bound to hit the mainland sooner or later. I confidently aimed towards Cumbria, the sea was calm and we made steady progress.

Then, after fifty minutes and when every horizon was water, we ran out of fuel.

*

Laughter is a lonely business. Everyone loves to laugh but no one loves a comic. They say they do, but what they love is the laughter. The reason that everyone loves laughter is because laughter is love. It is the love of your life because it is the love of life.

Laughing is kissing bliss.

I have been a purveyor of laughter but even if everything was to return to normal I would never take money in return for laughter again. All entertainers are whores. You pay for the pleasure we provide. Comedians are the worst kind of whore, for we prostitute true love. From now on, from me, it's free.

We all like to laugh and we all like to make other people laugh. You can laugh anywhere, any time. People sometimes say there's nothing to laugh about. That's an old excuse. Adam used it.

Then look what happened.

*

Nineteen: Lemon.

27th April 2006.

We drifted, nudged by the swell and pushed by the strengthening wind.

"Don't worry," I said. "It's a westerly. We'll hit England eventually. Or Scotland." I didn't mention tides and currents. I secured the cabin door and sat in the seat of the once proud, now drowned, weekend captain. I toyed with the wheel, but of course it had no effect. She sat on the bench-seat to my left. The baby cried. Kirsty fed it.

"What is she called?"

"All sorts of things. She hasn't got a name."

"Why not?"

"Because I haven't given her one. It's kind of important isn't it?"

"March 11th?"

"Scary isn't it?"

"Exactly one year after conception?"

Kirsty nodded. The boat jostled and the child lost her purchase on the nipple and wriggled and snuggled in protest. Kirsty guided her breast back into place and the hungry suckling continued.

"Can you be sure?"

She looked at me with a caged glare. "I'll check for you just as soon as I can find my diary."

I could have escalated the uncomfortable atmosphere but couldn't see the point. Instead I let the lap of sea provide percussion and tried to adjust my body rhythm to the irregular sway as we bounced on the waves. We sulked out the silence, then Kirsty said, "I'll need to change her."

I searched the cabin compartments and found a first aid kit. Kirsty used that to improvise a new nappy. I helped to hold the baby steady on the seat. Her skin has a strange texture. It is smooth and warm, but doesn't look so. It is peach-like but a touch tougher and looks ever so slightly reptilian, though it is not in any way scaly. I can only revert back to the word rind, as on a citrus fruit, but much more delicate and subtle and soft. Her eyes have such power. In certain light they flash golden, though mostly are a soft creamy very pale brown, but there is a fight behind them. When she looks at you it is as if she knows everything about you.

It began to rain.

"Great!" said Kirsty.

"Don't worry," I said. "We are waterproof."

There were some emergency food packs next to the first aid kit. We nibbled on biscuits and shared an energy drink. I held the baby for a while and made grandfatherly gurgling noises. She looked back at me as if she'd just read the Odyssey. Gradually as our situation worsened, Kirsty softened. We discussed the birth.

"I'm glad you came through it all right."

"Yasmin was wonderful."

"She's waiting for us."

"She'll have a long wait."

The boat bobbled.

"How did Steve treat you?"

"He wasn't such a bad person."

"He killed Thistle."

"We'll never know that for sure. Anyway I killed Clita."

"Why?"

"That's the most stupid word ever invented. There's no such thing as why. People just do, that's all. You don't stop and think 'why am I doing this?', you just do it." She looked piercingly at the child in my arms. "She made me. She rules me."

"Do you mean that?"

"Do you mean what you believe?"

An eccentric wave dropped the boat and Kirsty and I bumped together.

I breathed deeply. "I've given up believing anything and everything. I just do now. I just do what has to be done."

Kirsty smiled. "Me too."

"You had to do some pretty extreme things."

We rose, we fell.

"Look," she said, "when we first met I was screwed. Completely screwed. Screwed in every way you could imagine. Not only was I walking through a dead world, I had a child inside me. The more I realised how bad things were, the more desperate I got. You were the first person I met that . . . well, I don't know, you just felt safe. People were losing it and you kept calm. You talked sense. So I latched on to you, or got you to latch on to me. It felt the right thing to do. And it was. I was so glad you came with us and I ended up being with you. After a while I began to doubt the pregnancy test. I took another. That was positive too. But nothing else changed. You can imagine what it was like. Maybe I was, maybe I wasn't. If I wasn't I wanted to stay that way, and you were the only man I felt I could trust. So I wanted to stay with you even more. Did I love you? Yeah – course I did."

I wanted to ask a supplementary question, but the boat nudged me away from it. Kirsty went on.

"And then, gradually but suddenly, I knew the baby was still there. There would be little signs. I felt sick, then I didn't. My waistline changed. Each realisation hit like an electric shock, but nothing was definite, so I was able to deny it. I might have been sick for all kinds of reasons. And with all that pre-packed stuff, why shouldn't I put weight on? So there was ages when I was and I wasn't. And that was very hard. But eventually, at Clitheroe, I knew for sure. I also knew it was controlling me, and had been for ages. It would never have been my idea to burn your house down. It was the child, it was Lemon, inside me, making me. I thought it was me who was desperate to make you join us, to be with me. But it wasn't me, it was she. She wanted you with us. She knew that you were good for her too. You'd see her safely born. But she knew that even more when Steve came and found us again. Then she wanted to be with him, though I still wanted to be with you. But she was in charge. She ruled." There was acid in Kirsty's eyes. "Once I knew for sure that she was there, and I looked back and saw the things I'd done, then I knew that she'd not only occupied my body, but also my mind. I saw what power this child had over me. That's why I tried to kill us."

"Us."

"Lemon and me."

"And Thistle and me."

Kirsty stared into her own history of that night. Her inner focus found what she was looking for before her voice did. "I didn't want you to rescue me. You were both asleep. I spread the petrol around outside. I came inside and pushed a match through the loo window, before joining you in the bedroom. I tried to breathe the smoke, the monoxide, before the heat came, but something woke you, woke Thistle. Must have been the sound of the fire, or something."

"Or something."

"She sees things. When Steve took me to Yasmin, then of course I was glad, but not just me, she, she was glad too. I felt her gladness. I clamped on to the Cordelia like a limpet shell, but when the birth was done and we moved boats to go to the Isle of Man somehow it felt more than right, it felt necessary. I was compelled. She compelled me. She knew the island would be the safest place for her. She wanted the move and when we were there she wanted to stay, and she made me want to stay too. She was no longer inside me, but she still compelled me. She still does. She can't speak, but she tells me what she wants. She knows what she needs and what she doesn't. She always has. She got me to get rid of Clita, because that made sure you came to me and she wanted you with me as long as you were useful to her."

I questioned Kirsty with a stare.

"Don't look at me like that Dan. I'm not making this up. She has such power over me."

I rode the smile for a wave, then rode its memory for three more, then I let the sea fill the soundscape for as long as I could then did what had to be done, which was to say what had to be said. "You're scared of her aren't you, Kirsty?"

"I think I always will be."

"Always?"

"Yes."

The sea nudged me like a dumb prompter, knowing what must be said, and knowing that I was the only person who could say it. So I spoke. "You could just slip her over the side. Let the sea take her."

I braced myself for one of Kirsty's Braveheart explosions, but she sat listening to the sea and hearing me, and after four waves said, "I've just fed her."

Rain lashed with new venom. I looked out at the gathering storm and said, "Well maybe that's where all three of us will end up."

Kirsty scanned the spray and rain as it splattered the glass of the windscreen. "She'll save us," she said. "You just wait. She'll save us. She'll save herself."

The most remarkable thing was not that less than an hour later a boat appeared on the horizon, or that she saw us and changed course for us even before I had fumbled a distress flare into the sky, or that she was crewed by the party from Caton embarking on their Golden Fleece mission, or that she was captained by the retired Chemistry teacher George White, or that despite the ever-worsening conditions they took the three of us easily on board, no, the most remarkable thing was the name of the vessel emblazoned on her prow: the Ocean Queen.

"Lancaster has some very good bookshops," said George, resplendent in his cabin. "Sparks drip fed what he knew about The Bosun's Tale, though he never admitted to having a copy. I went in search of it and lo, found the sequel." He waved his copy of the Sea of Troubles. For a burning instant, I lusted for it, as mine had been incinerated in God's apocalyptic chopper. "We're off in search of the sequel to that, the third part of the trilogy. Hence the name of our ship."

"To Tibet?" I asked.

"To Tibet."

The child in Kirsty's arms squawked. Mother comforted daughter by slipping a finger between the child's gums. The ship, a fine twin-masted yacht rolled but with much more finesse than the cabin cruiser we had abandoned. George grinned and said, "Do you want to come?"

"Very much," I said, and to my delight Kirsty snapped a stare in my direction. "But I can't. I've a child to think about."

"Ah yes," said George and he gazed upon the infant as a magus might.

Needless to say the baby had caused a great deal of interest on board. Everyone could see that she was not quite delightful and her slightly unusual appearance was sufficiently blatant to provoke guarded but cutting comments. "Novel complexion." "Touch of jaundice?" "Lovely hair." "Wonderful eyes."

The vessel was crewed by some of the muscular males I knew well from the fencing teams at Caton, but there were also experienced sailors that I did not recognise, from Kendal and from Windermere. There were twelve on board in total, including three women, two from Caton, one from Windermere. They in particular fussed round the mother and child, especially Lara who Kirsty knew from the laundry team. Geoff had the good sense to secure us in his cabin. He also immediately changed course. They had sailed, not from Lancaster as I presumed, but from Barrow. They were initially heading for the Isle of Man and were then planning to set foot in Ireland and then France, Spain, Portugal and so on, replenishing supplies as they went. They thought they might mount an expedition to Alpine villages to test George's altitude theory, but their ultimate aim was the high plains of Tibet.

"Monsieur Gerard is the prophet, and that's where he went. We're going to look for him."

"Beware false prophets," I said.

"How can you doubt him? He's got so much right."

"Doesn't make him prophetic, just inspired."

"Prophecy is not foretelling the future but seeing the truth," said George. "So much of what he wrote has come true."

"Age of reason?" I said in reference to George's group at Caton. "How could he have known?"

"I don't know. But he did. Someone or something must have told him."

"That sounds less like science and more like superstition."

"And what else is science, but demystified superstition? I want to meet him. You're a good man, Dan. Come with us."

"You didn't treat me like a good man at Caton."

George shifted uncomfortably. "Sparks held a lot of sway with some people, and well, Kirtsy is a lovely young woman."

I smiled. Kirsty looked at her child. Then George said something remarkable. "You're not the father, are you?"

Kirsty did nothing.

I said, "What makes you say that?"

"I don't know. But something does. And she doesn't look anything like you."

"Or me," said Kirsty.

Although George seemed much less rational than he had been when I last knew him, he seemed much more reasonable. Towards the end of my time at Caton I felt that he and the whole community had turned against me, but he was especially considerate on the Ocean Queen, and indeed all on board were warm, engaging and welcoming. George was not a seafaring man but he'd appointed his own bosun, Ken from Windermere, and as soon as we told him what had happened on the Isle of Man, George told Ken to avoid the place, and soon after that he instructed that we set an entirely different course. The sea was no place for a newborn baby, he said, especially this one.

The next day we sailed up the Ribble estuary. They launched a small inflatable with an outboard motor and put us ashore. Before we disembarked from the Ocean Queen, I gave George an envelope.

"If you meet a woman called Teresa, ask her what her childhood surname was and where she was born. Depending on her answer, you might like to give her this."

"I will," he said. I climbed down the rope ladder to join Kirsty, child and a sailor on the launch. George called after us. "Oh, and Thistle sends her love."

"What?" I said. But he refused to elaborate, and the outboard screamed into propulsion and pushed us for the shore.

The launch took us right up the Ribble and put us ashore in docklands. We made our way across the western fringes of the city to Ashton. We passed many cadavers on the way. Some of them had moved.

The corpses on the streets had become part of the architecture of the city, and just as how you get used to certain pavement furniture or billboard advertisements in certain location, so key junctions and landmarks had become associated with certain human bodies. The ones that had moved, had not moved very much. Perhaps an arm had shifted, or the torso was repositioned, not much more than that, so perhaps it was the effect of a particularly strong gust of wind or even some strange temperature-induced muscular contraction or something, but I am sure that movement had happened.

Yasmin was not around when we arrived at the Nora. She had said that whilst we were away she would probably return to the Cordelia. This frustrated me, because we'd been very close to the docks when we were put ashore and we could have looked for her then, but the thought hadn't occurred to me. My narrow boat was in good order, and I welcomed Kirsty aboard. She lingered on the aft deck, holding her child, and didn't come into the cabin. I wondered why.

"Come in," I said. I'll make a drink.

Still she stayed.

"Come in," I said.

"Have you seen this?" she said.

I rejoined her on the deck. "What?"

She was clutching one of the small plant pots under my improvised rooftop cloche. I swallowed hard. Blinked. Stared. It was a deception. Must be. Had to be. Wasn't. There, tiny but stately, minute in reality but mammoth in significance, was a green shoot.

"What is it?" she asked.

"I planted a pip," I said. I looked at the place from where she'd lifted the pot. "That one's a lemon pip. The compost is from the latrine in my garden."

"It's not a lemon pip any more," said Kirsty. "It's a lemon tree."

The child in her arms saw what her mother was holding and angled an unsteady head towards it. Kirsty put the pot to the baby's hand and tiny rind-patterned fawn fingers closed round the rim in reflex.

"There's no choice now. That's what we have to call you," said Kirsty. "Lemon."

And so the child was named.

Kirsty put the pot down and went inside. I repositioned it in line with its companions, examining each in turn. I found three more shoots. Two more were lemon and one was orange. I looked in the bag of fruit and nuts that I'd left next to the pots, but they seemed as dry and dead as ever, except for one lemon that I'd sliced open to extract pips. I looked closely at the surface of the cut flesh. It was dry, but there was a microscopic powder coating there. I could not be sure. It might just have been dry lemon flesh debris. Or it might have been mould.

1st May 2006

It was another two days before Yasmin returned. She brought her boat. In the meantime, Kirsty and I caught up with each other. I learned about her life on the Isle of Man, where a combination of the skills of Sparks' team and the quality of the property in which they were living meant that her life was by far the most comfortable she had known since the Event. They had solar and wind power and an oil-burning Aga. She had her own room in a spacious and luxurious villa. She had begun to cement friendships with some of her companions, though she admitted having reservations about others, including Steve, who she described as 'unpredictable'. She admitted that her relationship with her child was ambivalent. She felt a deep attachment as a mother, but also felt threatened. This baby was patently alien. The fear of childbirth was over. The dread of childhood was rising.

I filled her in on all that had happened to me in her absence, including my dreams. These conversations took most of a day and as I began to prepare a meal for us we slipped back towards the routine warmth we had known in the winter months. There was even a hug or two. It became clear, however, that something between us had irrevocably changed. We would always have the memory of a special bond, but that intensity of union would never return. In our renewed companionship I found a new loneliness.

The Nora was a considerable step down in comfort for Kirsty but we made sensible arrangements to adjust the living space. We each would have our own cabin. We did not speculate on what may have been the consequences to those she left behind on the Isle of Man. In this new future there is immediacy about the past. When it has happened, it is over. We move on quickly and without sentiment. Life in the present is too challenging to indulge in the luxury of living in the past. We were both buoyed by the sight of my sprouting crop. The infant Lemon tree had grown perceptibly by the second day, and a fifth plant appeared. The next morning brought an even more uplifting sight.

Lemon slept in Kirsty's bunk. I was watching her, studying her skin, observing her breathing whilst Kirsty stepped onto the park for some air. She came back swiftly. "Come and see this."

I followed her and she pointed at my message carved in the dead grass: GOD HELP ME. It was a lovely spring morning, with just a hint of rapidly evaporating frost everywhere, and at first I couldn't see anything that had changed. She squatted next to the initial G and pulled me down next to her. GOD was growing grass. In fact the whole message was peppered with a blanket of green spikes. I squeezed her hand and felt myself wanting to cry.

We danced around and began hunting for other growth, but the rest of the park seemed as dead as ever, and we began to think about divine intervention, until I spotted more signs where God's helicopter had disturbed the brittle carpet. "It's coming back," I said. "She's recovering! The Earth is getting better! " And we danced around kicking up the grey dust like some frantic ritual in honour of Jack in the Green, and then baby Lemon began to cry, so we returned to the Nora and celebrated with coffee for us, and breast milk for her. We got drunk on caffeine.

"I thought it was the shit," I said.

"What?"

"Harvest the latrines. I thought it was the bacteria we'd carried in our guts. That's what's in the plant pots: soil and shit. But it's happening everywhere."

"Not everywhere," she said.

"But it will. It's starting first where the soil's been cleared and the sun can get through."

"Thank god, thank god!" said Kirsty her accent kicking strongly, her eyes joyously wet, and with a tyrannosaurus smile.

"Thank God and his helicopter," I said, and then a new thought, or rather an older thought, brought us back down to earth. "This is what happens in the book."

"What book?"

"The Sea of Troubles. New growth happens. Another cosmic wave restarts things. Not just plants. Animals. People."

"What?"

"That's happening too." This was Yasmin's voice. She had stepped on board and was walking into the cabin. She'd brought her boat and quietly moored it along the canal from mine whilst we'd been raucously brewing coffee. Her face was heavy. She took a quick glance at the baby and then described what she'd encountered in the previous two days.

"I saw people trying to move. At first I was spooked out. But I saw it in animals too. A dead swallow, down by the docks, on the roof of one of the boats. The wind had blown it against the rail and I thought the wind was blowing it again, but there was no wind. It twitched, I watched it spasm, then it stopped and it hasn't moved since. And that's what happens to people. But some get further. They move limbs. They look. One old woman by the door of Morrison's tried to crawl. I went to her. She tried to speak. Sounds. No sense. Then she died. Died in my arms."

"Oh god!" said Kirsty.

"Is it happening everywhere?" I asked.

"No, no. Just here and there. I think it may have been happening for some time. Just that we haven't seen it till now."

"Oh god!" said Kirsty.

"Don't worry," said Yasmin, "They don't last long. Their bodies can't cope. They're too damaged."

"But what about their brains," I said, "Their brains have had no oxygen for a year."

Yasmin shrugged. "No bacteria either. No rotting."

I thought about the lemon on the roof above our heads. "I think bacteria might be back too."

"Could be, I suppose," said Yasmin. "There's a terrible smell down by the docks."

"Oh hell," said Kirsty.

"This is what happens in the book," I said.

"This is no book," said Yasmin. "This is us."

It is very hard not to believe that Michel Gerard is a true prophet. I am beginning to grasp how that might be the case, in fact Gerard himself offers the explanation. In The Sea of Troubles the Bosun's Tale becomes the boson tail as Gerard clarifies the nature of the cosmic stream that brought the pivotal disaster in his fiction. A river of subatomic particles sears through the universe, colliding with stars and planets at random. It passes right through whatever it hits and in ninety-nine per cent of cases has no effect, but sometimes it strikes a planet with life and then it acts as a fundamental parasite, immobilising its victims and planting the seeds of a new life. The tail is thin but light years long, and consists of different sections. The pioneer particles are what Gerard calls the Bosun's boson, but he suggests scientist might name them sterilisation bosons. They do not kill, for killing involves living, as dead material is consumed by bacteria and other living organisms, whereas the boson stops all life, suspends it, pauses it, freezes it. The planet becomes sterile. Some time later the latter part of the particle tail arrives, but this section contains another particle, what Gerard calls the fertilisation boson. This latter particle has two effects; it unlocks the previously paused material, and implants its own code in the host's atomic structure, changing its DNA. Not all life can be re-started. Some will have been irrevocably damaged by the natural climactic forces of the planet during its sterile period, but that loss is part of the boson tail's legacy, partially clearing the planet of rival species.

Gerard argues that by concentrating its effects at low level, the tail maximises the life potential of its passenger implants. A few specimens of a few species will escape the full effects of the first wave, and some of those will be pregnant. The low concentration of sterilisation bosons will slow the development of the unborn without noticeably affecting the parent. The fertilisation boson will then hijack the foetus and cause it to be born as a hybrid creature with attributes of two worlds. The crossbred children in Gerard's story have extraordinary powers, exotic knowledge and malevolent drives. They become the undisputed despotic rulers of their adopted world. It is the most pervasive and potent invasion that mankind has experienced. It arrives without warning, and there is no defence. Gerard does not imply there is an intelligent force behind it. The tail does not know what it is doing. It is simply a very advanced form of evolution, but he takes his theory to an extraordinary level by revising his assertion that the sterilisation boson is at the leading tip of the tail. He says that the vanguard is actually pure knowledge in the form of a wave of understanding carried in a subatomic code that affects the minds of some of the recipient species, provoking them to move to higher ground and await the arrival of the tail. They may even consciously or subconsciously welcome the invaders into their own wombs and worlds. Such benefactors would be rewarded by being associated with the new dominant species. That is why Gerard left Morocco and went to Tibet.

I'm sure all who read Michel Gerard's prophecy found it entertaining or absurd or both of those things. I find it to be neither.

And so our whole situation changed again. And once again it was better and worse. There was new growth, and that was the best news of all. Life had stopped, and now it had started again, but in life there was the death we used to know, things began to decay and suddenly our larder was even more depleted. Furthermore I soon developed new concerns about the new growth. Without insects how would things pollinate? But insects reappeared. They simply started again. Whether these were adult invertebrates that recovered, or pupae or eggs that had sat out the dead phase I simply don't know, but the same day that Yasmin returned, so did flies. I dug the soil, and in among the worm casts and still exoskeletons I found living beetles and a millipede. I could not accept that a human brain could function again after minutes, let alone months of no nutrition, but I have to accept that our presumption that brain death had universally occurred might have been wrong. Perhaps the whole world had simply been put on pause in a way that we are not destined to understand for another millennium?   Neither I nor Kirsty saw any humans returned to life at that time, but we did not doubt Yasmin's word, and within a day or so we began to detect obnoxious odours on the wind. It was evident that for a time life was going to become much more unpleasant.

I really didn't try too hard to understand how it had happened. For all I know the sub-atomic theory contained in Gerard's fiction might be completely wrong. With the world in the state that it now is, I cannot envisage any deep scientific research happening in the near future that will clarify things. All I can tell you is what I have lived through and what I have seen with my own eyes. Part of what I have seen, the most pertinent part to me, was not real at all, of course. I refer to the visions and dreams. Throughout this year I have spent a great deal of time reflecting on them. Where they just in my head or did they really occur? Did I actually have conversations with my dead family? Did the ghost of my wife appear to me? Was that apparition in my eye, my mind or in the space before me? Until now I have deliberately tried to avoid words like 'ghost' or 'spirit' because I do not think they are appropriate. I certainly encountered the essence of those people. Perhaps consciousness is a better word. Claire's consciousness and mine overlapped and interacted. Whether that was actual intercourse, or simply a mixture of memory and creativity on my part, I do not know, but it happened, and it helped. Most people would say that consciousness cannot live on outside of the brain, especially a brain that has died, but I remember a television programme where eminent scientists considered the opposite. Perhaps our consciousness is not in the brain at all? Or perhaps it exists beyond the sub-atomic boundaries and can move from the brain? If so, perhaps it could return to a brain that has been in hibernation? Maybe that was what Yasmin had seen in action?   That prospect deeply troubled me, for if Claire tried to return to her body, she would be unable to move, as I had buried her. And she now lay in soil that was no longer sterile.

The three of us have talked exhaustively. We have a plan. We have realised that the greatest of all of our enemies, and the one that has been most persistent in pursuing us, might provide our salvation. Fire. To be among so much that will slowly rot is not an appealing prospect, but if God was telling the truth and most of Wales was razed then all the cadavers in that country will have been incinerated, the vegetation will have been burned off and new growth will have a clean start. That, after all, used to be the way great expanses of farmland were managed. We will sail to Wales. The drawback will be that the fire will probably have devoured all the habitation and there will be no supplies of sealed food – something we will need for several months. So the plan is to take several barges of supplies with us and set up camp just over the burned border, wherever that may be. We will plant and try to grow new food. In the meantime we can embark on expeditions to top up our supplies. We're going to start our preparations tomorrow.

Through all that, of course, we'll have to nourish and educate our newest companion. I wonder what delights she holds in store for us? And because of what Yasmin has reported, I can't rid my mind of Claire's spirit and how it might have returned to her revived, but buried, body.

*

Twenty: Encore.

15th May 2006

I walked the mile to my back garden. It was night. We spent the rest of that day, the day of Yasmin's return, discussing and planning, but Claire remained at the forefront of my thoughts. I looked for her consciousness everywhere, in the skeletal trees, walking on the water of the canal, behind the windows of the houses on the other bank, and especially behind my eyelids. I wanted to talk to her and to ask her what to do. Each of my adult companions knew of my dreamed encounters with Claire, so of course I mentioned my fear that she might return to her buried body. They made reassuring noises, and Yasmin stressed that all she had observed were very short-lived attempts at resurrection, all of which resulted in a peaceful termination, but that did nothing to pacify my pain. I had imprisoned my wife and my two sons. That evening I sat with this laptop and brought my account up to date. That night as the women and the star-child slept, I walked home.

It was a clear night. It fell to a cool crispness barely on the damp side of frost. The sky was solid with stars, and every billion of them were keeping watch on me, and the babe on the boat. It was as if our barge was an ark, holding their treasured future. The moon was rising and looking back along the canal all was tinged with silver. Yasmin's boat had a golden sheen about it. That's where the child was. We would take both boats. It had been agreed. Kirsty and the child had moved out of mine and in with Yasmin. The stars knew. That's why they gave Yasmin's boat the golden glow. But the moon was rising and the moon was with me. The moon was silver and she gave me silver: silver paths to light my way, silver breath to exclaim my urgency and, silver skin in which to wrap my slender hope.

Once again I exhumed my lifeless wife. I dug slowly, religiously, using her favourite trowel, easing it into the ground and releasing it with tenderness, carrying the soil with reverence, piling it around in a sacred loop. When I reached her clothing I discarded the trowel and worked with my hands. I found her head and uncovered her face. I brushed all the earth from her and there she lay, in a Claire-shaped hollow with just me, the moon and half of the universe gazing upon her. I prayed. I prayed to the earth to give her back, I prayed to the moon to lift her up, I prayed to galaxies to give what only they could give. She lay, still and grey.

I brought water in bucket from the water butts she used to collect the rain that quenched her plants, and washed her face with my hands. I tried to kiss life back into those ten thousand kissed lips. She lay, still and white.

I washed her hands. I cleaned the soil from beneath her nails. I lifted her head and brushed her wet hair. She lay, still and cold.

I raised her from the ground. It was hard. It was awkward. She was heavy. I sat her in the summerhouse in her favourite garden chair, reclined back, facing the apple tree, where she could watch the birds. She lay, still.

I sat with her for a while.

Moon shadows moved, marking the passing of time. The whole garden was a moondial. When the shadow of the apex of our summerhouse touched the first stepping stone embedded in the lawn I said out loud, "Right. I'd better see to the boys."

I returned to the graves at the end of the garden. Which first? Paul. The youngest. Youngest first, as in all our family games. I took the trowel and began to break the soil over Paul's resting place.

Glass smashed.

I turned and there was Claire. Not spirit, but body. Body and soul. She was standing precariously, holding very unsteadily onto the door of the summer house that had swung so wildly open that a pane had cracked, fractured and fallen to the floor. The shards sparkled in the moonlight.

I was frozen, then I ran towards her, then I slowed, stopped a few feet from her. Her eyes were half open, the lids overwhelmingly heavy, her pupils searching for focus. Her breath was shallow and slow as if her lungs were learning to breathe. I moved the final few feet and caught her in my arms. I looped her arm round my shoulder and she gripped me with old woman claws. The pain was glorious. Gradually her breathing deepened, the breaths took longer, became more regular and her grip eased. She straightened and tried more steps. Our motion was staccato and awkward like some insect dance. We walked six yards towards our children's graves. She breathed in an acre of air.

"Leave them," she said.

"The boys?" I asked.

"Leave them," she said. She sucked another acre in. "They've moved on."

"Through the doors?"

She smiled, once for our boys, then once for me, then she concentrated on standing and breathing again. We turned and, as the moon carved out time with its shadows, I took her back to the summerhouse and sat her in her favourite garden chair again. I rubbed her hands, her face, her feet. Slowly she regained flexibility. She breathed better. She asked for water. All I had was the bucket and the rainwater, but she drank eagerly and thankfully. For hours we sat. We worked on each limb. We worked on breathing.

"How are you?" I said.

"It hurts," she said. "But I knew it would."

"Where does it hurt?"

"Everywhere." But she smiled. We both smiled. She cried. We both cried.

I took Claire back to the boat in our wheelbarrow. What else was there? I wasn't going to fuss around trying to find a serviceable car with keys on hand. I wasn't going to let her out of my sight for more than six breaths. It was undignified and I nearly died, but it worked. Here and there she had to get out, for example while we negotiated the steps from our garden, and down onto the towpath, but somehow we managed it.

We had said goodbye to our boys first. Claire did not find that as difficult as I. She knew things that I didn't.

I woke Yasmin and Kirsty. They each went into mild shock I think, for even though neither of them had known Claire, they could tell that the person before them was a mixture of the macabre and the miraculous. They came round fairly quickly though, and Yasmin's medical background kicked into place. I wanted to put Claire to bed, but Yasmin said it was probably the worst thing we could do. We concentrated on building up her circulation and getting her breathing and her pulse steady. We got some dilute soup down her. We did not pound her with profound questions but kept the conversation simple and pragmatic. She talked more and spoke more easily, but said very little during that first day. She told us how she felt physically. There were pains, aches and frustrating stiffening of joints and muscles, she felt bilious and nauseous, but all in all as the day wore on, all those things eased.

Throughout that day, baby Lemon, cried a lot and made a great deal of fuss, but Kirsty had little time for her.

I fought sleep. I feared sleep. I did not want to sleep, and I did not want Claire to sleep in case she did not wake up again. She didn't want to sleep either, but each of us did. I slept first. I woke in a sweat and a panic to find Kirsty watching over the snoozing Claire. She slept smoothly and when she woke felt better and was hungry. More soup was given.

And so we continued for a week or so, concentrating on managing Claire's convalescence. To say that she recovered completely would be to lie, and throughout this account I have not lied to you. Claire lives. She lives again, or maybe she never died. I don't know. What do I know? I know nothing. Claire knows things, but she's reluctant to tell. They can't be told, she says. They can't be told. They can only be known and one day we'll all know them, because one day all we will be is knowledge.

We stocked up our narrow boats and sailed south. We found the boundary between stale earth and burned earth and sailed seven miles beyond it. That is where we now live, on a river, in north Wales. We have planted crops. They are growing. Grass is growing. Vegetation is returning.

We have been very busy, which is why I kept putting off completing this, but today it has to be finished. Today is exactly one year since the Event. One year since I flew into Heathrow for the final time.

The child Lemon is doing well, a little too well, perhaps. She is putting on weight and becoming more and more aware of what I think she already knows. I am fearful for her future, for all our futures, and for the natural challenges we will have to face. The most terrible thought I harbour regarding Lemon is that all this, all of it, was in some way commanded or engineered by her. Could she have selected her own surrogate mother, and then manipulated the minds and lives of all of us who had contact with Kirsty? Not only the lives, but also the afterlives? That is too terrible a thought to entertain, but it is not too terrible to conceive as a possibility. I do not know if there are any other children like Lemon on our planet. Michel Gerard forecast that there would be, and from the moment of their arrival it would no longer be our planet, but theirs. It will be some years before I know whether the Bosun's boson has done what Gerard predicted. It will be some years before Lemon is old enough to demonstrate the powers he says her kind have. All I can do is wait. That is another story for another time.

For now we have our recovering planet. We will see how she turns out. Some things, I hope, will be the same, a great deal more has gone for good. The weather will always be fickle. Fire will always stalk us. Disease is back, so sooner or later we will have to face that. Insects have returned but we have not yet seen any living mammals or birds. Our future looks to be largely, vegetarian but we have seen, though not yet successfully caught, fish. Yasmin thinks she saw a frog.

We have not seen any more resurrected humans.

I often wonder about George and the Jason expedition. I often think about Teresa and wonder if she really is alive in Tibet. I think Claire knows, but she isn't telling. When I mention Teresa, Claire smiles, and that is my only answer.

I also think about Thistle, and about what George said, or what I think he said as the noise of the Irish Sea spray lashed between us. Is Thistle where Claire was? She was fatally struck, then drowned and then cremated. There is no way back for her. Has she moved on or did George converse with her in the way I did with Claire? I think she may still be with us. She loved to roam free, and now she can roam more freely than ever. I shall keep an eye out for her. I consulted Claire on this quandary, but it is another piece of knowledge that can only be expressed as a smile.

Claire seems bound, physically or mentally, by some supernatural code. There are things that she simply cannot enunciate. The knowledge is in her mind but she is unable to put it into words. There is a wonderful peace and glory behind her eyes. She has been to a remarkable place, and she has returned. She carries joy but her return remains painful. Her body causes her considerable discomfort and that, she tells me, is why many others in her situation chose not to return. That is why she would not let me unbury our boys. She does not want them to come back to this. So why has she? Why has she come back?

I asked her.

"Because you wanted me to."

"Many other survivors want their loved ones back. Will they come?"

"You tasted the choice," she said.

"That was just a dream."

She looked at me through a tangle of obligation and love. There were things she thought she ought not to do, but the desire to do them raced through her like a fire in dry thicket. We were alone on our boat. She drew a deep breath through loving lips. "Dreams are not just dreams. They extend your wakefulness. They are journeys in a true sense. They take you places."

"In your mind."

"Where is your mind?"

I sniggered and shrugged. "In your brain."

She smiled with a hint of kind condescension. "My brain died. I dreamed on."

I stuttered over my reply to say a word I had long since rejected. "Your . . . soul?"

There was the merest hint of a head shake. She breathed deeply again, as if about to disobey some supreme discipline. The radiance in her eyes rose to a lemon-gold intensity as she spoke. "The supernatural is sub-atomic. Dreams taste that state. When the body dies, the mind dreams on. Then there is a choice. A choice. A choice." Her eyes found her hands. Her hands found each other. "You tasted that choice."

"The door." I re-experienced the awful wonderful pull of the handle my mind had touched. "What's on the other side?"

"You know as much as I", she said. "I haven't opened it either. You called me back." She found the same memory as I, and felt also that terrible terrific seduction. The memory became a thought, the thought became a decision. "Everything."

"Everything?"

"Everything." With her waking eye she saw the inadequate man she had chosen and with her dreaming eye she saw the arc of all knowable experiences that she had postponed.

"And there is a choice."

"There is a choice," she said.

"Reincarnation?"

"If the body is not too damaged. You had protected mine. You had laid me flat. You had covered me with soil. Kept me from the frost. Shaded me from the sun."

"So you could return?"

"I could. I have."

"But why? When you could have had everything?"

"Not had everything. Known everything. Knowledge is the only possession. Your value is you. Only you know what you know. Only you have lived your life, and had your particular experience. The door is the gift. Through the door and you give what you are and receive the same from all others who have given."

"Everyone who has lived."

"Every thing," she said.

"And you gave up all of that for me?"

She smiled an engagement acceptance smile and said, "Not given up. Delayed."

"Why?"

"Because I still have work to do. And so do you."

Right on cue, close by, on the deck of the Cordelia, or on the riverbank, Lemon, the cosmic child, cried. Claire's eyes flicked in the direction of the sound and she put the child firmly in both of our minds. Then Claire's voice cast a shadow across my soul.

"And you are going to need my help."

**

About the Author.

Pete Hartley is based in northern England where he has taught drama since 1984. He has written extensively for the stage. Some fifty of his plays have been performed by professional, amateur and student companies. Six have won prizes, and one, Mitigating Circumstances, was broadcast by BBC Radio. He has also had short stories published and broadcast.

By the same Author:

Christmas Present
Seven Seasonal Ghost Stories